A Kiss of Salt & Sea

Darkstone Academy Book 1

Bliss Devlin

Philtata Press, LLC

Copyright © 2023 Bliss Devlin

All rights reserved

The characters and events portrayed in this book are fictitious. Any similarity to real persons, living or dead, is coincidental and not intended by the author.

No part of this book may be reproduced, or stored in a retrieval system, or transmitted in any form or by any means, electronic, mechanical, photocopying, recording, or otherwise, without express written permission of the publisher.

Cover design by Jacqueline Sweet
Maps by Sapphire X Designs

Author's Note

This book contains explicit content and darker elements, including mature language, death, threats of sexual violence, and domestic violence. It is not intended for anyone under 18 years of age.

Maps

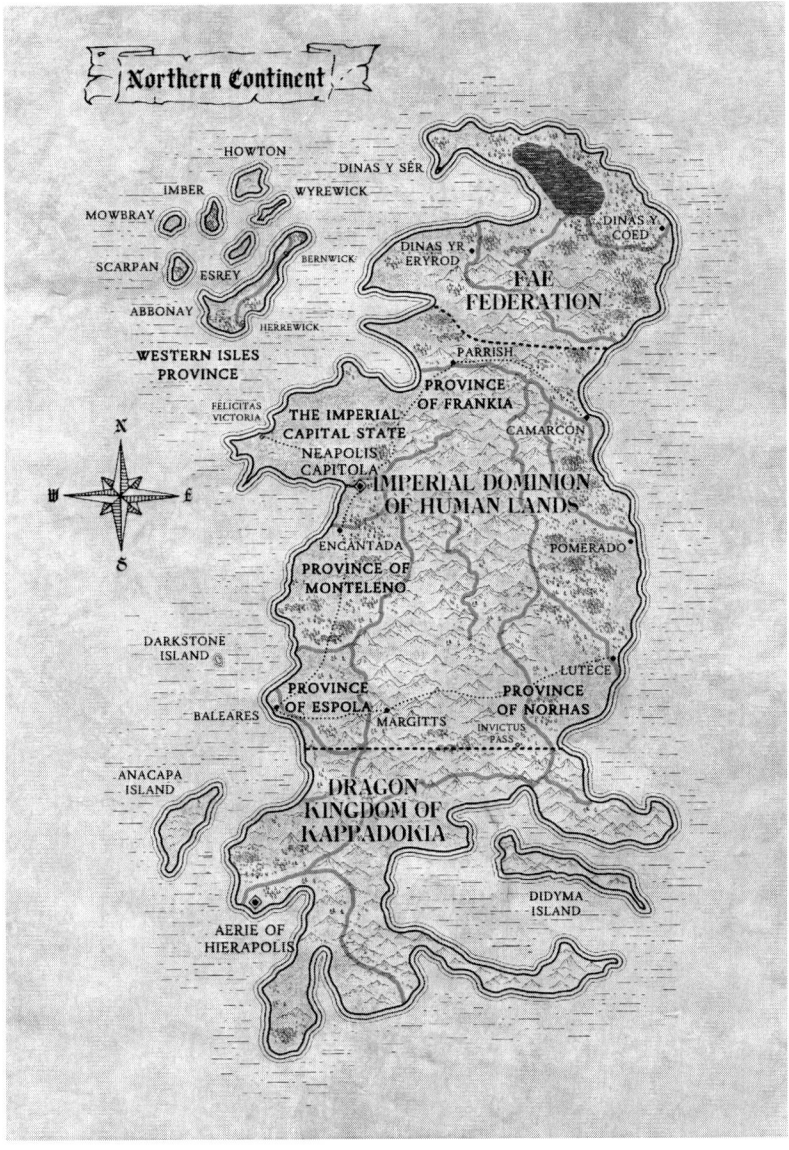

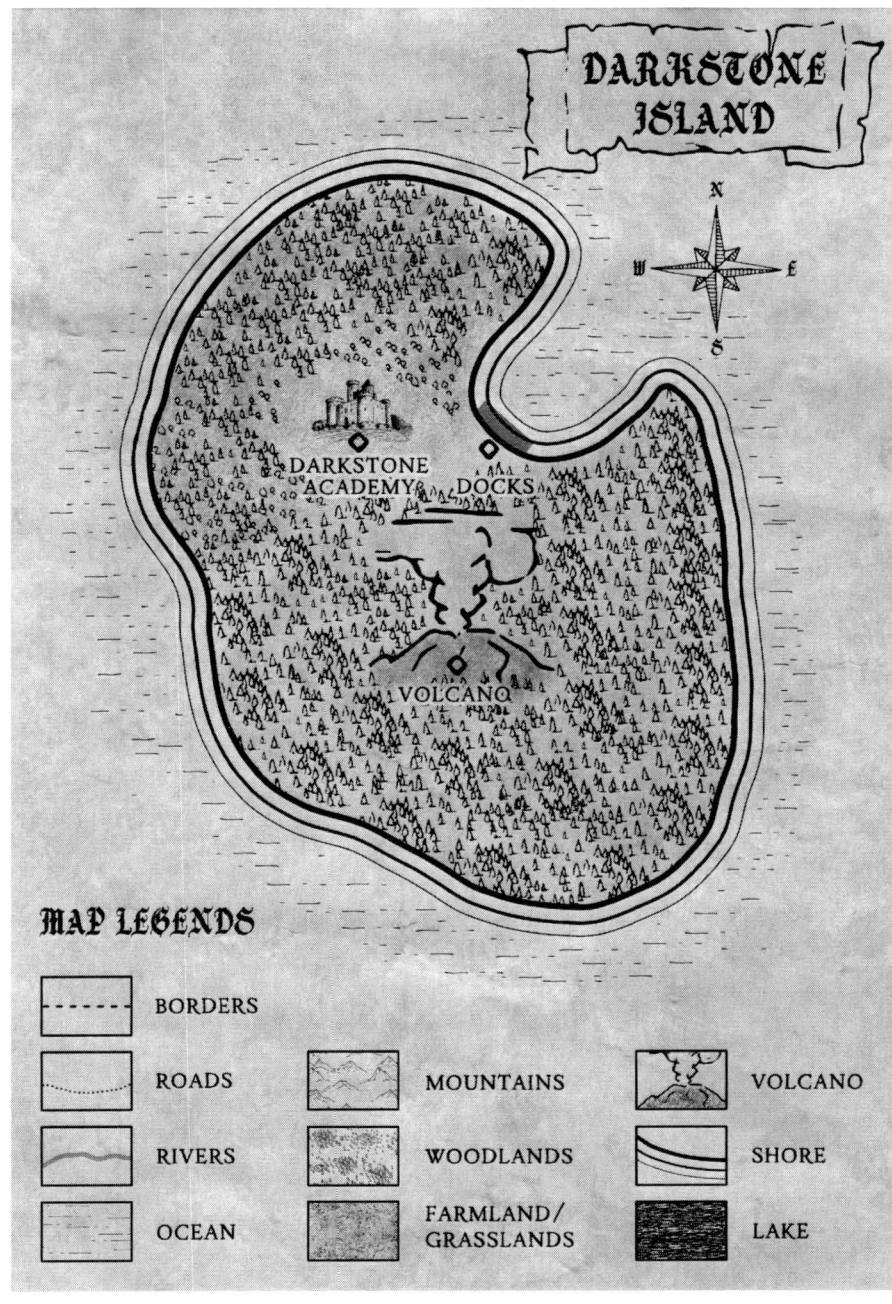

Prologue

Jacinthe

Bernswick
Isle of Abbonay, Western Isles Province
First Day of Autumn

"I sense nothing," declared Lady Adalburga, frowning as she dropped my hands. "Jacinthe has no magic. None."

The Provincial Magecraft Aptitude Examiner was an older woman with a face set in kindly lines and palms as dry and cool as snakeskin. Like most of the native-born islanders, she had bright blue eyes above ruddy cheeks. Wisps of graying golden hair stuck out from beneath her old-fashioned starched white widow's cap.

Disappointment coiled like a cold lead snake through my gut at Lady Adalburga's pronouncement.

Mama hadn't been the only one hoping desperately for a miracle. Throughout my childhood, I'd never shown the faintest spark of magic. But sometimes there were late bloomers in old mage-blood families like ours.

Just not *this* late. My seventeenth birthday had passed two months ago. If magic hadn't manifested by now, it never would.

My younger half-sister Talisa snorted. "*Told* you," she whispered loudly to the twins, Juno and Mira.

The twins snickered. "Knew it!" they whispered back.

All three of them had passed the Magecraft Aptitude Examiner's assessment with signs of strong magical talent and an affinity for Wood, the aspect of magic associated with the manipulation of living things. As was to be expected with two healer-mage parents.

Wood mages often trained as healers, but they could train as plant-mages or shaper-mages, who could fashion anything out of organic materials without saws or chisels or any tools except magic.

I ignored my siblings' taunts. I only had eyes for Mama. I had feared she'd be upset. Oddly, though, her expression looked... *relieved?*

Then she turned to me. "Oh, Jacinthe, my dearest, I was so *hoping...*"

Tears welled in her beautiful eyes. She pulled out a delicately embroidered handkerchief and dabbed at her lids, careful not to smear her eyeliner.

All right, maybe she really *was* upset, and I'd misread shock for relief.

But I was usually very good at reading people. Even people as controlled as Mama.

Like me, she was hazel-eyed, with a tall, curvaceous build. But that was where the resemblance between us ended.

Where Mama had the smooth, light olive skin and straight dark hair typical of someone born in the Imperial Capital State on the Continent, my long-dead father had gifted me deeply-tanned skin and red hair of a shade derisively known as "dragon fire."

My stepfather Baldwin cleared his throat. "It's a good thing we put aside money for Jacinthe's dowry, my love," he said to

Mama. "Since she won't be attending the Imperial Academy for the Magical Arts with *my* girls, after all."

His tone was mild, but he shot me a disapproving glare over Mama's bowed head.

I gritted my teeth at yet another reminder that he didn't consider me his daughter. I was another man's child, and he *never* let me forget it. Though usually not where Mama could overhear him.

"Since your three younger daughters all have strong healer-mage potential," Lady Adalburga said, clearly relieved to change the subject away from the disappointment I'd given everyone, "it is both my pleasure and my duty on behalf of our beloved Dominus Victor Augustus the Eighth to offer them full scholarships at the Imperial Academy in Neapolis Capitola. That's the capital of our Dominion," she added condescendingly.

"I'm well-acquainted with that city." Was that an edge in Mama's voice?

I perked up at this tidbit.

Mama never talked about her past, but her looks and her accent revealed she'd been born somewhere on the Continent.

Not for the first time, I wondered whether she'd actually grown up in Neapolis Capitola as well as attended the Imperial Academy there. But I knew it would do no good to ask her.

"I see." Lady Adalburga shot her an inquiring glance. "Are you from the capital, then?"

Mama arrived on the Isle of Abbonay seventeen years ago, when I was still a babe in arms, claiming to be a Dominion-certified Mage of the Healing Arts, and a recent widow. But she had never spoken my father's name, or provided any meaningful details of her life before coming to the island.

Bernswick was a small, close-knit town. Throughout my childhood, everyone had gossiped and speculated wildly about Mama's mysterious past.

Then, two years ago, a new mage had arrived to establish a rival herb shop and clinic in the next town over, and Narcissa of Camarcon quickly became the new object of discussion.

A born islander would have leaped on Lady Adalburga's question as an excuse to spin a tale filled with details of the capital and travels on the exotic Continent.

Mama merely folded her hands and gazed back at the Magecraft Aptitude Examiner with a tranquil, closed expression. The silence stretched uncomfortably.

Finally, Lady Adalburga cleared her throat. "Well, then, Mage Isabeau, the last student transport vessel of the year sails from Port Herrewick to Neapolis Capitola in a week. See that your girls are on it."

"So soon?" Mama looked horrified. "We'll have to find space on a riverboat heading down to the port, and you know how busy they are this time of year! And before that, there's all the packing and preparing to do. And then there's my business!" She shook her head. "Impossible. The girls have waited this long already. Can't they enroll in the spring?"

I thought she had a point. The twins had just turned twelve last month, the official age for magical talent assessment. But Talisa was nearly fourteen. She should have been tested two years ago.

The Western Isles were the remotest province of the Dominion. It had been difficult for our governor to recruit a qualified mage to fill the post of Magecraft Aptitude Examiner after the last one died.

The new Magecraft Aptitude Examiner shook her head. "You know the law, Mage Isabeau. Youth identified as Potentials are required to report to the nearest academy *immediately*."

Mama's beautifully rouged mouth set into an unhappy line. Her fine dark brows drew together over her large eyes. "Fine. Baldwin and Jacinthe can mind the shop—" Her gaze rested on me, and I flinched from the deep emotions I saw there. "And I'll escort the girls to the academy."

"All the way to the capital, Isa?" my stepfather protested. "You'll be gone all winter! I'll miss you terribly," he added, putting his arm around Mama.

His glacier-blue gaze flicked in my direction, and I saw his distaste. He usually kept it hidden better than that, helping Mama to pretend we were all one big, happy family.

"I'm the only one who can go. You nearly died of seasickness the last time we took the ferry to Imber." Mama spread her hands helplessly. "There's no help for it. It's the law." She sighed. "Besides, Jacinthe knows how to brew all the medicines and tonics. She can help you with our patients. And she's a good cook, too. The two of you will be comfortable enough."

It was true. I might not have an ounce of magic running through my veins, but I'd inherited Mama's touch with potions and foodstuffs, and she'd trained me well in the non-magical healing arts.

Baldwin's mouth twisted in distaste as he surveyed me.

In return, I raised my chin and looked him straight in the eye.

It was going to be a *very* long winter.

Chapter 1

Jacinthe

Bernswick, Isle of Abbonay
Six months later

When the messenger bearing news of Mama's death arrived, I was perched at the top of a very tall ladder, replacing roof slates.

One week after the Magecraft Aptitude Examiner's visit, Mama and my sisters had boarded a riverboat for Herrewick. It was the first stage of their long journey to the Imperial Academy for the Magical Arts in Neapolis Capitola.

Despite my worries about Mama leaving me alone to deal with my stepfather, the long weeks of winter had passed quickly.

The seasonal influx of patients kept Baldwin and me both too busy to have the time or energy to argue. I fell into my bed every night too tired to think, and rose again at dawn to bake bread and cook breakfast for us.

Besides coughs, fevers, and the grippe, there were the inevitable injuries from chopping wood, building fires, and walking on icy cobblestone streets.

Baldwin healed the injured with his magic as best he could, though he wasn't nearly as skilled as Mama. He also dealt with customers and grudgingly ventured downriver to Herrewick at intervals to purchase fresh stocks of herbs, syrup of poppies, and other imported drugs.

Meanwhile, I kept house and tended the ill. I brewed gallons of Mama's special honey-and-herbs cough remedy, compounded painkilling salves, and made other medications as needed. All the while, I counted down the days until she returned home.

A few days ago, a winter gale had roared down from the Polar Sea. It swept through the islands, leaving a broad swathe of uprooted trees, collapsed buildings, and wrecked fishing vessels in its wake.

The walls of our old, slightly off-kilter, three-story half-timbered house had withstood many storms over the course of two hundred years. But the wind's grasping fingers tore away many roof slates. It also sent a thick tree limb crashing through the front window of the ground-floor medical clinic.

That very expensive plate-glass window had been Mama's pride and joy. She'd commissioned it from a glassworker in Herrewick. I remembered the day it was painstakingly transported upriver. She would be heartbroken when she returned home and found it gone.

This morning had dawned cold but clear, with pale blue skies, weak sunshine, and scudding clouds.

After I finished cooking breakfast, Baldwin ordered me up on the roof to undertake the most dangerous and difficult of the post-storm repairs.

Meanwhile, he remained safely on the ground. After spending the winter with him, I wasn't surprised. In the weeks following Mama's departure, he'd gradually shifted all of the tedious, difficult, or dangerous work to me.

As I lay on my stomach on the steep slope of the roof, nailing fresh slates over bare patches, Baldwin made a big production of stretching oiled canvas over a wooden frame to keep out the rain and snow from coming in through the large hole left by the shattered window.

Given the amount of damage in the village and on the riverside docks, it would take a while before Gymi Carpenter and his apprentices could build us a set of wooden shutters to keep out the rain and snow.

"If Isa thinks I'm going to pay to replace this thing," Baldwin grumbled loudly as he lifted the canvas-covered frame into place, "she needs to think again."

I knew better. If Mama insisted on replacing the window—which I knew she would—Baldwin would crumble like a dike made from sand under the pounding of the surf.

"Mage Baldwin? Miss Jacinthe?" someone called.

I wriggled cautiously backwards until my toes found the ladder.

From my vantage point high on the roof, I saw a stranger, a young woman near to my age. She came trotting up the street from the riverside docks, where the ferry from Herrewick had pulled up a short time ago.

She had a sturdy build, with the golden hair and rosy cheeks of an islander, and wore a familiar uniform.

"Yes, I'm Mage Baldwin," my stepfather said, turning to face the newcomer.

I had just enough time to wonder why someone from the Herrewick Harbormaster's Office had traveled upriver to visit us when the newcomer began speaking in a rush.

"Mage Baldwin, the Harbormaster sent me to convey sad tidings." The young woman looked away, then squared her shoulders and straightened her warm cloak before continuing. "We've received news that the ship bearing Mage Isabeau went down in the gale, lost with all hands aboard."

High above Baldwin and the messenger, I gasped. The world started spinning around me, and I clung tightly to the ladder.

Mama's gone? It can't be true. It can't!

The messenger added in a breathless voice, "I'm so very sorry. Mage Isabeau saved my little sister when she caught the red fever. May the Mother of All cherish and keep her."

"Isabeau is gone? *Drowned?*" repeated Baldwin now.

From my perch, I saw him rapidly blinking his pale blue eyes. His face looked chalky under his bushy brown winter beard.

"But how can that be?" he demanded. "I thought Air and Water Mages protected Dominion vessels!"

The messenger shook her head. "I'm so sorry, Mage Baldwin." Her gaze darted up to me. I didn't trust my shaking knees to climb down the ladder. "And Miss Jacinthe," she added.

Then she returned her attention to Baldwin. "The Harbormaster said that Mage Isabeau took passage on a merchant ship, not a government vessel. He guessed maybe she wanted to get home faster than a Dominion Postal ship would take her."

Knowing Mama, I could believe that. The mail ships sailed with mages' protection, but they also stopped at every port, large and small, along their routes to pick up and deliver letters and packages.

"Y-yes," Baldwin said, echoing my thoughts. "Of course. She would've wanted to return to us—to *me*—as quickly as possible."

The messenger bobbed her head. "Yes, well, I am very sorry for your loss." She looked around nervously, then patted a large leather satchel slung over her shoulder. "Please excuse me. I have to deliver the mail before the ferry departs for Oswy's Ford."

When she had disappeared down the street, a long period of silence followed, punctuated by Baldwin's choked sobs as he buried his face in his hands. His shoulders shook.

I looked away to give him some privacy.

My own eyes were still dry. Numb disbelief shrouded me as birds sang in the trees and the distant sounds of passengers crowding the docks drifted on the chilly breeze coming from the river.

This can't be happening. It has to be a mistake, I thought, gazing over the thatched roofs of our neighbors. *Mama's coming home in a few days.*

"Jacinthe!" Baldwin shouted hoarsely.

I looked down and saw tear-tracks glittering on his cheeks. His expression twisted as I met his gaze. "Get back to work, you lazy wench!"

My mouth dropped open. I could only stare at him.

"Well?" he demanded. "There's more rain coming tonight, and that roof isn't going to fix itself."

He wiped angrily at his wet cheeks and picked up his hammer.

The mourning period was apparently over.

Chapter 2

Jacinthe

Six weeks later

As I entered the house, lugging a big willow shopping basket filled to the brim with the first strawberries of the season, tender green vegetables, and a nice fresh catfish, a sugary female voice called from the parlor, "Oh, there she is, Baldwin!"

The parlor door stood open. Inside, I glimpsed Narcissa of Camarcon on the red velvet couch normally reserved for Mama's most important guests.

I froze. *What's she doing here?* The widowed mage with the silver-gilt hair and generous bosom spilling over the top of her tightly laced bodice lived one town over, in Dunsthorpe.

Like Mama, Mage Narcissa had come to Abbonay from the Continent, though Narcissa hailed from the northern province of Frankia. She was Mama's biggest business rival.

"Well, don't stand there gawking like an idiot," Baldwin barked. "Come here and pay your respects to Mage Narcissa."

With an effort, I bit back a sharp retort. After Mama's death, Baldwin no longer tried to hide either his temper or his dislike of me. He was quick to anger, and even quicker to use his fist or any weapon at hand to punish me if he thought I was being insolent.

And to him, anything less than instant obedience counted as insolence.

"Yes, sir," I murmured, and carefully set down the heavy shopping basket while wishing a plague of itching sores on him.

If only I had some magic, I thought despairingly for the thousandth time. Even a crumb of power might've helped when dealing with Baldwin.

The week following the messenger's devastating news had been the most difficult I'd ever known. I'd spent the first few days in a numb daze, moving mechanically through my daily tasks. If Baldwin hadn't been there to demand his meals, I wouldn't have remembered to eat.

My tears finally came when Baldwin ordered me to clear out Mama's armoire. I climbed the stairs to her bedroom and opened the tall, carved oak cabinet to confront the row of summer gowns she'd left behind. Her familiar perfume of herbs underlaid with rosewater came wafting out to surround me like a ghostly embrace.

That was when I finally, really, *truly* understood that Mama was gone. She was never coming home. Never coming back to me. I was all alone now, stuck with a man I loathed and who loathed me in return.

The frozen mass of grief and shock had finally melted and rushed out of me in a flood of tears. Sobs had racked my body as I sank to my knees in front of the armoire.

I don't know how long I had stayed there. Baldwin had left that morning to run some mysterious errand, so at least I could grieve in blessed solitude.

Then, feeling a hundred years old, I rose and forced myself to sort through Mama's clothes.

She'd packed all of her warm winter gowns for the trip, as well as her best midnight-blue velvet dress and her jewelry, so that she would have something fitting to wear to the official welcoming ceremonies for incoming students and their families at the Imperial Academy. But her summer gowns were all still in good shape. With a bit of alteration, they would fit me just fine.

I didn't want them. Didn't want to wear a constant reminder of my loss. But I also knew that I needed clothes and Baldwin was unlikely to spend a farthing on me. He already grumbled about the cost of feeding me.

As the days grew longer and the snow melted, Baldwin had left the house for hours at a time—which was just fine by me—returning hours after sunset in a cloud of beer fumes.

I should have resented the extra work, but honestly, I welcomed his absences. I was happier when free of his sullen presence.

And now Mage Narcissa was here, visiting him. That couldn't be good. Did she want to buy the shop and take over Mama's business?

Dreading unwelcome news, I entered the parlor and did my best to greet Mama's rival politely. "Would you like some tea, Mage Narcissa? I baked some lavender shortbread yesterday," I offered.

"That would be lovely," she crooned, looking me over like a housewife examining a chicken on market day.

When I returned from the kitchen with the tray of refreshments, I served them, then prepared to leave. I needed to put that catfish on ice and make a crust for a berry tart.

"Jacinthe, stay," Baldwin ordered in the same tone he used on dogs and children.

Wondering what he wanted from me now, I tucked the empty tray under my arm and turned to face the pair from the parlor doorway.

"At least you have some useful skills, child. I heard about the Magecraft Aptitude Examiner's visit," Narcissa said, taking a bite of the shortbread. Her tone was sweet as a poisoned apple. "Everyone expected all Isabeau's children to be magical prodigies. My condolences, Baldwin." She patted his arm with disturbing familiarity.

"Lady Adalburga assured me that Talisa, Juno, and Mira would excel at the academy," Baldwin countered defensively.

"Well, I suppose three gifted children out of four isn't bad," Narcissa observed, less apple and more poison in her tone now. Her green eyes flicked over my plain homespun dress in cool assessment. "And when will you be sending Jacinthe to her father's kinfolk?"

My stomach tightened in surprise and apprehension.

"If only I could." Baldwin sighed loudly and hunched his shoulders. "Truth is, my love, we don't know anything about the wench's father. Isa told me he was dead, but never shared any other details." He shrugged and gave her a sheepish smile.

My love? Alarm bells began jangling in my head. *What in Dragon-fire is going on here?*

"Ah, yes, Isabeau the famously tight-lipped," Narcissa jibed. "She certainly enjoyed being mysterious, didn't she? Why, I never even heard which academy she graduated from! *If* she graduated at all…" she added in a malicious tone.

"Neapolis Capitola," I snapped. At Baldwin's baleful look, I made an effort to soften my tone. "Mama graduated from the Imperial Academy at Neapolis Capitola. She wore their golden badge, the one with the Dominus' imperial eagle."

"That's the same academy my girls are attending right now," Baldwin added smugly.

Narcissa's generous lips thinned. Pinned to her bodice was a silver Mage's Badge enameled with the coat of arms for the Provincial Academy for Magical Arts in Camarcon.

It was an old and well-respected school, but not nearly as prestigious as the original Imperial Academy at the capital.

"How very nice for you," she said with a dismissive wave of her hand. Her jeweled rings glittered coldly in the light from the window. "In any case, Baldwin, you are truly a generous soul to raise another man's child at your expense like this."

I bristled. "Generosity" had nothing to do with it. Baldwin worked me harder in the shop than any contracted apprentice, and I did all the household work, besides.

He puffed out his chest and smiled ingratiatingly at Narcissa. I noticed he'd trimmed his beard and dressed it with lilac-scented oil.

"Yes, it's a trial," he said in a mournful tone. "But at least the wench is of some help with potions and cooks a passable meal."

Now I was furious. I was an *excellent* cook and I knew it.

Not only that, but my potions were good enough that before she departed on her ill-fated journey, Mama had trusted me to brew nearly all of them.

Same with Baldwin. He usually returned from his afternoons at our local tavern, the Eagle & Anchor, to perform the last step of adding the enchantments before dispensing them to our patients.

Not caring about how my stepfather might react, I opened my mouth to give them both a dose of the unadulterated truth.

But before I could commit this foolish and dangerous action, Baldwin announced, "Narcissa has done me the honor of accepting my suit. We just signed a betrothal contract. She and her four lovely daughters are moving here next week, and I want you to prepare all the bedrooms for their arrival."

"Betrothed?" Shocked to the core, I blurted, "To *her?* But it's not even the end of the mourning period!"

Swift as a rushing boar, Baldwin lunged up from the sofa.

His open-handed blow numbed my cheek and mouth, and sent me stumbling back through the doorway.

"What did I tell you about keeping a civil tongue in your head, wench?" he snarled.

"Baldwin, my love," Narcissa said. "Come back. We were going to discuss Jacinthe's future, weren't we?" Her eyes were bright with malice as she surveyed me from the sofa. "She can't stay here in the shop forever, and since she has no dowry—"

"Wait, what?" I interrupted, still reeling. "I don't need a dowry! I have my apprentice fee!"

After the Magecraft Aptitude Examiner's devastating report, Mama had assured me she'd saved a respectable amount for my further schooling as a healer.

Baldwin smirked at me before returning his attention to Narcissa. "Oh, Isa and I had a small sum laid aside for emergencies," he told her in a dismissive tone. "But I spent it all to repair the house… and to pay for a few other things."

"Oh, like this?" Narcissa asked in a breathy voice, showing off a gold filigree ring set with a large, gleaming pink pearl.

The promise of escape via an apprenticeship somewhere far away from my stepfather had sustained me through the long dark weeks of grieving. And now it was *gone*?

"Don't look at me like that, you spoiled wench," Baldwin snapped. "Haven't I fed you and clothed you for years out of the goodness of my heart? Isa *owed* me that money for your maintenance!"

Angry words rose in my throat, choking me. Mama once told

me I'd inherited my father's temper. It was one of the few things I knew about him.

I snarled, "Mage Narcissa, do you really want to marry a man who'd steal his stepdaughter's inheritance? If he's low enough to do it to *me*, he'll do it to—"

A second vicious blow cut me off. "You ungrateful little bitch!"

White-hot pain exploded through my jaw and tongue and sent fiery sparks of agony darting through my head. I went down hard on the hall tiles, my mouth filled with the iron and salt taste of blood.

Narcissa looked down her nose at me. "So arrogant! Just like your mother. She always considered herself above us," she said softly. "But she was a mage. You? You're *nothing,* girl. Just a kinless, penniless orphan dependent on the charity of your betters. How *dare* you slander the man who's feeding and housing you at his own expense?"

She turned her gaze to Baldwin. "Darling, my girls are all accustomed to having their own bedrooms."

Breathing hard, his face flushed with rage at me, Baldwin nodded. "Of course, my love. Jacinthe will move herself to the attic before you and your girls arrive."

"Good," Narcissa said serenely. "We'll need that extra room for Kazetta." She pursed her lips. "And just how long *will* we have to support Isabeau's daughter?"

"I'll see about finding the wench a husband," Baldwin promised, to my horror. "I'm sure someone will take her without a dowry."

After Narcissa and her spoiled daughters arrived and took possession of my mother's house, my life became every bit as miserable as I'd feared.

The dark, cramped attic where Baldwin had banished me was crowded with old drying racks, crockery, empty crates, and other junk. I improvised a pallet by sewing together old sheets and stuffing them with old rags. The resulting mattress was lumpy, but more comfortable than sleeping on bare boards.

From the first day, Narcissa and her spawn treated me like an indentured servant instead of Baldwin's stepdaughter. I labored from dawn to bedtime seven days a week, cooking, cleaning, and doing the laundry for seven people.

She allowed me to eat only after everyone else had finished their meals, and restricted me to the leftovers… *if* there were any.

For the first time in my life, I experienced hunger pangs gnawing relentlessly at my stomach, sapping me of strength and will.

I sneaked food where I could. The whippings whenever Baldwin or Narcissa caught me were bad, but still better than being hungry all the time.

Still, I grew gaunt and weak. I stumbled through the long summer days, fatigue dragging at me like stone weights tied to my arms and legs. I realized I had to get away from my stepfather and his new family before they starved and worked me to death.

But how? I had no money, and nowhere else to go. I knew what happened to penniless young women who ran away from home, and I wasn't that desperate. *Yet.*

Despite Baldwin's threat to marry me off, neither he nor Narcissa ever mentioned it again. Maybe no man would take me without some kind of dowry. Or maybe the two of them simply enjoyed having an unpaid servant around the house.

For Midsummer Feast, I spent days scrubbing every inch of the house, then cooking and baking a feast for a crowd of Narcissa's friends and cousins.

In the following days, Baldwin and his new bride began a series of urgent, low-voiced conversations that always broke off abruptly when I came into the room.

I should have been worried about what they were scheming. But I simply didn't have the strength. Each day was a slog of unending chores until I collapsed into exhausted sleep.

A fortnight later, Baldwin cornered me in the kitchen as I washed dishes.

"I'm taking the ferry down to Herrewick tomorrow morning," he announced. "Narcissa needs ginseng root, orris powder, cardamom, and a dozen kinds of herbs for her vivifying tonics."

I looked at him, wondering distantly why he was telling me this. "Yes, and?"

"You're coming with me," he said impatiently. "Isa trained you well. You're good at spotting the fake ginseng and stale spices."

My surprise must've shown on my face, because he added with a grudging scowl, "You get me the best prices on those herbs, and I'll treat you to lunch at The Dolphin." His expression softened. "Isa always loved the fried fish there."

My mouth watered at the memory of The Dolphin's crisp, piping-hot crab cakes topped with a sweet-and-spicy mustard-apple cider sauce.

The thought of escaping this house—and Narcissa's demanding presence—for a few hours felt too good to be true. For the first time in weeks, I felt a spark of excitement.

Even stranger, Narcissa fed me a generous breakfast the next morning: a whole egg and a thick slice of toasted bread with butter. It tasted like the Divine Mother's heavenly ambrosia.

While I ate, she watched me avidly, a strange, almost triumphant smile curving her full lips. That should've been a warning to me.

But I was so worn down that I didn't care about anything but the sensation of warm, velvety egg yolk sliding down my throat, and the richness of the melted butter soaking the bread. It was the biggest portion I'd eaten in weeks.

A full belly put a spring in my step as I followed Baldwin to the dock and boarded the ferry. It was a beautiful summer day. I sat on a wooden bench and enjoyed the breeze on my face. On either bank of the river, lush barley fields stretched out to distant, forested hills.

Several hours later, we disembarked in Herrewick, the bustling walled town located where the River Rouse flowed into the Northern Sea. I knew it well from countless shopping trips with Mama.

"Look! It's one of the merfolk!" someone shouted as I stepped onto the rough planks of the ferry dock.

I stopped and looked at the river, but didn't see anything in the water.

"Not there, dear," said an older lady who stood near me. She wore a linen tunic embroidered with summer flowers, and her graying golden hair wrapped around her head in a coronet of braids. Her tone was kind. "Over there. See?" She pointed to the end of the dock.

I spotted a group of four ordinary-looking humans dressed in imperial livery carrying an open-sided palanquin on their shoulders. They were surrounded by harbor guards, and appeared to be headed for the seaside docks.

The palanquin's passenger had drawn back the curtains, and was looking around at the passing sights with open curiosity.

My first impression of the merman was of lean strength.

Long, shining silver hair flowed over his bare, muscular chest and shoulders. Above his waist, his skin was pale and smooth, utterly hairless. From the hips down, his body tapered into a long, powerful tail. Under the noonday sun, it looked like a dolphin's tail, but glittered with iridescent scales like a fish.

The merman turned his head to stare at the flood of passengers disembarking from the ferry. His features were beautiful and utterly inhuman, with great dark eyes like a seal's. Around his neck, he wore a mass of braided cords strung with beads, whale's teeth, and pierced gold coins. A close-fitting mask of glass and metal covered his mouth and nose, with long hoses connected to a large water-jar.

Streams of water pulsed from feathery gill-slits on either side of his neck and ran over his shoulders and chest in gleaming rivulets.

The breath caught in my throat as I met his cold, predatory gaze.

It stole my breath. I instantly understood he was proud, and hated the need for humans to carry him around because he was helpless on dry land. And he would have happily slaughtered every single person gawking at him as his procession passed through the city.

I shivered. All my life, I'd heard stories of the merfolk that painted them every bit as ruthless and bloodthirsty as the Fae or Dragons. Suddenly, I believed it.

Then the palanquin moved past the riverside docks. I lost sight of it as it disappeared into a street leading from the plaza.

Ahead of me, Baldwin turned his head. "Stop lollygagging,

wench! We haven't got all day!"

Without waiting for my reply, he strode briskly to the end of the dock.

Then instead of heading left to Import Row, where a long line of tall stone buildings stood shoulder to shoulder facing the seaside quays, he led me across the plaza at a brisk march.

We wound our way around fruit and vegetable stalls and long tables heaped with shining silver fish. I wondered if Baldwin wanted to buy something for Narcissa, but his pace never slowed.

We passed Herrewick's crooked, half-timbered City Hall and the huge new Sailor's Guild Hall before he halted in front of an unfamiliar two-story stone building. Its façade was grimy with age, and its windows were tall and very narrow.

Above a plain oak door hung a painted sign, topped with a small imperial gilded eagle. It read, *Dominion Bureau of Apprentices.*

"What—?" I began.

I'd heard of the DBA. And nothing good. Mama had promised me a private apprenticeship with a healer somewhere in Frankia on the Continent.

Quick as a striking snake, Baldwin grabbed my wrist with bruising strength, pushed open the door, and dragged me inside.

The building's narrow entrance hall was dark after the bright sunlight, with dingy white walls and an equally dingy floor tiled in a black-and-white diamond pattern popular two hundred years ago. A plain staircase of worn oak rose at the back of the hall.

Facing the door stood a wide desk manned by a single, bored-looking elderly clerk wearing a moth-eaten black velvet cap.

Wire-rimmed spectacles perched on his beaky nose, and an imperial civil service badge gleamed dully against his dark coat.

The clerk gave me a bored, cursory glance. His gaze lingered on Baldwin, taking in the enameled pin fastening his linen summer cloak.

"Your business, Mage—?" he asked in fluent Capitolan. His voice was as dry and creaky as old boards.

"Baldwin," said my stepfather, switching from Abbonethy to Capitolan. He squared his shoulders but didn't release his hold on me. "I'm Mage Baldwin of Bernswick, and this dowerless orphan—" He yanked hard on my arm, bringing me stumbling against his side. "—Jacinthe of Bernswick wishes to apprentice herself."

"What?" I asked in Abbonethy. Confusion and incredulous hope vied for space in my head.

Was he really offering me escape from the hell that my life had become?

Baldwin gave me an oily smile. "Narcissa and I have decided that since you have no suitors and no dowry, this would be best for you," he said in Abbonethy.

Thank the Divine Mother! Relief surged through me at the thought of escaping my miserable servitude.

Then I remembered with whom I was dealing. "What *kind* of apprenticeship?" I asked warily. "And what about the apprentice fees?"

His smile widened. "What about them?"

I went cold.

To the clerk, Baldwin said in Capitolan, "Miss Jacinthe wishes to indenture herself to His Imperial Majesty in return for an apprenticeship in an honest trade."

I staggered as the import of his words sank in.

By long custom and guild laws, parents or guardians of a young person paid a generous fee to an artisan, merchant, or other tradesperson in return for an apprenticeship.

Those who couldn't afford to pay an apprenticeship fee could indenture themselves to the government. Originally a program designed to allow the children of the poor a fair opportunity to receive training, indentured apprenticeships were now just legalized slavery, and only for the truly desperate.

Especially since it was common knowledge that the DBA frequently sent female indentured apprentices to work in brothels. Knowing Baldwin and Narcissa, they intended exactly that fate for me.

"No!" I shouted in Capitolan, frantically trying to free myself from Baldwin's steely grip. "I won't!"

I addressed the clerk. "Sir, I don't consent to this!"

A hot bonfire of rage threatened to consume me, making my skin prickle and my hidden tattoo itch. After everything he'd already done to me, I was determined not to let my stepfather assume false authority over me. Not now, when the stakes were so high.

The clerk's lips thinned. "Silence, girl!" he ordered. "I don't like anyone making a fuss in my office."

Then a burly young man wearing Imperial livery emerged from a back room. He moved swiftly around to my back and grabbed my elbows, immobilizing me.

Chapter 3

Jacinthe

Dominion Bureau of Apprentices
Herrewick, Isle of Abbonay

I struggled against the guard's grip.

"Let go of me!" I demanded, which did absolutely no good. I kicked backwards, but the guard dodged my clog while still holding onto me.

"Now, miss, calm yourself," he rumbled in Abbonethy as his grip slid down to my wrist.

He deftly wrenched my arms up behind my back and bent them at the elbow to fold my wrists under my shoulder blades. In this position, my shoulders strained and popped with every movement. So, I stopped fighting him. I wasn't stupid enough to court a dislocated shoulder—or two.

Instead, I took a deep breath and tried to push down my temper. I needed a cool head right now to consider my options. I decided to appeal to the clerk. "Sir, this man—Baldwin—has no right to indenture me! He's not my father. He's not any kind of blood relation at all!"

The clerk peered at me over his spectacles before moving his gaze to my stepfather. "Mage Baldwin, is that true?"

Baldwin drew himself up and crossed his arms over his chest. "I married the wench's mother fifteen years ago. After my wife died this past winter, I've been feeding and housing my ungrateful stepdaughter out of the goodness of my heart."

"I see." The clerk pursed his lips, then turned his attention back to me. "So, girl, you're fluent in Capitolan?"

I nodded.

"How old are you?"

"Seventeen," I replied.

"And have you been living under Mage Baldwin's roof, supported fully by him for the past fifteen years?"

I hesitated. I didn't like where this was going.

"Think very carefully how you answer me," the clerk warned. "Lying to a government official is a crime."

"I don't live under *Baldwin's* roof. The house belonged to my late mother, Mage Isabeau of Bernswick," I said angrily. "Baldwin married Mama and came to live with us. It was *her* business that feeds and keeps me, not his. What's more, he's lying about being good-hearted. I work hard for my keep. After my mother's death, I single-handedly ran the business for months while this man spent his days at the tavern or courting rich widows. Now, his new wife starves me and treats me like her servant. I'm no kin to him, and I don't want to be!"

"You insolent, lying little bitch," growled Baldwin in Abbonethy, uncrossing his arms. His fists clenched. I wondered if he would dare hit me in front of the clerk and the guard.

Would that help my case? If so, maybe the temporary pain of a blow might be worth it.

To my dismay, the clerk said, "Girl, you ought to be grateful to Mage Baldwin that you, an orphan, had a bed to sleep in and bread to eat."

I scoffed. "A *bed*, sir? He took my bed away and gave it to one of his new wife's brood. I sleep on the floor now, up in the attic."

The clerk's mouth tightened further in disapproval. With a sinking heart, I realized he didn't care how Baldwin had treated me, just that we'd both established he was my stepfather.

Dragon-fire consume them both, I thought, a toxic mix of anger and despair churning my stomach.

"Be that as it may," pronounced the clerk, confirming my fears. "As you are an orphan and still a minor, your stepfather, Mage Baldwin, is your legal guardian. Under Dominion law, he has the right to indenture you for an apprenticeship once you reach the age of twelve."

I gasped. "That—that's not *fair!*"

I remembered Mama's cool voice chiding me whenever I said the same thing to her. *Life's not fair, sweetheart. That's why you have to fight like a Dragon for the things you want and need.*

Think, I told myself. *Find some way to get this clerk to reject the indenture.*

"So, Mage Baldwin," said the clerk, "what useful skills does your stepdaughter possess?"

Baldwin shot me a venomous sidelong look. "None at all," he spat. "She's a lying, lazy, useless wench."

Terror flowed through me in an icy torrent as panic tightened my chest. My heart began pounding. What if this clerk believed Baldwin?

Forget wriggling out of this indenture. In my heart, I knew it was hopeless. I needed to prove I could be useful to the government as more than a prostitute!

"That's not true!" I sputtered. "I can read and write in both Abbonethy and Capitolan, and keep accounts. Mama—that is, Mage Isabeau—trained me as a healer. I know herbal remedies and have some surgical skill."

What else? I thought frantically. *What else can I do? How else can I keep myself out of the brothel?*

I added breathlessly, "Oh, and I'm an excellent cook and baker."

Baldwin scowled and opened his mouth. No doubt to contradict me.

But before he could say anything, the clerk snapped, "How good of a cook can you possibly be, girl? You look half-starved."

"That's only because I'm not permitted to eat the food I prepare," I retorted, then added desperately, "But I swear to you by the Mother of All that I told you the truth about what I can do!"

"Just send her to the whorehouse and be done with this nonsense," Baldwin snarled. "She's a liar, and of no use except on her back."

No! I drew in a shuddering breath. If the guard hadn't been holding me upright with my arms twisted up against my back, I would've fallen to my knees to beg.

The clerk pursed his lips again and examined me from head to toe.

I hung in the guard's hold, my breath rasping in my throat and my heart hammering so loudly that I was sure everyone else in this chamber could hear it, too.

Finally, the clerk said, "That would be a waste... *if* she truly has the knowledge she claims. Only one way to find out." He reached out with his pen and tapped a small silver bell sitting on one corner of his desk.

The sharp, clear chime cut through the air like a dagger. Before the last echo had died away, someone began stomping down the stairs.

A silver-haired man with a short, neatly trimmed gray beard appeared. Like the clerk, he wore a long, dark blue gown with a golden DBA badge pinned to his collar.

"Yes, Clerk Petri? What do you want *now?*" he demanded in an irritated tone as he reached the bottom step.

"Healer Reynaud, this apprentice applicant claims to have knowledge of the healing arts. I want you to test her claims." The clerk shoved a blank sheet of paper across the desk and plucked a fountain pen from a cup sitting next to the desk-bell. "Write out your answers, girl. That way, we'll see if you're actually literate, and possibly snag two fish on a single hook." He jerked his chin and said to the guard, "You can release her, Ivar. Fetch her a stool."

Ivar obeyed instantly. The he strode to the hall's far wall and dragged a worn-looking wooden stool across the tiles with an ear-splitting screech.

Rubbing my aching arms, I sagged onto the hard seat in relief. I was confident I could pass a fair test.

Clerk Petri looked at Baldwin. "You might as well take a seat, too, Mage Baldwin."

"This is a waste of time," declared my stepfather. "You'll see."

"We'll see. And if she passes the test, I'll fine you one hundred silver denarii for lying to a government official."

That sum was equal to a farm laborer's weekly wage.

"Are you calling me a liar?" Baldwin demanded with a ferocious scowl. "And what happens if *I'm* right?"

Unperturbed, the clerk shrugged. "If you are, Ivar here will give the girl thirty lashes before we decide whether to take her as a Dominion apprentice. We'll find out soon enough which of you is telling the truth."

Healer Reynaud blew out a loud breath. He clearly thought we were wasting his time. "All right, girl. A patient comes to you complaining of sore throat. How should you examine and treat?"

Oh, good. An easy one! I uncapped the pen and began writing out my answer. For good measure, I added the recipe for Mama's soothing honey syrup infused with slippery elm bark, licorice root, and ginger.

As my pen scratched across the paper, I felt Baldwin's glare burning into my skin. If he'd been a Dragon, he'd have incinerated me on the spot. But luckily for me, humans couldn't wield fire magic.

Now that I had a chance to avoid the brothel, the prospect of an indentured apprenticeship didn't sound quite so bad. One way or the other, I needed to escape his baleful presence in my life.

When I finished writing out my answer, I looked up to see Healer Reynaud leaning against the nearest wall, studying me with a thoughtful expression. "Now, give me the symptoms and treatment for a broken arm."

Another basic question. I thought back to the time I'd diagnosed and splinted a neighbor's broken wrist under Mama's watchful eye. Then I wrote out everything I did that day, finishing with a poultice of sunflower to reduce inflammation, and an infusion of comfrey to speed the bone's healing.

And so it went for an hour, with Reynaud's questions growing increasingly more difficult.

I answered them all in detail, except for his final question, which had to do with how to craft and apply an anti-aging treatment. For that, I could only answer, "This procedure involves mage-craft," and hope that sufficed.

When I looked up, Clerk Petri asked, "All done?"

I nodded. He scooped up the papers, then quickly scanned them. "Hmm."

From his expression, I couldn't tell whether he was pleased or disappointed.

He handed the pages to Healer Reynaud. "Read this and tell me what do you think."

Reynaud grunted and began reading. I held my breath and prayed to the Divine Mother that he'd give me a favorable assessment.

Clerk Petri returned his gaze to me. Though his expression remained serious, I swear I saw his eyes twinkle.

"One more question, Miss Jacinthe," he said, using my name for the first time instead of calling me *girl*, "to test your culinary knowledge. Write out the recipe and steps for making a strawberry and custard tart."

He handed me a fresh sheet of paper. I wrote furiously, struggling to keep my handwriting neat as my fingers cramped around the pen.

When I was done, I handed him the sheet.

Then I snuck a look at Reynaud. The healer was frowning as he squinted down at my handwriting. Apprehension made my stomach churn.

Clerk Petri cleared his throat and placed the recipe carefully on his blotter. "Your recipe looks near to my wife's. Though she doesn't put mint and basil on her strawberries." He cleared his throat. "I'm satisfied that you have at least a basic knowledge of household cookery. Healer, what's your assessment?"

Reynaud looked up. "Well, the young lady appears to have had *some* training in the healing arts," he admitted in a grudging tone. "Her recipe for honey balm comes straight from the Imperial Academy's handbook of herbal remedies."

Petri folded his hands primly on his desktop. "Well, then. Seeing that Miss Jacinthe has easily passed the skills assessment, I rule that her statements to me were honest and complete."

He leaned over, opened a drawer, and pulled out a sheaf of papers. He slid them across the desk to me.

I saw that they were printed, rather than hand-written, with a gold-foil seal stamped with the Dominion's imperial eagle at the very top.

"The term of an indentured apprenticeship is seven years," he explained. "During that time, His Imperial Majesty will provide you with food, clothing, housing, and a small monthly stipend to cover any additional needed items. In return, you will be apprenticed in an honest profession at His Majesty's pleasure. You are obliged to go where you are assigned, and work in good faith and to the best of your abilities." He gazed sternly at me over his wire-rimmed spectacles, and raised an admonitory finger. "Be warned: if you recklessly incur debts with your master during that term, they can legally extend your indenture until those debts are satisfied."

Which meant that if Petri placed me with someone who was greedy or unethical, I might be indentured forever.

On the other hand, I thought, *how much worse could it be than my current situation?*

"Assuming that you are indeed of sound mind and body, I believe that His Imperial Majesty can make use of your skills and talents as demonstrated here," Petri continued. "If I assure you that you won't be placed in a brothel, will you sign this apprenticeship indenture of your own free will?"

I hesitated, caught between Dragon-fire and Fae poison, or so the old saying went.

If I return to Bernswick, Baldwin and Narcissa will make sure

I have a tragic accident soon. As soon as the thought popped into my head, I realized it was true. A cold shiver raised goosebumps under my gown.

I nodded. "I'll sign it," I said, before I could talk myself out of it.

Despite knowing I had no actual choice about agreeing to the terms, I still read the document carefully. All was as Clerk Petri had told me, just in legalese. I picked up the pen and signed my name, then pushed the contract over so that Baldwin could sign it.

His jaw was clenching under his beard, and his brows were drawn into a thunderous frown. Apparently, he hated that Petri wasn't sending me to the brothels, as per his plan. I wondered if he would refuse to sign out of sheer spite.

And then what? One way or another, I was dead-sure I wouldn't be returning to Bernswick with him.

To my relief, Baldwin leaned forward and countersigned the contract as my legal guardian. Apparently, sending me to a brothel was less important to him than getting rid of me.

Once Petri had witnessed and stamped the document with his official seal, Baldwin rose to take his leave. "Well, that's it, then," my stepfather announced, without looking at me.

"Not quite." Clerk Petri raised his hand to halt Baldwin's exit. "We have one more piece of business to settle, Mage Baldwin." He pulled out another form, scribbled furiously, then handed it over.

"What's this?" Baldwin glanced down at the form. "Is this a *joke*?"

"It's no joke when you lie to one of His Imperial Majesty's officials and attempt to cheat this office out of skilled labor by deliberate misrepresentation," Petri replied. "You are hereby notified in writing that you owe this office the sum of a hundred denarii, due and payable before the Harvest Festival."

"But—" Baldwin sputtered. "You can't *possibly*—"

"Failure to pay this penalty will accrue a five percent penalty each month it remains unpaid," the clerk interrupted him smoothly. "Should you fail to pay within a year, Governor Julius' office will seize your home and possessions, and sell them. Any amount above the penalty will be confiscated for failure to comply with a writ of penalty. Do you understand, Mage Baldwin?"

"You—you're nothing but a thief!" he blustered.

I couldn't help grinning at his discomfiture. It was the first time I'd ever seen my stepfather held to account for *any* of his actions, and I was determined to enjoy it while it lasted.

"Do you understand?" Petri repeated calmly.

"Fine. You'll have your money before Harvest Festival," Baldwin muttered, crumpling the writ and stuffing it in his belt-pouch.

Even though I knew it was hopeless, I couldn't help asking, "And where should Mage Baldwin send my belongings?"

If I'd known what he planned for today, I would've packed. As it was, I had only the clothes I wore, and nothing else, not even a comb or a change of underwear.

As expected, his mouth twisted. "What belongings? You're lucky I'm leaving you that gown and those shoes."

"So, you're keeping everything?" I asked bitterly. "Even the things I inherited from Mama?"

"You greedy wench!" His voice rose as his face flushed purplish red, like a ripe plum. Was it too much to hope for an apoplexy? "That house and everything in it is *mine* now. Isa owed me that much for my generosity in caring for you."

As he spun on his heel and stalked towards the door, I glimpsed Ivar's expression. The tall young man looked appalled.

Clerk Petri busied himself with tucking away my apprentice contract in a large wooden filing cabinet standing against the wall behind his desk. Meanwhile, Healer Reynaud scurried upstairs again.

"Fine," I snarled at my stepfather's retreating back. "May you enjoy all the happiness and luck you deserve, Baldwin of Bernswick, and may your treatment of me return to you threefold."

My tattoo prickled, as it did whenever I lost my temper.

Without breaking stride, Baldwin reflexively crossed his fingers and made the traditional sign to ward off a curse.

But of course, I had no magic with which to fashion a curse. Just a fervent desire to see that he and Narcissa received their just desserts.

I added, "Just wait. I'll be back someday, and both you and that woman will regret everything you did to me."

Baldwin stopped dead just before he reached the door. "You're vowing revenge on me?" he asked, sounding incredulous. "*You?*"

Instead of the anger I expected, he laughed. He was still chuckling as he stepped through the door and pulled it closed behind him.

I let out a breath of relief. I suddenly felt lighter, as if I'd just shed a suit of heavy, constricting armor.

Clerk Petri reseated himself behind his desk.

"Miss Jacinthe, let's discuss what happens next. I have here a listing of all the current openings for indentured apprentices." He shuffled through a thick pile of papers, looking increasingly uncomfortable.

I waited impatiently, fighting the urge to squirm on the hard stool. Where would I be going, and what would I be doing for the next seven years?

At long last, Petri cleared his throat and looked up. "I regret to inform you that there aren't actually any apprentice healer spots available in Dominion infirmaries right now."

My heart sank. The fear returned. Why hadn't he told me that *before* I signed that damned contract? Where was he sending me?

"But there are several openings for kitchen apprentices at various institutions," he continued reassuringly. "You could choose to work for a cook, saucier, baker, cheese-maker, or butcher."

Feeling battered by the abrupt rise and fall of my fortunes over the past hour, I just stared at him.

As the silence stretched, his brows lifted. "That's not acceptable to the fine young lady?" he asked, his tone thick with sarcasm now. "Or would you prefer the dockside brothel, after all? They always welcome new apprentices, even skinny ones like you."

"N-no!" I protested. "Any position in a kitchen would be fine, but I'd prefer to work with a baker or pastry-cook."

I wasn't afraid of hard work, and at least apprentices were fed and housed. For the next few years, I could count on having a full belly and a roof over my head.

Clerk Petri nodded. "Excellent. Just what I wanted to hear."

My relief at dodging the brothel was short-lived, though. "Where were you thinking of sending me?"

His gaze dropped back down to the sheaf of papers. "Darkstone

Academy is in dire need of all classes of apprentices, but especially kitchen workers. In fact, there's a vessel departing for there on the afternoon tide. It's carrying a royal hostage as well as a group of apprentices. As soon as you pass your physical examination, Ivar here will escort you down to the dock and see you on board The Silver Dolphin."

I gulped. Despite its name, everyone knew that the Darkstone Academy for the Magical Arts wasn't a proper mage school at all. It was actually a fortified prison, built on an otherwise-uninhabited island. The students were the high-born rejects from other academies and rogue mage-blood youths who'd tried to evade the law regarding training.

The government considered commoners with mage potential who failed their training too dangerous to live, and promptly executed them. But nobly-born failures got a second chance at Darkstone Academy.

The prison island was also the place where the dominus kept his supernatural hostages.

I flashed back to my earlier glimpse of the merman. Was he being sent to Darkstone Island, too?

Two hundred years ago, a powerful and charismatic Neapolitan general named Severus Cavalieri di Corredo united the human kingdoms of the Northern Continent and Western Isles, and rallied their armies to defeat the Dragons and the Fae living in the eastern islands and Southern Continent.

The victorious general was crowned as Dominus Victor Augustus the First, and he ruthlessly kept the peace by exacting punishing tribute from the conquered nations and demanding the children of their rulers and nobles as hostages for the peace terms.

By the terms of the peace treaty that ended the Great War, the Dragon, Fae, Sea People, and Djinn rulers were required to send their heirs to the Dominion to prove their good faith. These high-born hostages stayed as the Dominus' official guests for a term of one to two years before being permitted to return home when their replacements arrived.

Great. I'd finally escaped the toxic atmosphere of Baldwin and Narcissa's household, only to find myself condemned to spend the next seven years working in a distant prison filled with crazy mages deemed too dangerous to live in normal society and captive supernatural nobles who hated humans.

As Clerk Petri directed me upstairs for my physical examination, I wondered briefly if going to a brothel wouldn't have been a better fate after all.

Chapter 4

Jacinthe

Herrewick, Isle of Abbonay
Three hours later

As I followed Guard Ivar through the maze of narrow streets leading from the DBA building down to the seaside docks, I nervously patted my new belt-pouch.

I might not have a single coin to my name, but I had a full stomach—for the second time today!—and a dense, freshly baked rye roll I'd saved from the midday bowl of vegetable soup with bacon that Petri had shared with me at the DBA. The roll's presence in my pouch reassured me I'd have something for supper.

That was a level of security I hadn't had in months.

Even better, Clerk Petri had issued me a change of clothing and a traveling kit for my journey to Darkstone Academy. My new belongings hung over my shoulder, neatly packed in a sailor's sack made from waterproof oiled canvas.

Ivar caught my movement from the corner of his eye and gave me a sympathetic smile.

"Don't you worry, miss, they'll feed ye aboard the ship," he reassured me. Then he sighed. "That stepfather of yours... a right piece of work, he was. I've a daughter of my own, and if something happens to me, I hope my wife will find a *decent* man to marry."

"I hope so, too," I said, then added glumly, "but Baldwin adored my mother, and he was always good to her."

Ivar just shook his head and continued walking.

The past few hours had passed in a whirl of activity.

After Baldwin left the DBA office, Clerk Petri sent me upstairs to undergo a physical examination.

To my relief, Healer Reynaud's wife, Healer Emritte, conducted the examination rather than Reynaud. She was a tiny woman with silver hair and a no-nonsense attitude. She noted my age, height, hair color, weight, and asked me whether I'd borne any children.

Then she ordered me to strip and noted each of my scars, moles, and other marks. She grunted in disapproval as she examined the small tattoo located discreetly below my belly button. I ignored her.

Islanders considered inked women scandalous, but Mama came from the Imperial Capital State, where both men and women proudly displayed intricate designs on their skin.

She had designed and inked my tattoo herself shortly after we'd arrived in Bernswick. I didn't remember much about the occasion, but she always told me it was to celebrate our narrow escape from a fire that threatened to burn down our new house.

The stylized hyacinth inscribed on my skin, surrounded by a short blessing in the ancient calligraphic Saba script, was now my only keepsake from my mother.

"Well, you could use some feeding-up, that's for sure," Emritte said when she was done. "But at least you're not ailing or pregnant. We get a lot of families trying to fob off their unmarried girls on us when the babe's fathers deny parentage or simply vanish." She motioned to the neat pile of my folded clothing. "Get dressed, then I'll take you over to Mage Blaedswyth's place to get you fitted with your collar."

"Collar?" I asked with a stab of apprehension.

Emritte's dark brows rose, as if my question surprised her. "Yes, the DBA requires each indentured apprentice to wear a collar. It marks you as an imperial servant." She gave me a narrow-eyed look, and added, "It will also prevent you from leaving your assigned duties until the term of your contract is complete."

"Oh," I said.

It made sense that the Dominion would take steps to prevent runaways. But dread clawed through me at the prospect of being trapped in a dangerous situation with no way of escape.

The mage's shop was located a few doors down from the DBA office. It was an old, narrow, three-story half-timbered building, a little crooked from age, squeezed between newer stone buildings on either side. It reminded me of my home.

The mage who answered the shop looked like she was fresh out of the academy, with two thick golden braids framing a round, pleasant face with rosy cheeks.

"Oh good, an easy one," she said when she heard Emritte's request. "My last job, a rush request from the governor, took a lot out of me."

I wondered what kind of major working she'd performed for the governor, but she offered no further details.

As she ushered us into her ground-floor shop, I breathed in the scent of herbs and exotic drugs, mixed with the faint brimstone trace of recent magic. The smells transported me back to pleasant afternoons spent in Mama's company, mixing up medicines and her popular anti-aging cream.

The actual collar fitting took less than ten minutes. Mage

Blaedswyth had a stock of slim silver circlets hanging on a wall-hook, each engraved with a repeating pattern of imperial eagles on the outside and a line of spell-runes on the inside.

The mage lifted one of the hinged circlets and murmured an invocation. I saw the spells woven into the runes activate, making the collar glow with bluish magical energy.

Not everyone could see that energy. It was what had given me hope that I'd pass the Magecraft Aptitude Examiner's examination. But, alas, simply being sensitive to magic didn't mean I had any of my own.

Mage Blaedswyth snapped the collar shut around my neck and said simply, "Lock."

As the mechanism clicked, a tingling rush of warm magic raced over my skin, pooling in a brief, painful flare of heat over the tattoo on my belly.

The sensations died away almost immediately.

"And that's that," the mage declared, stepping back.

Magritte signed a government payment voucher, then I followed the old healer back to the DBA office, where Clerk Petri issued me clothes and some other necessities for the journey ahead.

Once I'd eaten a hasty lunch, Petri dispatched Guard Ivar to take me down to the seaside docks.

We approached the row of broad stone quays that jutted into Herresund Bay. The city of Herrewick stood on the site where the River Rouse flowed into the bay. It had become wealthy as the Western Isles' main hub for transferring riverboat and inter-island trading ship cargoes of lumber, ores, dried fish, and furs to larger ocean-going vessels headed for the Continent.

"Ah, there it is!" Ivar exclaimed, pointing at a big, single-masted wooden ship pulled up alongside of the quays. "And isn't she a beauty?"

The ship that would take me south across the sea to Darkstone Academy was a typical wooden trading cog, with high sides and raised platforms at the front and back. It had a broad, square sail dyed a faded blue, and flaking gold paint outlining an imperial eagle.

My steps slowed as we approached the narrow gangplank.

"Oh, no need to worry, Miss Jacinthe," said Ivar, misinterpreting my hesitation. "Ye'll be safe enough in that ship. Look at those fortified bow and stern castles!"

I nodded, though I didn't have the faintest idea of what bow and stern castles were, or why they were useful. I guessed they were the elevated platforms at the front and back.

"And no danger of being becalmed, either," Ivar continued. "Look—it's got oar-ports, for rowing if the wind fails." He pointed at a line of small, square holes along the side of the ship, about a man's height above the waterline.

To my eyes, the ship looked like a super-sized version of the sturdy flat-bottomed river traders, which could carry bulky loads even in shallow water, and beach on riverbanks without harm in places that had no docks.

"I won't lie," Ivar said, a note of longing in his voice. "I wish I was going with you. After the ship delivers you and the other apprentices to Darkstone, it's supposed to continue on to Neapolis Capitola. I've never been there, but I've heard stories."

I sighed. It was clear he saw adventure and excitement when he looked upon the ship. But all I saw was a long exile from the only home I'd ever known.

At the base of the gangplank, Ivar cupped his hands around his mouth. "Hallo, the captain!" he shouted in heavily accented

Capitolan. "Permission to board one more passenger for Darkstone Academy!"

A black-bearded man with skin as brown as my own stomped to the railing. He peered down at us and spat over the railing in disgust.

"*Another* one?" He shook his head. "It's bad enough that His Excellency sent me that damned fish-man without warning, but now Petri is loading me up with *more* mewling children?"

Undeterred, Ivar pulled a document from beneath his leather breastplate and waved it at the captain. "I have a travel voucher for Apprentice Jacinthe of Bernswick, bound for Darkstone Academy."

"And how am I supposed to feed all these extra mouths with no notice?" grumbled the captain. "Never mind, I'll send one of my boys for extra food, and make sure he collects the reimbursement from old Petri before we set sail." He waved towards the gangplank. "Well, girl, do you speak Capitolan?"

I nodded.

"What are you waiting for, then?" he demanded impatiently. "Come aboard and bring me that paper!"

"This is where I leave you," Ivar said, handing me the folded document. "Best of luck to ye, Miss Jacinthe. If nothing else, ye'll be getting meals regular-like now."

"Thank you, Guard Ivar," I said, then added, because he'd been kind to me, "I hope you get to visit Neapolis Capitola one day."

His face creased in a smile, and his blue eyes twinkled. "I hope so, too. It'll take some doing to convince my wife, though."

I turned to walk up the steep gangplank. It was frighteningly narrow, had no railings, and bounced alarmingly with every step.

When I reached the deck, the captain was waiting for me. "I'm Captain Bartolmi." He surveyed me with dark, piercing eyes. "Apprentice Jacinthe, is it? At least you're not bringing a ton of baggage with you."

He snatched the document from my hand and tucked it into his broad, worn leather belt without reading it. "Follow me," he ordered, turning on his heel and marching across the deck.

The planks beneath my shoes looked worn and weathered, but still in good condition. All the crew members stopped working to gawk at me as I followed Captain Bartolmi towards the structure Ivar had called "the stern castle," which was built on two terraced levels. I heard someone wolf-whistle, and a couple of comments.

"She's a real looker. Wonder if she'd be up for a bit of sport wi' us?"

"—wish I could bend her over and—"

The captain whirled around with a ferocious grimace. "Get back to work, you lazy sods!" he shouted. "And I'll not have you lot bothering the passengers. *Any* of 'em!"

To me, he said, "And I'll not have *you* wandering around my ship, getting into trouble. My men are hard workers, but they're the rough sort and not to be trusted around young ladies. Or boys," he added.

"Yes, Captain," I answered, shooting the sailors a nervous glance.

I didn't like the prospect of being trapped on board with a gang of lecherous ruffians for a fortnight, or even longer if the winds failed.

"This is where all the passengers' and officers' cabins are," the captain said, gesturing up to the stern castle's terraces. "My cabin's on the second level, along with our noble guest." His mouth twisted as he said the last, as if he'd bitten into a green apple.

He led me up a series of narrow steps to the first landing. From here, I could see the entire ship. It hummed like a beehive with activity.

I spotted one sailor climbing the rigging, while dockworkers trundled wheelbarrows piled high with sacks up the gangplank and onto the deck. Sailors shouted and swore as they wrestled the sacks down a hatch, presumably to store them somewhere in the hold.

"Absolutely no going belowdecks unless I'm with you," he continued. "For any trips up to the deck for meals, to use the heads, or to get fresh air, I want you kids to always pair up—hell, come out in a group, if you can." He turned his head and fixed me with a stern glare. "And any of you get seasick, you're in charge of cleaning up the mess."

I nodded. "How many other apprentices are there on this voyage?"

"Seven, including you. You and the other girls will bunk here." Captain Bartolmi marched over to one of the four doors facing the landing. "The boys are next door."

He turned the knob and revealed a small room crowded with hammocks.

Six dark wooden clothing chests stood against the walls beneath the hammocks, along with a collection of chamber pots. A small porthole window let in light and fresh air.

A group of children looked up as the door opened. Some lay in hammocks and others sat on the floor and the tops of the chests, playing a card game. They all looked young, somewhere between twelve and fifteen years of age.

"These are the other apprentices headed for Darkstone

Academy," the captain said to me. "Since you're the oldest of the lot, I'm putting you in charge of 'em. You watch over 'em and keep 'em outta trouble."

My heart sank. I was used to watching over my three younger sisters, but now I was going to be responsible for six strangers?

The captain glared at the children and jerked a callused thumb in my direction. "This here is Apprentice Jacinthe. If she tells you to do something, you do it. No questions, no back-talk. Understood?"

The youngest, a pair of wide-eyed girls seated together on a chest, shrank back. A tall, dark-haired boy wearing a farmer's plain linen shirt and dirty breeches stared defiantly back at the captain. All of them wore the same silver collars as me.

Captain Bartolmi raised his voice. "Do. You. Understand? Or am I gonna have to throw one of you lot overboard to feed the sharks and fish-men?"

All the children nodded. "Yes, sir," whispered one of the girls lying in a hammock.

"Good. We're settin' sail on the afternoon tide. You stay put and listen for the ship's bell. It'll call you to supper. You got any questions, you save 'em until we're clear of the harbor and well out to sea."

He stomped away and swiftly descended the ladder-stairs leading down to the main deck, leaving me alone to face my new charges.

"Um, hello," I said to them, lowering the bag with my new belongings to the floor. "Are you all headed to Darkstone Academy?"

"Yeah," said the younger-looking of the two boys. Short, curly amber hair curled around his face. "I'm Kenric, and I'm gonna be apprenticing with the academy's metalsmith."

"Pleased to meet you, Kenric," I said, and received a long, thoughtful look in return.

"I'm Elswyth and this is my little sister Rheda," said one of the wide-eyed girls seated on a chest. "Our dad was the village baker, but he died. So Mam apprenticed us. We'll be working in the academy kitchens."

"That's where I'm going, too," I told them. Both girls brightened immediately, so I added, "My mama was a healer-mage, and she taught me all about herbs and cooking."

The tall boy wearing farmer's clothes said, "My name's Toland. I've ten brothers and sisters, and my ma and da canna feed the lot of us, so they apprenticed me an' two of my sisters, 'cause we're the youngest."

He tilted his head toward the final two girls, both as dark-haired as he and lying in hammocks. They were pale and looked unwell, but smiled tentatively at me.

"Those're Sunniva and Winifred. Ma told the DBA clerk they're good at needlework, so they're to be apprenticed to the academy's tailors. I'll likely be sent to the academy's kitchen gardens and orchard."

"I'm sure we'll all be good friends by the time we arrive at the academy," I told them with more confidence than I felt. Sunniva and Winifred already looked seasick, and we were still moored in the harbor. I dreaded the moment we actually set sail. "Have any of you been on a ship like this before?"

They all shook their heads. "Nah, just the river ferries," Kenric said.

"Same," I told him. "So, I have no idea if I'm going to be seasick or not."

"I don't like this ship," Sunniva complained. "I wanna go home!"

"You canna, so just shut up about it, will ya?" Toland snapped.

I gave the girl a sympathetic smile. "Everything will be okay," I reassured her.

"Would Captain Bartolmi *really* throw us overboard to the fish-men if we're naughty?" Elswyth asked in a hushed voice.

Kenric laughed. "He don't need to do that. We got a fish-man of our own, right here on the ship! I saw him come aboard right after I got here." He frowned. "He didn't have any shark's teeth or tentacles, though. He just looked mad." The boy sounded disappointed at the lack of teeth and tentacles.

"The merman is *here?*" I exclaimed in shock. "On this *ship?*"

I realized he was the "noble guest" and "royal hostage" that Petri and the captain had mentioned.

Why else would one of the merfolk allow himself to be paraded through the city's streets on a litter, and why else would the governor's guards have accompanied him?

No wonder he looked so angry, I thought with unwilling sympathy. *Trapped on a ship with a bunch of humans when he could swim to the academy on his own!*

Hampered by his tail, the poor merman wouldn't be able to get around on his own. I wondered which of the sailors were assigned to carry him around the ship.

All of my new friends nodded vigorously.

"He's in the cabin *right above us!*" Elswyth said in a whisper, as if she feared the merman might hear her.

∞∞∞

Much to my fellow apprentices' disappointment, there was no sign of the merman at supper, which was served in the ship's main cabin on the lower deck.

As I'd feared, Sunniva and Winifred became violently seasick as soon as the ship cast off and left the sheltered waters of the bay.

To my relief, I and the rest of the apprentices only felt queasy, a sensation that vanished when the dinner bell rang and we got some fresh air, walking across the deck to the ship's main cabin.

There were a few leers and smirks from the sailors as I herded my charges into the dining hall, but the captain's quelling glare suppressed any unwelcome comments.

The crew dined at a long table, crowded elbow to elbow on benches. Our little group sat with the captain and his officers at a smaller table with chairs.

The furniture was all bolted to the floor of the cabin, and the drinking-glasses all had odd, bulbous shapes. Captain Bartolmi explained that in heavy seas, these arrangements kept liquids from spilling and chairs and tables from being flung around.

To my surprise and pleasure, supper was roasted chicken, served with lightly boiled vegetables in a butter sauce and crusty, freshly-baked bread. It was the best meal I'd eaten in months.

After everyone finished eating and a pair of young cabin boys cleared the dishes, Captain Bartolmi escorted me and my charges back to our cabin, since his own quarters were on the terrace above us.

On the way, he pointed out the ship's most important features, including the location of the latrines, which he called "heads." They were at the very front of the ship, located in the narrow bowsprit just behind the figurehead.

As we neared the stern castle and our cabins, Kenric exclaimed,

"Look! There he is!" and pointed up to the stern castle's upper deck.

The merman stood at the railing, gazing out over the water. His long hair whipped across his face and streamed out to one side like a silver banner. His skin was pale and luminous as a pearl, gilded now by the slanting rays of the setting sun.

He wore human clothing now, a rich, sea-green velvet tunic, with a gilded leather belt and close-fitting golden silk leggings that disappeared into fine leather boots. Unlike the last time I'd seen him, he was unmasked, his beautiful, inhuman face bared to the salty wind.

He shouldn't have been able to hear Kenric's comment over the sound of the waves hitting the ship's sides, the creak of timbers, and the loud thrum of the sail stretched taut with the wind.

But he turned to face us. To face *me*.

The breath caught in my throat as I met his huge, dark eyes. My heart began hammering in my ears. This powerful supernatural creature, one of mankind's ancient enemies, stared at me, his gaze unblinking.

Terror... and something else... dried my mouth and the inside of my throat.

I looked away and tried to calm my racing heart. A lock of hair escaped my loose braid and caught in my eyelashes, covering my nose and tickling my lips. I desperately wanted to push it aside, but was afraid to draw the merman's attention any further.

Then the strangeness of the scene finally struck me. The merman was *standing* on the ship's deck. On *legs*.

"What happened to his tail?" I croaked.

With a look of disgust, the merman turned his back to us.

"Shape-changing spell," answered Captain Bartolmi. "His Imperial Majesty requires that all royal hostages take human form while residing in the Dominion."

A sailor coiling rope nearby guffawed and said cruelly, "And now the fish-man can't swim any better than the rest of us!"

I stared at the merman's wind-whipped hair and resolute back, and noted how tightly he gripped the railing, as if he needed its support to remain upright.

Mama had told me that shape-changing spells were incredibly agonizing. They used brute magical force to rearrange bones, muscles, and flesh into a shape they were never meant to take.

Horror and pity replaced my instinctive terror at coming face to face with one of the dreaded merfolk, those cold and ruthless predators who ruled the underwater kingdoms. The merman's original form this afternoon had been sleek and powerful, perfectly adapted to life in the water.

No wonder he seems so angry! By the Divine Mother, seeing him tortured by magic and then condemned to a life above the sea's surface made *me* angry, too. And deeply sad on his behalf.

He's a lost soul cast into exile, just like me and my fellow apprentices, I realized.

Perhaps I was being the fool, just as Baldwin always accused me. But at that moment, I vowed to become his friend.

Chapter 5

Jacinthe

"I'm so happy Sunniva and Winifred finally stopped puking," Elswyth said the next morning as we emerged, squinting from the cabin's gloom into bright sunlight. "Maybe they're done with being seasick," she added hopefully.

"Or maybe they just don't have anything left to vomit," I responded.

My throat felt scratchy and my eyes were gritty and watering in the piercing morning light. I knew I looked like a slattern with my gown stained, dark circles beneath my eyes, and my hair coming out of its braid.

It had been a long, sleepless night. And I feared it was just the first of many.

The girls' bouts of violent sea-sickness had taken their toll on all of us. I wished futilely for the store of herbs I kept stocked back home in Bernswick. Some ginger, or even peppermint or chamomile, might have helped.

Eventually, the stink of vomit had triggered the rest of us to throw up, too. Yuck.

I staggered over to the railing, and emptied the chamber pots over the side. Elswyth and Rheda did the same. We descended to the main deck, then rinsed the pots out in the washtub of seawater fastened to the deck, before returning to the dim, stuffy cabin.

The ship's bell rang, summoning us to breakfast.

Sunniva and Winifred were finally asleep, their faces pale and their hair matted with filth. I decided to not wake them, and just bring back dry bread and something to drink.

Back outside, I encountered Kenric and Toland. Both boys appeared to have slept well, and greeted us with disgusting cheerfulness.

An hour later, our little group returned from a hearty breakfast of strong tea, fresh bread, and fried ham. The ship's cook had given me a stone jug of lukewarm tea heavily sweetened with honey, and a package of dry, hard, ship's biscuit wrapped in a napkin.

As we emerged from the dining hall, I spotted the merman standing at the railing on the highest deck, which also served as the roof of the stern castle.

He had not joined us for either supper last night or breakfast this morning, and I wondered whether he'd eaten at all since boarding the ship yesterday.

The merman was alone. I glanced around and saw all the sailors gathered near the front of the ship, eyeing him and muttering nervously.

Just like yesterday, the merman was once again gazing out over the endless expanse of waves. Though his face was expressionless, he radiated pain and utter misery.

He turned his head to watch us cross the lower deck and climb the stairs to our cabins.

He's in danger. He's thinking about jumping, Mama's voice warned me inside my head.

Over the years, I'd learned to listen to that voice. It was never wrong.

On impulse, I waved at the merman and called, "Good morning!"

He recoiled in apparent surprise.

The sailors guffawed.

At my side, Toland hissed, "Miss Jacinthe, what are you doing? He's *dangerous!*"

I made my decision. I thrust the jug and packet of biscuit into his hands. "I need to talk to him about something. You and Kenric make sure that your sisters at least try to eat and drink a little."

Then, heart pounding, I climbed the stairs to the next level of the stern castle, then grabbed for the ladder leading up to the stern castle's deck.

The merman's great dark eyes locked on mine as I reached the top of the ladder.

Today, he was all in blue. He wore a sleeveless, midnight-blue wool tunic decorated with a flowing pattern of silver embroidery over a sky-colored linen shirt with matching linen leggings. Long, freshly healed pink scars ran down the sides of his neck and disappeared under the collar of his tunic.

The sight of them alarmed me. *Did he already try to kill himself?* With cuts that deep, he should've bled out in moments. Apparently, someone—probably a healing mage—had intervened in time and saved him.

I crawled a few inches forward, then rose unsteadily to my feet as the deck rose and fell beneath me with the motion of the waves.

Then, suddenly, a cool hand closed around my wrist, steadying me. Startled, I jumped. I hadn't seen the merman move, but he stood right in front of me now. An embarrassing squeak escaped my throat.

"What do you want?" he demanded in fluent Capitolan. His voice was low and intriguingly husky.

He didn't let go of my wrist. I was acutely aware of his hard grip, and the smooth, uncalloused skin of his webbed fingers. I glanced down, and saw that his hands were webbed and clawed like an otter.

My gaze returned to his disturbing scars.

"It won't do you any good to jump overboard," I blurted.

He gave me a look that made me acutely aware of my flyaway hair, stained gown, and the lingering odor of puke. My face heated as I realized how I must look, standing next to his elegant clothes and glossy silver hair.

His beautiful mouth twisted in a sneer. "I was *born* to swim, Drylander," he said in the same tone that he might have used on a toddler. "I have spent my entire life living underwater."

"Yes, but not like you are now," I retorted. I pointed at his left ear, where a small silver walrus with long, curving tusks hung from his pierced lobe. An imperial eagle had been engraved on the walrus' side.

The earring glowed with magic, and I guessed that this was the anchor for the shape-changing spell. "Won't you drown without your tail and gills?"

His mouth thinned. "I suppose." He sounded disinterested, but his hand rose to touch his scarred neck, and his shoulders slumped by the barest degree.

Then I realized those weren't scars from a failed suicide attempt. They were the remnants of his gills after the shape-changing spell.

"Besides, they're going to undo that shape-changing spell once your period as an imperial hostage ends, right?"

"What do *you* know about magic, Drylander?" His gaze devoured me. My heart, already pounding, sped up. "You're no mage. I sense no power in you."

"You're right. I'm no mage. But my mother was," I replied. "Her name was Isabeau of Bernswick, and she treated any living thing that came to her for help. She trained me as her assistant, so I know a lot about magic… in theory."

"In theory," he repeated coolly. But I could sense that his interest in our conversation was dispelling some of the dark clouds hanging over him.

And he was still holding onto my wrist, his grip firm but not painful. That meant he wanted me to stay, right?

Somehow, his touch made me feel oddly safe.

"Um, are you headed to Darkstone Academy, too?" I asked.

I already knew the answer, but I wanted to keep him talking as long as possible.

"Of course. Aren't all the emissaries to the Drylanders now imprisoned at the academy?"

I nodded. "I'm sorry. I know it's not fair."

"But if it isn't fair," he spoke the word with contempt, "then why are you Drylanders doing it?"

I sighed. "It's because of some tremendous scandal a couple of decades ago. Something to do with a Dragon hostage at court, and one of the imperial princesses." I frowned, trying to remember the details. It had been a long time since I heard the story. "I think the princess died. Maybe the Dragon killed her?"

That was the only explanation that made sense: a supernatural had murdered one of the Dominus' family members, and he'd banished them all to the most secure and isolated location in the Dominion.

"And now your ruler punishes all the supernatural races for the Wind-Walker's transgression?" the merman asked, reasonably enough.

"I said it was unfair," I pointed out, then tried to think of a way to steer the conversation back into safer waters. "Um, I forgot to introduce myself. I'm Jacinthe of Bernswick, and I'm headed to Darkstone Academy, too."

"I know," he said. "I overheard the captain and the younglings calling you Apprentice Jacinthe and Miss Jacinthe. Which form of address do you prefer?"

"Um, just Jacinthe is fine," I said, unnerved that the merman had been paying such close attention to all the conversations on board. His ears must be really, *really* keen. "I didn't catch your name."

"Because they only refer to me as 'the merman' or 'the fish-man,'" he said, his tone dangerously bland. "You may call me Tama."

"Just Tama?" I asked. "No honorific?"

Even commoners were addressed by the honorific of their professions. And weren't all the imperial hostages supposed to be nobles or the rulers' heirs?

He raised his chin. "You're a Drylander. What do you know of Sea People clans?"

"Nothing," I confessed.

He nodded. "Then Tama will do. 'Warrior Tama,' if you must."

"Girl, what the hell are you doing with that thing?" The captain's shout rose from the lower deck. "Get back to your cabin. *Now!*"

"Ah, I'd forgotten I was also 'thing,'" murmured Tama with no trace of irony.

His fingers remained clamped resolutely around my wrist. I tugged gently. "I'm sorry, Tama, I have to go. But I'd like to speak with you again."

I met his eyes, and saw a flash of suspicion. His hand briefly squeezed my wrist before he released me. "That would be acceptable."

As I climbed down the ladder, I saw Tama had already turned his attention back to the waves.

He didn't say no, I thought in triumph. Which meant he *was* lonely, but probably too proud to admit it.

I smiled to myself as I returned to the cabin to tend to my seasick charges.

∞∞∞

Tama

The next day

"Fucking fish-man, thinks he's better than us!" one of the sailors whispered to his companion.

He and his comrade were scrubbing the deck some distance away, so I don't know whether he thought to keep his conversation private.

But my new Drylander ears were sharp… painfully so, on a vessel built from dead trees that constantly creaked and screeched and thumped like something undergoing death-agonies.

I knew exactly how the ship must feel. My body felt caught in invisible weighted nets that dragged on joints and sent spears of pain through bones and muscles with every movement. Simply standing upright, precariously balanced on my new legs, was torture.

I'm a man now, not a mewling child, I told myself. *I must appear strong and fierce, a true Walrus Clan warrior of the Sea People.*

But I wanted off this damned Drylander ship. I wanted to sleep, rocking and mercifully weightless, in Mother Sea's cool embrace. I wanted it more than I ever wanted anything in my life.

And I'd fought hard and trained long to become the youngest clan member ever to gain full warrior status.

When Grandmother selected me as the current clan representative to the human Dominus, she informed me it was a great honor. I was to spend two summers in the Drylander realm, representing all the Sea People clans in the Seas-That-Freeze.

Our undersea territories were harsh places, but filled with great beauty and abundant food. We prided ourselves in being tougher and fiercer than our cousin clans, who dwelled in the warmer southern waters.

But so far, there'd been no honor in the way I'd been treated. Instead, I was a prisoner rather than an emissary.

Immediately following my arrival in the Drylander city, I'd been paraded through the streets. I lay on an elevated platform like a beached porpoise, breathing stale water while crowds jeered and insulted me.

Then one of their mages had tortured me for hours, stealing my tail and gills and imprisoning me in Drylander form. But I'd refused to give the creature the satisfaction of hearing me scream. I'd bitten through the inside of my cheeks, trying to remain stoically silent, as befitted a warrior.

Now, I was being sent to a prison island, far from the imperial court, to serve out my time as emissary. Even if I'd been willing to sacrifice my honor and escape this hell I found myself in, I could never reach home.

Mother Sea would devour this weak, air-breathing form in minutes.

Speaking of which—how in the name of Great-grandfather Whale did they bear it? Breathing this toxic thing they called "air" burned my new-made lungs and constantly sucked the life-giving moisture from every inch of my body. It dried my throat and mouth until they shriveled like storm-flung seaweed on a beach under the merciless sun.

Only two nights had passed since the mage had imprisoned me in this shape. How was I going to endure two whole *years* of this constant torment?

I had a sudden, horrible thought. Had Clan Grandmother *known* what the Drylanders would do to me? That they would force me to change shape and then exile me to a prison island?

Had she deliberately condemned me to this torture?

Of course she had, I realized. I wasn't the first emissary to the Drylanders, after all. Many others had gone before me. But the ones who survived the experience and returned never spoke of their time in the Dry Above.

I didn't want to think she had betrayed me. My clan's loyalty to our Clan Grandmother depended on everyone trusting that she knew best and would always act in the clan's best interest.

But what if that "best interest" required her to sacrifice her youngest warrior to the Drylanders?

I shuddered and looked around for a distraction.

And found it when the flame-haired Drylander female—*Jacinthe*—emerged from the cabin she shared with the group of younglings.

I watched avidly as she flung the contents of a metal pisspot into the sea. Then she slowly and carefully descended the stairs to the main deck, heading for the large tub of seawater there.

I thought back to my conversation with her. She had treated me differently than any other Drylander I had encountered—with respect, as if I were a real person to her. And while we conversed, I'd been able to forget about the torment of being exiled on dry land.

My gaze lingered on the thick, flame-colored braid hanging halfway down her back. I imagined it unbound, floating weightless around her face underwater.

But it wasn't just her full lips or sharp features that held my attention. It was her eyes, the striking combination of rich browns and greens like kelp shimmering in the sunlight at the water's surface. There was something somber and captivating about them, like someone who had been through many trials.

I remembered the heat of her sun-kissed skin beneath my fingers yesterday, and imagined running my hands all over her naked body.

What would mating her feel like? Was her sex as hot and dry as her skin? Or was it smooth and wet, like the inside of her mouth?

My sex stirred inside its protective pouch at the prospect of sliding into her hot, slippery flesh while we kissed and I explored every part of her.

Such relationships were forbidden, but they still happened. Everyone knew the stories about Sea People who'd taken Drylanders as lovers.

And all of those stories had ended badly for the couple.

I won't be so foolish, I told myself.

And yet, I couldn't look away from Jacinthe. I scrutinized every detail of her being; her firm jaw and dignified bearing, and the way she moved with a grace that resembled the gentle sway of kelp fronds beneath the waves close to shore.

Then the serenity of the moment shattered when two burly seamen cornered her. Their body language screamed predatory intent. As a predator myself, I knew the signs.

One sailor caught her braid in his meaty fist while the other roughly grabbed her right breast.

Instant rage surged through me, but I forced myself to stay where I was. I didn't like what I saw, but I wasn't familiar with Drylander mating customs.

But what happened next made things very clear for me. My claws sank into the wooden railing as Jacinthe cried out in anger and fear. She slapped away the hand grasping her breast and tried to free herself from the hold on her hair.

The sailors' advances were unwelcome. That pleased me, though I didn't understand why. I'd just met this Drylander. She had no claim on my protection.

But that didn't matter.

Her defiance seemed to amuse the Drylander males. They laughed heartily before flinging their arms around her and dragging her towards the open hatch leading down into the cargo hold.

I drew on my power, the deep well of magic inside me rising to my call. I prepared to slice these fools into ribbons, just like the orca I'd battled and defeated for my initiation into warrior-rank.

Then my new earring flared to painful life, as hot and bright as the merciless sun burning overhead.

It swallowed my magic down to the last drop, sucking me dry

like a helpless clam in the grip of a starfish.

I sagged in horror. An invisible tentacle, strong as a giant squid, closed around my chest and squeezed the breath out of me.

The Drylander mage hadn't just stolen my tail and my gills. She'd taken *everything* from me!

My claws sank into the wooden railing as I fought to remain upright. And it reminded me I wasn't *completely* helpless.

I quickly strode towards the edge of the stern deck and bellowed: "Get away from her!"

Three faces tilted up to look at me. Jacinthe looked angry and terrified, and her beautiful eyes pleaded for my aid.

The two sailors scowled. One of them shouted, "You want in on the action, fish-man? You can have a turn when we're done."

"No!" Swift as an ambushing shark, Jacinthe's head whipped around. She broke one of her captor's noses. He released his hold and stumbled back, blood dripping onto the planks of the deck.

Then she spun and sank her teeth into the arm of the sailor gripping her braid.

"You little bitch!" Undeterred, he wrapped her hair around his hand and kicked the back of her leg, sending her down to her knees. "You're gonna pay for that!"

Clan Grandmother had warned me not to make trouble among the Drylanders. But as I leaped to the lower deck, I told myself I'd given the sailors fair warning.

Besides, *they* were the ones who had made trouble, not me.

I was only putting a stop to further trouble.

Chapter 6

Jacinthe

How could I be so stupid? I thought angrily, doing my best to kick and bite the sailor who'd grabbed me. *Didn't Captain Bartolmi warn me about going anywhere on this ship by myself?*

Not that I had much choice at this point. Overnight, the waves had gotten higher, and the ship began to pitch and roll in the most disturbing way.

Sunniva and Winifred were the worst off, but after a few hours, even Elswyth and Rheda had fallen victim to seasickness. And the pitiful sounds of gagging and vomiting coming from next door told me that the two boys were no better off.

With some fresh air to clear the stink of puke from my nose, I was the only one who seemed immune to the ship's wild rocking and swaying.

Thus, it fell to me to visit the galley and beg the cook for jugs of heavily sweetened ginger tea. Mercifully, he had a store of precious ginger root on hand, and was willing to part with some of it. He also gave me slabs of dry ship's biscuit, in hopes the children could keep at least some of it down.

Now that everyone had had at least a few sips of the tea and a mouthful of biscuit, I set about cleaning what I could. First, the overflowing chamber pots, and then I'd ask Captain Bartolmi for a mop. After that, I either needed to get clean sheets from the ship's store, or do laundry in the seawater tub.

As I slogged through these tasks, I was so tired I didn't notice the two sailors sneaking up on me.

My first warning of danger was someone yanking hard on my braid. I stumbled backwards, dropping the chamber pot, and crashed into a hard, lean form.

Divine Mother! I thrust a hard elbow backwards to free myself.

A sailor appeared in front of me. Without a word, he grabbed my breast.

How dare he! I shouted and slapped away the offending hand. Instantly, someone locked my arms behind me in an iron grip.

"Give us a kiss, sweetheart," the breast-grabbing sailor growled. Leering, he leaned in. His grin exposed stained teeth.

"Release her!" a familiar, husky voice rang out above us.

The sailor holding me from behind shouted, "You want in on the action, fish-man? You can have a turn when we're done."

"No!" The protest ripped from my throat.

I took advantage of my captor's distraction. I whipped my head forward and smashed his nose.

He cried out and stumbled back, clapping his hand over his face. Blood smeared his fingers and dripped onto the ship's deck.

Then I twisted around, caught the arm of the sailor holding me from behind, and bit down as hard as I could.

"You little bitch! You're gonna pay for that!" shouted the second man, who still held my braid and my arm in a steely grip.

Instead of letting go, he only pulled harder on my hair. Then, while he had me off-balance, he kicked the back of my knee. My leg collapsed beneath me and I hit the deck hard.

A flash of sudden movement directly in front of me startled me.

I gasped as I recognized the shimmering figure of my new friend Tama standing there.

His dark eyes absorbed the sunlight like the lightless ocean depths as his hands moved lightning-quick towards the sailors. His long claws caught them off guard, slicing through their throats with ease and sending streams of blood fountaining into the wind.

The sailors' bodies folded lifelessly and collapsed. But before their corpses reached the planks, Tama caught them, lifted them effortlessly, and flung them over the side of the ship.

Still on my knees, I watched in horror as the limp bodies hit the waves and sank instantly.

In the blink of an eye, only he and I remained on deck. Deep scarlet splattered his pale face and fine green tunic. There were drops caught in his silvery hair, too.

I glanced down and saw that my once-clean gown had fared no better. All around me, blood pooled on the decking and speckled the railing.

I swayed, my stomach roiling, and steadied myself with a hand placed carefully between patches of glistening red. I'd seen people die—patients too injured or too far gone in wasting illness for even Mama's magic to heal—but never violently like this. It had all happened too quickly to follow.

"Are you unharmed?" Tama's voice was low and raspy.

He reached down, offering me his hand.

I noticed his fingers were coated in fresh blood, and I shivered.

"Fine," I lied.

Steeling myself, I took his sticky hand. He'd just saved me from rape… or worse.

As he helped me to my feet, I took in my surroundings.

The decks were eerily deserted. No one had come up on deck to investigate the commotion. Or to intervene in the attack.

Were the other crew members aware of what their comrades had planned to do to me? Were they waiting in the hold to join in the attack once my two attackers dragged me belowdecks?

I started shaking helplessly as the enormity of what I'd just escaped hit me.

Tama surprised me again by folding me in his arms. His body was all hard muscle beneath his rich garments. Under the rusty scent of fresh blood, he smelled of clean seawater and salt breezes.

For an instant, I wanted to melt against him and soak in his strength.

Then the moment of insanity passed. Sure, he'd rescued me… but in doing so, he'd revealed he was a terrifying monster who'd slaughtered two grown men in the blink of an eye, and with little effort. And all this while bound into human shape, too!

What was Tama capable of in his true form and with his powers unchained? I'd heard horror stories about what happened when sailors or fishermen offended one of the merfolk. But until this moment, I'd never believed they were more than cautionary fairy tales.

Instead, I struggled to free myself. "Thank you, I'm fine!" I lied. "Really! They didn't hurt me."

Tama grunted skeptically. Instead of letting me go, his embrace tightened. "Stop fighting me, Jacinthe," he ordered sternly. "The battle-shock will pass soon, but you require my aid to stand right now."

He was right. I was trembling violently. My knees felt as strong as a tea-soaked ship's biscuit, and my pounding heart made it difficult to breathe.

I closed my eyes and sent a prayer up to the Divine Mother: *Please don't let me faint.*

That would be the ultimate humiliation… and it would leave me dangerously helpless out here.

Tama might've just saved me from the sailors, but he was a cold-blooded killer. And not human. Who knew what he'd do next?

With dazzling speed, he shifted his hold on me and lifted me. I found myself cradled against him with one of his arms around my back and the other under my knees.

Startled yet again, I tilted my head back to look him in the face. Our lips were so close we were breathing the same air.

For one tense moment, I thought Tama was going to kiss me.

Did I want him to?

Was my heart pounding from terror? Or from something else?

I was seventeen years old, almost an adult woman in the eyes of the law… and I'd never had a sweetheart. Never even been kissed. None of the village boys I found attractive had ever reciprocated my interest.

Perhaps they found my brown skin, red hair, and foreign features off-putting. Or maybe they didn't want to risk angering Mama, the most powerful mage for miles around. Even Narcissa, trained on the Continent and highly skilled, didn't have the raw magical power that Mama could call upon in a crisis.

Then the moment shattered with the pounding of multiple feet on deck and shouts of "Men overboard!"

A dozen or more sailors gathered at the railings and peered out over the waves.

Then one of them noticed us… and all the blood.

He made a warding gesture, then shouted, "Someone get Cap'n Bart!" Immediately followed by, "I don't give a rat's arse if he's sleepin'! That fish-man's gone and killed someone!"

"Did it eat 'em, too?" piped a terrified voice.

The crowd turned towards us, fear and disgust. "It's got the girl!"

"I'm all right!" I called. "He doesn't want to hurt me!"

I glanced up at Tama. As usual, his expression was impassive, perhaps even coolly amused, though his gaze fastened unblinkingly on the sailors.

"Your captain ordered all of you to stay away from this female," he said, his tone as cold as a winter wind. "Those two disobeyed that order. So, I swept them away to feed the children of the deeps."

"Turn the ship around!" another of the sailors shouted. "We can't just leave 'em in the water!"

Then Captain Bartolmi stormed out of his cabin, half-dressed in a long shirt and tugging a pair of breeches up over his hips.

"What in the name of the Seven Divine Disciples is going on out here?" he demanded.

Below him, I saw the doors to both the girls' cabin and the boys' cabin open slightly. A line of pale faces crowded the opening, eagerly looking for the source of the excitement.

A flurry of replies rose.

"That fish-man attacked Fawkes and Munis!"

"—killed and ate 'em!"

"Threw 'em overboard!"

"That girl's to blame! Lookit 'er! She's that thing's whore!"

"SILENCE!" thundered the captain.

His men looked at each other, then subsided into low mutters.

"Your excellency," Captain Bartolmi continued, clearly addressing Tama. "What happened here?"

Tama, still holding me, turned his back on the sailors and faced the captain. "You neglected your duty towards Miss Jacinthe. I acted to protect her from two of your men."

Captain Bartolmi scowled, then pointed down at the bloodstains surrounding Tama and me. "You killed both of them?" He sounded incredulous. "Munis *and* Fawkes?"

"Yes. They ignored my warning and persisted in attacking Miss Jacinthe," Tama said levelly. He sounded almost detached, as if killing were an everyday occurrence for him.

Maybe it was.

"Throw it overboard!" a sailor demanded.

"Yeah, before it kills the rest of us!" another seaman pleaded.

"Flog it till it bleeds!"

I tensed. Was my mistake in coming on deck alone going to cost Tama his life, too?

"You storm-born pack of fools! I can't punish an imperial hostage!" shouted Captain Bartolmi. "And didn't I tell you lot not to bother the girl or the children? Well, now that those two troublemakers got what was coming to 'em, maybe you'll listen when I give you an order!"

I breathed out a sigh of relief. They weren't going to hurt Tama for trying to rescue me.

Then the captain glared down at me. "As for *you*, girl—didn't I warn you not to come on deck by yourself? Thanks to you, I'm two hands down now, and the rest of my men will have to work extra shifts."

He's blaming me *for what happened?* My temper rose. I hadn't asked those two louts to stalk and attack me! They'd acted of their own free will.

"Captain, *you're* the one put me in charge of the younger apprentices," I snapped. "In case you hadn't noticed, they're all seasick." I pointed out to the empty metal vessel rolling around the heaving deck. "*Someone* has to empty the chamber pots and bring those children something to eat and drink."

"Well, as of this moment, *Miss* Jacinthe," Bartolmi snarled in return, "you and those kids are all confined to quarters. I or my first mate will bring you your meals. Set your chamber pots outside your cabin door when they're full and keep your doors locked. That's an order." He glared down at me.

"Yes, sir," I whispered.

Tama abruptly loosened his hold. He plunked me feet-first on the deck, but kept his arm around my shoulders.

"I do not wish Miss Jacinthe held prisoner in her cabin," he declared.

Turning to me, he reached down into his tunic and brought up one of his necklaces. It was a conical carved whale's tooth as long as my hand from the base of my thumb to my longest fingertip, strung on a braided seaweed cord. He pulled the necklace one-handed over his head, deftly sliding over and down his long, bloodstained hair.

He put it around my neck. The heavy ivory pendant thumped against my stomach.

"From this moment, Miss Jacinthe is under *my* protection." He didn't raise his voice, but somehow his words carried to every listening ear. "Because she is the only interesting one here. She will attend me daily and amuse me with her conversation."

His arm tightened around me possessively. And I wondered whether I'd just jumped from a burning house into Dragonfire.

Chapter 7

Jacinthe

The next morning, as ordered, I joined Tama on the top stern castle deck after breakfast.

The seas had calmed yesterday afternoon, and the children's seasickness had retreated. We had all gotten our first good night's sleep since the voyage began.

When the ship's meal bell rang just after dawn, I opened the cabin door to find trays of food and jugs of ginger tea placed there.

Below, on the main deck, a pair of sailors worked industriously to remove the last of the bloodstains from the railing and the decking.

One man was on his hands and knees, scrubbing the planks industriously with a large chunk of gray pumice-stone. The other was applying a pungent mixture of linseed oil and mineral spirits to the railing. I recognized the smell from applying the same stuff to our front door and wooden furniture at home.

The sailor at the railing glanced up at me. His face twisted in disgust. He said something to the other man, who stopped scrubbing and craned his head around to look at me.

Then, deliberately, both men spat on the deck before returning to their tasks. The venom emanating from them made my throat tighten.

It wasn't my fault their friends died, I told myself.

If I repeated that thought often enough, I might believe it, in time.

"Are you finally awake? Come join me now," Tama called from above.

"I need a few minutes," I replied, picking up the first tray.

When I'd made sure that everyone had gotten their fair share of tea, hard-boiled eggs and bread, I hastily gobbled down my own portion, combed and braided my hair, and checked the front of my plain, dark blue apprentice's uniform gown for stains.

My other gown, the blood-stained one, had spent the night soaking in a bucket of soapy seawater. I hoped I could get it clean.

When I reached the top of the ladder, I saw a small table with two chairs near the railing.

Tama was already seated, with two large bowls set before him. One was heaped with glistening, pale-brown strands of seaweed. The other bowl was piled high with translucent, pale-pink chunks of raw fish.

"You may join me for my meal," Tama said, indicating the empty chair opposite him.

I fought to control my expression of revulsion. I didn't want to insult my new friend.

"No, thank you. I've already eaten," I said, politely and truthfully.

To my relief, he shrugged and didn't insist. He dipped a webbed hand into the bowl of seaweed, and lifted a broad, amber-colored piece of kelp to his lips.

"I wish to know about this Darkstone Academy," he demanded,

as soon as I'd seated myself.

"I don't know much about it," I confessed. "The only thing I know is that it's a reform school for well-born young mages who've broken the laws governing use of magic. It's their last chance to prove they're not a danger to society. The place is located on a remote island, which is supposed to keep them out of trouble, I guess."

Tama sat back and glowered at me. "'Reform school' sounds like another word for 'prison.' That is unacceptable. My Clan Grandmother told me the terms of the peace treaty specify that emissaries sent to the Dominion will be considered honored guests and treated as nobles."

"Well," I suggested dryly, "since Darkstone Academy seems to be the place populated by nobles' children, perhaps sending the imperial hostages there is observing the letter, if not the spirit, of the treaty."

Tama gave me a long, level look from his intense dark eyes. "Given my treatment so far, I guessed as much from my so-called hosts."

He scooped up a handful of the raw fish and ate it. His eyes never left mine as he chewed. Foolishly, my face heated under his scrutiny.

"Tell me about yourself," he ordered when he'd finished chewing. "Are you and the younglings headed for the academy to train as apprentice mages? And what does that training involve?"

"I'm contracted as an apprentice, yes, but not as a mage," I replied. "My mother was a famous mage, and my younger sisters are all mage-gifted, but I don't have an ounce of magic."

Even after all these months, the reminder of how I'd been tested and found wanting still stung.

I added, "I'm going to apprentice with one of the cooks at the academy."

There. Now he knew I was just a commoner without anything to distinguish me, like mage potential.

Even worse, I was going to be a mere servant at the academy, rather than a student.

He might not be human, but Tama was a prince of the merfolk, or he wouldn't be here.

I braced myself for his dismissal. He surprised me by making a dismissive gesture.

"But how can that be, if you're mage-blooded?" Tama sounded genuinely curious. "Is your father also a mage?"

It was my turn to shrug. "I have no idea. He died before I was born. All I know is that he had red hair, like me. But I'm sure my mother was disappointed when I was tested for magical ability and didn't have any."

I tried to keep my tone unemotional. I didn't want my new friend to see how much I'd always hoped for *some* magical talent, no matter how small.

Growing up, I'd often caught Mama studying me closely, even anxiously, while she worked magic. Afterwards, she always asked me if I'd felt anything stirring inside me.

I never had, though I desperately wanted to. But I could see the colorful auras generated by spells and charms, so that gave me hope, right up until Lady Adalburga had shattered them.

Though Mama never treated me as anything but her beloved eldest daughter, I wondered sometimes if she was relieved when my half-sisters manifested their mage potential while they were still young.

"I see," Tama said thoughtfully. "Among the Sea People, there are no such things as mages, because *everyone* has magic. Some people have strong magic, and others weaker magic, but to us, magic simply helps us fulfill our duties within the clan. I have strong magic—*had* strong magic before your mage stole it," he corrected himself, "and it aids me in defending my clan against raiding pods of orca or other Sea People clans. Grandmother, who rules the clan, is a powerful healer."

"So your grandmother isn't really the queen of all the Sea People?" I asked, surprised. Weren't the imperial hostages all supposed to be royal heirs?

"I am told she is equivalent in rank and responsibilities to a Drylander duke, but she is one of many Clan Grandmothers and Grandfathers among the Sea People," he replied. "Unlike your dominus, we have no single ruler who unites all the clans."

There was a short lull in the conversation as Tama ate more raw fish and seaweed.

When he spoke again, his gaze rested on the front of my gown. "I see you wear my *Kujiranokiba*, my warrior pendant. Good."

"It's beautiful." I touched the tooth, which had been engraved with an intricate design of interlocking whorls and spirals. "But what do you mean when you call it a 'warrior' pendant?"

Tama polished off the last of the fish, then sat back. "It commemorates the day I fought an orca in honorable single combat and graduated from apprentice warrior status."

I gaped at him, hardly able to believe what he'd just told me. "You fought a whale, single-handedly, and *won?*"

I'd sometimes glimpsed the pods of the black-and-white whales that fishermen called "sea-wolves" when Mama and I took a sea-ferry to the annual Herb Fair on the neighboring island of Imber.

Imber was known for growing the finest meadowsweet, the primary ingredient in Mama's painkilling and fever-reducing potions. They also had white-poppy farms, and sold dream-cakes made from the gummy resin collected from the poppies.

The sea-wolves, which Tama called orca, were smaller than some of the other kinds of whales. But compared to a human or merman, they were *enormous*.

Tama nodded gravely, but I could see my astonishment pleased him. "Yes, and the orca I defeated fed my clan for weeks. Clan Grandmother awarded me one of his teeth as my warrior pendant. From that day on, I was considered a grown man rather than a boy."

"Do your people hunt whales for food?" I asked.

"Not usually," he said. "But we never waste fresh meat."

I shuddered. I'd heard stories of merfolk devouring unfortunates caught in shipwrecks.

Though, to be fair, there were many more stories about merfolk rescuing humans and bringing them safely to shore.

"Among my people," Tama continued, "warriors defend clan members against the orca. The orca hunt in large packs, preying upon the Sea People when they can. The young people who wish to become warriors join the older warriors and train with them until the time comes for the apprentices to either prove themselves in single combat or perish in the attempt. That has been our way since time immemorial."

I shivered at the thought of a youth single-handedly going up against a whale, fighting it… and actually winning the fight.

Tama was possibly the most terrifying person I'd ever met. And yet, I liked him. The fact that my heart began pounding whenever I met his gaze wasn't *all* due to fright.

Now that I knew how much his pendant meant to him, I

couldn't possibly keep it.

I pulled the cord over my head and offered him the necklace. "Here."

He stared at me and made no move to take it. "Why? Don't you trust me to protect you?" His voice had gone cold again.

I swallowed hard, realizing I'd somehow insulted him.

"No! That's not the reason!" I protested. "It's just that I now know this is very important to you. And we just met…" I stumbled to a halt. From his unblinking gaze, I could tell he wasn't buying my explanation. I blurted, "Tama, what if I lost it? I'd feel terrible if something happened to your pendant!"

His eyes burned into me. "Yes, the *Kujiranokiba* is very important to me." His voice was soft. I strained to hear it over the rush of the wind and the sound of the waves. "But I trust in your honor, Jacinthe. You will do everything you can to safeguard it, yes?"

"Yes." I really wished my reply hadn't emerged as an undignified squeak.

For the first time since we'd met, Tama smiled. It made my breath catch in my throat as something squeezed my chest.

"Then all is well," he said serenely. "I have seen how diligently you care for the younglings. You are a person of strength and honor. I trust you."

He gently took the necklace from my shaking fingers. He slipped it over my head once again, gently lifting my braid out of the way. His cool fingers brushed against my neck as he tucked the cord under my silver indenture collar. I felt the shock of that contact arrow like lightning down to the pit of my belly. My face heated and my pulse raced.

"Jacinthe, come quick!" Toland shouted from below. "Kenric fell and bumped his head!"

Alarmed, I jumped to my feet. "I'm sorry, Tama, I have to go!"

Tama nodded. "You are the younglings' protector. Go," he ordered gravely. "Bring your morning meal here tomorrow and we will dine together."

As I hurried down the ladder to check on Kenric's injury, I knew that Tama the Whale-Killer should scare the skin off me.

But notwithstanding everything I'd learned about him today, despite his alien appearance, intimidating aura, and brusque speech, I felt oddly comfortable with him in a way that went far beyond his declaration of protection.

I'd been in peril for months now, ever since Mama's death. My situation had gone from bad to worse, until I was little more than a slave, bound for a distant and dangerous place. But Tama made me feel *safe*, somehow.

∞∞∞

"Sing me one of your human songs," Tama ordered when I met with him on the stern castle's upper deck again the next day.

Luckily, Kenric's injuries had been minor, needing only a bit of salve. Even better, the seas remained calm, so even Sunniva and Winifred were able to rise from their hammocks, eat heartily, and join the others for fresh air and exercise on the lower deck.

At dawn, Captain Bartolmi knocked on the cabin door, and informed us that he'd decided to relax his orders confining all the apprentices to the cabins for the duration of the voyage.

The captain treated me to glowering looks, and informed me that I remained banned from the dining hall and confined to quarters except for when Lord Tama requested my presence.

I felt relief. At least the other apprentices weren't being punished anymore for my perceived misdeeds.

Now, I plunked my plate of eggs and fried fish on the table, along with one of the jugs of tea delivered to the cabin for my breakfast. I also had a freshly baked roll with salted butter. The generous portions thus far had been a pleasant surprise.

The captain might be displeased with me, but at least he hadn't reduced my rations to dry biscuit and water. After the third meal at sea, I'd stopped stashing away extra portions of bread in my belt pouch. No matter what fate awaited us apprentices at Darkstone Academy, it was clear Captain Bartolmi didn't plan to starve us before we arrived.

"Tell you what," I said. "I will sing you a song, if you sing me one of the Sea People's songs," I replied.

He considered this for a moment, then nodded gravely. "Very well. You go first."

I thought for a moment. I was not a trained singer, but I'd been told that my voice was clear and on key. I picked something I knew well, an old but still popular love song that told the story of a young man taking leave of his sweetheart before he departed to fight in the Great War.

Tama listened politely through all five verses, which chronicled the young man's tragic death in battle while his sweetheart waited futilely for his return, pregnant with their child. In the final verse, she finally received the news of his demise, and drowned herself because she could not live without him and knew her family would cast her out for bearing a fatherless child.

When I finished the song, my new friend scowled.

"Why would he do that?" Tama demanded. "Mate with a woman when he knew he was marching off to die? And why would her clan not care for the woman and his baby in his absence?"

"It's considered shameful to bear a child out of wedlock," I told him. "He didn't marry her before he left for the battle, so her family would have punished her for falling pregnant with no father to take responsibility."

I'd always wondered if Mama's family had cast her out for falling pregnant with me. That would explain why she never spoke of her kin, nor sent or received any letters from them.

Tama shook his head. "Then that man was selfish and dishonorable. He manipulated his intended mate for his own gratification, then abandoned her to her fate."

I blinked at him. "I've never thought of it that way."

I'd sung that song a thousand times, but never stopped to think about it beyond the sweet tragedy of the sundered lovers.

Now, I realized Tama was right. And I didn't like it.

"Thanks for ruining my favorite song," I muttered peevishly.

He looked at me blankly. "How so? I merely observed what was already there."

I bit my lip in frustration, and saw his dark gaze dip to where my teeth caught my lower lip.

"But it's not about the logic of his actions," I said finally. "It's about the feelings. The emotions. The tragic *love* between the soldier and his sweetheart!"

"That so-called love was very selfish." Tama shook his head slowly. He gazed out over the glittering surface of the ocean. "My grandmother says that lust and affection without trust and honor cause the most trouble." He turned his head to look at me, and the intensity of his regard made my breath catch. "Don't you agree?"

I opened my mouth to deny it, then stopped to reconsider. *Why did Mama choose to marry Baldwin, of all people? Did she allow her feelings to override her assessment of his faults?*

I didn't like the conclusion I reached.

I'd always worshipped my strong, wise, mysterious mother, so beautiful and so skilled in mage-craft. I didn't want to think that she'd fallen pregnant with me because she'd trusted the wrong man. Or that she'd misjudged Baldwin's character because he'd turned her head.

But it was difficult to ignore the pattern of ill-luck when it came to Mama's mates.

Then Tama sang his song, which he described as an ode to dolphins.

I couldn't understand any of the words, but the melody used an unfamiliar scale of notes, with a fluid, sliding quality that was foreign to my ear, but somehow beautiful.

"Why is the captain holding those birds captive?" Tama asked immediately after he'd finished singing, and before I could offer any comment.

"What birds?" I asked. "The chickens belowdecks? Those are for fresh eggs."

"No, these birds." He pointed at the large, circular pigeon coop built around the base of the main mast. "Are they fresh meat for when our supplies run out?"

His mouth twisted, showing what he thought of that prospect.

"Those are messenger birds," I explained. "They're trained to fly to various locations on our route. If this ship runs into trouble, the captain can use them to send out a distress call. That's how I found out that my mother's ship sank last winter, on her way home from the capital."

"Where exactly did it sink?" Tama demanded, with odd

eagerness.

The merfolk apparently don't believe in empty words of condolence, I thought wryly.

"Off the coast of Lusitania, near the Port of Felicitas Victoria. It was a cargo ship coming from Neapolis Capitola, bound for Herrewick."

I didn't want to think about Mama's final, terrible moments as she drowned. At least my sisters were safe at the Imperial Academy in Neapolis.

Tama shook his head. "You're mistaken," he stated. "No human ships have descended to our realm from that region since last summer."

"How would you know?" I asked sharply. Was he really trying to dispute the facts?

He shrugged. "My Clan Grandmother is cousin to the Sea Lion Clan Grandmother who claims that stretch of ocean. If a ship had gone down in Sea Lion territory, we would have received some of the salvaged goods."

I felt sick at the thought of merfolk eagerly combing through the shipwreck for prizes. I only hoped they hadn't eaten the corpses. Tama's comment yesterday about his people never wasting meat sat uneasily with me.

"Maybe the other clan lied to you," I suggested. "And kept all the goods for themselves. I heard the ship carried a cargo of fine glassware from Veneto."

"Sea Lion Clan would not do such a thing." Tama sounded offended. "Unlike you humans, merfolk don't lie. No ship sank anywhere near that port last winter."

"Then what happened to my mother?" I demanded, unable to stop the dizzying sensation of sudden hope.

He shrugged again. "I don't know. Perhaps your mother's ship sank elsewhere, and there was a mistake in the reports you received."

My hopes collapsed, and a burst of anger filled the void in my chest.

How dare he raise my hopes like that! Mama was dead, I told myself. *Or else she'd have come home to me. She would never have abandoned me like that!*

A mistake in the ship's reported location was the only explanation that made sense. A storm could've blown the vessel badly off-course before it went down. Or some clerk assigned to write the report sent to the Herrewick Harbor Master could have made an error.

It didn't matter. Mama was still dead.

A fresh wave of loss with knife-edged shards of grief rolled over me, reopening wounds barely healed.

I didn't want Tama to see my pain, so I turned away from him. I pretended to study the endless glittering waves beyond the ship's railing while I regained control over my breathing and my emotions. I'd had a lot of practice doing that in the past few months. Baldwin had reprimanded me with sharp words and sharper blows whenever he caught me crying.

Then I saw Elswyth and Rheda emerge onto the deck directly below me. "Miss Jacinthe! We need to use the head!"

"Excuse me, Tama," I choked out.

"Later, you will teach me how to play human card games," he commanded.

Rising, I hurried down the ladder and made my way over to my charges.

I'd spent many years caring for my younger half-sisters. They had frequently annoyed me, but after they departed for the academy, I'd found myself missing them.

Now, watching over this gaggle of young apprentices gave me something to do and distracted me from worrying about what lay ahead at Darkstone Academy.

As I escorted the girls to the bow of the ship, where a pair of box-like latrines were screened off with a large square of sailcloth tied to a wicker frame, I felt Tama's gaze burning into the back of my neck.

So what if the merman made my heart beat faster every time I saw him? And if I spent a lot of time thinking about him when we were apart?

But he'd made it clear that he despised humans.

And then there was the law. After the Great War, the first Dominus had passed a series of legislation regulating human-supernatural interactions, with harsh penalties for violators.

Yet I couldn't help wondering if our tentative shipboard friendship would continue once we arrived at Darkstone Academy.

Most likely, the royal hostages would be sequestered away from the academy's student body and human servants while I worked from sunrise to sunset in the academy's kitchens.

This voyage was simply an interlude before my exile began in earnest. I should enjoy my last fortnight of relative freedom while I could.

Chapter 8

Jacinthe

Ten days later

My first glimpse of Darkstone Island was an ominous gray volcano, its top wreathed in white clouds, rising from the waves in the far distance.

The days had steadily been growing warmer during the voyage south. After my uncertain start with sea-sickness and slaughter, the rest of the journey passed smoothly, even pleasantly.

I was still officially confined to quarters, but thanks to Tama, I didn't actually spend many of my daylight hours inside the cabin. We conversed and played cards, and I filled up the rest of my days reading or tending to laundry and the children's intermittent bouts of sea-sickness.

This was the first time in years I'd had this much leisure time. Even better, I could fill my belly at every mealtime.

I guessed that a grim routine of unending drudgery that would rival Baldwin and Narcissa's treatment of me awaited at the academy. But for right now, I was happier than I'd been since Mama departed on her doomed voyage.

Tama had quickly grasped the rules of all the card and board games I knew, and played with a cold, calculating ferocity. Within a couple of days, he'd surpassed my skill level.

Not being stupid, I refused any further wagers with him after losing a bet that cost me a week of teaching him every song I knew, the bawdier the better.

Despite his impassive expression as he listened to me, I couldn't help but thinking that my obvious embarrassment at singing some of the verses—especially with the sailors listening in and guffawing at intervals—amused my merman friend.

I'd learned he had a sense of humor despite his outward stoicism. It was very dark and dry, but he frequently made me laugh during our talks.

He then moved on to playing cards with the ship's crew, and quickly accumulated a collection of winnings that included books, coins, clay pipes, and a truly eclectic assortment of charms, amulets, beads, colorful bird feathers, and shells.

Oddly, for all his determined pursuit of winnings, he seemed to care little for his prizes once he got them.

He freely gave them away to me, the other apprentices, and the sailor assigned to clean Tama's cabin and do his laundry.

By the time Darkstone Island's cinder-colored cliffs and verdant slopes came into view, the children each had a collection of baubles, and I had a growing library of books.

I cried with joy when Tama gave me the first volume. It was a copy of the prized herbal reference Baldwin and Narcissa stole from me when they forced me to abandon all my belongings. He told me he'd won it from the ship's cook.

Mama's edition had been bound in fine leather and handsomely illustrated with color plates of each plant. This herbal was cheaply printed and bound with thin, painted boards. But tears of joy still stung my eyes and rolled down my cheeks upon receiving it.

My reaction to his gift puzzled Tama to no end. But after that, he attempted to win every book aboard the ship.

Most of them were novels and collections of printed ballads belonging to Captain Bartolmi. Seeing them in my hands didn't endear me any further to the gruff seaman, and I silently vowed to leave behind all except the herbal when we finally disembarked at our destination.

Tama would probably be unhappy if he discovered that I'd "forgotten" most of my new library on board, but Captain Bartolmi had treated me well on this voyage despite his anger at losing two of his crew.

On the last afternoon of our voyage, Tama rose from his seat after we'd finished playing a card game. I'd lost to him, as usual, but I'd made him work hard for his victory this time.

"This is for you." He tossed a heavy leather pouch, jingling with coins, in my lap.

I gaped at this unexpected bounty. "I can't accept this!" I protested automatically.

Even if the pouch held only copper pennies, that was still more money than I'd seen in months. Back home, a penny could buy a loaf of bread or a dried salt-fish.

He straightened and glared down at me. He had an extensive collection of glares. This one meant I'd hurt his feelings.

"As a warrior of the Sea People, it is my duty to share my prizes with my people," he declared haughtily.

Well, that explains a lot, I thought. "But this is a lot of money," I explained. "Won't you need it when we arrive at the academy?"

He smiled and reached down to stroke my cheek with his cool fingers. As always, his touch sent a shock of heat through my belly. "I appreciate your care for me. But would you deny our connection by refusing my gift?"

I inhaled sharply at the combination of his caress and words. "Connection?" My voice came out in a whisper.

He feels it, too? That strange sensation of a deeper current flowing beneath the surface of our every conversation?

He frowned. "No, that is not the correct word. I meant, would you deny our friendship, Jacinthe?"

"Of course not, Tama."

Ah, so it was just friendship he felt for me.

It's safer that way, I told myself, trying to ignore the stab of disappointment.

"And thank you. Having a little money of my own will make me feel a little more…" I paused, trying to think of a reason that would make sense to him. "It will give me a little security, if I can pay for something I need."

My indenture contract had specified a stipend of five silver denarii per month, but I didn't know when that sum would be paid out… *if* it was paid at all.

After all, as an indentured apprentice, to whom could I reasonably complain?

His frown deepened. "You will come to me if you need anything." His tone brooked no argument. "You are *mine*, Jacinthe. Remember this."

Mingled with the disappointment I tried to suppress was an unexpected burst of joy.

Bereft of my mother and sisters, and having no other living kin I knew of, discovering that this beautiful, often terrifying man now considered me one of "his people" kindled an unexpected happiness deep inside my soul.

Likewise, over the course of our fortnight at sea, my fellow apprentices had quickly become like younger siblings to me.

Despite being torn from their homes and families, and sent far from their island home, they were cheerful, helpful, and often sweetly affectionate with me.

The girls had all started giving me hugs and demanding a goodnight kiss on their cheeks or forehead before going to sleep. Kenric and Toland joined the girls in sneaking me dessert—sweet custards, spiced honey cakes, and steamed puddings made with dried fruits—to supplement the adequate but plain rations delivered to my cabin three times a day.

On impulse, I leaped to my feet and embraced Tama's steely form. "Thank you, Tama. Thank you for everything you've done for me. This journey would've been a lot harder without your friendship and the books."

He stiffened for an instant, then his arms wrapped around me. I felt him stroke my back and tug gently on my braid. I inhaled his scent, brine and clean salt breezes, and rested my forehead against his hard chest.

Why did he make me feel so safe?

Then I heard someone hiss, "Whore! Fish-man's whore!"

Tama released me so abruptly that I stumbled forward. With a terrifying expression, he spun and pointed at a sailor climbing the rigging. Sunlight gleamed on the long, curving claw tipping Tama's finger.

"How *dare* you insult Miss Jacinthe?" he snarled. "And how dare you insult me?"

"S-sorry, milord!" the man shouted, frantically scrambling up the mast to put more distance between himself and us. "I didn't mean nothin' by it, honest!"

"Liar." I could almost feel an icy wind blowing across Tama's words. "You will apologize to Miss Jacinthe. Now."

"Sorry, Miz Jacinthe. Really, I am!"

Tama turned to look at me. "Are you satisfied with his apology?"

I gulped, imagining what might happen if I said no. "Yes!"

Now, all of us crowded the railing of the lower deck as the ship approached the island. Bundles of our meager belongings sat at our feet, and we watched intently as our new home drew closer.

Captain Bartolmi shouted orders and his crew scurried around, hauling on ropes and muscling the ship's rudder to bring us close to Darkstone Island.

Waves frothed white at the feet of steep, dark gray cliffs that wore vibrantly colored headdresses of flowering bushes and thick grass. A cloud of soaring, darting seabirds emerged from white-streaked perches on the cliff sides, and circled the ship, filling the air with their mournful cries and demanding squawks.

Ahead of us, a lush forest rose halfway up the slopes of the volcano that dominated the center of the small island, broken by an irregular patchwork of cultivated fields and orchards, the trees lined up and standing at attention like a regiment of soldiers.

Passing through a narrow opening in the cliffs, the ship dropped anchor in the middle of a small cove with calm water.

I caught my first glimpse of Darkstone Academy.

The old castle, dating from the days of the Great War, nestled between the cove and the base of the volcano. Built from the same black stone as the island's cliffs, the high walls and round towers looked grim and foreboding.

Fields and orchards surrounded the castle, and a narrow dirt road led from the castle gates down to a simple wooden dock built onto the cove's black sand beach.

A small group of people, most of them clad in tunics and leggings dyed the dark indigo of imperial livery, stood on the dock, apparently awaiting our arrival. Three of them looked like men-at-arms, wearing polished parade armor.

"Passengers, it's time to go!" Captain Bartolmi shouted.

I bent to lift my bundle, and made sure that the other apprentices had theirs as well. The captain had assigned a pair of sailors to carry Tama's large sea-chest. They stood as far away from him as they could.

Then, one by one, we stepped over the railing and into a large rowboat hanging from lines at the ship's side. Once everyone seated themselves, the two sailors loaded Tama's chest onto the boat and took their places at the oarlocks.

The remaining crew released the pulleys and slowly lowered the boat.

Elswyth, Rheda, Sunniva, and Winifred clutched the sides of the boat and squealed with excitement during the creaking and swaying descent to the mercifully calm waters of the cove.

Tama and I sat together at the bow. I caught his fleeting expression of unvarnished longing as he gazed over the side of the rowboat. Then he quickly schooled his face back to impassivity.

Unlike the opaque, gray-green seawater in Herrewick Harbor, the sea in this cove was clear as glass. I could see all the way down to the black sand and coral-encrusted rocks far below. Vividly colored fish darted around the boat in flashes of red, yellow, and twilight-blue.

As the sailors rowed us over to a low wooden dock that extended from the beach, I saw half a dozen people waiting for us there, some of them men-at-arms wearing what looked like parade armor.

"Who are those two people?" Tama asked, pointing at a man and a woman standing a little apart from the others. They were more richly dressed than the others gathered near them.

The man was tall and imposing, dressed in a gold-embroidered indigo tunic and polished leather boots. A day's worth of stubble shadowed the lower half of his face and a wealth of dark curls fell to his collar. An enameled gold mage badge pinned to his tunic over his heart proclaimed he'd graduated from the Imperial Academy for the Magical Arts, just like Mama.

Beside him stood an equally tall woman wearing a matching indigo gown with gold embroidery around her neckline and around the edges of her long sleeves and stiff, gold-laced bodice. She, too, wore the Imperial Academy's mage badge.

Her features were beautiful, but her expression severe, her black eyes cold and disapproving as she watched our boat approach the dock. An indigo ribbon loosely tied her long chestnut curls at her nape.

One sailor snorted. "That's Lord Roderigo de Norhas. He's the fellow in charge of this place. The woman standing next to him is his sister and second-in-command, Lady Erzabetta."

The other sailor manning the oars snickered. "Wonder who they pissed off at court to end up on this mother-forsaken rock?"

Even growing up in the Dominion's most isolated province, I'd heard of the de Norhas. They were one of the Continent's most famous and powerful noble families.

Rolando, the first Duke de Norhas, was famous for holding the mountain pass of Invictus against an army of Djinn who'd sailed up from the Southern Continent and landed on the shores of the Kappadokian Peninsula. His actions had prevented the Djinni Emir from joining his forces with the Fae

High Lords and the Dragon King Pyrrhus, who were battling the allied human forces on the plains outside the city of Lutèce.

Thanks to de Norhas' courage and tenacity, General Severus Cavalieri di Corredo, the scion of an ancient Neapolitan ducal family, had led the united human army to victory in the Battle of Lutèce. His troops promptly crowned the victorious general as the Dominus Victor Augustus the First, and he spent the next two decades of his reign unifying the independent fiefdoms of the Continent into the Imperial Dominion of Human Lands.

I'd often wondered how the Duke de Norhas had felt about seeing a man from a rival duchy raised to the throne after the victory he'd helped ensure.

Just like I wondered now about why two officials of such prestigious lineage would come down to the docks to meet a gaggle of commoners indentured to service at the academy.

Then I remembered that despite the reality of his situation, Tama was still an official guest of the Dominus. Alerted by a messenger bird, Lord Roderigo and Lady Erzabetta were here to welcome Tama to his new home.

At the sailors' urging, Tama was the first to disembark. He immediately extended his hand to help me step from the boat onto the dock, then steadied me when I swayed.

Though it appeared motionless, the dock felt like it was rolling like the ship's deck beneath my feet.

"It's just your sea-legs, lass," a man-at-arms said kindly. "It'll wear off right quick."

Tama then helped the children onto the dock one by one, before turning to face the group of strangers.

The fine lord and lady stepped forward.

"Lord Tama of the Sea People, I presume?" The gentleman

made a courtly bow while the lady sank into a deep curtsey.

"I am Tama." Tama put his palms together in a formal gesture and inclined his head. "You are Lord Roderigo and Lady Erzabetta, yes?"

She smiled brilliantly at him, flashing perfect white teeth and a pair of charming dimples, but her eyes remained cold. "Welcome to Darkstone Island, my lord Tama. My brother and I will endeavor to make your stay with us as comfortable as possible. Please, come with us now, and we'll show you to your quarters."

She took his arm, and I fought an inexplicable clench of jealousy as this poised and elegant noblewoman led Tama to a carriage waiting just beyond the narrow black-sand beach.

Lord Roderigo snapped his fingers at the men-at-arms before turning to follow his sister and Tama across the sand. Two of the guards lifted Tama's chest and carried it over to the carriage.

Then they all drove away in a cloud of dust, leaving me and the children to face the remaining people on the dock by ourselves.

Chapter 9

Jacinthe

A dour-looking woman with frost-colored hair and a chilly gaze stepped forward. Her dark blue imperial livery was made from the same expensive fabric as Lady de Norhas' clothing, with the academy's emblem embroidered in gold thread over her left breast. She wore heavy gold earrings set with polished sapphires.

She addressed the sailors who had ferried us over from the ship. "You have the documents for these young people?" she demanded.

"Here you go, ma'am." One sailor pulled a packet from inside his jerkin. It was bound with string and sealed with dark blue wax. "We'll be heading back to the ship now."

Apparently absorbed in unsealing the packet, she waved him off without glancing up.

"Good luck to ye, kiddies," the sailor said as he untied the mooring rope. Then his tone turned venomous. "As for you, Miss Jacinthe, I hope ye find the fate ye deserve. Jack Munis was a good mate o' mine."

I gritted my teeth and made no reply. It didn't matter, not now. With luck, I'd never see Captain Bartolmi or any of his crew again.

He cast off. Then he and his comrade rowed rapidly back to the waiting ship.

Meanwhile, the woman had extracted a sheaf of documents from the packet. She frowned over the papers, then lifted her head to scan us. "Which of you is Kenric of Astonburg?"

Kenric squared his shoulders and stepped forward. "That's me, ma'am."

"I am the Baroness Margitts, Assistant Chatelaine of Darkstone Academy. You will address me as Lady Margitts," she snapped, marking the paper in her hand. "Smith Barclay, your new apprentice."

A big, broad-shouldered man with a drooping mustache and a shaven head gestured at Kenric. His face creased in a smile that looked friendly enough. "Come wi' me, laddie, and I'll show ye around and tell ye what I expect of ye."

There was a brief delay as the girls crowded around Kenric, hugging him and pleading with him not to forget them. He and Toland shook hands awkwardly, then Kenric turned to me. His face had turned scarlet from the girls' attentions.

"Thanks for lookin' after us, Miss Jacinthe," he said. I saw him swallow hard, then he rushed into my arms and hugged me with unexpected strength. "I'll see you around, yeah?"

"I'm sure we'll see you at mealtimes." I actually had no idea whether the apprentices ate communally in a dining hall, but I wanted to reassure him.

He chuckled, ducked his head, and let Smith Barclay lead him away.

No carriage for the commoners, I thought, watching them trudge up the narrow dirt road that led to the castle.

Sunniva and Winifred were the next to be called. The academy's Master Tailor was a pretty woman who looked near to Mama's age, with the olive skin and dark hair of a Neapolitan. Like the smith, she waited patiently for the girls to take their leave of us and their older brother Toland.

Toland was the next to depart. The academy's Master Gardener was an elderly, slightly stooped man with deeply weathered skin and a fuzzy wreath of silver hair circling his sun-spotted scalp.

Now, only Elswyth, Rheda, and I remained.

Lady Margitts called our names, one by one, marking her list as we responded. "I'm assigning you three girls to Master Chef Brigitte Vollkorn."

I breathed a sigh of relief. Clerk Petri hadn't lied to me about what kind of apprenticeship I'd be serving! Based on all my previous disappointment, I had been bracing myself for the worst.

The academy's Master Chef was an extremely tall woman with a solid build and a short mop of wavy sun-streaked brown hair touched with silver.

"Girls, welcome to Darkstone Academy," she said in a high, warbling voice. "Follow me."

Without waiting for our response, she set off down the dock with long, swift strides. Elswyth and Rheda clung to my hands and jogged frantically as we struggled across the fine, warm sand to the grass.

By the time we reached the dirt road leading to the castle, Chef Vollkorn was just a distant figure.

Then she noticed we were lagging, and waited for us to catch up.

After that, she slowed her pace. "Before we reach the castle, there are a few things you need to know," she began as we continued our walk towards the castle. "I pride myself on treating my apprentices fairly, but there a few things I absolutely will not tolerate."

She ticked off points on her large, long-fingered hands. "Dirty hands. Laziness. Theft. Unexcused absence from duty. Coughing, sneezing, or spitting in food."

Chef Vollkorn whipped her head around to glare at us. Elswyth and Rheda shrank back from her stern expression. I merely nodded.

So far, the chef struck me as stern but fair. My ordeal with Narcissa and Baldwin had taught me what truly monstrous treatment was like.

"Good. Before starting work each day, you will tie back your hair and wear the caps we issue you," Chef Vollkorn continued. "You will wash your hands thoroughly with soap and hot water before work, and after each visit to the latrines, the storehouses, or the compost heap. You will carry out the tasks assigned to you by any of my assistant cooks to the best of your abilities. Do you understand?" she finished, giving us all another look.

"Yes, Chef," I said. Elswyth and Rheda echoed my response.

"Very good," warbled Chef Vollkorn. "Now for the more pleasant part. Under imperial regulations, you will all receive one day of leave per week. My senior apprentice will assign you each a day, to ensure that the kitchens are always adequately staffed."

She eyed our travel-stained clothing and the pitifully small bundles of belongings slung over our shoulders.

"After I give you the tour of the kitchens, storehouses, and other essential places in the castle, Lady Margitts will issue you aprons and uniforms, linens, and any essential toiletry items you need. You will receive three meals a day, and take turns with the other apprentices in preparing the staff meals. We serve the students, professors, and officials first in the Great Hall, then we eat in the servants' hall with the rest of the staff."

She paused for several steps, clearly waiting for us to acknowledge her.

"Yes, Chef," we all said again.

"Speaking of the students," Chef Vollkorn's expression turned sour. "Let me make one thing clear: you and the other apprentices are only obliged to follow orders from the academy staff. *Not* the students." She heaved a gusty sigh. "There have been… *incidents* where our students test the new apprentices by ordering them to pilfer from the stores or break the rules in other ways. If this happens to any of you, you will report it to me immediately."

"Yes, Chef," we chorused once more.

Despite speaking non-stop, Chef Vollkorn's steady pace never faltered nor did she sound breathless at all.

The further we got from the beach, the steeper the road grew, and the breath began to rasp in my throat. Two weeks of inactivity aboard the ship had taken its toll on my legs.

The castle's black stone walls and towers loomed over us now.

"One more thing, and this is very important. As you already know, the castle hosts the imperial hostages. Be warned, girls, they may look handsome enough, but they're all monsters in disguise," Chef Vollkorn said.

We passed through the open castle gates, flanked by impressive watchtowers on either side of the huge arched gateway. We emerged into a space crowded with a jumble of three- and four-story buildings in a variety of architectural styles, but all built from the same dark volcanic stone as the castle's defensive walls.

She lowered her voice and added, "Now, this happened before my time here, but I heard they actually *ate* some of the students!"

I couldn't help but roll my eyes at this. Tama had taught me that the hostages might not be human, but they weren't monsters either.

"But Lord Tama wouldn't do that… would he?" Elswyth piped up.

"He wouldn't," I replied firmly. "He's our friend."

Chef Vollkorn's brows rose in surprise. "You sound very certain of that, Apprentice Jacinthe."

"I am."

She made a skeptical "hmm" sound as she led us across an open courtyard with a large fountain in its center. Chickens scattered at our approach, and I heard the distant lowing of cattle drifting over the castle walls. The rest of the open space was planted with herbs and flowers between graveled paths.

"We are mostly self-sufficient here," she told us, sounding proud. "You'll be tending this garden and gathering eggs from the hens as part of your duties."

As we headed for a row of two-story buildings lined up against the castle wall, she asked, "Do you girls have any questions?"

Elswyth and Rheda both shook their heads shyly. But, encouraged by what I'd heard so far, I spoke up. "Back home in Abbonay, the clerk told me I was going to apprentice with a pastry chef."

To my dismay, Chef Vollkorn scoffed. "Those clerks! They'll tell you *anything* to get you or your guardians to sign that indenture!" She shook her head. "In my kitchens, all apprentices start at the bottom as junior staff. Now, if you're a hard worker and you prove that you've learned the basics, then and *only* then will I promote you to the rank of Chef's Apprentice. For most new apprentices, that takes at least two years."

Another disappointment, but one I'd been expecting this time. I vowed I would prove myself to this woman and quickly work my way up from whatever menial position she initially assigned me.

In the meanwhile, Chef Vollkorn's orientation lecture assured me I'd be fed, housed, and clothed, just as my indenture contract specified. That was good enough… for right now, anyway.

The next hour and a half passed in a blur as we followed the Master Chef's brisk steps around the castle.

In rapid succession, she pointed out the location of the huge underground cisterns, the rain-fed water tanks in the watchtowers, the latrines, and the line of storehouses against the back wall.

Then, finally, she led us through the castle's vast kitchens, where a bustling scene greeted us.

Two massive stone fireplaces, their cavernous interiors blackened with centuries of soot, crackled and blazed, casting flickering light and shadows on the plastered stone walls. Inside the fireplaces, a framework of sturdy iron racks and spits held succulent-looking cuts of roasting beef.

Sturdy wooden beams supported the high, painted wood ceiling. A squadron of cooks in dark blue uniforms and long white aprons labored at long stone counters, chopping, rolling, and mixing with precise and purposeful movements.

The rhythmic clamor of metal against metal filled the air as cooks stirred, whisked, and pounded ingredients with mortar and pestle. The staccato rhythms of knives and cleavers against wooden chopping boards echoed through the kitchen, counterpointed by the buzz of lively conversations between cooks and apprentices, punctuated by occasional bursts of laughter, adding a melodic backdrop to the symphony of sounds.

Shiny copper pots and pans hung from hooks embedded in the walls. Tiers of shelves held jars of herbs and spices, utensils, and stacked bowls.

Adjacent to the hearths, a bank of charcoal-fueled tile stoves held bubbling stock pots and sauce pans.

The girls and I halted as Chef Vollkorn paused her tour to consult with a sauce-cook.

I inhaled deeply, breathing in the enticing medley of aromas. The warm, savory aroma of roasted meats mingled with sharper fragrances of fresh herbs and the perfume of pepper, cinnamon, anise, and nutmeg.

This place exuded a bustling energy, filled with the harmonious symphony of clanging utensils, crackling fire, and animated conversation. It was simultaneously frantically busy and cheerful.

It felt *safe*. Even welcoming, in a strange way.

Something inside me loosened for the first time in months, and long-dormant hope rose and began to blossom.

Maybe this place wasn't the awful purgatory I'd been fearing. Maybe everything would be okay.

The tour resumed as we moved through the brewhouse, thick with the smell of malt and hops; the bakery, hot from the stone ovens and smelling of yeast and freshly-baked cinnamon bread that made my mouth water and my stomach growl; the larder, cooled by channels in the stone floor that ran with water, and crowded with great sides of beef and pork; the confectionary room, with sacks of flour, sugar, and nuts leaning against the walls and jars of honey and preserved fruits gleaming like polished gems on the shelves; and finally, the dry goods storerooms, dark and crowded with sacks, barrels, crates, and boxes of every imaginable seasoning and foodstuff.

It was an astounding bounty. I didn't think that anyone back home, not even the governor, had this amount and variety of food.

After she finished giving us the tour, Chef Vollkorn brought us over to the Assistant Chatelaine's office, located near the Great Hall.

"Lady Margitts, I've brought you the three new kitchen apprentices for intake," Chef announced as she herded us into the office.

It was furnished with a polished wooden desk set on slender gilded legs, with matching wood-and-gilt bookshelves crowded with bound ledgers and reference books. Colorful woolen tapestries depicting beautiful gardens crowded with flowers and exotic birds concealed the stone walls.

The Assistant Chatelaine rose from her seat behind the desk and pulled a familiar-looking packet from beneath a stack of papers.

"They know the rules, Brigitte?" Lady Margitts demanded.

"I gave them the full orientation," Chef Vollkorn replied, sounding a little huffy, I thought. She turned to us. "Report to me first thing after breakfast tomorrow, and I'll assign you to your stations."

Once she had departed, Lady Margitts pointed at the bag slung over my shoulder. "Open that disgusting sack and empty it on the floor." Her gaze shifted to Elswyth and Rheda. "You, too. I want to ensure that none of you brought contraband items."

We obeyed.

She examined our pitiful trove of belongings with thin-lipped disapproval.

"Rags," she sniffed, extending a booted foot and sweeping most of the clothing into a pile.

The girls' spare chemises and skirts were faded and threadbare. I hadn't succeeded in completely washing the bloodstains from my spare gown, but it was still perfectly serviceable, with no holes or frayed seams. And it was wrapped around my precious herbal.

Lady Margitts raised her voice and shouted, "Steward!"

A hearty looking man promptly appeared in the office doorway. He had bright gray eyes and thinning hair combed over his pink scalp. A bulging paunch strained the seams of his indigo tunic. "Yes, milady?"

"Take this trash away and burn it. All of it." She pointed at the heaped garments on the floor.

"No!" I protested.

Lady Margitts fixed me with a cold stare. "I will *not* have any of the castle staff looking like beggars."

"But I have a book—" I began. Maybe she hadn't noticed it wrapped in the folds of my stained gown.

In response, she toed aside the fabric to reveal the volume.

"An herbal? You don't need *that* for washing dishes and chopping vegetables," she declared.

She bent and lifted it between her fingertips like a dead rat. She riffled quickly through the pages, as if searching for contraband.

"Cheap *and* outdated," she sniffed, then tossed it back onto the pile. Her cold eyes surveyed me from head to toe. "Your paperwork states you can read and do sums?"

I nodded.

"Well, those skills aren't anything special, not *here*," she said. "We are an institution of higher learning, after all." Her long finger rose to tap my indenture collar. "And you are *not* a student, but a servant. Remember that, girl."

Her gaze shifted to the steward. "Potts, three sets of standard issue uniforms and linens, if you please, plus aprons and caps, since these girls all belong to Chef Vollkorn."

Potts bowed. "Yes, milady." He gestured at us to follow him to a large storeroom next door.

In a daze, I received a pile of clothing and linens, including two uniform gowns, chemises, aprons, caps, bedsheets, and towels, as well as an assortment of other items necessary for daily life.

I felt overwhelmed by my introduction to the castle. The kitchens alone seemed to contain more people than lived in all of Bernswick!

And we hadn't even seen the places yet where the mage students lived and studied, nor the imperial hostages' quarters.

Once we were suitably equipped, Potts led us to the kitchen apprentices' female dormitories, a wide, high-ceilinged hall located above the bakery.

Our new home was very basic, but clean and spacious. A double row of beds stretched the length of the plank-floored hall. Each bed featured a wooden sea-chest at its foot, and large metal hooks in the wall above the beds provided a place to hang clothing and towels.

At either end of the dormitory were the garderobe chambers, each with a set of latrines that flushed with water from tanks mounted high on the castle walls. A large tiled bathroom was furnished with deep stone sinks, metal tubs, and showers with water heated by the bakery's ovens.

Thanks to our meeting with Lady Margitts and the castle steward, we had missed the evening meal with our new coworkers.

We settled into the three empty beds next to the bathroom, and put our new clothes and meager personal possessions in the chests.

I was happy to see that the chests locked, so I tucked the coin-pouch Tama had given me beneath my clean chemises. We had just finished making up our new beds with the linens issued to us when Chef Vollkorn sent her senior apprentice up to the dormitory.

The young woman, red-faced with a few sweat-dampened tendrils of dark hair escaping from her cap and stuck to her forehead, carried a tray laden with bread, cheese, fresh cherries, and a jug of weak ale.

"My name's Malia, and Chef says this is the last time you're getting meals delivered to you, so don't get used to it," she told us cheerfully. "Unless you're sick or injured, of course."

She plunked the tray down on my clothing chest. "Welcome to the kitchens, girls. Chef Vollkorn will work you hard, but she's fair and don't beat us like the last Master Chef here."

I noticed that, unlike us, Malia didn't wear a silver collar. I guessed she'd been properly apprenticed, with a fee paid by her parents or guardians.

"Thank you for bringing us supper," I said. "My name's Jacinthe."

"I know," Malia said with a cheeky grin. "Everyone's heard about *you*." She leaned forward. "Is it true about that merman?"

"Is *what* true?" I asked sharply.

"That he killed a bunch of sailors on the voyage here?"

"Lord Tama's *nice!*" Elswyth piped up before I could answer.

"Yeah, he gave us presents and kept the sailors from bothering Miss Jacinthe!" Rheda added.

"And we played cards with him every day after lunch," Elswyth added. She wrinkled her nose. "He always won, though."

Malia's brows shot up in surprise. "Well, now, aren't you all his loyal defenders?"

I decided not to mention that Tama had actually killed two men aboard the ship.

"I meant no insult to your friend. Forget I asked." Malia flapped her hand dismissively. "Bring the tray and dirty dishes down to the kitchen when you're done eating, and leave 'em in the sink. Likely as not, you'll be washing them *and* everything else tomorrow."

And on that cheery note, she departed.

As we sat on our beds and ate our supper, I asked the girls, "So, what do you think of Darkstone Academy so far?"

Both girls had been mostly silent during the tour, and quickly looked overwhelmed.

"I don't like this place!" Rheda exclaimed around a mouthful of bread. "Chef said there are monsters here who eat people!"

Elswyth nodded. "It's scary." She darted a nervous glance up at the stone-vaulted ceiling. "Do you think it's haunted, too? Ma used to tell us bedtime stories about castles with ghosts."

I smiled at them. "I don't think there are really monsters here. *Or* ghosts," I said, trying my best to be reassuring. "And you liked Tama, right? I'm sure that the other imperial hostages are just like him. Not monsters, just… *different* from us."

The girls traded doubtful looks, then nodded. "Tama was nice to us," Elswyth agreed.

"I hope I get to work in the bakery, like I did back home," Rheda said. "Da always called me his best assistant."

"That's the spirit," I told them. "I'm not going to lie to you. Our apprenticeship is going to be hard work and long days, for sure, but Chef Vollkorn didn't strike me as mean, and Malia said she's fair."

Brusque, yes. And definitely no-nonsense. But nothing like Narcissa and Baldwin. Not anywhere close.

I concluded with, "Overall, this place doesn't seem so bad."

Even though Lady Margitts had confiscated my herbal, Darkstone Academy still seemed a thousand times better than the Herrewick Harbor brothel.

And who knew? I might learn a lot here and use that knowledge to find a good job somewhere after my indenture ended.

Not for the first time, I vowed I was not only going to survive my indenture term, but I was also going to get revenge on Baldwin and Narcissa. I didn't know *how* yet, but I had plenty of time—seven years, in fact—to figure it out.

The girls nodded solemnly. Then Elswyth yawned. So did I.

A short time later, I drifted off to sleep on my new bed, wondering how I was going to tell Tama about what had happened to the book he'd given me. At least I still had his precious whale-tooth pendant, hidden securely under my clothing.

Chapter 10

Jacinthe

My first day of work at Darkstone Academy began well before sunrise the next morning.

I woke with a start as Senior Apprentice Malia marched through the dormitory, banging a metal saucepan.

"Rise and shine, kitchen mice!" she shouted with disgusting cheerfulness.

All around me, my fellow apprentices, who I'd met only briefly during yesterday's tour, were stretching and yawning and rising from their beds.

Feeling revived after a good night's sleep, I made sure that Elswyth and Rheda were up and getting ready. Then I combed and re-braided my hair, washed my face and hands, and donned one of my new dark blue uniforms, complete with a linen cap and a long white apron.

Dressed and presentable, I followed the example of the other kitchen apprentices and made my bed before going downstairs.

There, Senior Apprentice Malia took attendance, introduced Elswyth, Rheda, and me, then assigned us to different apprentice work groups.

The four other apprentices in my work group weren't exactly unfriendly, just extremely focused on their work. As the hours passed swiftly in round after round of chores, I understood why no one had the energy to chat or trade jokes.

My work group's first task was to help bake the day's bread.

While the baker's six apprentices swiftly formed rows of evenly sized rolls and loaves from the giant bowls of dough left to rise overnight in the warm bakery, I and the other junior apprentices used wooden paddles to shove the floury loaves into the enormous, beehive-shaped stone bread ovens that took up one wall of the large bakery.

Most of the loaves were the same plain, whole-grain bread I'd eaten every day back home.

But one batch of dough had been made from expensive white flour. The baker's apprentices spread rectangles of this dough with butter, sprinkled it with a sweet spice mixture, crystallized honey, and raisins, then rolled it up and cut it into sections, each with a neat spiral of filling.

"For Lord and Lady de Norhas," one of the apprentices explained when he caught me watching him work, "and the other nobles here."

Long wooden work tables filled the rest of the bakery. Sacks of flour, sugar, and salt lined the walls, and wide, shallow wooden kneading bowls were stacked on the lower shelves, along with baskets of dried herbs and fresh eggs, jars of olives in brine, and boxes of raisins, dried apricots, dates, and other dried fruits I couldn't identify.

Once all the loaves were in the ovens, we scurried to stoke the multitude of charcoal stoves and reawaken the banked fires in the enormous fireplaces of the main kitchen.

I followed the other apprentices in my work group outside the castle walls to the woodpile and charcoal shed. My arms piled high with fragrant applewood, I paused for a moment to watch the sun rise over the island in a glory of scarlet and gold.

As the first rays touched the leaves of the wild forest covering most of the island, a vast cacophony of shrieks, squawks, screeches, and hoots rose through the mist-shrouded treetops.

It was beautiful, but utterly alien compared to summer dawns on Abbonay.

While my workgroup and I fed the fireplaces and stoves with fuel, Elswyth and Rheda were dispatched to the huge courtyard chicken coop to gather eggs.

Meanwhile, other apprentices fanned out to the storerooms and gardens to fetch the remaining ingredients for breakfast.

Once we revived the kitchen fires, the cooks arrived and set to work cooking the first meal of the day. In short order, the smells of frying bacon, eggs frying in butter, and freshly baked bread filled the air.

Senior Apprentice Malia and two others delivered baskets piled high with the fragrant raisin rolls up to the Great Hall. The rest of us kitchen apprentices then carried trays of food and baskets of warm loaves to the servants' dining hall, where we joined the rest of the castle's staff for breakfast.

There, I was happy to see Toland and Kenric. They both reported they liked their new masters and fellow apprentices, which made me happy for them.

After breakfast, the *real* work began.

First, Malia assigned my work group to wash all the breakfast dishes, pots, pans, trays, and utensils.

Once we'd completed this gargantuan job, we spent the next two hours peeling and slicing sacks of assorted vegetables.

We spent the remaining time before the midday meal weeding the courtyard herb and flower garden. Other apprentices went outside the castle walls to the orchards and kitchen gardens to harvest fruits, vegetables, and nuts.

Then we gathered in the servants' hall once again for the midday meal, before washing the next batch of dishes and pots.

It seemed like the work would never end. Not even the endless drudgery under Baldwin and Narcissa had prepared me for the overwhelming number of tasks involved in feeding an academy and castle staff.

By midafternoon, I was starting to doubt that I would make it through the day.

But then, as I scrubbed out the final pot, Chef Vollkorn strode over to me.

"Apprentice Jacinthe, Lady Margitts tells me you can read, write, and do sums," she warbled. "Is that true?"

"Yes, Chef."

"Wonderful!" She clapped me on the shoulder. "I need you to work on a special project for me. It's time to conduct our half-yearly storeroom inventory." She paused. "You remember where the storerooms are located, yes?"

"Yes, Chef," I replied, feeling a spark of excitement at possibly escaping my work group's endless list of menial tasks for a few hours.

"Wonderful! I want you to list all the dry goods storeroom's contents and note their condition and quantity, and report back to me before the evening meal. If you find any sign of vermin infestation or damage, note that also."

"Yes, Chef," I repeated.

"Accuracy is important, Apprentice," she said sternly. "I need a complete list of items to re-order before the academy's commissioners dispatch the next supply ship from Neapolis Capitola."

She reached into her apron pocket and pulled out a bound ledger book and a pencil. I hastily dried my hands on a dish towel and accepted it from her.

Then I escaped the crowded, noisy kitchen with an overwhelming sense of relief.

Hoping that Chef Vollkorn's special project signaled a promotion from the worst of the drudgery, I completed the inventory in a couple of hours. I even summarized the obvious shortages and highlighted the items I thought questionable.

To my dismay, once I'd completed this task, it was back to the kitchens for yet more menial tasks as the cooks began preparing the evening meal. I washed and peeled tubers, chopped herbs, and turned the spits with their rows of succulent roasting chickens as ordered.

By the end of the day, when all the apprentices gathered after the evening meal to clean the kitchens from top to bottom, my body was beyond exhausted.

All I wanted was to collapse into bed. The long days of leisure aboard the ship were already a distant memory.

After the kitchen had been swept and scrubbed, and the fires banked for the night, Malia and other senior apprentices handed out bread rolls smeared thickly with butter and honey.

"Rough first day?" she said, sounding sympathetic as I staggered up to her to claim my share of food.

"I've had worse," I replied honestly. I raised the soft roll with its sweet filling. "At least it doesn't seem I'll go hungry here."

She smiled approvingly. "It's always good to look at the bright side."

When all the junior apprentices were busy chewing, she cleared her throat. "Good job today, everyone. As we all know, the Victory Day festival is coming up next week. Starting tomorrow, Chef Vollkorn wants the apprentices and cooks to prep all they can for the feast."

A quiet chorus of groans rose all around me.

"Ugh, more work!" someone behind me complained.

"Here are the extra tasks I want you to complete tomorrow, besides your regular duties," Malia said, ignoring the complaints.

She then read out a bewildering list of tasks that involved everything from harvesting honey to grinding spices to churning extra portions of butter.

She assigned Elswyth, Rheda, and I to shelling and blanching ten sacks of almonds in-between our other chores over the next week.

Once the almonds had been briefly boiled then rinsed with cold water, we would have to slip the skin off each nut one by one.

Another set of apprentices would then grind the blanched almonds into almond meal.

From experience, I knew this was the first step in making the marzipan the confectioner needed to create the edible sculptures of Dragons, Sea People, Djinn, and Fae for the academy officials' banquet.

The cooks would turn the rest of the ground almonds into almond milk. Next week, the kitchens were tasked with preparing a vast quantity of the traditional victory pudding for the students and castle staff. This was one of my favorites, a creamy dessert made from almond milk thickened with boiled rice, then flavored with saffron, cardamom, and rosewater, and topped with candied rose petals.

Having just spent an entire day frantically scurrying from task to task, I wondered how we'd find the time to prepare the time-consuming holiday treats, in addition to feeding the officials, professors, students, and staff of the academy three times a day.

∞∞∞

Note delivered by one of the castle staff to the Kitchen Apprentices' Female Dormitory:

From Tama of Walrus Clan to Apprentice Jacinthe of Bernswick: Greetings.
We have been parted for six sunrises now. I have seen the two male younglings working outside the walls, but I have not seen you or the female younglings. Are the preparers of food treating you well? If not, let me know and I will come to you.
You wear my Kujiranokiba; I am your warrior. You have only to send me word.

∞∞∞

On my first day off work, seven days after I arrived at Darkstone Academy, I slept through breakfast, then took a long, luxurious bath and washed my hair.

When I finally left the dormitory, I headed downstairs to the bakery, where I managed to snag a leftover roll.

Now that I had caught up on my sleep, I planned to explore the castle grounds, and maybe even sneak into the academy's library and do some reading.

Over the past week, when I'd occasionally encountered the mage students while running errands for Chef or the senior apprentices, the students had acted like my blue livery made me invisible.

Maybe I could use that invisibility to my advantage.

On the way out of the kitchens, I encountered Charmaine, another of the junior apprentices.

She was staggering under the weight of an enormous wicker basket piled high with unidentifiable lumps wrapped in waxed paper. I caught a strong whiff of seaweed and fresh fish.

I exchanged greetings with her, then asked, "What's that basket for?"

"Meal delivery to two of the prisoners. Chef Vollkorn says they're refusing to eat bread or anything except raw meat or fish." She grimaced. "This is the worst job they've given me so far!"

I came alert. "Is one of them Tama of the Sea People—I mean, merfolk?"

My chest squeezed with mingled excitement and pain. Yesterday's note from Tama, delivered while I was at work, hadn't mentioned anything about how he was faring here. All week, I'd heard the increasingly wild stories about his bloodthirstiness, and my heart ached for my friend.

"Yeah, him." Charmaine shuddered. "I heard they locked him up because he tore ten sailors to pieces and ate them!"

"That's a lie!" I exclaimed indignantly. The stories about Tama were getting more and more ridiculous with every re-telling. "He only killed *two* people. And they both deserved it!"

Her eyes widened. "So, the stories are true? You've actually met the merman?"

"Yes. We were on the same ship. He's my friend."

"You made friends with a monster like *that?*" she asked in open disbelief. I knew that there would be some more interesting gossip circulating at the midday meal in the servants' hall.

Then I had a flash of inspiration. "Why don't you let *me* bring him this basket?" I suggested.

"If you *really* want to work on your day off…" Charmaine looked and sounded relieved. "Lord Tama gets the fish and seaweed. The Dragon gets the raw haunch of beef and the liver."

"There's a *Dragon* here?" I asked in disbelief.

"Yeah." She thrust the basket into my arms.

As I staggered a little under the unexpected weight, she pointed at the gatehouse, with its three stories of narrow windows above the castle's arched gateway. "The prisoners are all lodged up there. Thanks!"

Then she turned and fled back into the kitchens. Maybe she was worried I'd change my mind about delivering the food.

Eager to see my friend again, and intensely curious about an actual live Dragon, I hurried towards the gatehouse, the heavy basket of food carefully balanced on my hip.

The scent of blooming roses filled the air as I neared the courtyard garden. I spotted Elswyth and Rheda harvesting petals for rosewater distillation and candying.

Not wanting to stop and talk, I skirted around the garden, smiling at the prospect of seeing Tama again.

I was nearly at the gatehouse when I heard Elswyth exclaim, "We can't! We'll get in trouble if we do that!"

I turned to see my two young friends cornered by three people who looked to be my age. There were two young women and a young man. All wore the long black robes of mage-students, which had earned them the nickname "crazy crows" from the castle servants.

The trio's avid expressions as they loomed over my young

friends were all too familiar. Narcissa and her daughters had worn those same looks while they inflicted their petty cruelties on me.

Both Elswyth and Rheda looked terrified.

I dropped the basket and rushed towards them, my heart pounding with anger and fear.

"What do you mean you can't?" the leader of the trio, a slender, dark-haired girl, sneered. "Do you little mice *know* who I am?"

Frightened, Elswyth and Rheda both shook their heads.

"I'm Lady Cresta of Pomerado. My father is the Count of Pomerado—you know, the Imperial Treasurer. And these are my friends, Lord Bernardo de Espola, son of the Imperial High Admiral, and Lady Alondra of Parrish. Her father is the Duke of Frankia."

The girls stared at her, wide-eyed.

Cresta snapped her fingers. "Now, mice, go fetch us those pastries!"

I slowed my pace as I approached them and set my jaw. "What's going on here?" I asked loudly.

"*Another* kitchen mouse?" Cresta tucked her long, dark hair behind one ear and sneered.

Bernardo added, "We heard there's fresh-baked *pakhlava* and we want some."

I and six other apprentices had spent all of yesterday painstakingly rolling out a hundred paper-thin layers of dough for the special Victory Festival pastries filled with ground walnuts, spices, saffron, rosewater, and honey.

Anger bubbled up inside me at their selfish cruelty. I couldn't suppress it, despite knowing that these were noble mages and I was just an indentured commoner without an ounce of magic.

"Leave them alone," I snapped, using the same voice I'd used on my younger sisters when they misbehaved. "They've got work to do, and those pastries are off-limits to everyone. You'll get your share tomorrow at the banquet."

"Ooh, so insolent for a servant!" Smirking, Bernardo flicked his fingers at me.

A sudden, violent gust of wind nearly knocked me off balance. I managed to stay on my feet, but only barely.

My mouth went dry as Cresta stepped forward, her eyes narrowing.

"No one says 'no' to me, and especially not a dirty servant mouse!" she hissed. "Kneel, mouse, and kiss my shoe before you apologize to us."

She raised her hand and turned the palm in my direction. It glowed with blue magical energy.

My stomach clenched in sudden terror. I'd grown up with mages. I knew what they were capable of. And the students here were all *delinquent* mages, expelled by the more respectable academies.

"Run!" I shouted at Elswyth and Rheda.

As they turned to flee, I braced myself for the pain and humiliation that would surely come next.

Chapter 11

Jacinthe

As the torrent of Cresta's power hit me and swirled around my body, my silver indenture collar chimed like a bell and the hyacinth tattoo hidden beneath my skirts flared with sudden heat.

The spell coiled around me like a snake, relentlessly pushing and tugging at me. A thousand invisible needles pierced my skin wherever the magic touched me.

Her power felt much stronger than Bernardo's. Nevertheless, it failed to force me to my knees.

Cresta's eyes widened. "What…? How are you *doing* that?" she demanded.

I wondered the same thing. My collar vibrated madly against my collarbones. Was it protecting me?

"No kitchen mouse is going to beat *me!*" she declared with a fierce frown.

The coils of blue magic winding around me thickened. I gasped as the burning sensation increased over my belly until I was sure the skin there was blistering from the heat. Afraid that my skirt was going to ignite, I clapped a hand over the spot. But the fabric was cool against my hand.

Then, a giant, red-headed man appeared and stepped between us.

"Enough of this, students!" he bellowed. He leveled a fearsome glare at the trio of bullies. "How dare you attack these servants!"

He towered over us, broad-shouldered and muscled like a metalsmith. I saw he was younger than I first thought from his commanding presence and deep voice, maybe just a year or two older than me.

Like me, his skin was a rich brown, and his hair was blazing red. His eyes were several shades lighter than mine, green-gold rather than hazel. His richly embroidered sleeveless red jerkin and cream silk shirt marked him as someone important.

Bernardo snarled, "Stay out of this, Dragon!"

Dragon? I thought in shock. Unlike Tama, this man looked completely human. Maybe it was just a nickname?

Then I saw he wore an enameled earring in the shape of a red dragon. Like Tama's earring, it glowed with magic. Looking more closely, it struck me that his eyes had vertical pupils, like a cat.

"Do I need to teach *you* a lesson about respect, too?" Cresta snapped. She raised her hand again and pointed it at the newcomer.

The blue coils of magic squeezing me abruptly vanished. The awful prickling and burning torment instantly stopped, too.

She can only maintain one spell at a time? I thought in astonishment.

Cresta's magic was powerful, but I'd seen Mama effortlessly perform three simultaneous magical workings when a scaffold collapsed and our neighbors rushed several injured workmen over to our shop for healing.

Like before, blue power pulsed and glowed in Cresta's palm.

But before she could release her spell, a fireball suddenly

sprang into being. For an instant, it floated in front of the giant's face. Then he blew out a mighty breath.

The fireball hurtled towards Cresta. Just before it hit her, it divided and engulfed all three bullies.

The trio screamed as their hair and clothes burned away, leaving them naked and sooty, but otherwise unharmed.

Now that's some extremely fine control of magic, I thought in admiration.

I couldn't help snickering. Cresta looked considerably less intimidating without her fancy hairdo or eyebrows.

"You monster! How *dare* you! Do you know who I am?" she shrieked.

"Apparently, no one here knows who you are," I said, with all the sweetness I could muster. "It must be *so* very inconvenient."

As her face twisted in rage, I grinned at her. It was a foolish thing to do, but I was giddy with the realization that both she and Bernardo had hurled powerful spells at me… and they'd been utterly ineffective.

The giant grinned, too, a hungry, predatory baring of his teeth that made all three mage-students take an involuntary step back.

"You are a student," he rumbled. "And 'students are expressly forbidden to work spells without the supervision of an academy instructor or official.'" His bass voice was heavily laced with irony as he spoke, presumably quoting from the academy's rules.

"You fool!" shouted Bernardo. "Throwing fire around like that! You could have *killed* us! Or burned down the castle!"

The giant laughed. "Nonsense. Unlike *you*, earthworm, *I* can cast a proper spell."

"Hey, everyone!" someone called from the colonnade that ran around the garden's perimeter. "You *gotta* see this! That Dragon burned off Lady Cresta's clothes! She's naked! And so are Bernardo and Alondra!"

Black academic gowns flapped as students leaned out of windows and others appeared in the archways, racing towards the courtyard garden to see what was going on.

The trio of naked, bald bullies began glancing around wildly, trying to cover themselves with their hands. Beneath the sooty smears, their faces flushed deep red.

Then Cresta seemed to snap out of her panic. She screeched a short incantation and summoned a shimmering silver robe out of thin air.

Alondra's spell produced a primrose-colored cloak, which she wrapped around herself from neck to knees.

Bernardo's attempt only invoked another wild gust of wind, which scattered the rose petals from Elswyth and Rheda's basket in a whirl of pink and red.

As the three bullies turned to flee towards the students' apartments on the other side of the castle, Lady Cresta shouted, "I'll make you regret this! All of you!"

The red-headed man scoffed loudly, and jeered, "Fine words from a naked, scorched ass running away!"

Laughter, hoots, and jeers erupted from the crowd of black-robed mage students who had gathered to watch the confrontation.

I sighed in relief when the last of the trio vanished through an arch.

Elswyth and Rheda rushed over to me and flung their arms

around me.

"Miss Jacinthe, I thought they were going to kill you!" Rheda began sobbing.

I patted her back reassuringly and turned to our rescuer.

"Thank you," I said to him. "I'm grateful for your help."

I received a fearsome scowl in reply. "Don't take it personally—" His burning golden gaze dropped to my neck. "Apprentice. I hate all you humans but I fucking *loathe* little earthworms like that most of all." He planted one meaty fist on his hip. "Those fools could've hurt you or destroyed something, flinging all that power around like that. So, what are you going to do about it?"

His tone was challenging and his burning gaze raked me from head to toe, as if judging me and finding me wanting.

What could *I do about three noble-born students?* I wondered.

Now that the confrontation was over, a steady tide of anger rose inside me, pushing out all the residual terror. "I'm going to tell Master Chef Vollkorn that those students tried to extort Elswyth and Rheda, and then attacked us when we refused to back down."

Chef had told us to tell her immediately if any of the students gave us trouble. I didn't doubt that she'd go straight to Lady Margitts.

"You do that." Then our savior strode away before I could ask him his name.

I stared after him as he vanished into the gatehouse, where the imperial hostages' apartments were located.

"Who *was* that?" Elswyth asked.

"I don't know, but I'm guessing one of the imperial hostages," I replied.

"He was scary but he made Lady Cresta and the others run away," Rheda said gleefully. "She looked funny without her hair!"

Only two supernatural races could wield fire magic: the Anemodareis, as the Dragons called themselves; and the Djinn.

And Cresta had called him "Dragon." Combined with his earring…

"I think we just met an actual *Dragon*," I breathed.

I wondered whether our rescuer was the person I was supposed to deliver food to.

Dragons were the villains of every fairy tale and historical account. They were the age-old enemies of humanity, and they'd nearly wiped us out several times in history.

So why had this Dragon helped us?

He could have simply watched Cresta and her friends terrorize us with an illicit display of magic, like everyone else.

That thought led to another puzzle. *If he's a hostage like Tama, then why wasn't his magic bound, too?*

Now that the excitement was over, the gathered students quickly dispersed.

As I helped my two young friends pick up the scattered rosebuds and petals, I considered whether I should tell Tama about the incident.

I could only imagine how Tama would react when he heard we'd been attacked. I remembered Munis and Fawkes aboard the ship, and shuddered.

If I *did* tell him, I'd have to make certain not to mention any names or identifying details to my merman friend. The last thing I wanted was for Tama to execute Cresta and her two hangers-on.

Besides, I felt that my Dragon rescuer had already doled out a satisfying punishment.

Tama would be angry and hurt, though, if I said nothing and he heard the story from someone else.

And if there was one thing I'd learned about Darkstone Academy in the week since I arrived, it was that gossip spread even more quickly here than it had back home in Bernswick.

I continued to debate with myself as I retrieved my basket of food and continued on my errand.

Maybe I should deliver the other meal first, and hope that some better solution occurred to me before I arrived at Tama's rooms.

Chapter 12

Boreas

Burning the clothes off those sniveling little earthworms was the most fun I've had since arriving here, I thought. I settled back into my quarters and opened the book I'd borrowed from the academy's barely adequate library.

My captors let me out of my rooms for a few hours every day so that I could exercise and visit the library. That was better treatment than some of my fellow hostages received.

My apartment wasn't entirely unpleasant. It comprised two spacious rooms: a bedroom and a sitting room. The bedroom's solid stone walls reminded me of my clan's mountain aerie back home. The sitting room had a window that provided light and gave me a view over an endless expanse of sea.

Courtesy of my predecessors, all the furnishings were made from fireproof materials. Even the hangings were woven from hair-thin metal threads.

Today, that view just taunted me with just how far in the middle of fucking nowhere I was right now. If I still had wings, I could climb onto the wide stone sill, launch myself into the air, and ride the trade winds south and east, towards home.

Except I couldn't, of course. And not just because some earthworm mage warped me into this puny, weak, defenseless human shape.

When the time rolled around for the next hostage to depart, my Clutch Mother chose *me* to fulfill this important duty. She was the High Lady Aeolia, the Royal Vizier to King Menelaus of the Anemodareis, the Wind-Walkers, as my people called ourselves.

Humans called us "Dragons," and I liked it. Especially when they said it with awe and fear and proper fucking respect.

I gave my word of honor to my Clutch Mother and the king that I would obey the terms of my imprisonment and stay with the humans until my release.

"And whatever you do, don't kill any of the humans," Aeolia had warned me during our last meeting before I departed for my journey to the Dominion.

"No problem," I'd answered cockily. "As long as they don't mess with me, I won't mess with them."

Unfortunately for me, that "don't mess with me" clause didn't get me out of being shape-changed as soon as I landed on this island.

In what felt like the worst torture anyone had ever undergone, one of the human mages whittled me down to human size.

Luckily, they kept my excess mass against the day my term of imprisonment ended and they restored my true shape. It was a coal-black Dragon statue, currently locked away for safekeeping in the castle's chapel to the humans' Mother of All.

Despite this and other indignities heaped on me since I arrived, I was determined to do my Clutch Mother and the rest of my aerie proud.

After all, I wasn't anything like our esteemed ruler, the great Dragon of Hierapolis, King Menelaus the Third.

Back when he'd served his time as a hostage at the human imperial court, he'd ignited an enormous scandal because he hadn't been able to keep it in his human pants.

From what I'd heard, good old Menelaus had gotten some human noblewoman pregnant. The humans had reacted badly. *Really* badly. They banished Menelaus to this island in disgrace, and I heard they executed both his lover *and* the baby, because it had been "born a crime."

By Primal Fire and the Unconquered Sun, these humans were the worst!

After that, the human authorities sent every imperial hostage to this same forsaken place to serve out their terms. Thanks to Menelaus and his uncontrollable cock, the human ruler no longer wanted the hostages anywhere near the imperial court.

No doubt Menelaus' father, King Zephyros, and his Clutch Mother both ordered him to behave himself while in the human realm. But male Dragons are really fucking *terrible* at following orders.

Our independent, combative streak is why we were the best individual warriors in the fucking world.

And our absolute inability to actually organize into a cohesive unit, like the humans did, is what led to our defeat in the Great War.

To be fair, the Fae couldn't do it, either. Working together in groups for long periods of time proved impossible for them. Their tribes were even more quarrelsome than the Dragon clans, and that was saying something.

So here I was, the latest Dragon to serve as a living guarantee of that damned peace treaty the humans shoved down our throats after they slaughtered old King Notos and his most experienced warriors on the battlefield.

But what really defeated us were the mage-crafted birds infected with plague sent to the mountains of Kappadokia to kill off the clans. The humans came damned close to wiping us out that time.

The one bright spot in my world was that the old human mage who performed the shape-changing spell hadn't managed to lock away *all* my magic.

It was only a tenth of what it used to be, but it was enough to teach those little black-robed earthworms who called themselves "students" a lesson when they needed one.

I was only a few pages into my new book when I heard the clank of a key unlocking my door. I shot up, my fists clenched, ready to attack whoever dared to disturb me.

Guard Machry opened the door, then instantly backed away into the corridor. As always, he reeked of fear, and that stirred my inner predator.

Then I saw he'd brought that red-haired human with the silver slave collar I'd rescued from the mage student bullies a short time ago. She had a large wicker basket looped over her arm.

"What do you want now, human?" I demanded.

To my surprise, she smiled at me. Why wasn't she afraid of me like the other servants who had come to my cell before?

"I've come to deliver your meal," she replied calmly. "Guard Machry told me that your name is Prince Boreas of the Anemodareis." Then she dipped into an actual fucking curtsey. "I'm Jacinthe, one of the kitchen apprentices. Thank you again for taking our side against those three students."

I grunted in response. Her gratitude made me deeply uncomfortable.

She took that as permission to step into my apartment. Moving unhurriedly, she set the basket on the table in my sitting room. That intrigued me. All the other servants in this place had just dropped their baskets and run away.

"How long have you been here on the island?" she asked, lifting packets out of her basket and unwrapping them.

"Since winter solstice." My mouth instantly began watering as the scent of fresh beef—not that burned shit or that vile bread-crap they'd been trying to feed me—filled the room.

"I only arrived here last week," she offered.

I didn't care about that. I was suddenly *starving*.

"Is that fresh tuna I smell, too?" I asked hopefully.

She shot me an apologetic glance. "Sorry, but the fish is for Tama. Um, *Lord* Tama, I mean. I'm delivering his meal next. He's one of the Sea People, and a hostage—I mean, imperial guest here."

At least she wasn't trying to pretend he wasn't a prisoner here. I already liked her better than most of the other humans.

"Oh yeah, *him*," I said with admiration. "I've heard a lot about that guy. Killed a bunch of sailors on his voyage here. Good for him."

The guards couldn't stop talking about Tama of the Sea People. They were all scared shitless of him, which amused me to no end. I used to be the only one who could make the guards piss themselves in terror.

But Tama had really flipped their wings and sent them into a spiral, like fledglings caught in a tornado.

I thought about being trapped on a ship for weeks with a bunch of smelly, noisy humans and no fresh meat, and shuddered.

If I hadn't flown here on my own, I might've killed a bunch of humans, too.

Jacinthe blew out an exasperated breath. "He did *not* kill a bunch of people!" She sounded frustrated. "Just two. And it was self-defense."

"Well, that's disappointing," I commented.

I laughed. The stories I'd overheard the guards telling about the merman had been fucking *wild*. Too bad they weren't true, after all.

"Killing people isn't funny!" Now the human girl was mad. Which I found adorable for some weird reason. "It was *awful!*"

Despite myself, she interested me. I studied her as she continued to lay out the first acceptable meal I'd seen since I arrived on this forsaken, earthworm-infested island.

She was tall and attractive, for a human, with the same red hair as my human shape, and curves in interesting places. Best of all, she bore herself with a warrior's confidence.

And she smelled delicious, like a healthy human woman, but with a tantalizing hint of something else. Something familiar that I couldn't pin down.

I decided I liked her. She was a lot more interesting than the other human servants in this place. Speaking of which…

"So, Jacinthe, are you a slave here?" I asked, pointing at the silver metal collar she wore.

In the months I'd lived here, I'd noticed that most of the servants wore them, but not all.

"Not exactly." She grimaced. "I'm an indentured apprentice in the kitchens." She shrugged. "At least they feed me, and I have a comfortable place to sleep. It could be a lot worse."

Not a whiner. I liked her more and more.

"If any of those black-robed little earthworms bother you again, tell me and I'll take care of it."

Damn. I hadn't meant to say that. It just kind of slipped out.

It earned me a smile so warm it felt like sunlight against my skin. "Thank you, Prince Boreas. I appreciate that. But Tama already offered to protect me, so I won't trouble you further."

Her response irritated me. I wasn't used to having my generosity rejected. And especially not by a human slave girl.

And how in the name of the Unconquered Sun had she gotten the protection of one of the Sea People? Those fuckers hated humans even more than Dragons did.

The longer we talked, the more interesting Apprentice Jacinthe became.

"Tama's locked up tight," I told her. "They're not letting him go *anywhere*. And in case you haven't noticed, the students here are completely unhinged. You need all the help you can get, human."

The guard, still hovering in the doorway, made a choking sound that might've been agreement.

"You know what?" Jacinthe asked, her eyes lighting up. "You and Tama should meet! I'm sure you could be friends."

What the fuck? I stared at her in astonishment, then growled, "I don't need any fucking friends. And if I do, I'll find my own."

She shrugged, apparently unintimidated.

Yeah, this one definitely had a warrior's spirit.

"Have it your way," she said. "But Tama could use another friend here, and I think he's too proud to make the first move. I worry about him, especially if he's locked up all the time and not able to talk to anyone."

She bit her lower lip.

I couldn't look away from the sight of her teeth indenting the soft flesh. What would it feel like if I did the same thing? Caught that delectable lip between my own teeth? I bet she'd taste as delicious as she smelled.

My cock pulsed, reminding me how long I'd been alone.

But humans were off-limits. Strictly taboo. Bad news.

"Yeah, poor bastard," I said, feeling sorry for him despite myself.

If I hated it here, then it was probably a hundred times worse for one of the Sea People stranded on dry land.

"I really think you two could be friends," she persisted. "I mean, you're both kind and nice. Sweet, really. And *very* protective," she added, noticing my scowl.

She thought I was *kind?* By the Northern Wind, I was a prince of the fucking Anemodareis. *A Dragon.* I was supposed to be ferocious and fearless. Terrifying.

Not kind. Or *nice*. Or *sweet*.

Fuck.

I opened my mouth to tell her exactly what I thought of her calling me "kind," but her wide-eyed, hopeful expression made the words dry up in my throat.

"Fine," I said, exasperated. "I'll meet him. At least he sounds interesting. But I'm not making any promises about friendship. And since Tama's in lockdown, you'll have to petition Lady Margitts to let him out of his cage."

"I've met her," Jacinthe said. Her tone suggested the meeting hadn't gone well.

"She's like the Clutch Mother of this aerie," I observed.

Jacinthe looked puzzled at my reference, but didn't ask. Instead, she said, "All right, I'll ask her. My next day off is a week from now. If Lady Margitts says it's okay, I'll introduce you then."

I grunted, and damned if she didn't give me one of those warm, wonderful smiles again.

It made me want to stretch out and preen for her. But that would just look stupid in human-shape. I needed my wings and feathers to make a proper impression.

The guard cleared his throat and shot me a nervous glance. "Come along, Apprentice. I'll take you over to the fish-man's apartments now."

She grabbed her basket. "It was nice meeting you, Prince Boreas. I'll see you next week."

As the door swung shut behind her and the lock clicked, I sat down to enjoy my first decent meal in months.

It looked like my hunger strike had actually worked, because there wasn't a single piece of charred meat, nasty bread, or any fucking vegetables in those packets. Just sweet, raw flesh, with a succulent fresh beef liver for dessert. It all tasted fucking amazing.

I'd heard there was someone new in charge of the kitchens. If this food was any sign, it looked like Master Chef Vollkorn was going to be more reasonable than that vindictive old earthworm Tessler who'd finally dropped dead in the middle of beating the shit out of an apprentice.

While I chewed, I thought about Jacinthe. Why the fuck had I offered to protect her?

I fucking hated all those little earthworms in their black robes, so stepping in to stop those three from frying Jacinthe to a crisp hadn't required much thought.

But then, when I offered to become her protector just now... what in the name of the North Wind was I thinking?

Especially since she seemed to be mighty interested in Tama.

I wondered what the story was between them, and by the Unconquered Sun, was I actually *jealous?*

No, that's ridiculous, I told myself. *I'm just bored out of my mind, and Jacinthe is the most interesting thing to happen in fucking weeks. Besides, even if I* was *jealous—and I'm definitely* not— *no way am I going to be stupid enough to repeat King Menelaus' mistake.*

But I was still looking forward to seeing Jacinthe again next week.

Chapter 13

Jacinthe

After leaving Prince Boreas' quarters, the guard led me up a narrow spiral staircase to the top floor of the gatehouse. He'd cheerfully introduced himself as Machry when I arrived at the gatehouse, and produced a constant stream of commentary as he guided me upstairs to where the imperial hostages were lodged.

"The only reason you wasn't afraid of that one, Apprentice," he declared as I followed him up steep, twisting stone stairs, "is because you didn't see him *before*. When he was still a real Dragon."

"What was he like then?" I asked, remembering the woodcuts and paintings I'd seen of Dragons.

Torchlight sparked off the guard's polished helmet as he shook his head. "Teeth as long as my dagger here, an' no lie. And claws long as those curved swords the Djinn use. Those Dragons are a nasty piece o' work, to be sure. They ate my great-great-great grandpa during the Great War. I'm dead-sure that Prince Boreas 'ud do the same to me, if the mages hadn't cut 'im down to size," he concluded.

I felt a surge of compassion for Prince Boreas as the guard led the way from the stairs down a gloomy hall, past a long row of closed doors on either side.

What's it like to be shrunk to a sixth of your former size and confined to human shape, no longer able to fly or breathe fire?

The shape-changing spell must've been as torturous as stripping Tama of his tail and gills. Maybe more so.

No wonder he was so rude and grumpy.

At the end of the hall, we stopped in front of a rust-streaked door set into a stone archway.

I studied it with apprehension. Boreas's apartment had had an ordinary wooden door, like any other chamber in the castle. *This* door, though, looked like something better-suited to a dungeon.

The guard drew his dagger and used the pommel to pound on the door. "Lord Tama! Mealtime!"

"Leave me be, Drylander!" came the sullen-sounding reply from within.

The guard shot me a glance. "You sure you want to go through with this, Apprentice? I know you said you're a friend o' his an' all, but I'd hate to see a pretty young thing like you get ripped to shreds and eaten." He clicked his tongue against his teeth, and shook his head. "That other apprentice, the little blonde, she was so scared of him she wouldn't stop cryin'. Near broke my heart, it did, to see her in such a state."

"I'll be fine. And Tama doesn't eat people!" I shot back.

How often had I said that since arriving here?

"Jacinthe?" Tama asked, his voice faint behind the locked iron door.

My friend's hearing was apparently as keen as ever.

"Yes, it's me!" I called. "And I've brought you fresh fish and seaweed." I turned to address my escort. "Guard Machry, please open the door."

He shot me a speculative glance, then he pulled the big keyring from his belt and unlocked the door.

"If'n you don't mind, Apprentice, I'll just wait out here. You need anything, just scream." He smiled thinly and stepped aside to let me enter.

He'd been afraid of Boreas, too. Interesting.

As Machry shut the door behind me, he joked under his breath, "Maybe a spot of humpty-rumpty'll sweeten that monster up a bit."

My face heated as I turned to glare at the guard through the rapidly narrowing space between the door and its frame. I worried about the stories he'd tell his fellow guards and the next visitors to the gatehouse.

If those stories reached the wrong ears, Machry's baseless gossip could get me into serious trouble.

"Now, don't be takin' my little jest so hard, Apprentice." Then metal slammed against stone, and the lock clicked loudly into place.

I turned to survey the room. Unlike Prince Boreas's apartment, which was richly furnished, Tama's quarters were as stark as a prison cell, with unadorned whitewashed stone walls, a crudely-made wooden table, and a pair of equally crude chairs.

Then I caught sight of Tama. And instantly forgot about the potential damage to my reputation.

Mother of All, I'd missed him this past week… when I'd had time to think between the endless parade of tasks.

He was sitting in the deep window embrasure as I entered his rooms, but immediately rose to greet me. Today, he wore a long-sleeved tunic and leggings dyed a green so dark it was nearly black, thickly embroidered with shining silver thread at the neckline and cuffs, and down the outside seam of the leggings.

"You look well," he said with one of his rare smiles as he came to stand in front of me.

I wished I could tell him the same. But a week of captivity with food he couldn't or wouldn't eat had taken its toll on my friend. He was visibly thinner, his formerly pearly skin had lost its luster, and his sharp features looked gaunt.

My chest tightened with mingled joy and concern.

He studied me in return. His gaze dropped to my hands, chapped and sore from near-constant exposure to hot water and harsh soap as I battled an unending parade of dirty pots, pans, and cooking spoons.

Before I could hide them behind my apron, he seized them in his cool grasp and examined them closely.

"I'm well enough, really I am!" I protested in response to his wordless inquiry. "It's hard work, but Chef Vollkorn and her cooks treat me better than my stepfather and his new wife ever did."

His shoulders relaxed slightly. "It pleases me to hear it."

On impulse, I let my basket drop to the worn plank floor and hugged him. "I've missed you, Tama. And I've been worried about you. They tell me you haven't been eating."

"I have also missed your company, Jacinthe." His arms came around me, and clasped me firmly.

"How have you been?" I asked, turning my cheek to press against his hard chest. His heart pulsed slowly beneath my ear. "What was your first week in the castle like?"

He was silent for a long time. My heart sank. It had been bad for him, then.

When he finally spoke, he said, "I dislike this place intensely. They keep me locked in this stone box, so far away from the water. And… I am alone. Always." His arms tightened around me.

"Oh, Tama, I'm so sorry," I said, my heart aching for him.

Elswyth and Rheda had cried themselves to sleep for the first few days of the voyage, and still occasionally suffered from fits of homesickness. But they had me and the rest of the apprentices to comfort them and help them adapt to their new circumstances.

Tama didn't have anyone. Thanks to all the wild stories, all the humans were terrified of him. And there were no other Sea People hostages in the castle right now. Just a few Fae and Djinn, and Boreas, of course.

"This prison would not be so wearisome if I was not alone all the time," Tama murmured. "At home, my people live communally. We are always together." He drew a shuddering breath. "The ship was uncomfortable, but at least I had you and the children to keep me company. Now I am in solitary confinement."

I squeezed him in sympathy. "They don't let you out of your chambers for exercise and fresh air, like the other hostages?"

The other apprentices had told me that the Fae and Djinn were given the liberty of the castle, and even permitted to attend classes with the human students. And when I'd first met him, Prince Boreas had been out of his chambers and walking freely around the castle grounds.

Tama sighed. "Apparently, after reading the captain's report of what happened during the voyage, the chatelaine and castellan decided it would be too dangerous to allow me to mingle with the Drylander students or the other prisoners."

"Having met some students just now, I'm pretty sure they can fend for themselves," I said dryly.

Tama loosened his embrace. He took a step back and stared

down at me, though he kept his hands on my shoulders. "What do you mean by that?" he demanded.

I took a deep breath and reminded myself to downplay the situation. "Well, on the way over here with your food, I saw some students trying to intimidate Elswyth and Rheda into stealing holiday treats from the kitchens."

His fingers tightened. "Did these students injure the younglings?"

"Not at all," I said, as breezily as I could. "There was a tense moment or two when I intervened and told the students to stop it. They tried to throw a spell at me, but it didn't work. Luckily for me. I guess they failed basic spell-casting."

My light tone wasn't working. Tama's look of concern had darkened into a glower. "They tried to *hurt* you?" he growled.

"Tried and failed," I replied quickly. "And here's the funny part—one of the other hostages came to my aid. He used fire magic to burn off the bullies' clothes and hair. He didn't harm anything but their pride." I snickered. "They had to run away naked through a crowd of their fellow students. I'd say the punishment more than fit the crime."

Tama's glower didn't lessen. "*I* should have been there to protect you and younglings, not that other prisoner. You wear my Kujiranokiba, after all."

"Everything turned out all right," I assured him with more confidence than I felt.

Lady Cresta had sworn to get revenge on us for her humiliation, but I wasn't going to tell Tama that.

"This fire-magic user who helped you," he said. "Was it the Djinn, the one they call Arslan?"

I'd heard about the Djinn but hadn't met him yet. I shook my head. "No, a Dragon, by the name of Prince Boreas. Speaking of which, would you be interested in meeting him? He lives one story below you, and he seems a little lonely, too. I told him I thought that you and he might become friends."

"You spent time with this Wind-Walker Boreas?" Tama looked even less happy than before. "You *visited* him in his rooms?"

Was my friend actually *jealous* of the Dragon?

"Only because I had to deliver his food," I said reassuringly. I bent and picked the basket up from the floor. "Speaking of which, I have fresh fish and seaweed for you." I patted his arm, which was still rock hard with muscle. "I heard the kitchens were sending you bread and vegetables before."

"And cooked fish." Tama shuddered. "I tried to eat what they sent, but it made me ill. I would rather be hungry than sick."

"Well, hopefully you won't have to be either of those things from this point forward. I'll talk to the cooks and make sure they send you only fresh, raw seafood. Can you eat shellfish? Crabs? Shrimp?"

He nodded. "I enjoy all those foods."

"I'll ask the cooks to request them for you when the fishermen make their deliveries." I put the basket on the table. Unlike Boreas's quarters, these rooms had no carpets or hangings to soften the worn plank flooring or the whitewashed stone walls.

"Sit, eat," I urged him, reaching into the basket for a packet and unwrapping a thick, dark-red piece of raw tuna.

Tama's hand darted forward and hooked around the braided seaweed cord of the necklace he'd given me. The brush of his clawed forefinger against my neck sent a pleasant shiver arrowing straight down to the pit of my belly.

He tugged gently, pulling the whale tooth pendant up from where I'd tucked it inside my bodice. "Why have you hidden my Kujiranokiba?" he rasped. "How will anyone know you are under my protection if they cannot see it?" His liquid black eyes narrowed. "Or have you found another protector? The Dragon?"

I blinked at him. *Is Tama jealous? No, I probably just hurt his feelings.*

"Tama, I'm only trying to keep your pendant safe," I explained. "I'm afraid that it might get damaged while I'm working in the kitchens." I decided not to mention that I feared it might suffer the same fate as my book if Lady Margitts or any of the other castle officials saw it.

His glower lightened, and he let the heavy ivory cone drop against the front of my gown. "Has anyone in the kitchens threatened or harmed you in any way?"

I shook my head. "Everyone has been—" Not exactly kind, but fair, certainly. "—too busy to pay any attention to me, as long as I keep up with my work."

From what I'd heard about the former Master Chef Tessler, that hadn't always been the case. All the cooks and apprentices who'd known him agreed that Chef Vollkorn was an enormous improvement over that vindictive old man.

"Very well," Tama said, his hands returning to my shoulders. "You may continue to protect my Kujiranokiba while you are working in the kitchens. But you must display it as soon as you venture anywhere else in the castle."

"All right. I'll do that." It seemed like a small thing to promise if it made him feel better.

"And you do not need a Wind-Walker to protect you." To my shock, he bent and pressed his mouth against mine in a hard kiss.

His lips tasted of clean brine, cool as seawater against my

mouth, and yet the sensations that surged through me in response were anything but cool. Every part of me suddenly came alive with an intense, burning heat that I'd never felt before.

It felt like being pulled into the ocean, swept away by the undertow of a powerful, passionate desire that I'd only ever read about. It was terrifying and exhilarating at the same time.

I went up on tiptoes and looped my arms around his neck as I eagerly returned his kiss. As fire ran through my veins and coalesced in a ball of throbbing heat between my thighs, I shamelessly pressed myself against his lean, hard body.

His large, webbed hands clamped around my hips, pulling me even closer as he deepened the kiss.

Dizzily, I realized that our friendship had abruptly become something more. Something forbidden by every human law and custom.

And I didn't care. I only wanted to keep kissing Tama as he aroused all my senses.

Endless, blissful moments later, I was rudely jolted back to reality by the guard's voice. "Time to go, Apprentice!"

A bolt of sheer terror shot through me, and I pushed Tama away. My face flaming with embarrassment, I grabbed for the basket and turned away, suddenly unable to meet his dark, liquid gaze.

The lock clicked. An instant later, the door swung open and Guard Machry stuck his head inside. "Ready?"

I nodded, sure my flushed cheeks and rapid breathing betrayed exactly what had just happened.

But Guard Machry didn't seem to notice. He just waved me over with a sharp, impatient gesture.

"I'll see you soon, Tama," I managed. "And I'll ask about getting you some time outside these rooms."

∞∞∞

Wrapped in a warm glow, I left the gatehouse and headed back to the castle's kitchens. I felt as though I were floating, and that everyone who saw me could see my joy and arousal.

Hot, pulsing sensations continued to course through my body. I could still feel the imprint of Tama's lips against mine. I craved his delicious, arousing caresses more than I'd ever wanted pastries or spiced sweetmeats. I finally understood why so many songs, poems, and stories revolved around the love between two people.

Am I in love? I wondered. I liked, trusted, and respected Tama. And his kisses had only made me crave more.

Then, as I continued walking, the overwhelming need slowly subsided in my veins. Rational thought slowly returned.

Laws with harsh punishments forbade humans from intimate entanglements with non-humans.

Guard Machry's joking, scandalous comments about my visit sweetening Tama's mood now seemed ominous.

If anyone found out that Tama had kissed me, the consequences could be disastrous. Especially since I'd discovered there were already stories floating around the castle regarding our friendship. I couldn't afford to feed those rumors any further.

What punishment could be worse than being indentured on this island for the next seven years? a subversive voice in my mind wondered.

How about a public flogging? I asked myself. *Lady Cresta and her friends would certainly relish that! Or the chatelaine could lock me up in the castle's lightless dungeons.*

The old dungeons were now used as wine and ale cellars, but a few iron-barred cells still remained. They were currently used as keep-safes for the most expensive vintages and liqueurs, but it wouldn't take much work to restore them to their original purpose.

I shuddered.

But I couldn't stay away from him, either. Not when he was clearly suffering in his solitary confinement.

The difficulty was that I only had a single day off from work each week. The rest of the time, Chef Vollkorn, the cooks, and the senior apprentices kept me busy from before dawn until long after sunset. I couldn't exactly sneak away from the kitchens without someone noticing my absence.

It was a dilemma I was determined to solve somehow.

Despite the dire threat of punishment, I couldn't help but replay the memory of Tama's kiss over and over in my mind.

My feet carried me back to the kitchen while my head remained in the clouds.

To my surprise, Chef Vollkorn was waiting for me at the entrance to the kitchen, her expression stern. "There you are!" she barked.

I fought my instinctive urge to flinch. I reminded myself that this was my official day off work.

"Chef?" I asked warily. "Is something wrong?"

A hundred disastrous scenarios rushed through my brain, most of them revolving around Tama, and guilty terror tightened steely bands around my chest, making it hard to breathe.

Chapter 14

Jacinthe

"Apprentice Jacinthe, I've been informed of the trouble you encountered earlier," Chef Vollkorn said.

Mother of All help me! I prayed, my gut clenching in apprehension. I hadn't done anything wrong, but that had never mattered to Baldwin. He'd always found a way to fault me for whatever went wrong.

"Elswyth and Rheda told me what happened," Chef Vollkorn continued. "Now, I want to hear your version of the incident."

"Of course, Chef," I said, feeling the clouds of impending doom gather around me.

Would Vollkorn punish me for making trouble?

I told her about the confrontation in the courtyard garden, and how Boreas had unexpectedly come to our rescue and taught Lady Cresta and her two friends a lesson.

"I know I shouldn't say this, but good for him!" Vollkorn grimaced. "This is the third time this week those three have waylaid the younger apprentices. This time, they've gone too far with an unauthorized use of magic."

She was taking my side? Relief rushed through me. Feeling giddy, I nodded in agreement. "Yes, Chef."

"I want you to come with me now to Assistant Chatelaine Lady Margitts' office. I intend to file a formal complaint." She paused, and then added in a bitter tone, "For all the good it'll do."

Elswyth and Rheda crept out from the kitchen to join us.

The three of us followed Chef Vollkorn as she marched towards her goal.

On the way, she informed me, "Apprentice Jacinthe, seeing how you're more… *comfortable*… with the castle's non-human residents than the other apprentices, I'm assigning you an extra duty. From now on, you will deliver the special meals to the Dragon and merman imperial guests twice a day, after breakfast and before supper."

"Yes, Chef!" I responded, with more enthusiasm than a work assignment merited.

But joy sang through my veins at the prospect of being able to visit Tama twice a day, every day. And without undue suspicion falling on me, since I'd be doing it under direct orders of the castle's Master Chef.

"I'm glad you're pleased," Vollkorn said dryly. "This will free up Apprentice Charmaine to take over your post-breakfast pots and pans cleanup."

That was even better news.

"Yes, Chef!" I said, even more enthusiastically than before. "Thank you, Chef!"

She chuckled. "Just so we're clear—you're not off the hook for lunch and dinner clean up, Apprentice."

The assistant chatelaine glanced up at us with an air of weary resignation as we entered her office a few minutes later. "Brigitte! I was just about to summon you."

"Lady Margitts." Chef Vollkorn sounded wary.

Lady Margitts' next words made my blood boil. "Lady Cresta, Lady Alondra, and Lord Bernardo were just here, looking positively frightful. They told me that a gang of kitchen apprentices, aided by Prince *Boreas* no less, attacked and nearly killed them a short while ago."

I gasped in outrage and sudden terror. Maybe Chef Vollkorn had believed me, but that wouldn't matter if Lady Margitts took the students' side against us. "You're joking, right?"

That earned me a sour look from the assistant chatelaine.

"But that's a lie!" Little Rheda protested. "*They* attacked *us!*"

"Prince Boreas saved us!" Elswyth added. "They were trying to hurt Miss Jacinthe with magic!"

Chef Vollkorn clenched her fists at her aproned sides. "Those three students started this mess, not my apprentices, Lady Margitts! And it's not the first time, either! Lady Cresta, Lord Bernardo, and Lady Alondra have been extorting sweets and pastries from the youngest apprentices for months now." She took an audible breath and added, "As you know perfectly well from the last five times I've complained to you about those three. Today, though, they crossed the line!"

Lady Margitts' mouth thinned. "Is that so?"

Vollkorn demanded, "Tell her what happened, Apprentice Jacinthe."

I took a deep breath and recounted our version of the events leading up to Prince Boreas sending the miscreants fleeing.

I watched Lady Margitts' face carefully as I spoke, but she showed no reaction.

When I finished speaking, she merely nodded, and then said, "Well, that certainly sounds more plausible than the first version I heard."

"Will you at least ban them from the Victory Day banquet?" Vollkorn asked. "It would send a message to the other students to respect the castle's staff. And enforce the rules against casting spells outside of classes."

Lady Margitts drew herself up in her chair. "Brigitte, are you really asking me to punish the children of our most noble families on the unsupported word of three *commoners?*" She smiled frostily at me. "You apprentices are all common-born, is that not true?"

I fought to return her gaze without flinching. It was hard. Baldwin at his worst had never managed to radiate this kind of cold menace.

"My lady, you're setting the wrong example by letting these bullies off without consequences," Vollkorn insisted. "The castle's rules should be enforced!"

"Enough, Brigitte," ordered Lady Margitts. "I've made my decision, and you will abide by it." Her gaze raked us with contempt. "Perhaps you should take pains to ensure that your apprentices don't come in contact with the students from here on out."

It was an impossible request, and we all knew it. The students were allowed to roam anywhere they wanted in the castle, with the exception of the wine-cellars. It was just lucky that few chose to visit the kitchens.

Chef Vollkorn's shoulders slumped in defeat. "Yes, my lady," she muttered.

I clenched my teeth in outrage. I had hoped that Lady Margitts would at least reprimand the mage students for casting unauthorized spells.

"Good," Lady Margitts said. "Now, if there's anything else…?"

It was clearly a dismissal. But I couldn't leave here without making my plea on Tama's behalf.

I took a deep breath and gathered my courage in the face of

Lady Margitts' icy indifference. "I have one more request, my lady."

Lady Margitts stared at me in astonishment. Chef Vollkorn shot me a worried sidelong glance.

"State your request, but I cannot promise to grant you any special favors." The assistant chatelaine's lip curled.

"The favor isn't for me," I clarified hastily. "I'm concerned about Lord Tama, the imperial guest who arrived here last week."

Lady Margitts' brows shot up. "The merman? What has he done now?"

"Nothing," I replied. "But I know he's being held in solitary confinement. After what happened on the ship, I understand why you're taking precautions with him, but it's not fair to keep him locked up this way. When I delivered his meal to him just now, he was clearly ailing from loneliness and lack of exercise and fresh air."

I paused, hoping for some kind of reaction.

"And?" Lady Margitts asked forbiddingly.

Not good. But I couldn't give up now. Not when Tama's welfare was on the line.

"He needs some company," I continued. "Would it be possible for him to attend classes or spend some time with the other hostages or students? Or even just leave his rooms for a while every day, to get some fresh air?"

The assistant chatelaine's expression was unreadable. Then she asked me a question that made my heart skip a beat. "Captain Bartolmi's report had some *interesting* things to say about your acquaintance with the merman."

I felt my face heat as Tama's kiss sprang vividly to mind. But all my meetings with him on board the ship had been conducted on the stern castle deck, where everyone could see us.

"We became friends on the voyage here," I said, determined not to betray myself. "He saved my life when two of the sailors attacked me."

"He's our friend, too!" Rheda piped up.

Elswyth nodded. "He was very kind to us on the ship. He gave us presents and played cards with us."

Lady Margitts' brows rose once more. "I see." Her colorless tone was impossible to decode. Then her gaze returned to me. "So, *friendship*, Apprentice? And nothing more?"

I nodded, my throat suddenly dry. I hated lying. And I knew I wasn't very good at it.

"Good. Because I don't need to remind you of the law forbidding intimate intercourse between humans and non-humans." She folded her hands primly on the desktop. "Now, is there anything *else* you want from me?"

"No, my lady," I said.

Chef Vollkorn echoed me.

"Then you may go." Lade Margitts lifted a paper from her desk and dropped her gaze to it. "Shut the door behind you when you leave."

∞∞∞

It was back to work the next morning. The sky above the castle was still dark when Malia entered the female apprentices' dormitory, pot and spoon in hand.

Yawning, I rose, quickly washed up, then dressed in my gown, with a fresh chemise, cap, and apron.

I followed the crowd of other apprentices downstairs to the kitchens. As I approached the entrance, Senior Apprentice Malia stepped out and grabbed my arm.

"Apprentice Jacinthe, you have a visitor," she hissed angrily.

Puzzled, I just stared at her. Other than Tama, I didn't really know anyone here who'd want to call on me. Then dread ambushed me. "It's—it's not Lady Cresta, is it? Or one of her friends?"

Had she returned for her promised revenge? Because I now knew that Cresta could do whatever she pleased, and Lady Margitts wouldn't lift a finger. After all, I was a mere apprentice. A *commoner*.

And even banished to Darkstone Academy in disgrace, Lady Cresta was still a member of the highest aristocracy.

To my immense relief, Malia shook her head. "No. And you need to tell him to go away. He's getting in everyone's way, especially the cooks."

He? My puzzlement deepened.

And why couldn't Malia order the unwanted visitor out of the kitchen? Or Master Chef Vollkorn? I was one of the most junior apprentices here.

Bewildered, I followed her into the main kitchen's strangely silent space. At this hour, it should have been noisy with cooks' shouted orders, the clang of pots and pans, and the sounds of knives beating out fast rhythms against chopping boards.

And stopped short, shock making my heart pound furiously as I spotted Prince Boreas on his knees inside one of the pair of cavernous fireplaces, heedless of his expensive dyed deerskin breeches.

A crowd of giggling female kitchen apprentices surrounded the giant red-headed man.

The older apprentices and the cooks were glaring at him, but apparently no one dared to order him out of the way.

As I watched, he snapped his fingers, and a burst of fire engulfed the pile of kindling stacked beneath the rotisserie spit.

"Oh, Prince Dragon, thank you!" Apprentice Jonitha exclaimed. *Was she actually fluttering her eyelashes at Boreas?* "If the hearths go out again, can we ask you for help?"

A chorus of agreement rose from her fellow apprentices.

"Yes, please, milord!"

"Milord, the flint and steel are so hard to use!"

"Pretty please, milord? We'll set aside some pastries for you!"

He sat back on his heels, smiling and clearly enjoying the attention. I snorted in disgust at the sight and wondered what in the world he wanted from me.

He's probably here to complain about the food I delivered, I thought glumly.

Then Boreas caught sight of me. "There you are, Apprentice Jacinthe," he boomed. "I've been waiting for you!"

The kitchen, already much quieter than usual, fell eerily silent as everyone—cooks and apprentices alike—looked at me.

"Why? What do you want?" I asked, puzzled. I didn't like that everyone was staring at me. Then I remembered he was royalty, and I was just a commoner. "I mean, how may I help you, Your Highness?"

A loud guffaw exploded from him. "No need for all this fucking formality. Call me Boreas. What do you say?"

I took a deep breath. "All right," I said recklessly, even though I probably shouldn't have encouraged him. "What do you want,

Boreas?"

"That's more like it! Yesterday, you told me I needed some friends," he said, cheerfully oblivious to our audience. "I slept on it and decided that I would rather have a pretty human girl than a merman as a friend. Therefore, I have chosen *you.* You shall be my friend!"

He then turned to wink at Malia. "You can be my friend, too, Senior Apprentice Malia!"

She recoiled, her face twisting in fear, but Prince Boreas didn't seem to notice.

He swept his hand in a wide, exuberant arc, taking in all the gathered female apprentices. "All you pretty human girls can be my friends!"

His gaze returned to me. He gave me a huge grin, white teeth flashing, his golden eyes alight with mischief. "But Apprentice Jacinthe shall be my *special* friend!"

I stared at him in disbelief.

Then I got mad.

How *dare* he come here and embarrass me like this, in front of everyone I lived and worked with?

Yesterday, I'd actually felt sorry for him!

But now, he seemed just like those men I'd known back in Bernswick, who saw every unmarried girl as fair game for pursuit. But it was clear that he wasn't going to leave unless I agreed to his outrageous request.

I gritted my teeth and told him what he wanted to hear.

"All right, I'll be your friend." Inspiration struck, and I added, "*If* you promise to give Lord Tama a chance to be your friend, too."

I'd always been much better at bargaining than either Mama or Baldwin, and I'd honed my skills over years of village market days and the semi-annual Herrewick Trade Fair.

Someone behind me snickered. "Ooh, look, Jacinthe's snared the Dragon *and* the fish-man! Wonder who she'll catch next? One of the Fae? Or maybe a Djinn?"

My face began burning. The rumors about me were even worse than I'd feared!

Then my temper rose. What business were my friendships to all these nasty gossips?

I whipped my head around to glare at the apprentice who'd spoken, and recognized Charmaine. She paled and shrank back.

I turned back to my uninvited, unwanted guest and put my hands on my hips.

"You need to leave now, Boreas," I snapped. "Can't you see we're busy preparing breakfast for the students and staff?"

I heard at least a dozen people suck in their breaths, either at my rudeness to a royal, or my foolhardiness in defying a Dragon. But I didn't care. I just wanted him *gone* and my morning routine to return to normal.

Boreas's eyes widened. He gazed slowly around the room. The cooks and apprentices stared back at him apprehensively.

"Very well, Friend Jacinthe," he declared. "We'll speak again shortly, when you bring my morning meal."

"One of the guards told me she spent an extra-long time alone in the fish-man's room yesterday… behind a closed door!" Norry, the sauce-cook's gangly apprentice, whispered loudly to Sauce Cook Paunto.

Paunto's eyes widened. Then he leered at me.

My eyes burned and my vision became blurry with hot tears of rage and humiliation.

"Jacinthe?" Boreas looked suddenly concerned.

"Go away. Leave me alone." Determined not to break down and weep in front of an audience, I turned and blindly walked out of the kitchen.

Once safely in the narrow alley outside, I sprinted for the shelter of the dry goods storeroom.

Slamming the door behind me, I sank to my knees, taking deep breaths as I fought to control my emotions.

Norry's words rang in my ears as my mind replayed the scene in the kitchen.

I want to go home. The thoughts I'd been suppressing over the past week welled up and overflowed, pouring down my cheeks in a flood of stinging tears.

But "home" was Mama and our comfortable routine of working together in the herb shop. And that was gone forever.

Damn Baldwin! And damn Ishkur the Storm-Bringer, who sank Mama's ship!

I wept and sobbed for a long time as months of built-up pain and grief rushed out of me.

Eventually, I heard the creak of the storeroom door opening. I scrambled to my feet, hastily wiping away the tears from my eyes and expecting to see Chef Vollkorn or Senior Apprentice Malia storming in to reprimand me for neglecting my work.

Instead, Elswyth and Rheda cautiously crept into the dim space. When they caught sight of me, both girls rushed forward to embrace me.

"Oh, Miss Jacinthe, they were so mean to you!" exclaimed Rheda, patting my back with her small, work-roughened hand.

"Are you all right?" Elswyth's blue eyes swam with concern as she looked me over. "You missed breakfast, so I brought you a cheese roll. I know you like those."

She offered me the roll, shiny with egg glaze and sprinkled with poppy seeds.

"Thank you," I said, accepting it with genuine gratitude. It was still warm.

I tucked it into my apron pocket, then blew my nose in my crumpled linen handkerchief, and used the bottom of my apron to blot my eyes and hot, puffy cheeks.

From experience, I knew my face looked blotchy and my eyes red-rimmed and bloodshot. Unlike some girls I knew, I'd never mastered the art of crying prettily. My infrequent bouts of tears were always noisy, snotty, and messy.

"Norry's always mean to me, too, when no one's looking!" Rheda declared stoutly. "You shouldn't listen to anything he says. He's a nasty, wicked boy!"

"After you left, Prince Boreas singed Norry's ears with his fire magic, and told him that if he heard Norry or anyone else saying bad things about you, he'd come back and burn off all their clothes and hair, just like he did to those mean students yesterday!" Elswyth added excitedly.

I groaned. It was Boreas's unexpected visit to the kitchens that had triggered my humiliation in front of my fellow apprentices, after all.

Absurdly, though, his unexpected support made me feel a little better. Even if he caused me yet more trouble in the long run.

That didn't mean I wasn't dreading this morning's meal delivery. Tama would notice I'd been crying, and he'd ask me questions. And possibly threaten Boreas.

The last thing I needed now was to become the excuse for a

fight between two of the imperial hostages.

The Dragon was huge in his man-shape, but I'd seen Tama fight and kill. He was fast, and his claws lethal.

"Men," I muttered under my breath. "Always making trouble."

"Why does everyone hate Lord Tama?" Rheda asked. "He was nice to us! Nicer than the sailors!"

"They don't hate him, they're scared of him," Elswyth corrected her sister before I could say anything. Then she brightened. "Oh! Miss Jacinthe! I nearly forgot. I saw Lord Tama just now while I was fetching firewood."

"He was outside the castle walls?" I asked, suddenly feeling better.

Elswyth nodded vigorously. "In the field by the barracks. Master Guisbald was giving him sword-fighting lessons."

Antoni Guisbald was the castle's master-at-arms.

Had my petition to Lady Margitts borne fruit despite her dismissive reaction to my request yesterday?

If so, it was a small repayment for the many kindnesses Tama had shown me during the voyage here.

My storm of tears had left me feeling wrung out and hollow. But this good news immediately lightened my spirits.

"I hope they let Tama—" I began.

Outside the storeroom, someone began screaming.

Shouts followed.

"There's a girl in the fountain!"

"She's dead!"

Chapter 15

Jacinthe

I rushed out of the storeroom, Elswyth and Rheda close on my heels. Ahead of us, cooks and apprentices streamed out of the kitchens. A buzz of speculation and questions echoed off the stone walls on either side of the narrow alley that led from the storerooms past the kitchens, and out to the courtyard herb-and-rose garden.

A crowd of apprentices and students had already gathered around the large fountain. I ruthlessly wielded my elbows with experience gained from years of battling the throngs at the Herrewick Trade Fairs, and worked my way to the front.

The sculpted imperial eagles perched on the branches of the tall, tree-shaped central pillar of the fountain spouted water from stone beaks. One clear, sparkling stream bounced off a figure floating face down in the center of the wide, scallop-shaped basin.

The sight of a pale, bald head and flowing dark academic robes made me stop short. A torrent of icy dread shot down my spine.

Lady Cresta! And she was indeed dead.

I caught my name a few times in the tumult of questions and comments, and felt sick to my stomach. By now, everyone in the kitchens had heard about my recent confrontation with Cresta and her two friends.

Dangerous bully or not, I knew I should feel sorry for the dead girl.

But in a tightening spiral of panic, all I could think about was: *Am I going to be blamed for this? How can I prove I had nothing to do with it?*

"All of you—back to your stations!" Chef Vollkorn bellowed from the corner of the courtyard nearest the kitchens. "And for the love of the Divine Mother, show a little respect for the dead and stop gawping at that poor woman!"

The crowd of kitchen staff fell silent. A few cooks and apprentices reluctantly began shuffling back to the kitchens, but most lingered, hoping to see what happened next.

I felt rooted to my spot in front of the fountain, too, but out of fear and worry rather than out of morbid curiosity.

A few moments later, a squad of castle guards trotted briskly into the courtyard, led by Master-at-Arms Antoni Guisbald.

They shooed us away from the scene. Reluctantly, we all returned to our various tasks.

The mood in the kitchens was livelier than I expected in the wake of a death. The cooks and other apprentices seemed almost gleeful as they speculated how Lady Cresta had died. I caught more than a few assessing looks cast in my direction, but I resolutely ignored them and continued working.

Luckily for my nerves, cleaning up from breakfast service kept me busy enough that I didn't have much time to worry about Lady Cresta. Or having to face Boreas again when I delivered his midmorning meal.

An hour later, Chef Vollkorn swept into the kitchen, where I was scrubbing yet another pot in an endless succession.

"Jacinthe, Elswyth, Rheda," she called, her voice easily cutting through the clamor. "Chatelaine Erzabetta has summoned us to the library. Come with me now."

The kitchen fell momentarily silent as everyone turned to stare at us, then a barrage of questions began to fly like a volley of arrows aimed in my direction.

"Did you really kill Lady Cresta, Jacinthe?"

"Or maybe the fish-man snuck out of his rooms and did it for ya?"

"No, the Dragon must've done it. You saw how sweet he was on her!"

"That crazy crow got what was comin' to her! She and her friends shook me down for candied almonds last month."

"Yeah, me too! She threatened to break my bones with one of her spells if I didn't do what she said!"

"Good riddance to one of those crazy crows. Only two hundred and ninety-nine left to go!"

"Is the high-and-mighty castellan finally going to move off his arse and finally punish someone around here?"

My stomach churned with renewed apprehension as Chef Vollkorn led the three of us to the castle library, located next to the Great Hall. I'd been longing to visit the library, but not like *this.* Not with a possible interrogation hanging over me.

Senior Apprentice Malia followed close on our heels like a sheepdog ready to keep us from bolting.

As we entered the library through a set of double doors, I stopped dead in my tracks, astonished at the opulence of this enormous hall in the otherwise stark castle.

The walls were lined with bookshelves stretching all the way up to the high vaulted ceiling, crammed with books and age-yellowed manuscripts. Spidery metal catwalks with narrow, spiraling wrought-iron stairs provided access to the upper shelves.

The wooden floors were polished to a gleam, and the wide aisles between the rows of bookshelves were filled with banks of study tables piled high with scrolls, quills, inkwells, and glass-and-gilt mage-light stands.

Tall arched windows set with clear glass on either end of the hall illuminated the space with a soft golden sunlight, highlighting the luxurious reading chairs upholstered in deep crimson leather.

I inhaled the fragrance of paper, ink, parchment, and scented beeswax floor polish, and fought the urge to go to the nearest bookshelf and examine the dusty volumes.

The library's walls were decorated with tapestries depicting the Siege of Lutèce and the victorious Final Battle that freed the city and ended the Great War.

"Took you long enough, Master Chef," a female voice said curtly.

I looked over to where the voice had come from. A large fireplace with a carved stone mantel stood empty and cold in the hall's far corner.

Before it, a group of richly-dressed, stern-looking castle officials sat around a study table, which had been cleared of clutter.

Chatelaine Erzabetta de Norhas sat at the head of the table. She gestured imperiously for our little group to approach.

I recognized Castellan Roderigo de Norhas sitting at Lady Erzabetta's side. His black eyes seemed to pierce right through me.

Lady Margitts was there too, her expression alive with suspicion.

I swallowed hard as I recognized Master-at-Arms Guisbald. Kitchen gossip delighted in describing how ruthlessly he punished the guards under his command. His presence only confirmed my suspicions about why we'd been summoned here.

All I could hear was the clang of certain doom: *They're going to find a way to blame me for Lady Cresta's death.*

"Lady Cresta is the daughter of the Count of Pomerado, our Imperial Treasurer," said Lady Erzabetta. "Lady Margitts informed me that Lady Cresta came to her in a sad state yesterday, complaining that three kitchen apprentices in the company of Prince Boreas waylaid her and attacked her, forcing herself to defend herself with magic. And now, she is dead, drowned under highly suspicious circumstances. Chef Vollkorn, what do you have to say about this grave matter?"

I wondered why Boreas hadn't been summoned to tell his side of the story.

Or maybe he had, just not at the same time as us. In any case, I was glad that I wouldn't be facing him here.

I waited tensely as Chef Vollkorn once again told our side of what had happened yesterday.

Lady Erzabetta pursed her lips. She wore a shimmering moonlight-colored satin gown, with her gold-and-enamel mage badge pinned to her bodice. Her glossy chestnut hair was caught in gold netting set with pearls, and more pearls the size of hazelnuts circled her long, elegant throat.

"I suppose there's only way to find out who is telling the truth." She opened a small jewelry box sitting on the table in front of her, and produced a large, colorless jewel set in a cage of gold filigree.

The gemstone glowed with the faint blue aura of an enchantment. Its many facets glittered in the light from the windows, and scattered a shower of rainbows across her pale bodice and over the polished tabletop.

"Lady Margitts reported you and your apprentices told her the same story yesterday, Master Chef. I want your apprentices to hold my Truth Jewel and swear that their version of events is what actually transpired."

I'd heard of Truth Jewels before, but I'd never actually seen one. They were extremely rare ancient artifacts. Over the centuries, countless mages had tried and failed to recreate the intricate spells used to craft the jewels.

According to legend, a Truth Jewel would ignite the hand of a liar and consume it utterly in unquenchable mage-fire.

I was the first apprentice summoned to step forward.

"Hand out, Apprentice Jacinthe, palm up," Lady Erzabetta ordered.

I knew I was innocent of harming Lady Cresta. But my throat still went dry and my heart began drumming against my ribs as the chatelaine placed the heavy gem in my cupped palm.

"Don't you dare drop it," she warned as my skin began to tingle with the same sharp sensations as when Lady Cresta had attacked me.

Beneath my skirts, the tattoo on my belly began itching furiously.

Was that a bad sign? Was the jewel going to hurt me even if I wasn't lying?

I didn't trust the chatelaine or her brother.

"Swear that you told Lady Margitts the truth regarding your encounter yesterday morning with Lady Cresta of Pomerado, Lord Bernardo of Espola, and Lady Alondra of Parrish."

"I swear by the Divine Mother that everything I told Lady Margitts yesterday was the truth," I said. "Lady Cresta and her two friends, Lord Bernardo and Lady Alondra, waylaid

Apprentice Elswyth and Apprentice Rheda and demanded that they steal pastries. When I intervened, Lord Bernardo and Lady Cresta both attacked me with spells, and only Prince Boreas' intervention saved me from serious injury."

The jewel flared briefly with a blinding flash of blue-white, then returned to its previous glassy appearance.

I flinched, but the tingling and burning both vanished.

"Passed. The wench was being truthful, after all." Was that disappointment I heard in Lady Erzabetta's voice?

I shuddered.

She took the jewel back and waved me away. "Apprentice Elswyth, come forward."

Elswyth and Rheda, though visibly nervous, also passed the test.

I had just begun to relax when Master Guisbald spoke up. "From the condition of the corpse, Lady Cresta died sometime during the night. Where were you last night, Apprentice Jacinthe?"

"Sleeping in the dormitory with all the other female apprentices," I replied, trying to hide my suddenly trembling hands beneath my apron.

"I can attest to this," said Senior Apprentice Malia, her voice strong and sure. "All of my apprentices were present at bed-check last night, and again at dawn."

"Hm." Guisbald eyed me with a skeptical expression. "Apprentice Jacinthe could have crept out and murdered Lady Cresta while everyone else in the dormitory was sleeping. I've been told the wench is sneaky."

"I'm not! And I didn't leave my bed last night!" Cold sweat dampened my chemise under my arms and down the middle of my back. "I didn't do anything to her! I haven't seen her since she attacked me."

I turned to the chatelaine. "I-I'm willing to swear to that on your Truth Jewel again, Lady Erzabetta," I offered, wishing my voice sounded confident instead of quavering.

"That won't be necessary," Lord Roderigo declared with a dismissive wave. "Antoni, the wench has already proved herself to be honest. In any case, I don't believe that she could drown someone in the middle of the courtyard without a sound or a struggle. And none of the students whose rooms overlook the scene reported hearing anything out of the ordinary."

Reprieved! I drew in a deep, shaking breath. My knees were as weak as a newborn foal, and my suddenly-aching head pounded in time with my heart.

Or was this really a reprieve? I couldn't believe the castellan was actually taking my side. It had to be a trick. Some kind of game. I braced myself for the next unpleasant development.

But Lord Roderigo merely turned to his sister. "Erzabetta, we've done our due diligence here, don't you think? Let's declare Lady Cresta's death for what it is—an unfortunate accident. I shall write an official report documenting Chief Healer Armand's complaint that Lady Cresta stole some of his medicinal mushrooms from the infirmary for recreational use. Don't you think her death could've been the result of eating too many of those mushrooms?"

"It's possible," Lady Erzabetta said grudgingly. Then she gave a loud sigh. "I suppose *I* will be the one who has to write to the Count and Countess of Pomerado about this. They will not be pleased, even if they are the ones who sent her to Darkstone Academy in an attempt to get her to mend her ways."

"I can draft the condolence letter for you," Lady Margitts said eagerly. "All you'd have to do is sign it."

"Very well. You do that, Baroness Margitts." Lady Erzabetta seemed to remember we were still there. "Chef Vollkorn, you may take your apprentices and go."

I bowed my head in respect and left the library with Elswyth and Rheda, Master Chef Vollkorn and Senior Apprentice Malia.

As we walked back to the kitchens, I couldn't help remembering what had happened to the sailors who'd attacked me.

Did Tama escape from his rooms and kill Lady Cresta?

I couldn't deny that I felt deeply relieved she was gone. Her threats had been hanging over me since yesterday.

But what has my life become, that I'm grateful to have befriended a cold-blooded killer?

It was food for thought. I'd been here for little more than a week, and Darkstone Academy was already changing me in uncomfortable ways.

Chapter 16

Jacinthe

An hour later, I was inside the castle's gatehouse once more, balancing a heavy wicker basket filled with packets of raw meat and seafood on my hip.

Guard Machry stopped in front of Prince Boreas' rooms, and unlocked the wooden door. "Here you go, Apprentice," he said, grinning broadly as he stepped aside. "Just knock when you're finished in there and ready to go."

I cast him a sour glance. "I won't be staying long."

I didn't want to be here at all. I'd been dreading my morning meal delivery since that mortifying dawn incident in the kitchens. I felt wrung out from my bout of weeping, followed by the nerve-wracking interview with the castellan and chatelaine. My plan was to drop off the packages of raw meat and immediately depart.

Boreas had embarrassed me and made my situation, already precarious because of my friendship with Tama, even worse.

And I still wasn't sure if it had been accidental or intentional on his part.

After more than six months of living in the castle, was the dragon really still as naive about human interactions as he appeared to be?

Or was he mocking me and playing some kind of twisted game to exercise his power over an indentured servant?

He certainly seemed to enjoy the attention from the other apprentices.

I told myself that I didn't know and didn't care about his motivations. It didn't matter what he intended. He'd humiliated me in front of everyone I worked with and lived with, and made me the object of crude gossip and speculation.

I squared my shoulders, shifted the basket to rest more comfortably, and stepped through the doorway.

And jumped in surprise as Boreas loomed over me.

"Ah, Friend Jacinthe," he boomed. "You came, after all! I was afraid I'd frightened you away for good."

He grinned at me, his golden eyes alight with good humor.

I scowled back at him. Someone so obnoxious shouldn't be so attractive!

I set the basket of food down on the table with a thump and glared at him. "I'm not scared of you. I'm *angry*."

"Ah, yes, you have a Dragon's courage." His grin didn't fade.

I bristled at his condescension. The anger I'd been suppressing for hours rose like a tide of hot lava inside me. I clamped my teeth together to prevent any further cutting remarks.

"But what did I do to anger you, Friend Jacinthe?" he continued.

"First of all, I am *not* your friend, Boreas." My simmering rage finally boiled over.

I would have never dared speak like that to Baldwin, Chatelaine Erzabetta or even Chef Vollkorn. But I wasn't afraid of Boreas, though I knew I should be. Despite being forced into human shape, he was still a fearsome predator, one of humankind's most dreaded enemies.

He flinched slightly at my bald statement, his golden eyes widening. "You *lied* to me?"

He sounded hurt.

Divine Mother preserve me. Did I actually feel a tiny bit sorry for him?

"You left me no choice this morning. You were making trouble, and I would've said anything to get you to leave," I snarled.

"So, how can I win you as my friend?" The Dragon was certainly persistent. "I didn't mean to make trouble this morning. Among my people, requesting one's friendship in front of their entire aerie is an honor."

What? It seemed ludicrous that he'd actually meant to honor me rather than embarrass me with his visit to the kitchens. I decided he was mocking me. And I wasn't having it.

"If you really want to be my friend, prove you're trustworthy." The words poured out of me like a torrent of bitter water. "So far, you've made me feel like I'm just an amusement to you. I'm sorry you are a prisoner here and that you're bored, but I am *not* a toy. Maybe you're telling the truth about wanting to honor me, but today, you made me the object of ridicule in front of my superiors and my fellow apprentices. That's *not* how friends treat friends."

I finished my speech, then swallowed hard as I realized what I'd just said. Never in my wildest dreams did I think I'd be chastising an actual *Dragon!*

To my surprise, Boreas dropped to one knee, took my hand and kissed my work-roughened knuckles with the aplomb of an imperial courtier.

His fingers were hot and his lips burned against my skin, sending a jolt of lightning racing up my arm and through my chest.

"Jacinthe, I truly didn't mean to insult you. And I am deeply sorry for causing trouble in your aerie. How can I make amends? I'll do anything you ask of me," he declared.

Was he mocking me?

But no. His golden eyes were filled with sincerity as he stared up at me.

I didn't know what to say.

He wasn't angry at my insolence. And he wasn't trying to brush aside the trouble he'd caused a humble kitchen apprentice. Instead, his apology and contrite offer seemed genuine.

What could Boreas possibly do to make it up to me? And did I even want him to? After a few moments of thought, I realized what I wanted.

"Actually, I have one thing I want you to do."

Boreas' expression lightened. "And then you'll be my friend, yes?"

"Maybe. I'll consider it," I said. "Remember what I asked you in the kitchens this morning?"

He nodded.

"I still I want you to meet my friend Lord Tama and give him a genuine chance to become your friend."

"Of course!" Boreas said without hesitation. "I asked the guards about him. This Tama's fearsome and bloodthirsty reputation more than qualifies him as a fitting companion to a Dragon like me!"

"I'm glad to hear it," I said dryly.

If Boreas wanted a friend with a 'fearsome and bloodthirsty' reputation, then what in the world did he see in *me*?

"When should I meet with Tama?" he inquired. "And are you going to be there also?"

"My work duties for this week include harvesting some herbs from the apothecary gardens outside the walls," I said. "Perhaps we can meet there tomorrow morning after breakfast."

Chef Vollkorn had excused me from afternoon pots-and-pans duty because of my herbal knowledge.

According to her, most of the apprentices couldn't distinguish basil from mint or dill from fennel. This was a problem because the upcoming Victory Day banquet required seasonings not normally used in the kitchen's everyday fare.

I was looking forward to spending a couple of hours outside the castle walls, surrounded by plants and fresh air.

"I'll be there," Boreas declared. "And I'll ask the guards to permit Lord Tama to accompany me."

"Thank you. And now I must go attend the rest of my duties," I said firmly as I picked up the half-empty and much lighter basket.

As Guard Machry opened the door for me, I wondered if I was doing the right thing by introducing Boreas and Tama. What if I was creating another disaster for myself?

Too late now, I thought.

And braced myself for my next task: delivering Tama's meal to him and finding out whether he'd killed Lady Cresta.

Mother of All, let it not be him!

∞∞∞

"You have been weeping, Jacinthe. Why?"

I stared at Tama like a startled deer. All the elaborate excuses I'd concocted over the past two hours fled from my mind as I met his concerned gaze.

As he approached me, I noticed he was limping. *He's injured!*

Had Castellan de Norhas already questioned him about the murder? Had the guards hurt my friend during the interrogation?

"Jacinthe, I displeased you." Tama stepped closer, his expression softening fractionally. "Believe me, that was not my intent."

I blinked at him. I had no idea what he was talking about. "What do you mean? You haven't done anything!"

And there was absolutely no chance I'd finger Boreas as the culprit. I knew Tama pretty well by now, and I didn't want to destroy any hope that the two prisoners might become friends.

Tama stopped in his tracks. "When I kissed you, I thought you enjoyed it. But then you pushed me away. And departed in great haste. I saw you were upset. And you are upset now." He bowed his head. His long silver hair flowed over his shoulders and formed a curtain around his face, veiling his expression. "I apologize for offending you."

"No! You didn't offend me at all. And I liked the kiss. A *lot*." I'd been so worried about getting caught, I hadn't stopped to think about how Tama might interpret my reactions. "When Guard Machry interrupted us, I didn't want to get in trouble."

"What sort of trouble?" Tama seemed genuinely curious. "It was none of his concern."

Doesn't Tama know about the law? I sighed. "Tama, what we did… isn't allowed. The authorities could flog me for breaking the law against relations with non-humans."

He shook his head. "I do not understand all these laws. But I will kill anyone who tries to hurt you, Jacinthe. And I am glad that my kiss pleased you."

His declaration sent mingled warmth and dread through me. I hoped with all my might that Tama would never hear about Boreas' disastrous visit to the kitchens.

I cleared my throat. "Speaking of killing… Lady Cresta of Pomerado is dead. Someone drowned her in the fountain last night."

Tensing, I waited for his reaction.

But Tama only stared at me blankly. "I do not know this person. Was she a friend of yours?"

I shook my head. "No. Remember those students who ganged up on Elswyth and Rheda a few days ago?"

"Ah. So, Lady Cresta was the one who attacked you? Well, no great loss," Tama said coldly.

I took a deep breath. "Everyone thinks you had something to do with it."

He stared down at me for a long moment. "And you think this as well." It wasn't a question.

"Did you?" I spread my hands. "I don't really believe you killed her, if only because you're locked up in here most of the time. And when they let you out for exercise and fresh air, I wager they watch you like hawks."

"Indeed," Tama said dryly. "No, I did not kill Lady Cresta. I have killed no one since arriving in this place. No matter how much they deserve it," he added savagely.

I believed him. Tama never lied. It wasn't in his nature.

"Good," I said, and felt relief coursing through my body.

He stepped close and took my face between his cool hands.

"You are under my protection, Jacinthe," he said, stroking my still-blotchy cheeks with his thumbs. "If anyone attacks you or makes life unpleasant for you, you will tell me. Immediately."

I looked up at him and nodded, unable to speak.

I didn't want him to hurt anyone on my behalf. But I'd been on my own for most of a year, facing daily hardships with no support or protection. It was comforting to know that *someone* was looking out for me, even a cold-blooded killer like Tama.

His eyes never leaving mine, Tama lowered his face until his cool lips met mine.

His kiss was gentle and firm. As before, it sent intoxicating warmth coursing through my veins, filling me with a hot longing I'd never experienced with anyone else. His arms came around me, and I melted against the hard strength of his body.

The kiss deepened as my lips parted beneath his. His mouth skillfully caressed and explored mine in a way that was simultaneously tender and demanding. His clawed hands roamed possessively over my back, my waist, and my hips.

His mouth moved to my neck as he bent me backwards in his muscular arms. He growled, and the sound thrilled though me. I felt the scrape of his sharp teeth as he nipped at the tender skin, leaving a burning trail of sharp caresses as his lips traveled down to my collarbones and the silver circlet resting there.

In response, heat blossomed in the pit of my belly and blossomed in a throbbing ache between my thighs. The tips of my breasts stiffened against the confines of my bodice as his breath teased the neckline of my gown. My heart pounded wildly, and I desperately craved more of his touch.

But then he staggered, his entire body tensing in pain. He released me and groaned as he clutched the edge of the table, holding himself upright.

I grabbed his arm to steady him, concerned that his face had gone gray beneath his pearly skin.

"What's wrong?" I demanded, pulling out a chair for him. "Did the guards hurt you?"

He shook his head. "They would not dare touch me."

"Then why were you limping? And what happened just now?"

"Nothing. It is nothing." Tama's expression reverted to his usual impassiveness. He ignored the chair and remained on his feet.

"By the Divine Mother, Tama, don't be a stubborn fool!" I raised my voice in frustration. Something was clearly very wrong, but I couldn't help him if he wouldn't tell me what was happening. "I'm a trained healer. Please let me help you."

He blew out a gusty breath. "Ever since that mage in Herrewick turned my tail into these legs, they have troubled me. On the ship, the pain was bearable. But coming here, with the stairs and now, the practicing with human weapons…" He trailed off, looking away in shame. "My legs are failing me. And without them, I cannot protect you as I have sworn to do."

I stared at him, my heart aching. If he was admitting to pain, then he must be in absolute agony. He was strong and proud, but even he had his limits.

"Why don't you visit the castle infirmary?" I suggested. "I'm sure they'll prescribe something to ease your discomfort."

He shook his head. "No. It is not the warrior way to show weakness to our enemies. I won't disgrace my clan."

I put my hand on his shoulder. "Then let *me* help you. My mother was a famous healer-mage, and she taught me how to find the cause of pain and how to relieve it."

When he didn't reply, I said with all the persuasiveness I could muster, "There's no disgrace in letting a friend aid you, Tama. That's what friends are for."

"Very well," he conceded, and finally sat in the chair. That alone told me how much he hurt.

I kneeled before him, and gently palpated each of his legs from his thighs to his ankles. His knees felt warm and puffy. He winced as I gently probed the joint. I removed his boots and saw that Tama's long, elegant feet were also swollen and tender.

"All right," I said when I finished my quick examination. "Here's what I think: your feet and legs aren't accustomed to bearing your weight on land. I think you've strained them badly with all the exercise you've been doing. Since you don't want to visit the infirmary, will you accept a potion from me?"

He hesitated before finally nodding. "Very well."

"Good," I said. My heart swelled with emotion. He trusted me to help him, even though it cost him his pride. "I'll be working in the apothecary garden tomorrow. I'll gather the ingredients and brew a potion to ease your pain and inflamed joints. Ask the guards if you can soak your legs and feet in a cold bath several times a day. Once the swelling eases, I will prescribe you gentle strengthening exercises. My mother found they helped patients recovering from broken legs, and I think it will help you, too."

I explained how do the exercises, but he stopped me.

"You will assist me with these exercises. I find your touch quite soothing."

My cheeks grew hot. Was that a twinkle in his huge, dark eyes? No, that would mean Tama was teasing me. And my serious merman friend was not the type to tease.

"I'll help you each time I deliver your meals," I promised.

"I will gladly accept any help you give me," he said solemnly. Then his expression hardened. "Now that the troublemaker is dead, you will tell me if anyone else in this place makes trouble for you again. No need to trouble the Wind-Walker."

Oh, so Tama was jealous of Boreas? That didn't bode well for their meeting tomorrow.

I forced myself to smile. "I promise. Oh, and speaking of Boreas, I almost forgot to ask you if you wanted to meet him. If you're not in too much pain, will you walk with us in the gardens?"

Tama scowled. "I will never be in too much pain to leave you alone with a Wind-Walker."

He pulled me down into his lap and his lips devoured mine in a hard, demanding kiss.

I closed my eyes and returned his kiss with enthusiasm.

"Apprentice, you done in there?" Without waiting for my reply, Guard Machry began unlocking the door.

I sprang out of Tama's lap like it was scalding hot. I grabbed for the wicker food basket and frantically scooped out the packages of fish, clams, and fresh shrimp.

I finished just as Machry pulled open the door with a squeal of badly oiled hinges.

"I'll see you tomorrow," I promised.

Tama rose from his chair with visible effort. "Until tomorrow, Jacinthe."

As I followed the guard out, I mulled over which of Mama's recipes for inflamed joints might work on a merman.

Chapter 17

Jacinthe

The next morning dawned clear and cloudless. After breakfast, I set out, armed with a long list of herbs and spices that included cardamom pods, sesame seeds, fennel, and fenugreek; a straw hat; a large but shallow trug basket; a pile of small cloth spice bags; and a pair of gardening shears.

As I passed under the gatehouse and emerged from the castle walls, I realized how much I'd missed being outside. For a moment, I felt oddly exposed, with no black stone walls rising around me to cage the endless expanse of sky.

Before Mama's departure, I'd spent most of each day outside during spring, summer, and fall. We had a large vegetable and herb garden in back of our shop, plus chickens, a pig, and a cow to tend to.

The voyage to the island had also offered me a bounty of fresh air and sun.

But since arriving at Darkstone Castle, I'd been locked in the kitchens from dawn to dusk. The only time I'd left the grim fortress was during hurried trips out the postern gate in the predawn darkness. Then, I was too busy fetching firewood or collecting eggs from the chicken coops to have any time to appreciate my momentary freedom.

I stopped a few steps beyond the castle's gates, closed my eyes, and drew in a deep breath. The salt air carried the scents of drying seaweed and fresh flowers, underlaid with the faint, familiar whiff of cattle and pig manure.

I opened my eyes, already feeling lighter and happier, and began walking. With luck, I'd finish gathering everything on my list with time left over to meet with Tama and Boreas in the privacy of the garden.

This morning had begun with a great deal of excitement, sparked by a grease-fire in a frying pan. It was a common occurrence, except this time, Charmaine had panicked and thrown water on the pan instead of salt. The wooden shelves above the stove then caught fire as well, and chaos reigned in the kitchen until the cooks brought the flames under control.

In the aftermath, everyone was busy assessing the damage and reprimanding Charmaine. When I asked the cooks for the apothecary garden's location, they told me to walk past the duck ponds and look for a walled garden at the very edge of the forest.

Ahead of me stretched the dusty road leading down to the docks. To my right, a large swathe of wheat and barley fields stretched towards a distant wall of living green. No sign of any ponds there.

To my left were wide pastures dotted with grazing cattle, sheep, and goats, as well as the castle's stables, guard barracks, and other outbuildings. A thick column of smoke fanned by the ever-present sea breeze marked the location of the metalsmith's forge.

I couldn't see anything resembling a walled garden over here, either, but I guessed I might find it hidden behind one of the other buildings on this side of the castle.

I wondered how Kenric was faring in his apprenticeship.

Sure enough, I spotted him a few minutes later. He stood at the entrance to a large shed just outside the forge, industriously shoveling charcoal into a wide-mouthed bucket.

"Kenric!" I called.

He turned and waved, grinning widely. "Miss Jacinthe!"

As I approached him, he put down his shovel and wiped his glistening face with a grimy bandanna, leaving behind broad black streaks.

"How've you been?" he called in Abbonethy. "And how's Lord Tama?"

After nearly two weeks of speaking nothing but Capitolan, the sound of my native language raised a pang of homesickness. Elswyth and Rheda had stopped speaking Abbonethy, even during our bedtime conversations.

"Well enough. I see Tama every day now," I replied. "How about you? Are your master and fellow apprentices treating you well?"

He shrugged. "I'm the junior apprentice, so I get all the shit jobs. But the food's good and no one beats me, so it could be worse. You?"

"About the same," I replied. "I've never scrubbed so many pots and pans in my life. I can't wait for the next batch of apprentices to arrive, so that I can move up to chopping vegetables and kneading dough."

He laughed. "You out here on your day off?"

I lifted my basket. "No, I'm actually working. We're in the middle of preparing for the big Victory Day banquet, and Chef sent me over to the apothecary garden to get a few things. You wouldn't happen to know where it's located?" I asked hopefully.

Kenric shook his head. "Sorry. I haven't had the chance to really explore this place yet. Toland and the other farm apprentices wanted to go swimming on our day off, so we all went down to the cove." He grinned. "It was fun! The water's much warmer here than back at home, and it's weird to see blue and purple fish." He heaved a sigh. "Well, I'd better get back to it. Smith's gonna yell at me if I take too long."

"See you at the banquet," I said, and turned to go. It pleased me to see him looking tanned and healthy beneath his layer of work grime, and I was glad that Toland also seemed to be doing well.

I walked further, past the guard's barracks and exercise grounds, and the squat stone milking shed and dairy. Ahead of me, the sparkle of sun on water alerted me to the location of the castle's duck pond.

As I approached the pond, I noticed a cluster of people on the bank. They were using big wooden paddles to beat water-retted flax stalks. It separated the fibers so that they could be combed and spun into linen thread.

Among them, I saw my young friends Winifred and Sunniva, who'd been apprenticed to the castle tailor.

They raced over to greet me. We regularly saw each other in the servants' hall at mealtimes, but they were still excited to see me.

Winifred held up a bundle of freshly separated flax fibers for me to admire. "Look at these! Once we spin it, it'll be perfect for embroidery work or a lady's dress."

I stroked the soft fibers, then asked, "Do either of you know where the apothecary garden is located?"

Both of them nodded. "It's right over there, by the drying shed." Winifred pointed to a distant outbuilding, right on the edge of the forest. Next to the drying shed, I saw a large open rectangle framed by half-height walls made from the same black volcanic stone as the castle.

My heart sank. I'd asked Boreas and Tama to meet me there,

but hadn't realized it was located so far from the castle. I knew Tama would insist on walking all the way out there despite his painful feet and legs.

But it was too late to turn back now, not if I wanted to complete my assigned errands and find the ingredients for the anti-inflammatory potion.

Then one of the other apprentices shouted, "More work, less gab, you two!"

Not wanting to get Winifred and Sunniva in trouble, I hastily took my leave.

I walked across a lush pasture towards the garden. The grass was dotted with a profusion of white, yellow, and purple wildflowers I couldn't identify. Ahead of me, a line of dense vegetation marked the boundary between the castle's cultivated acreage and the primeval forest.

As I walked, I marveled at how much life seemed to thrive on this isolated speck of land in the middle of the ocean. Birdsong filled the air. Now and then I would glimpse some small creature scurrying away from me through the grass and flowers.

When I reached the half-height stone walls marking the borders of the apothecary garden, I found a brightly painted wood gate.

I paused to admire it. Its wood panels were carved with intricate, lifelike scenes from nature–trees, flying birds, and flowers of all kinds. This level of artistry seemed out of place here on the fringes of the castle's estate.

I opened the gate and stepped into the garden with a sense of awe. Everywhere I looked, unfamiliar herbs, flowers, and shrubs beckoned, their sweet smells filling the air.

I inhaled deeply of the mingled perfumes, consulted my list, then began striding up and down the neat rows of plants in search of what I needed.

Tall white breadseed poppies crowded one flowerbed. I paused to admire them. I remembered seeing vast poppy fields on my outings to the island of Imber, when Mama and I had gone there to purchase poppy seeds for pastries and sticky medicinal cakes of dried poppy sap for use in painkilling potions.

Fruits and vegetables I'd never seen before grew in other beds. I tried to guess whether they were delicacies for eating or useful in compounding medicines. *Maybe both.*

When I reached the herb beds, I found them labeled with unfamiliar names. I only recognized a few of them from my books, and none of them matched the items on my lists.

Now I worried I wouldn't find what I needed to help Tama or fulfill Chef's request. I'd confidently told Chef Vollkorn that I knew a lot about herbs. But I hadn't stopped to consider that a much different assortment of plants grew this far south of my cold, wet northern home of Abbonay.

Just as I was about to give up and accept my failure, a movement out of the corner of my eye caught my attention. I turned my head just in time to see a figure come through the carved gate.

It was a Fae man, tall and beautiful, with silver eyes. Delicately pointed ears peeked out from his short, glossy, pale green hair. An enameled silver earring in the shape of a leaf pierced his right ear, identifying him as an imperial hostage.

To my surprise, instead of the expensive finery I was used to seeing on imperial hostages, he wore the plain, dark blue livery of the castle staff, like me.

"I thought I heard someone enter my garden." He smiled at me and bowed low with an elegant flourish. "I am Gwydion ap Pwyll, Senior Apprentice to Healer-Mage Armand. What brings you here to my garden?" he asked me, his Capitolan flavored with the lilting accents of the far northern Fae Federation.

"I'm Jacinthe of Bernswick, one of the kitchen apprentices," I introduced myself in return.

I'd seen Fae traders at the semi-annual Herrewick Trade Fair, but Gwydion was the first Fae I'd ever actually spoken with.

Faced with his effortless elegance, I suddenly became acutely aware of my sweaty, heat-flushed face and my red, chapped hands.

"Chef Vollkorn sent me to collect a variety of herbs and spices for the upcoming banquet." I pulled the list from my basket to show him. "I know all the herbs and plants back home, but I don't recognize any of the plants here."

"Ah, you look like a Djinn maiden, but is that the Western Isles I hear in your voice, Apprentice Jacinthe?" he asked with a flirtatious wink.

"Yes. I arrived from Abbonay just last week." My brown skin and flame-colored hair had garnered stares and comments from the fair-haired, pale-skinned islanders all my life. But no one had ever compared me to a Djinn before.

Did my father come from the deserts and sun-burned mountains of the Southern Continent? With Mama dead and gone, I'd probably never know the answer.

Gwydion chuckled and waved at all the unfamiliar foliage with an elegant, long-fingered hand. "Ah yes, many of these lovely plants are strangers to our northern climes. I'm from Dinas y Coed myself."

Dinas y Coed, the City of Trees on the east coast of the Fae Federation, was famed for its Forest Fae woodworkers. Now

I was sure Gwydion or one of the other Forest Fae imperial hostages had created that striking garden gate.

He stepped closer and plucked the list from my fingers. He smelled of sun-warmed honeysuckle and freshly cut grass. His silvery, enviably long lashes swept his smooth cheek as he bent his head to scan the paper.

"I can show you where to find everything on your list, if you'd like. In return, I ask only for a kiss."

My heart thudded in my chest at his unexpected offer. I'd gone for nearly eighteen years without being kissed, and now a second man within a week wanted to kiss me.

Maybe there's something about the island's air, I thought.

Gwydion winked and added, "After all, as one of the Fae, I need balance in every transaction."

I hesitated, caught between Dragon-fire and Fae poison... perhaps literally this time. Should I accept his help?

I'd always been told it was dangerous to owe a Fae a favor. And consorting with the Fae was also forbidden by law.

Besides, what about Tama? Did our forbidden kisses mean we were more than simply friends now?

But kissing Gwydion is such a small price to pay to get the ingredients for Tama's potion, I thought. *The kiss wouldn't mean anything except payment for a debt owed.*

And we were far enough from the castle that no one would see us within the garden's enclosing walls.

"Very well," I said, my heart beating even faster. "It's a deal. If you help me find all the items on my list, I'll kiss you."

"Deal." He smiled at me, his silvery eyes dancing in delight. I caught my breath at his sheer beauty.

He extended his hand. I took it without hesitation, then had to suppress a gasp as hard, icy fingers closed around my hand. Despite the heat of the day, his touch was so cold it instantly numbed my skin.

I'd never heard of the Forest Fae having that effect on humans. But with his pale green hair and his love of plants, what else could Gwydion be? The Forest Fae were renowned for their wielding of Wood Magic, power drawn from the earth and all living things.

Gwydion's earring marked him as one of the Fae nobles exiled here as an imperial hostage. If so, why would he want to serve as an apprentice like a human commoner?

He led me around the garden, pointing out each of the plants on my list. As we walked, we talked about how the plants on this island differed from the ones we both knew from our northern homes.

Within minutes, I felt like I'd known Gwydion for years. He was a kindred spirit, a healer and lover of plants, and easy to talk to. For the first time in weeks, I felt like my old self.

All the while, he continued to hold my hand in his steely grasp. He released me at intervals so that I could harvest leaves, blossoms, or seedpods, then immediately reached for my hand again as soon as I rose.

But I didn't mind. I liked him. And the sensation of burning cold gradually faded as we walked together from one section of the enormous garden to the other.

My basket quickly filled with fragrant greenery and flowers. By the time we reached the final few items, his skin had warmed against mine and felt completely normal.

Then Gwydion frowned down at the scrap of paper. "We don't have any meadowsweet right now. Someone left the garden gate open a few days ago, and those damned goats got in." He grimaced. "I stopped them before they did too much damage to the rest of my garden, but they ravaged the meadowsweet beds. I've reseeded them, but it will take a few weeks until we can harvest."

My heart sank. Meadowsweet, with its painkilling properties, was the key ingredient in the potion I'd promised Tama.

"Why do you need it?" asked Gwydion. "If it's for your menstrual cramps, there are several other herbs that work better."

"It's not for me," I said. "It's for an anti-inflammatory potion for one of the imperial hostages. He's a merman in severe pain from swollen joints and strained muscles."

"Ah, then I recommend you make a tisane with crushed fennel seeds and dried peony root to ease his discomfort," Gwydion said. "Those ingredients work better on the Fae and our cousins, the Sea People, than either meadowsweet or willow bark."

"Thank you," I said with genuine gratitude.

I waited as he went to the drying shed for the dried peony root. I already had a large quantity of fennel seed in my basket, because Chef Vollkorn needed it for her special onion and cheese tarts.

Our last stop was a cluster of long-leafed cardamom plants. I gathered a double-handful of tiny, intensely fragrant green spice pods and poured them into a small cloth spice bag.

Gwydion tugged gently on my hand, turning me to face him, then took the now-heavy basket from my arm and put it on the ground.

"There. All done," he said in his soft, musical voice. "You have everything on your list, and more. I'll take my payment now."

Feeling suddenly shy and gawky next to his elegant, flawless beauty, I took a nervous breath.

"Thank you again," I said, then leaned forward and gave him a quick, awkward peck on his lips.

Like his fingers, his mouth was cold and hard as winter frost.

When I stepped backwards, his hands darted out and caught my shoulders in a bruising grip.

Gwydion didn't frown or scowl, but suddenly, he looked terrifying.

"That's not a *proper* kiss," he chided me in the same soft voice he'd been using all along. But a vein of frost and darkness ran beneath it now, and his curiously light eyes burned into mine. "You're not trying to shortchange our bargain, are you?"

"No, of course not!" I protested. "I'm sorry. I didn't mean to do it wrong. I just haven't kissed many, ah, men." My face, already warm from the sun, felt even hotter as I stumbled through my confession.

His expression softened. Suddenly, he wasn't scary anymore. "Ah, so you're a virgin?"

His bald question shocked me. I just stared at him, my face burning like Dragon-fire now.

Gwydion's smile was sweet as honey. His silver eyes shone like moonlight. "Let me show you how to kiss properly, Jacinthe."

He drew me close and captured my lips with his.

A violent shock ran through me at his kiss, and I gasped against his mouth. I'd never felt anything like this before, not even when Tama had kissed me.

His arms tightened around me as he deepened the kiss. I lost track of time as his hands roamed my body, and bolts of sheer pleasure shot through me.

When he finally pulled back, I was panting. My knees were weak and my whole body trembled as fire and ice battled for dominance in the pit of my belly.

"That was *much* better, don't you think?" A satisfied smile played around Gwydion's flawless lips.

I nodded, then swayed dizzily. My heart was pounding, and I felt like I couldn't catch my breath.

"Now you've been kissed properly," he announced smugly. "Did you enjoy that?"

I couldn't speak; I just nodded dumbly in agreement.

Tama's kisses had been raw hunger and need, born of trust and friendship and loneliness. But Gwydion's kisses—they were *art* of the most beautiful and sensual caliber.

"I did, too. You taste every bit as delicious as I thought you would." His voice was deeper now, almost a purr. And his pale cheeks bore a faint flush. "Sweet as a ripe, sun-warmed peach, with velvety skin and bursting with sweet juice."

He drew a warm fingertip down my cheek, then traced the outline of my lips. I stood spellbound beneath his light, teasing caress. He smiled fondly down at me.

What it would be like to have him as a lover? I wondered.

"Thank you for brightening my day." He smiled wider and brushed my cheek again. Then he picked up the basket full of herbs and handed it to me. "Well then, Jacinthe, that concludes our business for now. I look forward to your next visit."

Reality returned with a rush as he took my arm and led me out of the garden.

I was just a penniless commoner, and he was most likely a Fae prince. No matter how much we had each enjoyed that kiss, the Fae had a reputation for being haughty and obsessed with status.

He'd had his fun, and I had everything I'd come for. And now it was time for me to return to the kitchens and my life as an indentured servant inside the black castle looming in the distance.

"I look forward to it." I was proud of how calm I sounded. I turned to go back the way I'd come.

Suddenly, a loud screeching noise filled the air, like a thousand nails scratching on chalkboards.

Gwydion and I both whirled towards the source of the horrible noise.

The wall of trees, bushes, and vines along the forest fringe a few dozen yards away shook violently. As we watched, a swarm of monkey-demons broke free of the dense vegetation.

I gaped at them, momentarily frozen in disbelief. Everyone at the castle had assured me that only birds and lizards lived in the island's forests.

And these most definitely *weren't* birds. They didn't look like anything I'd ever heard or read about. Their eyes glowed with black fire, and they shrieked like a thousand dying souls as they raced towards us in a blur of gaping fanged mouths.

Chapter 18

Jacinthe

As the creatures neared us, I saw that these could not possibly be natural creatures. No animal created by the Mother of All had green skin, purple fur, and scimitar-clawed feet and hands.

Each one was the size of a large dog, with a long, prehensile tail. Dozens of them swung out of the trees and swarmed toward us at terrifying speed. I recoiled in horror as their faces contorted in expressions of unadulterated rage and hate, revealing rows of long, jagged fangs.

They'd tear Gwydion and me to pieces within seconds.

At my side, the Fae man cursed under his breath in his native tongue before spinning to face me.

"Jacinthe," he said urgently, "I need your help. Loan me your power so that we can defeat these creatures!"

"But I don't have any powers," I protested.

"Who told you that?" He reached out imperiously with his left hand. "Jacinthe, your hand. *Now!*"

His tone and my terror both compelled me to obey. I grabbed his outstretched hand.

Instantly, a current of fiery energy surged through me. It felt like lightning racing through my veins. My indenture collar vibrated with a high, piercing note as Gwydion's voice rose above the din.

I couldn't understand what he was saying, but the cadence of his words sounded like a spell.

I gasped in surprise and pain as familiar and intensely painful needles pierced every inch of my skin, and my tattoo flared to agonizing life. I'd experienced the same sharp pain when Cresta and Bernardo attacked me a few days ago.

Without releasing me, Gwydion flung out his right hand. As his leaf-shaped earring flared with white-hot light, a scythe made from green mage-fire swept out in a wide arc.

It cut through the monkey-demon swarm in an instant, leaving a swathe of dead and dying creatures. He swung the blazing blade again and again, until only piles of dismembered corpses remained.

But instead of the blood I expected to see, a shimmering, translucent slime coated the grass. Then the dead creatures themselves faded into scattered piles of dark purple, wetly gleaming jelly.

The sudden violence, the onslaught of strange creatures, and the intense power of Gwydion's spell proved too much for me. As the mage-fire scythe winked out, I swayed on my feet as my heart raced and my legs shook. My ears rang and a flurry of black snowflakes obscured my vision.

Moving with lightning speed, Gwydion released my hand and looped his arm around my waist.

"Here, sit," he murmured, lowering me to the grass. "I apologize for drawing on your power like that, but I had no choice." He gave me a wry smile. "Better drained than dead, eh?"

I drew my knees up to my chest and wrapped my arms around them. My teeth chattered, and I felt frozen to the core, as if I stood in the middle of a blizzard rather than under the hot southern sun.

I had no idea why he kept talking about my power. Magecraft Aptitude Examiner Adalburga had assured me I had none. And Mama had agreed with Lady Adalburga's assessment.

They were both mages, so they would know, wouldn't they?

But whatever Gwydion had just done, it left me feeling like I'd just contracted a violent case of influenza.

"W-what happened?" I managed through my chattering teeth.

Before he could answer, I heard a familiar voice roar angrily, "What the fuck is going on here?"

I looked to see Boreas and Tama both sprinting towards us, their legs flashing with preternaturally fast movements.

I winced at the thought of Tama coming all this way with his painful, strained muscles. But he appeared to have no difficulty keeping up with the Dragon.

As soon as they reached me, Tama immediately fell to his knees in the grass. He wrapped me in a fierce, protective embrace. "You look ill. Are you injured?"

"I'm fine," I assured him. "Just shaken."

I saw he didn't believe me, and I didn't blame him. I didn't know what I looked like, but I was still shivering and too weak to get to my feet.

Boreas stepped between us and Gwydion, his golden eyes blazing with rage.

"Who the fuck is this pretty boy and what the fuck are those?" He pointed at the heaps of glistening jelly, now quickly evaporating under the tropical sun.

Every trace of the laughing, exasperating man was gone. In its place, I glimpsed the terrifying predator inside his human shell.

"What were those creatures charging out of the forest just now?" Tama added. He glared balefully at the slender Fae man. "And how did you destroy them?"

"Sea-brother, those were magical constructs," Gwydion said. "I borrowed some of Jacinthe's power and slew them with mage-fire."

"But I don't have any powers," I said once more. "A Magecraft Aptitude Examiner tested me last year."

"Is that so?" Gwydion asked. He tilted his head and studied me. "Interesting."

"What do you mean 'magical constructs'?" Boreas interrupted. "Are you telling us that those little black-robed earthworms tried attacking Jacinthe *again?*"

Gwydion looked surprised. "You've been suffering from mage assaults, as well?" he asked me.

"Just one, three days ago," I replied. "But the student who attacked me is dead now."

"Lady Cresta?" The Fae man looked at Boreas, then Tama, as if wondering which one of them had killed her. "Well, this isn't the first time someone's thrown a malicious spell my way. This has been going since I arrived here last summer, and I'm not the only one who's been attacked."

Boreas, Tama, and I exchanged dismayed looks.

"I haven't heard anything about these attacks," Boreas said. "And no one's attacked *me.*"

"Except for the mage who clipped your wings and swapped my sea-brother's fins for legs?" Gwydion asked snidely.

"Fuck you," snarled Boreas.

Gwydion appeared completely unfazed by the Dragon's anger. In fact, his lips curved in a small, delighted smile as he gazed at the giant towering over him.

Was the Fae deliberately provoking the Dragon out of some twisted sense of amusement?

"I am not your brother, Drylander," Tama said coldly.

I didn't like where this was going. But at least Tama and Boreas appeared to be united against my new Fae acquaintance.

Maybe they might become friends after all, just like I'd hoped. Mama always said I could find a silver lining in every situation.

But first, I had to defuse this angry confrontation.

If Gwydion could wield mage-fire to destroy an army of slavering monkey-demons, he could probably hurt or kill Boreas.

Despite my lingering annoyance with the Dragon, I didn't want anything bad to happen to him.

"Tell me more about these attacks, please," I asked, trying to divert the conversation away from the insults and posturing.

Gwydion shrugged. "Just mere annoyances at first, but then their severity escalated. After the second attack, I complained to the castellan. Lord Roderigo dismissed the incidents as student pranks and promised to investigate. But I doubt he's actually *done* anything." His mobile lips curled in scorn. "These magical constructs were the boldest and most blatant attack to date. And it was *not* a mere student prank. Whoever did this wielded high-level magic in broad daylight and within view of the castle." He shook his head. "If Jacinthe hadn't been here to lend me her strength, those things would have torn us to shreds and devoured every scrap of flesh and bone."

I shuddered. In response, Tama's arms tightened around my shoulders.

"We would have reached you in time," he assured me.

"Indeed," boomed Boreas. "I would've killed every one of those things before they laid a single claw on you or the pretty Fae boy here."

He narrowed his eyes at Gwydion. "Speaking of which, Friend Jacinthe, who is this, and why is he here?"

I decided it would be petty to point out that Boreas hadn't yet earned the right to call me "Friend." After all, he'd raced to save me, hadn't he?

"And how did he involve you in his affairs?" added Tama.

I felt a twinge of guilt as I remembered how much I'd enjoyed the Fae man's kiss.

"Gwydion ap Pwyll is—" I paused, not sure what his role was, then made a guess. "The apothecary garden's custodian."

Gwydion nodded. I'd gotten it right. "And you are Wind-Walker Boreas, and Sea-Brother Tama," he said. "You are both well-known in the castle."

I continued, "Gwydion was helping me find some herbs and roots I needed for—" Tama tensed, and I realized he wouldn't want me to tell the others about his weakness. "—the Victory Day banquet."

"So, you do not believe those creatures wanted to attack *you?*" Tama asked.

"I think they wanted to attack everything they saw." I shuddered at the memory of those glowing eyes and jagged fangs. "Gwydion, is there some reason that the mage-students would want to attack you?"

"Not that I can think of," Gwydion said. His smile returned. "The crazy crows avoid me, as a rule."

"An appropriate name for the black-robed troublemakers," Tama agreed.

"I prefer 'earthworms.'" Boreas' jaw jutted mulishly. "And if any of them ever try attacking *me*, I'll smash them to jelly, just like *these* things." He pointed at the rapidly shrinking piles of translucent violet jelly.

"Oh, would you now, Wind-Walker?" Tama asked, a sharp edge marring his usual calm tone. "I recall that when those three crows attacked Jacinthe, you let them off without spilling even a drop of their blood. If *I* had been there, none of those three would ever make trouble again. Because they would all be dead."

It wasn't an empty threat. He'd killed two sailors in the blink of an eye and with no regrets.

But he denied killing Lady Cresta, I reminded myself.

Boreas snorted. "Big words, fish-man, but it's funny how you weren't around any of the times when your precious Jacinthe needed help."

Tama released me and surged to his feet.

He poked his clawed forefinger at Boreas' broad chest. "Careful what you say, Wind-Walker. Unlike you, I don't just talk. I *act*."

Tama was more than a head shorter than the red-headed giant, but he radiated cold menace.

Smiling, Gwydion came to sit next to me.

"Oh dear, Apprentice Jacinthe," he said with a light, chiming laugh. "You've been claimed by a Wind-Walker *and* a sea-brother? What an *interesting* person you are, for a mere human." He cocked his head. "If that's what you truly are."

"Of course I'm human!" I protested. "What else would I be?"

He smiled enigmatically at me. "That's the question, isn't it?"

Boreas whirled to glare at us. "I have not fucking *claimed* her! You heard her, she's a *human*. And I'm not King-fucking-

Menelaus!"

King Menelaus ruled the dragon kingdom, I remembered. But what had the king done, and why was Boreas so angry at him?

"If that's true, then why are you and the sea-brother arguing over which of you is her true protector?" Gwydion asked, his eyes sparkling with malice.

He turned to me. "Or would you like to appoint *me* as your bodyguard, sweet Jacinthe?" His tongue darted out to wet his lips, and I couldn't look away from their shining perfection. "My price would be more than reasonable," he continued in a seductive tone.

Despite being exhausted and chilled to the bone, a treacherous throb of arousal stirred between my legs as I met his silver gaze.

"*You*, tree-hugger? Lord of Storms save me," sneered Boreas. "Or does a pretty boy like you have more tricks up his sleeve?"

"Oh, I do. But I wouldn't mind some help, if you're offering." Gwydion actually fluttered his sinfully long lashes at the big man. "And I certainly wouldn't mind spending more time with sweet Jacinthe here."

That won him a fearsome scowl from the Dragon. I was certain now that Gwydion was only flirting with me because he enjoyed goading Boreas and Tama.

"You did well enough against those creatures," Tama said unexpectedly. "Though the Forest Children aren't known for their warriors."

"I'm no warrior," Gwydion agreed. "Just someone high-born enough to satisfy the Dominus, but expendable. Just like you two fools fighting over this human girl."

"If *we're* the fools, then why are *you* so interested in her?" Boreas asked, crossing his heavily muscled arms over his chest.

The Fae sighed and draped his arm around my shoulders. Tama shot him a murderous look.

"Because I owe her a debt for her aid just now. I'm merely waiting for a chance to repay that debt." Gwydion smiled cheerily at Boreas and Tama. "It might take a while. I'm just a humble apprentice in the castle infirmary."

I couldn't help scoffing at this description. I'd known Gwydion for less than two hours, but I already knew that he was anything *but* humble.

He smirked at me, then continued, "At least it's better than being back in Dinas y Coed, watching my kin ceaselessly intriguing against each other. My dear father tossed me to the humans as a sop. Isn't that what happened to the both of you as well?"

I'd been feeling homesick, but Gwydion's words reminded me that my new friends were no better off. We were *all* stuck here, trying to survive until our various indentures ended and we could go home again.

Except I no longer had a home. Once I completed my apprenticeship here, where would I go?

Boreas interrupted my self-pitying train of thought. "It's none of your fucking business why I'm here, pretty boy! And I've had just about enough of your smart mouth."

As the dragon's fists clenched, I wobbled to my feet. Tama was instantly at my side, steadying me.

"Please don't fight," I begged, taking a wavering step towards the Dragon. "Maybe we can all work together to find out who's responsible for this attack."

Boreas growled in response. And Tama hissed softly between his teeth.

I guess that means no, I thought.

Then Gwydion flowed smoothly up from his seat in the grass.

He touched Tama's arm, and I felt the faint prickle of magic. "I would be honored to become your ally, sea-brother."

My friend's tense, angry posture immediately relaxed. He gazed at Gwydion with unaccustomed mildness. "I will consider it."

Then Gwydion went to Boreas and laid his hand on the dragon's forearm. Again, I sensed magic at work.

"And your ally as well, Wind-Walker. Forgive my teasing." His light voice sounded serious now. He glanced down, as if ashamed, and added, "Despite my wicked tongue, I have nothing but the greatest respect for you."

"Really?" But Boreas, too, seemed calmer now.

I was relieved that Gwydion had somehow defused the tense situation. But his uncanny skill in manipulating people and situations made me uneasy.

All my life, I had heard stories about Fae charms that could induce love, or hate, or calm raging beasts. Had Gwydion worked a charm on my two friends?

And what had he done to *me* during his defensive spell against those monkey-demons?

My teeth had finally stopped chattering. But I'd never felt this drained and exhausted before, not even after my worst day in the kitchens.

He smiled. "Indeed, Wind-Walker Boreas. I propose that the four of us work together to monitor the crows and figure out which ones were behind this morning's attack."

Tama and Boreas traded suspicious glances but then, to my surprise, both nodded in agreement. Was this also part of Gwydion's Fae charm?

"How do you propose we do this?" Tama asked.

"Oh, so you *are* going to help me?" Gwydion asked, sounding surprised.

Maybe my friends' agreement to work with the Fae wasn't because of magical influence. Gwydion's reaction showed that he'd expected to argue for our assistance.

"Whoever did this also attacked Jacinthe," Tama said, his tone as cold as Gwydion's touch. "I have sworn to protect her, and I will."

"I see." Gwydion's gaze flicked to me, then back to Tama.

"And I fucking hate sneak attacks, especially from those black-robed little earthworms," Boreas growled. "What's your plan, pretty boy?"

"Let's begin by making discreet inquiries. I want to know who's skilled at creating magical constructs," Gwydion said, ignoring the jibe. "I also need to know if any of them have grudges against the Fae hostages. Or—" He paused, as if a sudden thought had struck him. "If anyone at my uncle's court paid a mage instructor or mage student to get rid of me."

Boreas nodded in agreement, and both Tama and I followed suit.

"That sounds like a good place to begin," I said. "I can ask around the kitchens and in the servants' hall at dinner. The castle staff know *everything* that's going on."

Which was my diplomatic way of referring to the castle's rumor mill.

"But let's keep the castellan and chatelaine, and their assistants, out of it," growled Boreas. "If something else happens, I'll protect you and the pretty boy here."

Tama inclined his head in agreement. "It will do us no good

to bring more attention to this situation, especially if the castellan has done nothing to prevent the previous attacks on you. We will handle it without involving anyone else."

"I agree," Gwydion said. "And even if the castellan bestirs himself to investigate, I have no desire to put myself in debt to the authorities in this place. In fact, I'd rather die than owe any of the de Norhas clan a life-debt."

"But you don't mind possibly owing *me* a life-debt?" jibed Boreas.

That got him another flutter of lashes and a coy smile. "Not at all, Wind-Walker. I think you'd find my repayment… enjoyable."

Boreas growled and turned away, but I saw he wasn't truly angry. He just didn't want Gwydion to see him smile at the openly flirtatious offer. *Interesting.*

I swayed on my feet as another wave of dizziness rolled over me. In the next instant, I was off my feet and cradled in Boreas' arms.

"We're done here," the Dragon announced. "Friend Jacinthe looks awful. She needs rest."

He turned and began striding away.

"My basket!" I called, spotting it on the ground. I didn't want to return to the castle without it.

Not only would Chef Vollkorn be angry at all the time I'd wasted out here, but I wouldn't be able to brew Tama's potion.

With a sly smile, Gwydion picked up the full basket and handed it to Tama. "Here, you carry it for her."

My merman friend accepted it without protest.

Gwydion inclined his head at me in a courtly gesture. "When you get back to the castle, tell Chef Vollkorn that you're suffering from sunstroke and need to rest."

"Yes. You still look ill," agreed Tama. He turned to give Gwydion a stony stare. "What did you do to her, Gwydion of the Forest Brothers?"

"It's a side effect of the magic I used to destroy the constructs," the Fae man replied, sounding unconcerned. "A hearty meal and a nap will fully restore her, I promise."

Then Gwydion winked at me. "I'll see you soon, Jacinthe. Consider how I can repay my debt to you. The scales must balance, you know."

Boreas strode off, carrying me as if I weighed nothing. Tama kept pace with us, and I saw no trace of a limp.

Was he feeling better, or was he simply too proud to show weakness in front of Boreas and Gwydion?

I thought I knew the answer and felt a fresh stab of guilt at not realizing how far the apothecary garden lay from the castle.

All the way back to the castle, I battled mixed feelings of embarrassment at being carried like an overtired child and relief at being spared the long walk back.

But as we drew closer to the gates, a fresh worry sprang up.

"Boreas, put me down," I said.

He eyed me skeptically. "No."

"Please," I begged. "Just walking into the castle with the two of you is going to generate gossip. But if you're *carrying* me..." I shook my head. "They could punish me for inappropriate conduct with a non-human."

"By the Unconquered Sun, how is aiding you 'inappropriate'?" He halted, but still didn't lower me. "Are you sure you can actually walk?"

"Yes," I said, trying to sound confident despite my own doubts. "I'm feeling much better now."

Clearly unconvinced, Boreas scowled but set me gently on my feet. "I wonder if we should report what happened to the castellan, after all. Friend Jacinthe could have *died*."

"No. The forest brother was right." Tama sounded grudging. "Lord Roderigo will do nothing to aid us. Instead, he may use this excuse to confine us to our rooms. I wish to continue venturing outside that stone box." He looked at me. "We will protect you. Do not leave the castle again unless we are with you."

I had no wish to argue with him. "All right. I held out my hand. "My basket, please."

Tama gave me a long, assessing stare, then handed it to me.

I took one step, then another, willing myself not to stagger. Or fall over. I was keenly aware of two sets of intense eyes following my every move.

As I slowly plodded the remaining quarter-mile to the gates, with Tama and Boreas discreetly following at a distance, a set of troubling questions nagged at me.

Why had Gwydion been so certain that I had magical power? He'd done *something* to me to aid his spell, but what?

If he was right, then why hadn't Mama or the Magecraft Aptitude Examiner been able to detect these powers?

Chapter 19

Tama

"You will leave now," I told the Wind-Walker.

The guard had brought him to my stone prison-box just after sunrise, then locked the door and left.

The Wind-Walker Boreas glanced out the window, noting the position of the morning sun, as I had.

"Friend Jacinthe should be arriving any moment," he told me, cheerfully ignoring my attempt to banish him before she arrived. *If* she came. "And if she's all right." He shook his head. "I hope she's recovered. I wonder what that Fae pretty boy *did* to her."

The dragon hadn't stopped talking since he strode into my quarters and planted himself in my window seat.

Despite my irritation at the intrusion, any company was better than the silence and boredom that swallowed me when they locked me in here alone.

Now, it was nearly time for Jacinthe to bring my second meal. I hoped she would come this time. And I wanted the Wind-Walker gone before she arrived.

The Drylander female who'd delivered my afternoon meal yesterday had refused to enter my stone box at all.

The guard, who also stank of fear, had opened the door just far enough to shove a pile of fish and seaweed inside.

Neither of them answered me when I demanded to know how Jacinthe was faring.

She had been so ill and weak in the aftermath of that strange attack yesterday, yet her warrior's spirit remained undimmed.

Watching her struggle to walk on her own through the castle gate had tortured me. I badly wanted to lift and carry her despite the agony spearing through my own legs with each step.

But Jacinthe had been correct to remind us of the cruel Drylander laws that kept humans apart from all other races.

I vowed I would not be the reason for her punishment. No matter how tempting her warm lips and wet, welcoming mouth.

Dreams of burying myself in her hot, slippery sex had tortured me every night since kissing her.

But I could not—*would* not—endanger her. Not *here*, where our enemies kept us under constant surveillance and attacked us from the shadows.

"Forest-Brother Gwydion assured us she will recover," I reminded Boreas. "And if he does not, I shall punish him for what he did to her."

I had not liked the way he looked at her and touched her, as if she belonged to him.

And I didn't like the Wind-Walker touching her and calling her "Friend Jacinthe," either.

She was my friend. My *only* friend in this stark and inhospitable place.

"Oho!" Boreas grinned at me. "So, it's like *that*, is it, Friend Tama?"

Friend? The Wind-Walker considered me his friend, also?

Despite Boreas' irritating presence and my worry at seeing Jacinthe suddenly ailing, I had enjoyed my outing yesterday. Walking free outside for an hour had been worth the sleepless night that followed, racked by pain from my hated, useless legs.

My temporary escape from the loneliness and boredom of my imprisonment in this stone box had brought relief.

As had my unwanted companion. The Wind-Walker was interesting. A worthy opponent, if nothing else.

And surprisingly, so was Gwydion. The forest-brother wore a bespelled earring, just as I did, and yet his powers seemed undiminished. The next time I encountered him, I would ask him how he circumvented it to draw on his magic.

"It is not 'like that,'" I said, as icily as I could.

The sweet kisses Jacinthe and I had shared were for us alone. I would not betray her request for secrecy and risk having her punished.

I heard the dull clang of the guard's armor and his heavy footsteps creaking on the floor-planks outside my room long before the awaited knock came.

"Mealtime, fish-man! And for your dragon buddy, too!"

Boreas swung his legs down from the window seat where he'd curled up to bathe in the hot sunlight. I didn't understand why his skin didn't turn red and blister under that merciless searing like mine did.

We looked at each other, and I saw the same anticipation in his eyes. When that door opened, would we see Jacinthe?

Something loosened inside me when she walked through my door with her basket on her hip.

"Good morning, Tama," she said, smiling at me. It sent a

strange flood of warmth through my chest. "I heard—" She halted when she saw Boreas looming behind me. "Boreas!"

Her smile widened, as if seeing him brought her joy.

I didn't like it.

"Friend Jacinthe," he boomed, his large voice echoing from every corner of this small stone box. "I'm glad to see you looking revived!"

"I feel much better," she assured us, placing the basket on the table. Indeed, her skin had lost the alarming gray undertone and her breath no longer rasped and wheezed.

The guard hanging back in the stone doorway eyed us warily. "You sure you want to be in here with both of 'em at the same time, Apprentice?"

"Yes, Guard Machry," she responded, giving the Drylander the same smile she'd given us. I liked that even less than her smiling at Boreas. "Giving them both their meals at the same time is more efficient."

His eyes darted nervously to me, then to Boreas. "If you're sure…"

He backed away, his gaze never leaving us, as if he expected us to attack him at any minute.

My lip curled in contempt as the heavy door slammed shut.

If I wanted to kill Guard Machry, he'd be dead before he realized I was moving toward him.

But I had no desire to kill this Drylander. In carrying out his duties, he had never insulted me or forced me to defend myself.

Jacinthe began emptying her food basket, dividing packets. I studied her intently, assuring myself that she had truly recovered from yesterday's crisis. Relief lightened my mood when I saw her energetic movements.

Gwydion had been correct. Luckily for him.

"Friend Jacinthe." Boreas dropped into a chair and grinned at her. "Have you recovered from what ailed you yesterday?"

Her smile widened. "I'm feeling much better. Chef Vollkorn was worried when I went to deliver those herbs and spices. She made me eat and drink something, then she ordered me straight to bed. I slept all afternoon and through the night. I woke up feeling like my usual self." She stretched.

My gaze fastened on the rounded tops of her breasts as they rose from the top of the stiff bodice encasing them.

I longed to cup their soft warmth in my hand.

Then I noticed Boreas was looking at her, too. A fresh spurt of irritation rubbed me raw, like sand grains caught in a sensitive fold of skin.

I deliberately lowered myself into the second chair, next to him. "Jacinthe, will you stay and speak with us while we eat?" I pointed at the remaining empty chair.

"Of course."

Jacinthe shoved one pile of packages, reeking of dead cattle, in front of Boreas. The second pile, which smelled deliciously of the sea, was mine. Then she pulled a glazed clay wine-jug from the basket and handed it to me. "Here's the potion I promised you. Drink it with your meal. Gwydion recommended some ingredients that work better on Fae and Sea People."

Gwydion again. Feh.

Aware of Boreas' inquiring look, I uncorked the jug and sniffed at the contents, bracing myself for something vile. Instead, an unfamiliar but pleasant fragrance greeted me.

"Peony root and fennel seeds, and a few other things," Jacinthe told me as she seated herself. "I can bring more tomorrow."

I lifted it to my lips and drank it. "Not bad," I said when I had finished it.

Boreas' wide mouth turned down. "You didn't bring *me* anything special, Friend Jacinthe?"

I braced myself for her to expose my weakness. But my precious Drylander was quick-witted.

"I didn't realize Dragons drank tea," she shot back. "But I can bring you some tomorrow, if you like."

"No tea." Boreas grimaced. "Or bread. But if you come across a nice beef heart or some kidneys…"

"I'll ask the butcher," she promised.

After I'd eaten half of my fish and seaweed, I asked, "Do you think the surviving two crows of the group that attacked you summoned those creatures yesterday?"

She shook her head. "Lord Bernardo doesn't have enough power to create anything like that," she said, sounding confident. "As for Lady Alondra…"

Jacinthe pursed her full lips thoughtfully and paused, clearly thinking.

All *I* could think right now about was tasting her mouth again.

I sternly reminded myself that the Drylanders would punish Jacinthe if they caught us behaving improperly.

But no one here—servants, guards, or even my fellow prisoners—would ever catch *me* by surprise. Not when I heard everyone's movements, both inside this building and outside.

As long as I didn't leave marks on her delicate Drylander skin, Jacinthe would be perfectly safe, no matter what we did behind closed doors.

I began making plans for when Jacinthe and I were next alone together in my room. I looked forward to exploring her and discovering what lay beneath the garments that concealed most of her body.

Even changed to this clumsy shape, I had kept some of my original body parts. I knew I would bring her greater pleasure than any Drylander man or Wind-Walker could.

I shot Boreas a covert glance.

Would the Wind-Walker *never* leave?

"I don't know about Lady Alondra," Jacinthe continued. "She was with the others, but she didn't try to attack me. The only magic I saw her use was a fairly simple illusion spell to cloak herself after Boreas burned off her clothes, and it seemed like she had to work hard at it." She added dismissively, "Bernardo couldn't even manage *that* much."

"Any trouble with any other crows?" Boreas asked.

"No. Between what you did to those three, and Cresta turning up dead, the few students I've encountered since then avoid me like I'm infected with plague." She sighed. "I'm notorious now. Some of the castle staff refuse to sit next to me in the servants' hall."

A low growl escaped me. Shunning was one of the worst punishments I could imagine. Sea People weren't meant to be alone. Neither were Drylanders, from what I'd seen so far.

I reminded myself that killing those who shunned her wouldn't help Jacinthe.

"Speaking of the crows," Jacinthe continued, "I asked about them while working breakfast service this morning."

"And?" I prompted, hoping for some prey at last.

Sitting in this box, waiting for another attack, was no way for a warrior to live. I needed to *do* something.

"Pastry Chef Kalapania—she's worked in the kitchens the longest—said there aren't any truly gifted mages among the current crop of students."

Boreas and I both grunted in disappointment.

"Also, did you hear the castellan called a special meeting with the academy's professors and students yesterday?" asked Jacinthe.

I had not, but Boreas nodded. "The guards were speculating why."

"I heard a messenger bird arrived yesterday morning with a letter from Lady Cresta's parents. Everyone's wondering what they wrote Lord Roderigo and Lady Erzabetta. It can't have been pleasant." Jacinthe's eyes shone as she leaned forward and put her elbows on the table. "Anyhow, Lord Roderigo's temporarily banned all use of magic at the academy. For the instructors *and* the students. The only exceptions are Healer-Mage Armand and his staff, for obvious reasons. Isn't that *interesting?*"

"Lord Roderigo believes that one of the academy staff killed Lady Cresta?" I asked.

"It makes sense that a fully trained mage sent those creatures to attack you and Gwydion yesterday," Boreas said at the same moment.

"I agree," Jacinthe said. "I'm not a mage, but I grew up around them. Someone with strong powers and lots of skill created those monkey-demons."

"Someone who resents being exiled here." Boreas' tone was unusually thoughtful for someone so loud. "This isn't a place that a trained mage, or anyone else, would *want* to live."

"You're right," Jacinthe said, bestowing another smile on the Wind-Walker.

He grinned back, showing all of his blunt human teeth. "I'm *always* right, Friend Jacinthe. You will learn this."

I clenched my teeth. *She is my friend! Mine!*

And the Wind-Walker's presence here was preventing me from kissing her... and doing more.

And yet, I found it unexpectedly pleasant to share this meal with Boreas. For too long now, I had eaten alone, without the joy of conversation or even the presence of another living being to season my food.

I heard a familiar heavy tread approaching.

"The guard is coming," I announced. "Jacinthe, Boreas, we must discover which of the trained mages here sent those creatures yesterday. Can you find Gwydion and ask him whether he suspects anyone?"

Jacinthe frowned. "I can try the infirmary, but he told me he's in charge of the garden. I won't be able to go back out there until my day off." She sighed unhappily. "Chef Vollkorn gave my garden duties to another apprentice because she thought I had sunstroke. It'll be a while before she sends me outside the castle again."

She rose and began gathering the discarded waxed cloth wrappers, putting them back in her basket.

When Guard Machry unlocked and opened the door a few seconds later, Boreas got to his feet. "I enjoyed our visit, Friend Tama. I will return tomorrow to share the morning meal with you."

I stared at him, torn between frustration at not having Jacinthe all to myself and relief that I wouldn't be eating alone again.

A thought occurred to me. Could the Wind-Walker also be missing his aerie?

I lifted my hand to bid them farewell. "Until tomorrow, Friend Jacinthe and… Friend Boreas."

I hadn't meant to say that last part. But I didn't regret it either.

Being alone was far worse than the company of a loud, talkative, boastful yet good-natured Wind-Walker.

Chapter 20

Jacinthe

Two days later, the sound of loud, urgent voices outside the dormitory woke me long before Malia's pre-dawn wake-up call.

Before I even opened my eyes, I knew something was very wrong.

My fellow apprentices and I scrambled out of our beds, bleary-eyed and disoriented. I joined the crowd standing at the window, trying to see what was happening in the narrow alley below.

Senior Apprentice Malia entered the dormitory a few minutes later. She was always washed, combed, and neatly dressed for morning call. But this morning, she looked as disheveled as the rest of us. The apprentices greeted her with a volley of questions.

"What's happening?"

"Why are all those guards marching past the kitchen?"

"What's all that shouting about?"

"They found another mage student dead this morning. Something tore him to pieces just outside the postern gate," she said.

Everyone gasped. That was the gate all the kitchen apprentices used for fetching firewood and gathering eggs from the chicken coops.

I shuddered, remembering the slavering jaws of the monkey-demons a few days ago. If Gwydion hadn't been there to fight them with mage-fire, he and I would've ended up like this poor student.

Malia added, "The guards are saying it looks some kind of wild animal attacked him."

Another chorus of gasps rose from my fellow apprentices. We all knew that there were no animals native to this remote island other than birds and lizards. The only other animals here were livestock, and a few cats and dogs.

"Who died?" I called, an icy lump of dread forming under my breastbone.

Malia's reply confirmed my worst fears. "Lord Bernardo of Espola."

"Hey, wasn't he Lady Cresta's friend?" someone asked.

"Yeah," someone else answered. "And he was part of that group who attacked Jacinthe, Elswyth, and Rheda last week."

Everyone in the dormitory turned to look at the three of us.

"Don't mess with Jacinthe," someone joked. "Or you'll end up dead."

Nervous titters rippled through my fellow apprentices.

"I didn't have anything to do with it," I protested, though I knew it wouldn't do me any good. "You all know I was in here with you all night."

A violent storm had swept over the island at sunset, with howling winds and rain drumming hard against the castle's windows and roofs.

"But you've got your special friends to do your dirty work," Charmaine pointed out. "The monsters."

"Yeah, maybe you lured Lord Bernardo out of the gate so the fish-man could kill him," Jonitha added eagerly. "Prince Boreas would *never* lower himself like that."

Then she stopped talking and shot me a nervous look.

Everyone standing near me hastily shuffled back, leaving a wide gap around me. Only Elswyth and Rheda remained at my side.

I glared back at Jonitha and briefly fantasized about sending Tama or Boreas after her.

Not that I ever would, of course.

But she and Charmaine seemed determined to ruin my reputation in the castle, and I didn't know why. I hadn't done anything to them. In fact, I'd even helped Charmaine by taking over a job she detested.

Why did they dislike me so much?

"Charmaine, Jonitha, shut up and stop causing trouble," Malia ordered. "You're on ash bucket duty for the rest of the week."

The two of them would spend the next few days shoveling and hauling away ashes from the fireplaces, charcoal stoves, and ovens. It was the grimiest, sweatiest, dustiest job in the kitchens.

"Yes, Senior Apprentice!" both girls intoned dully. They both threw me evil looks, as if they blamed me for the reprimand they'd just earned.

I fought a smirk at the well-deserved punishment. I hadn't experienced the sweet taste of justice lately.

Malia put her hand on her hips and gave the rest of us an exasperated look. "No one knows what happened yet. The castellan and the guards are still investigating. If any of you saw or heard anything last night, please come forward."

I felt a chill run through me as I realized who the guards were likely to question first.

Anxiety consumed me as I quickly washed and dressed, then went down to the kitchen to start the day. I flew through my morning tasks, champing at the bit to warn Tama and Boreas that the guards were probably on their way to question them about Bernardo's murder.

Finally, I grabbed the prepared basket of raw fish, meat, and seaweed from the butcher and quickly made my way to the castle gatehouse.

As I walked, I wondered why Jonitha had instantly concluded that Tama was to blame. Who had she been talking to? Because it sounded to me as if someone at the castle was trying to frame him for Bernardo's murder.

A shaken Guard Machry led me to Boreas' rooms. There, I found Boreas and Tama sitting at the table, playing a card game.

The sight of them together, apparently enjoying each other's company, would have gladdened me if I hadn't been so upset by the morning's events.

"Friend Jacinthe! We have been waiting for you," Boreas greeted me with one of his wide grins. "What happened this morning? The guards are running back and forth, and they are all very upset. No one will answer our questions."

"It's Lord Bernardo of Espola," I said. "I heard that someone lured him outside the castle, then tore him to pieces. Do you think a pack of those monkey-demons got him?"

Tama shrugged. "If they did, no great loss."

"But I think someone's trying to frame one of you for it," I said urgently. "I've already started hearing rumors that you or Boreas killed Bernardo for attacking me."

Boreas crossed his arms over his chest. "Impossible. Everyone knows Friend Tama and I were both locked in our rooms overnight." He cast a sour glance at the tall but extremely narrow window-slit, impossible for someone his size squeeze through. "And there's no way out of here except by breaking down the door. Which I could do. Easily."

"I could also break my door and depart, if I wished," Tama agreed.

"Then why do you let them lock you up in here?" I couldn't understand it. Confinement in the gatehouse made both of my new friends clearly miserable.

Boreas gave me an incredulous, golden-eyed look. "I gave my word of honor to King Menelaus and Lady Aeolia to serve out my term as hostage."

Tama inclined his head. "And I swore the same to my clan grandmother. I must stay here until your ruler bids me leave to return home."

As was becoming my habit, I stayed and sat with them while they ate. But we didn't talk much.

I didn't know what Tama and Boreas were thinking, but I feared someone was trying to frame my friends.

I left them with a heavy heart.

As I walked back to the castle, I wondered who could be responsible for Bernardo's murder. Was it someone with a grudge against the student mages? Or someone with a grudge against my new friends?

Chapter 21

Jacinthe

Later that afternoon, I stood in a crowd cramming every inch of the castle's Great Hall. As we waited for the castellan to speak, a deafening roar of conversation rose to the painted stone vaults.

I caught snatches of speculation about Bernardo's murder, its connection to Cresta's death, and the sudden castle-wide ban on magic.

The Great Hall certainly lived up to its name. Located on the second floor of a building overlooking the courtyard garden, it was so grand I thought that all of Bernswick's cottages could have fit inside it.

The kitchen staff was preparing for dinner service when Castellan Roderigo summoned all the castle staff members for an important announcement. I'd stopped scrubbing pots and dried my hands. Then I joined the other apprentices as we followed the cooks and senior apprentices to the Great Hall.

Jonitha and Charmaine's caps and aprons were grimy with ash. They both conspicuously avoided me, as did a few of the other apprentices. But most of the others were too interested in speculating about what Lord Roderigo was going to say to pay much attention to me.

The castellan stood on the dais at one end of the hall, a scowl on his handsome, bearded face. Chatelaine Erzabetta and Assistant Chatelaine Margitts stood on either side of him.

I spotted Master at Arms Guisbald at rigid attention between a pair of fully armored guards holding long pole-axes at the foot of the dais.

I had an uneasy feeling in the pit of my stomach as I observed their grim expressions.

When the last servants entered through the tall double-doors, Lord Roderigo gestured at Master Guisbald. The guards pounded the butts of their pole-axes against the wooden floor. At this signal, the crowd quickly fell silent.

The castellan cleared his throat and began.

"It is with great sorrow I must inform you all that last night we found Bernardo of Espola dead in his chamber. We believe his death was an unfortunate accident." His powerful voice echoed off the high, vaulted stone ceiling.

A loud murmur of shock and denial rose from the crowd.

Thanks to the castle's rumor mill, we all knew how and where Bernardo had *really* died.

I held my breath, trying to make sense of what I was hearing. *Why* was the castellan lying about Bernardo's death?

The castellan continued, his voice rising to a stern tone.

"I will remind you all that intoxicants of any kind are strictly forbidden to the academy's students. We have always upheld this rule firmly. In light of the recent tragedies, I expect nothing less than full compliance from each and every one of you."

He paused and swept his black eyes around the hall, as if scrutinizing each of us for signs of rebellion.

"For the safety of the students," he continued, "I've ordered Steward Potts to lock the wine and ale cellars, effective immediately. Chief Healer Armand has put all medicines in the castle infirmary under spelled locks. And we are confiscating all alcohol from the kitchens and guard barracks."

A loud, protesting groan rose from the crowd.

"Fuck me," someone said loudly. "Beer's the only thing that makes this hellhole bearable."

A mutter of agreement rose.

"Silence!" roared Master Guisbald. "I'll give anyone caught with contraband liquor fifteen lashes." The angry muttering continued, but at lower volume.

Lord Roderigo's eyes scanned the crowd once more, as if searching for dissenters.

I felt shocked at his blatant—and utterly useless—attempt to cover up the cause of Lord Bernardo's death.

"Let us now have a moment of silence. May the Divine Mother guide the soul of this unfortunate young man to a happier afterlife," Lady Erzabetta intoned solemnly.

Obediently, we all bowed our heads. But not without sidelong glances and rolled eyes communicating that no one here believed the castellan's version of events.

"That is all," the castellan barked after the moment of silence passed. "You are dismissed."

As we streamed out of the Great Hall, I wondered why the castellan was trying to hide how Bernardo had really died.

Was he trying to quell possible tensions between the castle's human and non-human residents? Or was he trying to protect someone?

Was one of the academy's mage instructors the killer?

Or was it a student with hidden mage potential, shielded by powerful family connections?

Then an even worse possibility struck me. What if someone was attacking the children of nobles and the imperial hostages because they wanted to start the next Great War?

I shuddered and tried to dismiss that last possibility. Darkstone Island was too remote to influence politics. Wasn't it?

∞∞∞

Victory Day

After days of preparation and extra work for everyone in the kitchens, it was finally time for the big banquet.

Clear skies and a fiery band of dawn over the sea promised another hot summer day as I and my fellow apprentices rose and made our way downstairs.

We actually had not one but two banquets to cater today. First, the castle's administrators, academy professors, students, and the imperial hostages were expecting a parade of delicacies in the Great Hall. Once our betters had been served their multi-course meal, the castle staff would enjoy a banquet of their own, with humbler fare.

And, of course, the kitchen wasn't exempted from cooking and serving breakfast tomorrow morning, either.

Everyone in the kitchens dreaded feast days. Today, our work day began an hour earlier than normal, and we knew we'd still be cleaning up when the midnight watch bell rang.

The castle's kitchens echoed with the rhythmic clang of spoons against pots, loudly sizzling pans, and a symphony of orders. I was but a single cog in the clockwork engine of cooks and apprentices driven by Master Chef Vollkorn. Clad in a spotless white apron and cap over her imperial livery, she seemed to be everywhere at once. No detail escaped her attention in the main kitchen, the bakery, or the confectioner's rooms.

The sweltering air was thick with the delectable scents of roasting meat and chickens, steaming lobsters, poaching fish, herbed sauces, and baking bread.

As the time for the nobles' banquet approached, Chef Vollkorn drafted an army of castle servants to join the apprentices in delivering the food to the Great Hall.

Laden with baskets of bread, huge covered serving dishes, crocks of fragrant soups, sauce-jugs, and huge trays of delicate pastries and sweetmeats, we trotted through the castle's narrow service corridors.

Again and again, I made my way between the sweltering heart of the kitchens to the grandeur of the castle's Great Hall.

The first time I'd visited it, for Lord Rodrigo's assembly a week ago, it was impressive but stark.

Now, it was lavishly decorated in honor of the Dominion's most important holiday. Victory Day celebrated the final battle of the Great War. Defeated, the commanders of the allied supernatural forces had surrendered to General Severus Cavalieri di Corredo and his human army outside the walls of Lutèce.

Over the past few days, my young friend Toland and the other farm apprentices had harvested dozens of baskets of rose petals, lavender, and rosemary branches from the castle estates. These were now strewn on the flagstones. Enormous tapestries of red and gold hid the Great Hall's stark stone walls.

Long trestle tables draped in spotless linens embroidered with a repeating pattern of the blue-and-gold Imperial Coat of Arms stretched the length of the hall, set with gilded plates, glass goblets, napkins, and mother-of-pearl salt cellars filled with piles of glistening white crystals.

I saw rows of glass decanters filled with red and white wines. Despite his stern prohibition against alcohol, Lord Roderigo evidently had no intention of depriving himself or his guests. Only the castle staff and guards would be drinking water and fruit juice tonight.

As I passed through the hall, delivering yet another tray of succulent roast pork to the butlers' pantry beyond, I couldn't help but draw a comparison to the humble servants' hall, where I and the rest of the castle's staff ate our meals.

There, the benches were worn smooth by decades of use, the plain wooden tables stained by years of spilled wine and gravy, and the whitewashed walls adorned only with candle-soot and the occasional cobweb.

On a return trip from the Great Hall, I gasped as I rounded a corner and collided with a solid wall of muscle clothed in voluminous black student's robes.

The tall young man standing before me was broad-shouldered and solidly built. He had short hair the same sun-bleached gold as ripe barley.

Deep blue eyes locked onto mine. He examined me from my white linen cap to my sturdy wooden clogs.

Disturbed by the intensity of his gaze, I raised my chin. "May I help you, student?" I asked as coolly as I could. When he continued to stare at me, I snapped, "I'm a little busy right now."

"Are you Apprentice Jacinthe?" he demanded.

"Yes." I took a wary step back from him. I didn't like that he recognized me. Or that he knew my name.

"I'm Lord Ilhan of Parrish," he said, his tone clipped. "Heir to the Duke of Frankia." His body language communicated that he expected me to recognize his name.

"How may I help you, Lord Ilhan?" I repeated.

He scowled at me and exhaled loudly. Then he looked away. "I'm here to ask you to spare my sister Alondra."

Alondra of Parrish? Divine Mother spare me. I took another step back from him.

"Please." I saw the muscles in the corner of his jaw twitching as if he were clenching his teeth.

When I continued to stare at him, he ground out, "I'll get on my knees and beg you, if I have to."

I tried to imagine this big, proud young man falling to his knees in the middle of the corridor, and my face grew hot.

"I'm sorry, Lord Ilhan, but I don't know what you're talking about."

Ilhan smiled, but there was no warmth in his expression.

"I've heard that you've got this castle's resident monsters on your leash," he said flatly.

"What?" I gasped. My heart began pounding. "I don't. It's not like that!"

Oh, this is bad. Very bad. I looked around, but the corridor was deserted. We were alone.

"Oh, don't play innocent with me, Apprentice." Ilhan's lips twisted sardonically. "Everyone knows it's no coincidence that Cresta and Bernardo died after they attacked you. But believe me, Alondra isn't like that. She just fell in with the wrong crowd after we were exiled here because of the de Norhas plot."

His words felt like a punch to my stomach, winding me. Thanks to Charmaine and Jonitha, I knew some of the rumors about me, Tama, and Boreas circulating around the castle. But

I hadn't expected anyone to bring it up like *this*.

"What de Norhas plot?" I asked, still confused. "I thought the students here came from other academies for the magical arts, because of—" I hastily edited my words. "Um, certain difficulties there."

Ilhan let out a bitter laugh. "You can be honest," he said. "Some of the mage students here are dangerous criminals who should've had the magic burned out of them at their first offense. But not all of us are here because we committed a magical crime. Some of us, including most of the staff and administration officials, are political exiles."

I was taken aback. Growing up in the remote Western Isles province had left me ignorant of the political intrigues and power struggles among the nobles on the Continent.

But his comment explained a lot—like why a master chef of Brigitte Vollkorn's caliber was working *here*, of all places.

Ilhan seemed to sense my surprise. He snorted contemptuously.

"Don't you know *anything* about what's been happening lately?" he asked.

I shook my head.

Ilhan blew out a frustrated breath. "Domina Jacinthe exiled my sister and I here, along with our aunt Amella—that's Baroness Margitts to you. For some insane reason, Aunt Amella decided to join the Duke de Norhas and his family in plotting against the domina."

I stared at him in bewilderment. "Why would someone plot against Domina Jacinthe?"

She had always been popular. I was one of thousands of girls named for her after Dominus Victor Augustus the Eighth wed her and crowned her his consort. She was well-respected. I'd never heard the slightest breath of scandal attached to her name.

My question produced another heavy sigh from Ilhan. "Have you least heard that old Victor Eight is senile?"

"No," I said, shocked as much as hearing our distinguished dominus referred to as "Victor Eight," as by the news of his incapacity.

He had been on the imperial throne for decades, and must be ancient by now, but the news still surprised me.

"Right," Ilhan said, rolling his eyes. "Well, he hasn't made a public appearance in months, not since that incident at the state banquet for the Djinn Ambassador."

I wanted to ask him what had happened at the banquet, but Ilhan kept speaking with grim determination.

"After *that* disaster, Domina Jacinthe convinced the Imperial Council of Advisors to make her regent. That angered the Parliament of the Most Noble, who wanted one of their own declared Imperial Regent with an eye towards becoming Heir Apparent, since Victor Eight and Domina Jacinthe don't have any living children or grandchildren."

I nodded. I'd heard of Princess-Royal Jonquil's death in a tragic accident. She'd been in her early twenties, newly graduated from the Imperial Academy for the Magical Arts in Neapolis Capitola, and working as an official Court Healer.

"Well, long story short," Ilhan continued. "A group of nobles, including my father, conspired to proclaim the Duke de Norhas as Imperial Regent. The plot had failed, and Domina Jacinthe arrested and imprisoned the conspirators, including the Duke de Norhas and Father. She also exiled other members of his family, like Lord Roderigo and Lady Erzabetta, and their known associates, like Aunt Amella, to this place." He grimaced. "Alondra and I are here to keep my mother and the rest of our family in line."

Well, that explains a lot, I thought. I'd wondered why the castle's castellan and chatelaine were from such noble families, and why Lady Margitts acted so sour all the time.

I looked up at Ilhan, who was glowering down at me, as if everything he'd just told me was my fault.

"I'm sorry that you and your sister are here as hostages," I said, as sympathetically as I could. "But I assure you that Lord Tama, Prince Boreas, and I had *nothing* to do with the deaths of Lady Cresta and Lord Bernardo."

Ilhan scowled. "All right, if that's the way you want to play it," he muttered.

Before I could ask what he meant, he continued, "Is it money you want? Or some kind of special treatment? I can ask my Aunt Amella to get you and your *friends* anything you want, *if* you promise not to hurt Alondra."

He thinks I'm shaking him down for a bribe? Anger sent heat to my face.

Ilhan's only worried about his sister. I bit back my first outraged response, and took a deep breath.

"I'm sorry," I repeated. "But it's true. My friends and I didn't do anything to Lady Cresta or Lord Bernardo."

His dusk-blue gaze bored into my soul for a long moment. Refusing to be intimidated, I stared back at him.

"I thank you for hearing me out," he said curtly. "If you change your mind, you can find me in the infirmary most afternoons."

Then he turned on his heel and strode away, his black academic gown billowing out behind him like a cape in some heroic painting.

I watched Ilhan go, my mind whirling with questions. *Did I just make another enemy in this place?*

Is Lady Alondra truly in danger?

Who really killed Lady Cresta and Lord Bernardo?

And why are Tama, Boreas, and I being framed for the murders?

Chapter 22

Gwydion

The invitation to the Victory Day banquet came couched as an honor. But I knew Lord Roderigo and Lady Erzabetta really meant it as a humiliation. Why else would they want the representatives of the defeated nations to celebrate the humans' greatest military triumph?

This incensed my fellow hostages, though none dared refuse the invitation. But I was actually looking forward to it. It was going to be amusing to watch my fellow hostages torn between simmering resentment and forced courtesy.

And I knew the food would be good. The new chef had worked miracles in the kitchen since her arrival last fall.

And when emotions ran high, I could feed my *other* hunger, the bottomless pool of darkness inside me I tried to conceal.

As I crossed the threshold and entered the Great Hall, my fellow Fae immediately took notice. Three pairs of eyes shot loathing and pity at me.

"Oh, look," Princess Eluned of the Glass Fortress said loudly as I approached the small, round table where my fellow Fae hostages sat. "Prince Gwydion the Leech is here."

She and the others never passed up an opportunity to remind me of my cursed lineage.

Disdain rolled off her in waves as she made a show of drawing up the hem of her long, flowing velvet cloak so that my shadow wouldn't contaminate it.

"Find somewhere else to sit," she ordered, her voice dripping with contempt.

I glanced at the other two Fae hostages, Princess Angharad of the Eagles and Princess Branwen the Golden-Handed. They, too, regarded me with distaste and the tiniest bit of fear.

I understood their venom, even if I didn't like it. I loathed my family even more than they did. I'd spent my childhood and early youth dreaming of escape from my father's toxic court.

When Dominus Victor Augustus the Eighth's emissary arrived at Father's palace to deliver a demand for a high-born hostage, I'd eagerly volunteered. Anything to escape the nest of vipers I'd been born into.

My uncle had urged Father to agree. I was only a younger son, after all. If something happened to me while in exile, well, it *would* be a pity, wouldn't it? But not a crippling blow to our tiny kingdom.

Unlike the other imperial hostages in this castle, I actually liked it here. Best of all, Darkstone Island was far, far away from my family and their hangers-on. I could finally reinvent myself as a better person.

The only worms in this sweet apple of my freedom were my fellow Fae hostages. *They* never let me forget my cursed lineage. Or the fact I'd shamefully humbled myself when I apprenticed with a human mage.

Therefore, I spent as much time as possible away from my quarters. I passed the hours tending Healer-Mage Armand's apothecary garden and working in the infirmary.

Ignoring Eluned's insult, I passed by the three Fae ladies. I had no desire to force myself into their presence. They had made their feelings clear enough.

But where should I sit?

I stopped and looked around. Richly dressed human nobles, mage instructors, and students crowded the benches on both sides of the three rows of linen-draped tables stretching the length of the Great Hall.

Several smaller tables for the imperial hostages stood in each corner of the hall.

On the dais, at the high table, the darkly handsome but haughty Castellan Roderigo and his equally haughty sister, Chatelaine Erzabetta, sat looking out over the gathered guests.

Many of the human guests seated at the long tables stared at me curiously. But bright curiosity tasted far better than bitter fear or fetid loathing.

Over the past year, I'd built a reputation of being able to cure illnesses and relieve pain by laying my hands on a patient.

I had initially volunteered to apprentice with the doddering old Healer-Mage Armand because the castle infirmary promised me a steady supply of powerful emotions to feed on.

Pain and fear weren't nearly as nourishing as love and sex, but I took what I could get.

But once I began working, I realized that feeding on a patient's pain relieved their suffering. For the first time in my life, I was doing some good in the world, instead of spreading darkness and discontent, like my uncle Dyfan or my father, King Pwyll the Silver-Eyed.

If they knew what I was doing here, they'd be horrified and bewildered. No Dark Fae in a thousand years had ever wanted anyone to think of them as good or benevolent. Our power lay in the shadows, and our strength was the fear we inspired.

I knew I was a traitor to everything my bloodline represented. And I was happy about it.

If I had my choice, I would *never* return to Dinas y Coed.

"Gwydion!" A deep voice rose above the din of conversation. "Join us!"

Someone actually wanted my company? Well, *that* had never happened before!

I looked around and saw the voice came from a round table set apart from the others. This one stood in the corner of the hall furthest from the dais, next to the service door.

The huge, red-headed Wind-Walker I'd met last week waved at me. Prince Boreas grinned widely as I met his eyes.

"Come," he called. "Tama and I wish to speak with you."

Sure enough, next to him sat the sea-brother, Lord Tama of Walrus Clan.

The pair intrigued me. I'd never heard of a friendship between a Dragon and a merman. Fire and water rarely mixed.

Lord Tama's large black eyes shot me a wintry glance as I approached. "We have some questions for you."

I sighed. I could guess what questions they wanted to ask. But I was late arriving at the banquet, and there weren't any other places left at the other tables.

So, I accepted my fate. Everyone already seated at the table shifted places, leaving an empty chair between Boreas and Tama.

I felt the gazes of the three Fae princesses burning into my back from the other side of the hall as I seated myself.

Aside from the Wind-Walker and his friend, the round table held four other guests: three Djinn and another merman.

I recognized the Djinn hostages, though we had not yet met face-to-face.

Prince Arslan was clean-shaven, with eyes the deep color of dusk over the mountains. As he greeted me with grave courtesy, tiny flames danced within his irises.

He wore deep blue robes embroidered with gold thread and a matching round cap set atop his shoulder-length, sun-streaked dark hair. An enormous polished sapphire surrounded by small diamonds decorated his cap, crowned with three long white egret feathers.

Next to him, Princess Layla wore an exquisite, long-sleeved tunic of flame-colored silk set with clusters of tiny diamonds that flashed in the candlelight like stars. Beside her, Princess Karima wore a matching tunic, but in vivid peacock-blue silk.

Elaborate jewelry weighed down both Djinn women, beginning with gold-net headdresses hung with jeweled tassels that confined their elaborately braided hair.

Their flame-shaped restrictor earrings hung from piercings in the upper rim of their ears, allowing them to suspend huge, intricate gold filigree earrings from their lobes. Wide gold filigree collars with rows of stylized flower pendants circled their throats, and dozens of slim gold bangles chimed on their wrists.

Every piece was set with a plethora of multi-colored jewels that sparkled red, green, blue, and tawny in the dancing light from the chandeliers.

Next to Tama sat Lord Shuji of Dolphin Clan. The sea-brother had arrived three days ago, making him the castle's newest hostage.

Like Lord Tama, Shuji's enormous eyes were as dark and liquid as a seal's, and his face was framed by long, glossy hair that rippled in gentle waves down to his waist.

But where Tama's skin and hair were pearly-pale, betraying his origins in the cold Northern Sea, Shuji had dark blue hair and gray skin. His clan of the Sea People ruled the warm seas off the coast of the Dragon Kingdom of Kappadokia.

A silver restrictor earring in the shape of a dolphin's tail hung from Shuji's ear, marking him as an imperial hostage.

Unlike Lord Tama, with his fierce warrior energy, Lord Shuji radiated gentle strength as he inclined his head to me in greeting.

He wore a loose, wide-sleeved robe of ivory silk decorated with silver fish, and many necklaces strung with pearls and carved abalone shell pendants. On his head, he wore a gleaming diadem of mother-of-pearl.

"Have you found out who sent those monkey-demon things to attack you and Jacinthe?" Lord Tama asked.

I shook my head.

"We've been trying to find out which mages here are strong enough to work a spell like that," Boreas said as he poured me a goblet of wine from the painted and gilded glass decanter on the table. "I heard you've been here longer than any of us, Gwydion. Who here hates you—or hates the Fae—and has the power to work a spell like that?"

I noticed that he, Tama, and Shuji were all drinking water, and that they had already received their meals.

Chunks of raw, bloody meat formed a mountain on Boreas' plate, interspersed with the smooth shine of dark-brown internal organs.

Tama and Shuji each had an identical silver platter heaped with mounds of amber-brown and vivid green seaweed. Surrounding the seaweed were thin slices of raw fish that ranged from snow-white to blood-red.

Shuji and the three Djinn listened to our conversation with interest.

"Monkey-demons?" Prince Arslan asked in a soft, husky voice that reminded me of a sea wind blowing over sand dunes. "What monkey-demons?"

I glanced at his companions and saw only curiosity.

So, neither Boreas, Tama, or the intriguing kitchen apprentice girl had told anyone about the attack until now? *Interesting.*

Normally, stories about something this interesting would've raced through the castle's inhabitants like a plague of sweating-sickness.

I hadn't reported the incident, either, because after a year of steadily escalating attacks, I knew Lord Roderigo would mouth concerned platitudes but take no action.

I shrugged and answered the Wind-Walker's question. "I can't think of anyone."

At his scowl, I added, "I have three enemies in the castle." I couldn't help glancing over at the Fae princesses. "But I doubt that their magic could overcome the restrictions of their charmed earrings."

When I returned to my suite of rooms after the attack, I had watched the princesses' reactions closely. They were the only ones I knew hated me enough to want to kill me.

Instead, they'd greeted me with their usual contempt—but nothing else—as I entered the small dining room we reluctantly shared.

"Yet *you* cast a powerful defensive spell," Lord Tama pointed out in his cool voice. He touched his own silver earring. "How did you do that? I cannot summon my powers, no matter how hard I try."

I sighed. I didn't want to reveal my secret here, in public. And yet, as a Fae, I found lying nearly impossible.

As was my habit, I settled for a half-truth. "It was mostly desperation and fear for my life," I said, giving him a wry smile.

"Someone attacked you?" the Djinn Princess Karima asked. "These monkey-demons?"

"Yes, tell us what happened," Arslan ordered.

Prince Boreas looked around at the crowded hall. None of the laughing, chattering humans or Fae were paying us any attention. He leaned forward and began telling the story.

"What did you do to Jacinthe to make her so ill?" Tama asked in a low voice while his friend described what he'd seen. His tone turned accusatory. "You said you *borrowed* power from her."

Blight and ruin, the merman remembered my foolish comment! I'd been shaken by the attack and blurted more than I should have.

"I didn't harm her," I told him to avoid answering the real question.

Having seen how protective he and the Wind-Walker were toward the human girl, I didn't want to anger him. And I certainly wasn't going to mention my surprise that she survived my instinctive draw on her life-force.

The spell on the restrictor-earrings was a powerful one, meant to absorb magical energy. To summon mage-fire, I'd had to flood my damned earring with enough energy that I could use the overspill.

The drain on the human girl's life-force should have killed her. But it hadn't.

Instead, I'd touched a vast reservoir of power sealed behind an almost impenetrable wall. Even the thin trickle I extracted through a minute crack in that wall had been enough to power a defensive spell strong enough to destroy every single magical construct in the mob swarming out of the trees and toward us.

The girl had been sick and weak in the aftermath, but nowhere close to dead. And she seemed completely unaware of her power.

She was a fascinating mystery. And I still owed her a debt for what I'd taken from her.

The scales must always balance. Always.

Tama scowled at me, clearly unsatisfied with my reply.

The Wind-Walker finished his tale with, "And I would appreciate you all keeping this story to yourselves while we try to find out who did it."

Good luck with that, I thought, rolling my eyes.

Boreas had been here long enough to know that every imperial hostage within these walls would hear some version of the story before the sun set tomorrow. And probably the guards, too.

I gave it three days at most before everyone in the castle knew we'd been attacked outside the walls.

The Dragon's golden eyes, with their cat-like vertical pupils, fastened on me with a predatory stare.

"Friend Jacinthe recovered, yes, but you made her sick. *Weakened* her. Severely," he pointed out, having apparently heard Tama's question while he was still telling his story.

I shrugged and offered another uninformative truth. "My magic sometimes has that effect on others."

Time to divert the course of the conversation away from me. "Tell me about this Jacinthe. Is she human? Some kind of mage?"

She had protested she was human but no mage.

And even if she was a mage, no *human* mage had that kind of power. It certainly hadn't tasted human as it roared through me.

Both Prince Boreas and Lord Tama looked surprised by my question.

"Of course she's human," Tama replied immediately. "But she is no mage. She told me so."

"Why are you asking?" Boreas's eyes narrowed.

I shrugged. "I found her very interesting. I'd like to get to know her better."

As I spoke, I realized it was true. I was looking forward to meeting her again and unraveling her intriguing mystery. And maybe sipping from her delicious power once more.

The thought of that fiery, intoxicating energy flowing into me again aroused me nearly as much as the memory of her soft, innocent mouth and her ardent response to my kisses.

I knew I could seduce her. That was my family's greatest gift. I had only to meet her again, and she'd beg me to bed her. *Yes.*

Both Tama and Boreas glared at me. It reminded me they were the girl's suitors.

I gave each of them my sweetest smile and added maliciously, "Plus, I owe her a debt for her help. I want to repay her in a *truly* memorable way."

The fiery rage that instantly flowed from both of them bathed me in delicious heat, thawing my perpetually frozen bones. *Maybe I should bed all three of them. The Dragon, the merman,* and *the girl.*

It might even be fun to enjoy them all at the same time. Orgies were a favorite pastime in Father's court, but I'd never participated. I found all his courtiers repulsive, and it killed any desire I might've felt.

But *these* three… oh, that was a very different story!

"I want to get to know you both better, too," I said, letting some of my sudden desire flavor my words.

Then I reined myself in.

A Wind-Walker and a sea-brother willing to be friends with each other, and a human girl might also befriend me, *if* I didn't overstep.

More than the fleeting satisfaction of sex, I wanted friends. *Real* friends. I'd never experienced true friendship or loyalty. I wanted to receive some of what I saw between Boreas, Tama, and Jacinthe.

To ingratiate myself with them, I might have to drain off their hostility again, just like I had after the attack.

But someday, their companionship might be completely voluntary and free of my magical influence.

The Djinn princesses laughed. So did Arslan.

"An offer you shouldn't refuse," he joked. "The Fae make better friends than enemies."

Both Boreas and Tama switched their glowers to him. He returned a serene smile.

Boreas opened his mouth to say something. A deafening fanfare of trumpets interrupted him, announcing the first course of the banquet.

A parade of servants emerged from the service doors behind the dais and began circulating around the room.

They bore stacks of bread-baskets, giant soup tureens, and platters piled high with carved meat and mounds of vegetables. My mouth watered as the savory smells of seafood, roast beef, crisp-skinned chicken, and fresh-baked bread drifted to my nose.

Our table was the last served.

I was hungry, and the food was delicious. I devoured thick, tender slices of herb-crusted roast beef, crisp-skinned chicken quarters, and mixed vegetables in a smooth, garlicky sauce, with crusty fennel bread to sop up the savory juices.

Prince Boreas, Lord Tama, and Lord Shuji had politely refrained from starting their own meals until the rest of us received our food. Now, they finally began eating.

After chewing and swallowing a few disgusting mouthfuls of raw beef, Boreas turned to me. "I don't know what kind of game you're playing, pretty boy. But stay away from Jacinthe."

"Or what?" I challenged him.

His wide mouth twisted in a snarl.

I hastily clapped my hand over his wrist and siphoned off a potent surge of rage before he attacked me.

Then, both Lord Tama and Lord Shuji began coughing uncontrollably.

Lord Shuji's face darkened. His cough turned to a wheeze. Then he fell forward onto the table.

Thanks to my years at Father's court, I instantly recognized the cause.

Poison!

Chapter 23

Gwydion

I ruthlessly drew on the Wind-Walker's power as I chanted a vomiting charm.

Tama's coughing turned into a sputter. He promptly spewed a watery mix of fish, seaweed shreds and water over the table.

With lightning reflexes, the three Djinn sprang back from the table. They got out of range just in time.

"What the fuck are you doing?" Boreas roared, trying to yank his hand from my grasp.

His powerful voice ripped through the din of conversation, leaving silence in its wake. Everyone turned to look at us.

The hall fell silent.

All conversation in the hall came to a dead halt as Tama continued to cough in between spasms of vomiting.

Did I expel the poison from him in time?

Then I saw fat coils of pus-yellow magic winding around his chest and neck. And I realized that this was a two-pronged attack: poison *and* a powerful curse.

An assassination attempt worthy of Father's courtiers.

I drew more magic from the Wind-Walker and forced the curse back.

"What the fuck is going on?" Boreas demanded, still trying to free his hand. Moon and stars, the Wild-Walker was strong, even bound to human shape! "What are you doing to me?"

With Tama temporarily out of danger, I released him and shot to my feet. I ignored him and everyone else staring at us.

I raced around the table, to where Lord Shuji lay collapsed on the lavender and rosemary-covered floor.

Arslan was already kneeling next to the fallen sea-brother. Shuji's labored wheezes told me that the lethal combination of poison and magic was choking the life out of him.

On the dais, Lord Roderigo began shouting orders. A babble of questions and comments from the banquet's other guests almost drowned out his powerful voice.

I fell to my knees beside the merman.

"Will you help me save him?" I asked Arslan urgently.

The Djinn nodded. I took his hand and drew on him as I worked to expel the poison and push back the curse.

But my efforts came too late.

Instead of expelling the poisoned food he'd eaten, Shuji began convulsing and gasping pitifully for air. The evil yellow coils of magic continued to tighten inexorably around his throat, and I couldn't draw enough power from Arslan to loosen it.

If only we weren't wearing these damned earrings!

Then the sea-brother's convulsions stopped. He abruptly went limp. I heard his long, whistling exhale, and my heart sank. It was a sound I knew all too well.

His heart sputtered to a stop, and his spirit fled with the last of the air in his lungs. He did not inhale again.

No! I pounded his chest with my fist, willing his heart to restart as I poured power into him.

My damned earring flared with painful heat as I drew mercilessly on the Djinn's inner fires to reunite Shuji's spirit and flesh. Its glow cast cold blue-white light over the merman I was working to save.

Suddenly, Arslan's hand slipped out of my hold. The flow of life-saving magic instantly ceased, and the light from my earring winked out.

"What are you doing?" I reached for him again.

"Enough, Fae." Arslan's face looked bloodless beneath the smooth brown of his skin. His dark eyes were sunken and dull. The long egret feathers in his cap trembled as his teeth chattered. "The sea-brother is gone. He will not return now."

I hated that he was right.

Cursing, I sat back on my heels. Its task completed, the ugly coil of the strangling curse dissipated into nothingness.

I'd failed. Utterly.

But was Tama still alive? As I looked over at him, I found him slumped in his chair but still breathing, though his pale lips had a blue-gray tint to them.

Urgency drove me up to my feet.

As I sprinted around the table, Prince Boreas shoved back his chair and rose. He bent and lifted his friend in his arms, then gave me a baleful stare. "Fae, is this *your* work?"

I shook my head. "No! I swear to you, I'm trying to help him!"

"Apprentice Gwydion, what's going on?" asked a familiar voice, blurred with drink.

I turned to see Healer-Mage Armand staggering toward us. "What's happening here?"

With disgust, I noted the dark wine stains spotting the front of the ancient healer's russet tunic and drooping lace cuffs.

The old man wouldn't be any help to Tama in this state. Or to me.

Armand's advanced age and poor health made it too dangerous to draw on him.

"Go back to your seat, Healer Armand," I ordered him, too frantic to make my words sound anything like orders. "I'll take care of this patient. You go enjoy the rest of the banquet."

My lineage was famous for seductive wiles, and I'd learned how to bend them to persuasion and mild compulsion. I summoned what I could to thwart my earring's restriction and gave him a small push with my will.

"Never treated a merman before." Armand craned his neck to look at the table, then nodded blearily. "Very well, Apprentice. I'll check on you later."

With that, he turned and made his swaying way back to his seat.

I turned to Boreas. "If you want to help your friend," I snapped, "bring him to the infirmary."

The Wind-Walker gave me a sharp look, then nodded.

I opened the side service door. Behind me, shouts and the heavy tread of armored feet announced the guards had finally arrived.

Boreas strode past me, carrying his friend into the service corridor as if he weighed nothing. I shut the door behind us, cutting off the din of chaos and confusion.

Let the guards deal with poor Lord Shuji's corpse, I thought balefully.

I hoped his death ruined the human and Fae princesses' enjoyment of the banquet's remaining courses.

But I wasn't counting on it.

∞∞∞

"Prince Boreas, I need your help to save your friend," I told the Wind-Walker a few minutes later.

When we walked into the infirmary, he'd placed Tama in the bed nearest the door. I was now pouring a vile potion of activated charcoal and herbs down the merman's throat to neutralize any remaining poison in his stomach.

Boreas and my fellow infirmary apprentice, Lord Ilhan of Parrish, both hovered near the bed, watching my every move.

"Of course," he rumbled. "You don't have to ask."

I glanced at Ilhan. He'd followed us from the Great Hall to the infirmary, then fetched the ingredients for the antidote potion on my orders without protest.

Now, he hovered on the other side of the bed, studying Tama with a frown as the merman continued to struggle to breathe.

Up to this point, I'd concealed my ability to override my earring's restriction spell. But after my very public demonstration at the banquet just now, there wasn't any point in trying to keep it a secret from my fellow apprentice any longer.

"It's dangerous," I warned Boreas. "Someone not only poisoned Lord Tama's food or drink, they also placed a choking curse on him. I need to break that curse."

The Wind-Walker's eyes widened.

Ilhan nodded agreement. "It's true. I can see the spell. It's... ugly."

"Tell me how I can help," Boreas said.

"I must draw on your power again. It's a powerful curse, and thanks to these damned earrings we're wearing, I'll have to take more from you than I normally would." I met his golden eyes and added, "I already drew on you in the Great Hall to delay the curse. If I draw on you again now, I could take too much. You might even die."

There. I'd given him fair warning.

Which was more than I'd had time to do for the girl Jacinthe.

"No," Tama wheezed.

The Wind-Walker ignored the protest. His gaze narrowed. "This dangerous thing—is this what you did to Friend Jacinthe? Drained her of power?"

"I had no choice," I defended myself. "Those things were going to kill us both. It was the only chance we had to save ourselves."

He considered this for a long moment, then inclined his head. "Very well. Do whatever you need to save Friend Tama."

Tam struggled to sit up, propping himself with his arms. "No! Do not… endanger yourself… for me." Bouts of coughing interrupted his protest.

"Friend Tama," the Wind-Walker said sternly. "I will do whatever is needed. Now lie the fuck down."

The sea-brother continued to glare at Boreas.

The big man sighed, then placed his big hand in the center of Tama's chest and pushed him back down onto the straw-stuffed mattress.

Tama groaned and vainly struggled against his friend's imprisoning hold.

What depth of loyalty these friends had for each other!

I was now twice as determined to save the sea-brother and win both men's gratitude.

"Apprentice Ilhan!" I barked. "Bring a stool for Prince Boreas."

He obeyed without protest. Which was unusual for the proud young nobleman.

I pulled up another stool next to the bed and ordered Boreas, "Sit. And give me your hand."

He obeyed instantly. Our knees touched as we faced each other. I placed my other hand on Tama's chest, over his heart.

Then I took a deep breath and drew on the sun-like mass of corralled power roiling at the Wind-Walker's core. His fiery strength surged through me, and each of our earrings shone like stars as I flooded the restriction spells.

I fashioned a knife made of Dragon-fire and sliced through the swollen coils of the curse.

My desperation grew as time after time, the magic flowed together and re-knit after each cut.

I needed to burn it all away in a single blast. I reached deep into Boreas' rapidly shrinking sun to pull more power.

"Senior Apprentice Gwydion, stop!" Ilhan's powerful hands closed on my shoulders. He shook me hard. "You're killing him!"

I came back to myself. I looked at the Wind-Walker and swore. I tried to break his grasp.

But Boreas' fingers, now icy, clamped stubbornly around mine.

"No! Save him!" His powerful voice had dwindled to a raspy whisper.

He swayed on the stool, looking drained and strangely gaunt. A continuous shiver shook his powerful frame.

I shook my head. "I'll kill you if I take any more."

Boreas didn't let go. "But Friend Tama," he protested.

"I'll save him," I promised recklessly. "But you have to let go of me and lie down." I pointed at the empty bed next to us.

I racked my brain for what to try next. Ilhan, though a mage, didn't have half of the Wild-Walker's raw power. Drawing on him would do little good.

Then the answer came to me.

Neither Prince Boreas nor Lord Tama would like it. But they were both too weak to stop me.

"Apprentice Ilhan," I began. "I need you to do one more thing for me."

Chapter 24

Jacinthe

"Apprentice Jacinthe?" called a male voice with a Frankish accent.

I was in the main kitchen, elbows-deep in a tub of hot, soapy water, scrubbing a never-ending succession of used dishes and utensils arriving from the Great Hall.

If preparing for the Victory Day banquet had been bad, clean-up was proving far worse.

Earlier, I had scrubbed a teetering stack of soiled pots and pans, followed by a lengthy parade of serving platters. Every time I thought I was finally done, someone promptly filled the vacated space with a fresh tower of soiled items for me to wash.

Little Rheda was paired with me as my dish-dryer. She worked industriously at my side, her tall stack of clean, dry linen towels rapidly dwindling like a patch of spring snow in sunlight.

And I wasn't the only one on cleanup duty this afternoon, either. Tubs of soapy water for washing and clear water for rinsing stood at the work stations all around the cavernous kitchen, each with a pair of apprentices to wash and dry.

At the sound of my name, I turned. And found myself face to face with Lord Ilhan of Parrish.

The big, golden-haired young man had changed out of his

black academic robe. He now wore a close-fitting, knee-length jacket in rose-red velvet that strained across his wide shoulders. Wide white lace cuffs flowed over his wrists, and more lace trimmed his jacket collar.

He was handsome, even when he was frowning at me.

What does he want now? I groaned silently at the mage-student's persistence.

I'd already told him that neither I nor my friends had had anything to do with Lady Cresta and Lord Bernardo's deaths.

"Lord Ilhan, do you need something from the kitchens?" I asked, forcing a cheerful tone. I added hopefully, "Chef Vollkorn is in the dry goods storeroom, if you need to speak with her about something."

To my dismay, he shook his head. "I need you to come to the infirmary, right now."

I froze at the urgency in his voice. "Why? What's happened?"

And why does Healer-Mage Armand need a junior kitchen apprentice when he has apprentices of his own? I wondered.

Lord Ilhan's frown deepened. "Damned if I know why you're needed. But both of the Merfolk collapsed at the banquet, and one of them died."

He'd garnered a few curious looks when he entered the kitchen, but everyone was too busy working frantically to keep up with the flow of incoming items to stop what they were doing for a mere student.

Now, at this grim announcement, everyone halted to listen to us.

Tama! Shock punched my stomach and drove all the air from my lungs. I grabbed the edge of the counter to keep my suddenly weak knees from collapsing under me.

Lord Ilhan swept his brawny arm around my waist, holding me upright. "Lord Shuji's the one who died," he informed me. "Gwydion the Fae told me to fetch you. Says he needs your help to treat the *other* one." His handsome features twisted in distaste. "Lord Tama."

Tama is still alive! I remembered how to breathe. *Divine Mother, thank you!*

I tried to step away so that I could run to the infirmary. But Ilhan held onto me.

"I don't know what that Fae wants from you," he said, his voice low, urgent. "But he practically killed the Dragon just now with some kind of foul magic. The Divine Mother only knows what he plans for *you*."

I stared at him in disbelief. Ilhan was trying to *protect* me? But he thought I was a murderer who wanted revenge on his sister!

He shook his head, apparently misinterpreting my look. "Look, Apprentice, you don't have to go. I could always tell Gwydion I couldn't find you." He removed his arm from my waist and swept his hand around the bustling kitchen. "I mean, *look* at this place. It's busy enough that no one would question it."

"Lord Tama's my *friend,* Lord Ilhan," I said, grabbing for a dish towel and drying my hands. "I'll do *anything* Gwydion asks of me."

Ilhan shook his head. "'Never trust a Fae,'" he quoted, and added, "Especially *that* Fae. He's a sneaky bastard. I've worked with him for months, and just found out he's been hiding things from us. Important things."

"I don't care," I said.

I looked around and spotted Elswyth entering the kitchen with a fresh load of used serving dishes. "Elswyth, please tell Chef I've been called away. It's an emergency!"

"Is it Lord Tama?" she asked. "Everyone's saying that he and Lord Shuji fell suddenly ill at the banquet."

"Yes," I said. "Can you please take over washing these dishes?"

She nodded. "Anything to help Lord Tama."

Without waiting for Lord Ilhan, I picked up my skirts and ran out of the kitchen.

∞∞∞

All praise to the Divine Mother, Tama was still alive when I arrived, panting, in the infirmary ward.

Lord Ilhan was close on my heels as I reached the top of the stairs and burst through the open doorway.

The late afternoon sun cast its golden rays through the ward's tall arched windows. It glowed off plain whitewashed walls, bathing the room in a warm, peaceful glow that belied the tense situation.

Tama and Boreas lay unmoving in adjoining beds. They both looked terrible. And both were deeply unconscious.

Tama struggled to breathe, and the sounds of his painful, wheezing gasps tore at my heart. I saw a putrid yellow cloud of magic gathered around his chest and throat.

Gwydion sat on a stool between them, frowning in concentration. His earring glowed softly, and a faint silvery aura spilled from his long fingers as they rested lightly over the pulse-point on Tama's throat.

The yellow spell-cloud parted and drew away from whatever magic Gwydion worked, but his working appeared too weak to do more than hold it at bay.

He looked up at the clatter of my wooden clogs against the

flagstone floor. "You're here!" His relief was unmistakable.

"How can I help?" I asked, seating myself on an empty stool next to Tama's bed and facing Gwydion.

I reached out and took Tama's stiff hand in mine. I squeezed lightly, letting him know I was there. His clawed, webbed fingers twitched in response, but he didn't have the strength to close them.

Ilhan hovered nearby, arms crossed belligerently over his chest, scowling down at us.

Maybe he's hoping Tama dies, because then his sister will be safe.

But if that was the case, then why had he fetched me from the kitchens? He could've simply pretended he couldn't find me.

In response to my question, Gwydion licked his lips. His strange, beautiful silver eyes examined me gravely. "Remember what I did when we fought those monkey-demons?"

"*What* monkey-demons?" demanded Lord Ilhan. "What are you talking about?"

Gwydion and I both ignored him.

I nodded, suddenly understanding why Gwydion had summoned me. And why Ilhan was so worried.

I glanced at Boreas, noting his condition. If a Dragon's powerful magic couldn't banish the curse, then how could I? I wasn't a mage! Not anywhere close.

"Take whatever you need to save Tama," I told Gwydion recklessly.

Gwydion nodded. He held out his hand, and I took it without hesitating.

Just like before, his touch burned coldly against my skin,

numbing me.

"Ready?" he murmured.

I nodded, took a deep breath, and tried to relax.

Gwydion said something in his native language, and the same current of fiery energy I'd felt before surged through me like a torrent of molten gold.

Once again, hundreds of invisible needles pierced every inch of my skin, and my tattoo burned with an almost unbearable heat. My indenture collar vibrated with a high, piercing note that echoed through the long stone chamber.

Gwydion's earring sprang to brilliant life. His eyes half-closed and his head lolled back. He moaned, a low, sensual sound that thrilled through my nerves.

Blinding silver fire wreathed his free hand as he touched his fingers to Tama's throat once more. It instantly burned away the evil yellow fog of magic where it touched.

In response, the remaining cloud of magic billowed and surged to close the gaps Gwydion created.

He snarled another incantation.

The pain surrounding me suddenly increased tenfold. It felt like I was simultaneously being flayed and burned alive.

Gwydion's icy hand locked around mine in a bruising grip as I arched in spasms of agony. A scream tore free of my throat. Blinding flurries of blue and gold sparks raced across my vision as my world shrank.

"Stop it!" I heard Ilhan shout. He sounded so far away…

Darkness closed in around me, mercifully banishing the pain until it was only a distant tingle. I felt like I was weightless and floating in a freezing black winter sea.

Shockingly warm hands locked around my upper arms, yanking me back to the sunlit infirmary ward.

"Prince Gwydion, *you're killing her*!" Lord Ilhan growled in my ear. "Stop! Or I'll snap your scrawny neck!"

The rush of fiery energy abruptly stopped. The sharp tingling and burn faded.

I wanted to see what was happening, but I didn't have the energy to open my eyes. I drooped against the strong hands holding me upright.

"It worked." Gwydion sounded almost drunk as he added dreamily, "By the moon and stars, I've never felt anything like your power, Jacinthe."

I forced my eyes open. Tama lay peacefully asleep, his breaths free of that awful wheeze. No trace of the foul cloud remained.

"Oh, good," I breathed. "Thank you, Gwydion."

The hands still holding me upright gave me a tiny shake. "What are you thanking *him* for?" Lord Ilhan demanded. "He nearly drained the life out of you!"

"Hardly," drawled Gwydion, a foolish smile stretching his beautiful mouth. "You would not believe how much power she has! I've never seen anything like it!" He slanted a heated look at me through his ridiculously long lashes. "You are *delicious*, Jacinthe."

"Ugh, Fae pervert! Come on, Jacinthe." Lord Ilhan lifted me to my feet, but then had to hold me when my legs wobbled and collapsed beneath me.

"She'll be fine after some food and a nap," slurred Gwydion, still smiling. "They'll *all* be fine."

"Yeah, yeah, you're a miracle-worker," Lord Ilhan said in disgust. He picked me up and carried me over to the next empty bed, then gently put me down. "I'll get you some honey-water," he said in a much gentler tone as he drew off my clogs. "It'll help restore your strength."

I tried to smile up at him. "You're much nicer than I expected," I blurted.

Sleep dragged me under before he returned with the honey-water.

∞∞∞

An unknown time later, I opened my eyes to candlelight and a divinely savory fragrance.

Night had fallen while I napped. Shadows curtained the vaulted stone ceiling high overhead.

I blinked up at it, disoriented. Where was I? This wasn't the apprentice dormitory!

"How are you feeling, sweet Jacinthe?" Gwydion asked. "Ready for some soup? It will restore you."

He seated himself on the edge of my bed, a bowl and spoon in his hand.

Memory returned in a rush. I turned my head to look for Boreas and Tama, and found them in the neighboring beds.

Dressed only in his long linen undershirt, Boreas sprawled on his back, long arms and legs hanging off the edges of the mattress. He was snoring gently.

Beyond him, I saw Tama awake and sitting up against a pile of pillows. Lord Ilhan sat at Tama's side, offering him something from a glazed beaker.

"It was a close call, but Lord Tama will recover in a day or two," Gwydion said, following my gaze. "The Wind-Walker will be fine as soon as he wakes up and eats something. I'll send Ilhan down to the kitchen for meat."

Lord Ilhan turned to glare at us. "Get it yourself. I'm not your servant, *Prince* Gwydion."

"True. And your assistance was greatly appreciated during this crisis, my lord," Gwydion responded with a courtesy that bordered on mockery. "I will not ask you to humble yourself further to aid our patient's recovery."

He dipped the spoon into the bowl and offered it to me. I pushed myself up to a sitting position and reached for it, but Gwydion shook his head.

"Allow me," he said, touching the warm spoon to my lower lip.

I was too weak to argue with him. I opened my mouth and sucked the soup from the spoon.

It was a simple beef-and-barley soup, but I'd never tasted anything so delicious… or been so ravenously hungry.

A few spoonfuls later, I realized Gwydion's gaze was fastened to my lips as I closed them around the spoon.

And that I wore only my thin, nearly transparent, oft-laundered chemise. Someone had undressed me while I slept, and my apron and gown, with its stiffened bodice, hung from pegs on the wall.

Lord Ilhan snorted. "Fine. I'll go to the fucking kitchens as soon as I finish giving Lord Tama here his medicine."

He stomped out a few minutes later, leaving Tama peacefully asleep once more.

Gwydion finished feeding me. The warmth from the hot soup expanded from my stomach, relaxing me.

"You need more sleep," he said, setting aside the bowl and spoon.

I didn't resist when he pushed me back down on the mattress.

By accident or design, his knuckles brushed the tips of my breasts as he pulled the coverlet up to my chin. My nipples stiffened instantly, and a sensual jolt shot down to the place between my legs, instantly igniting a slow, hot pulse there.

To my embarrassment, Gwydion noticed my reaction. His mouth curved in a wicked smile that sent heat rushing to my cheeks.

He bent to brush his warm lips lightly against mine in a chaste kiss as gentle as the stroke of a butterfly's wing.

"Sweet dreams," he whispered against my mouth.

His perfume of meadowsweet and sun-warmed grass wound around my senses until I floated on a warm, sensual cloud.

Then he kissed me again. His mouth was still gentle, but not at all chaste this time.

"I can feel you burning for me, sweet girl." His voice was the merest breath of sound as his hand slid beneath the coverlet. "Here, let me give you what you need."

We shouldn't be doing this. Not with Tama and Boreas here, right next to us.

But that thought drowned in a flood of pure need as his hand cupped my breast and stroked the sensitive tip through the thin fabric of my chemise.

Heat shot through me. The hungry pulse between my thighs transmuted into a throbbing ache.

I whimpered and arched into his clever fingers, silently begging for more of that teasing, maddening, oh-so-pleasurable touch.

Gwydion's mouth returned to mine, his kiss harder, deeper, and more demanding now.

His hand left my breast and went lower, skimming over my stomach. His fingers curled at my hip, fisting the loose folds of my chemise. He tugged, trying to draw it up. I eagerly raised my hips to free the fabric.

Then Gwydion abruptly broke the kiss with a growl. He flew to his feet and frowned at the doorway.

"Stones and snow, who's visiting us at *this* hour?" he muttered angrily.

An instant later, I heard it, too: a heavy tread on the stairs, and the low murmur of voices.

He swiftly turned back to me and pulled the coverlet up from where it lay bunched around my waist, smoothing it over my shoulders and throat.

A moment later, a guard in an armored breastplate stepped through the door. "Her Excellency, Chatelaine Erzabetta de Norhas, honors you with her presence," he announced.

Lady Erzabetta glided into the ward with a sweep of her elegant golden satin skirts. Her gold-and-pearl hairnet gleamed in the candlelight, and more pearls shone at her ears and throat. She looked as if she'd come straight from the banquet—her cheeks were flushed with drink and her lips held a faded shadow of rouge.

Suddenly as cool and collected as if our heated encounter had never occurred, Gwydion bowed gracefully. "Lady Erzabetta, what brings you here at this hour?"

She blinked at him owlishly. "I am concerned about Lord Tama's health," she declared. "How is he?"

Your concern apparently didn't extend to leaving the banquet early, I thought.

"He survived a dose of poison *and* a curse-spell, and will make a full recovery," Gwydion reported, his tone as dry as dust.

An old man, his fine clothes stained with food and wine, and his velvet beret askew on thinning silver hair, staggered through the doorway. After a moment, I recognized Healer-Mage Armand, out of his usual robes.

He stopped, clutching the carved stone doorframe, and surveyed the ward and its three patients.

"Good, good job, my boy. Knew you'd save that poor creature," he slurred, flinging a hand in Gwydion's direction. His face swung towards the chatelaine. "Best damned apprentice I've ever had. Pity he's Fae."

Lady Erzabetta grimaced, put her hands on her hips, and said stiffly, "I cannot express the depths of my anger and concern over this unfortunate incident. Poor Lord Shuji." She sighed dramatically. "Poison, you say? And vile magic? Rest assured, Roderigo and I will investigate and discover how this tragedy happened."

She's a terrible actress, I thought. Either that, or the depths of her anger and concern were extremely shallow waters.

"The same way that you and Lord Roderigo investigated all the *other* attacks on your imperial guests?" Gwydion asked sardonically. "Your failure to take any kind of action to find the culprits and prevent further attacks caused this."

Lady Erzabetta gasped in outrage. "How *dare* you speak to me like that, Prince Gwydion!"

"Do you really want to help, my lady?" Gwydion didn't move, and his expression didn't change, but he suddenly seemed intimidating, even frightening.

"Of course!" Lady Erzabetta protested. But her gaze skittered away from him.

"Good," he said coldly. "Remove my earring, then. I might've saved Lord Shuji tonight if I'd been able to freely use my magic.

You forced me to take extreme measures and risk not only my own life, but the lives of Prince Boreas and Apprentice Jacinthe as well."

"I can't remove your earring," she protested. "It's against the law. If anyone found out, they'd brand Roderigo and me as traitors. And then we'd *never* leave this damned island!"

"Then how do you propose to balance the scales of your debt, Lady Erzabetta?" Gwydion's voice cut like the winter wind now. "You and your brother both owe Lord Tama a life-debt for failing to protect him while he is a guest under your roof. You owe Prince Boreas and Apprentice Jacinthe healer-fees for their heroic efforts to save Lord Tama. And you owe *me* for crafting a cure using what the Wind-Walker and the apprentice offered me."

"Yes," croaked Tama from his bed. "I agree. You have dishonored the law of hospitality, Chatelaine Erzabetta."

"Remove the Fae prince's damned earring, Chatelaine. He deserves it for saving Friend Tama," agreed Boreas, sitting up.

Lady Erzabetta's entrance had awakened them both.

"I cannot break His Imperial Majesty's law," Lady Erzabetta insisted. The wine-flush had vanished from her cheeks, leaving her smooth olive skin sallow. "Ask me for something else. Surely there is another way to recompense you for your troubles."

Gwydion's mouth thinned. He stared at her silently for a few moments, making her drop her gaze. Then he flicked a glance in my direction.

"Very well," he said finally. "If Prince Boreas and Lord Tama agree, you can pay your debt to us by transferring Apprentice Jacinthe from the kitchens to this infirmary."

"What?" Lady Erzabetta looked as startled as if he'd asked her to kick off her pearl-encrusted shoes, lift her skirts, and dance a jig in the middle of the ward.

"She has a special gift," Gwydion answered. "I want Jacinthe to apprentice *here*, under Healer-Mage Armand."

"I agree," Tama said.

"Me, too," Boreas boomed. "Friend Jacinthe is wasted in the kitchens."

Sudden hope flared as brightly as Gwydion's earring had earlier.

I hadn't dared dream I could ever work as a healer again. And I desperately wanted to escape the unending round of drudgery of scrubbing pots and the thousand other daily tasks.

"Now wait just a minute," protested the old man. "I already have three apprentices. I don't need any more. And certainly not a scullery maid!"

Hope died like a bright star winking out of existence in the night sky.

Gwydion was kind to think of me. Of course, it was too good to be true, I told myself as seven years of indentured servitude in the castle's kitchens stretched out before me like an endless wasteland.

But my new friend wasn't prepared to give up so quickly.

"You need all the help you can get, Mage Armand," he said in a cutting tone. "And Apprentice Jacinthe has already received training as an herbalist. She will be an excellent help to us for compounding medicines. My word on it."

Was Gwydion glowing with silver light? Or was it just a trick of my eyes?

Then my skin prickled and my collar chimed softly, signaling magic's presence.

"Oh, very well," Armand said grumpily a moment later. "But I'm putting *you* in charge of training her, Apprentice Gwydion. I haven't the time."

Gwydion had freed me from the kitchens, after all! Joy and relief warmed me more than the soup had.

"I hoped you'd say that." Another graceful bow. "Thank you, Healer-Mage Armand."

Gwydion turned back to Lady Erzabetta.

In a commanding tone, he told her: "You will amend Apprentice Jacinthe's indenture contract accordingly, and enroll her in the classes she needs to certify as a healer. She claims she's not a mage, but I intend to re-test her. In the meanwhile, she should attend Beginning Surgery, Intermediate Potions, and Intermediate Herbology."

Her mouth opened, but no sound came out.

He paused to think, then continued, "You will also supply her with academic robes, a library pass, notebooks, pens, ink, and everything else a student might need. And inform Master Chef Vollkorn that Apprentice Jacinthe is transferring out of the kitchen's dormitories immediately."

The chatelaine stiffened in shock and distaste. For a terrible moment, I thought she would refuse his requests out of insulted pride.

Then she raised her chin, looked at Gwydion, Boreas, and Tama, and sniffed like someone whose patience had been sorely tested. "And if I agree to all this, your precious scales will balance?"

Gwydion inclined his head. "They will."

"Your dishonor will be erased," said Tama.

"The wax melted and the tablet smoothed," agreed Boreas.

"Very well," snapped the chatelaine. "All will be done as you requested." She nodded stiffly at Tama. "My lord, I apologize for your trouble, and I wish you a full recovery from your ordeal." Her tone was flat, leached of all emotion.

Then she spun on her heel in a whirl of satin skirts and glided out of the ward. The guard followed, holding Armand's elbow to help the old man down the stairs.

I wondered if the chatelaine had even noticed my presence while Gwydion negotiated for my future.

"You will all sleep here tonight, where I can keep an eye on you," the Fae said briskly. "Jacinthe, if you're feeling fully recovered in the morning, you can move your belongings from the kitchen dormitory to your new quarters. The other apprentices live in student apartments, so you'll have your pick of rooms here in the infirmary building." His smile quirked. "With a door that locks for privacy."

A room of my own again! On top of all the other good fortune heaped in my lap just now! I couldn't believe this was really happening.

"Thank you," I said to my friends. "I don't know what to say, except all of you have made my dreams come true. My mother was a healer, and I've always wanted to be one, too."

"It was a fair reckoning, Friend Jacinthe," Boreas said with a dismissive wave of his hand. "Promise you'll still come to visit us in the gatehouse."

"Of course," I promised, then looked at Gwydion. "If that's all right with you, Senior Apprentice. I need to bring Tama his tea every morning."

Gwydion nodded. "I'll show you where to find the ingredients in the pharmacy."

"You risked much to save me," Tama said gravely. "And you will make a fine healer."

"And I owe *you* extra thanks," I told Gwydion.

His mouth tugged up into a smile. Unlike his previous smiles, this one seemed almost shy. "I'm happy I could repay you the debt I owed you for your help in fending off those monkey-demons. Now the scales are balanced, are they not?"

I wondered if his kindness just now had only been because of that debt.

Then I thought about all the things he could have requested from Lady Erzabetta. Yet, when she refused to grant him the thing he really wanted, his next thought had been to give me this precious gift.

Gwydion was a strange mixture of kindness, strength, unsettling flirtation, and strange power. Like Tama and Boreas, he was proud to the point of arrogance, and profoundly alien in some ways.

And like Tama and Boreas, I now felt I could trust Gwydion with my life.

I reached for his hand, which was burning cold once more. "Yes, the scales are balanced, my friend."

His smile blossomed into incandescence. He raised my hand to his lips and kissed my work-roughened knuckles. "I'm honored to be your friend, Jacinthe." His light, beautiful voice was roughened with emotion.

"You are my friend now also, for saving Friend Tama," Boreas said, grinning.

"I would gladly call you friend, forest-brother," Tama agreed.

"Friends." Gwydion beamed at us, glowing faintly silver in the flickering candlelight.

At that moment, Ilhan returned from his errand, carrying a

covered bowl. He looked at us and frowned. "Why is everyone awake? Did I miss something?"

Chapter 25

Jacinthe

Leaving the kitchen apprentices' dormitory on the morning of my eighteenth birthday was the best present I'd ever received.

At breakfast, Master Chef Vollkorn, the cooks and most of the apprentices wished me luck in my new apprenticeship. Only Jonitha, Charmaine, and their little coterie sent me sour looks from their end of the table.

I didn't care what they thought. I was Infirmary Apprentice Jacinthe now.

After breakfast, I returned to the dormitory and stripped my bed, taking the bundled sheets and pillowcases over to the dormitory's huge laundry sack.

On laundry days, the sack's contents were tipped out the window into a waiting cart below and taken away. If working in the castle's kitchens was hard, working in the hot, steamy laundry amidst giant cauldrons filled with boiling soap water had to be ten times worse.

Still dressed in my kitchen uniform of dark blue gown, long white apron and white cap, I packed up my belongings in a sack, and carried it downstairs.

Two small figures waited for me at the base of the stairs.

"Miss Jacinthe, I'm glad you get to be a healer now. But I wish you didn't have to leave us!" Elswyth said, hugging me.

Rheda came to hug me, too. Tears glistened on her cheeks.

"Please come back to visit us!"

"I'll miss both of you, too," I said, bending to kiss each of them on their foreheads. "And I promise I'll come see you on my first day off."

A short time later, I stepped into the infirmary ward, this time as an apprentice rather than a patient. My heart swelled with happiness and gratitude. I still couldn't believe I was finally free from the relentless toil of the castle kitchen.

A double row of beds lined the long room on either side of a wide center aisle.

Tama and Boreas had both been discharged from the infirmary this morning. Now, the ward held three new patients. I spotted a young man lying on his back, with a broken right leg bound in splints and elevated using a pulley and frame.

Nearby, a young woman wearing livery had a bulging lump on her jaw, likely an abscess. She was arguing with Lord Ilhan as he earnestly explained why he needed to pull her infected tooth.

"But how am I supposed to chew my bread!" she demanded. "I ain't got but two teeth left on that side of my mouth!"

"Ah, Jacinthe, welcome!" Gwydion looked up from his work and greeted me with a brilliant smile. "I'll be with you in a moment."

He sat on a stool, facing an older man with tanned, deeply-weathered features. Gwydion's patient looked like he'd been on the wrong end of a fight, with a black eye and a line of neat stitches across his forehead.

A curved suture needle flickered between Gwydion's fingers as he quickly stitched a second deep cut over the man's cheekbone.

I lowered my belongings to the floor and took a moment to

study my benefactor.

At this moment, Gwydion's features looked serene, and his low voice was soft with compassion as he reassured his patient that he was nearly done.

I hadn't been able to stop thinking about how sweetly he'd kissed me last night, or how eager I'd been for his touch.

Shame and curiosity battled inside me. A fortnight ago, I'd never even been kissed, much less imagined that two different men could awaken such intense needs in me.

Now, I dreamed of both of them. But neither of them was human. I was painfully aware they were both forbidden to me. And then there was Boreas… I loved his vitality, his brashness, his good humor, and his unabashed loyalty. I could easily fall for him, as well, if he ever displayed any sign that he considered me more than merely "Friend Jacinthe." Gwydion tied off the last suture. "Stablemaster, may I suggest you avoid the rear end of a mule in the future?" His tone was light as he dabbed a thick layer of salve over the stitched cuts.

"Prince Gwydion, I thank ye kindly for the advice, but mules can kick in all directions if they please," his patient replied dryly. His mouth pulled into a smile. "You've a fine touch, laddie. I've had more stitches than a quilt during a lifetime of working with yon temperamental beasts, and this is the first time without a bit of pain. Is it a Fae charm ye worked on me?"

Gwydion returned the man's smile with a mischievous one of his own. "Something like that," he agreed. "Keep those wounds clean, and we'll see you next week to have those sutures pulled. If you notice any signs of infection, come to us immediately."

He waited until his patient had departed, then turned to me. "Let's get you settled in your new room first, then I'll give you a tour of the infirmary building. We'll check in with Healer-Mage Armand, and then we'll discuss your duties and class schedule."

He picked up my sack and headed for a door set into the far end of the infirmary. It opened onto a corridor, with more doors set on either side.

"There's no dormitory here, since Armand never takes more than three or four apprentices at a time," Gwydion explained. "The four rooms on this side of the hallway—" He tucked my bag under one arm and pointed to the left. "Are all empty. Pick whichever you want." His hand swept to the right, and pointed to each door in turn. "Linen storage, cleaning supplies, infirmary kitchen, garderobe. As the junior apprentice, you'll be changing the bed-linens and cooking meals for patients as part of your duties."

He cast me an assessing glance, waiting for my reaction.

I nodded. "I used to do those things back home as my mother's assistant."

Preparing food for a few patients was light duty when compared to feeding an entire castle. And changing linens and bandages didn't bother me. I'd done plenty of that in Bernswick, and without the benefit of a castle laundry.

"Good." Gwydion led me to the last door on the left. "How about this room? It's far enough from the ward that the patients won't disturb you if you're off-duty. And the garderobe is just across the hall."

"Having my own room again will be a luxury," I said. That won me another smile.

He unlocked the door and presented the key to me with a flourish. "Don't lose it," he warned. "Lady Margitts has the only other copy."

We traded exaggerated shudders. I resolved to string the key around my neck, next to Tama's whale tooth pendant.

My new home was very spartan but clean and airy. A large window looked out onto the Great Hall and a sliver of the castle's second courtyard, this one cobbled. The walls were plastered a plain white, but someone had painted the ceiling-beams with leaves and flowers.

The room was furnished with a narrow bed and a straw mattress, like the ones in the dormitory, with a colorful rag-rug covering a section of the worn floorboards.

A desk and chair stood under the window, with a pair of glazed clay oil lamps on spindly metal stands on either side of the desk. A tall armoire with a cracked mirror had been placed against the wall opposite the bed. Next to it, a washstand with a chipped marble top held the usual pitcher and basin.

A long bookshelf fastened to the wall held a collection of books with worn spines.

Gwydion noticed my sudden interest. "The standard references you'll need for your classes," he explained.

He reached into his pocket and withdrew a small engraved brass plaque in the shape of a book. He handed it to me. "And here's your student library pass. After I finish showing you around the infirmary building, I'll take you over to the library to get your textbooks."

I felt the prickle of magic as my fingers closed around it. As I watched, the engraving writhed and changed. When it stopped moving, I read:

Infirmary Apprentice Jacinthe of Bernswick
Level 2 Library Access
Sponsored by Healer-Mage Niccolò Armand

"You won't need Level Three access until you're a senior student," Gwydion told me. "And Level Four access is restricted to academy instructors and mages with academy badges."

He set my sack down next to the bed, then opened the armoire. A single garment hung there: a black academic robe.

"Congratulations, Jacinthe. You've officially joined the crows."

Gwydion then proceeded to give me a quick tour of the infirmary building's ground floor, which consisted of a locked supplies storeroom and a large, well-lit work room with wide windows, long wooden counters, and glass-fronted cabinets crowded with marble mortar-and-pestle sets, beakers, pill molds, and other tools for compounding medicines.

"Time to formally introduce you to our master and remind him that you're one of his apprentices now," he said, shepherding me out of the room. He added with a roll of his eyes, "The wine fumes last night probably drove the memory out of his mind."

I felt a twinge of anxiety as Gwydion led me to Healer-Mage Armand's office. *What if the old man regrets agreeing to my apprenticeship and decides to send me back to the kitchens?*

After all the fuss made over my departure from the kitchens, if the Healer-Mage rejected me, Jonitha and Charmaine and their hangers-on would never let me forget it.

And my daily drudgery would be unbearable after this glimpse of the life I'd always wanted.

"Do you think he's still angry about being forced to accept me as an apprentice?" I asked, apprehensively.

To my relief, Gwydion shook his head. "Healer-Mage Niccolò Armand is old, doddering and nearly blind, but he's not mean-spirited. *When* he's sober, that is." He stopped walking and turned to face me. "He's brilliant, which is why I apprenticed myself to him. That, and the boredom of being an imperial *guest* was driving me mad. You'll learn a lot from him."

"I hope so," I said. I remembered what Ilhan had told me about

Darkstone Academy being a dumping-ground for political exiles. "Why is he here?"

"Ah, now that's an interesting story. I got him drunk one night and he told me all about it." Gwydion paused in front of a red door with gold lettering reading, *Healer-Mage Niccolò Armand*.

He lowered his voice and continued, "Long story short, he was the official court healer-mage to the current dominus. Apparently, he ended up on the wrong side of that huge scandal with the Dragon King Menelaus. That was almost twenty years ago, while Menelaus was still a prince and residing in Neapolis Capitola as an imperial hostage."

I nodded. "I've heard that's why all of the imperial hostages are sent here to Darkstone Castle instead of the capital."

"I wouldn't be surprised." Gwydion opened the door to the office and ushered me inside.

I entered a spacious room crammed floor to ceiling with books, bunches of dried herbs, assorted glass vessels, seashells, rocks, and all kinds of interesting knickknacks. Disturbingly, a human skeleton joined with wires hung from a hook next to the door.

The old Healer-Mage sat at a desk piled with papers and notebooks. He held a large magnifying glass, and was squinting down at a rumpled, water-stained paper covered with scrawling lines of handwritten text.

He looked up at our entrance. "Apprentice Gwydion, who's my guest?"

"Mage, this is Jacinthe from the Western Isles, come to study with you, remember?" Gwydion announced. "Her mother was a healer-mage and trained her well, from what I've seen so far."

I held my breath, waiting for him to banish me.

Instead, his clouded brown eyes met mine, and he offered a

surprisingly warm smile.

Gwydion had called the old man senile. But I wondered whether Healer-Mage Armand might simply be going blind from cataracts on this remote island, without another qualified healer to operate on him and restore his vision.

"Ah, yes! My newest apprentice. Welcome. If you're honest and a hard worker, I'll treat you well."

I dipped into a deep curtsey, feeling dizzy with relief at his acceptance. "Thank you, Mage Armand."

"So, your mother was a Healer-Mage in the Western Isles?" he asked, shuffling through the stack of papers directly in front of him. "Tell me her name and which academy she attended. Perhaps I knew her."

Last night, he'd seemed a crotchety, doddering old man. But maybe that had been the fault of the wine. And his proximity to the unpleasant chatelaine.

"My mother is dead," I began. "But her name was Isabeau of Bernswick, though she came from somewhere in Capitola Province. She attended the Imperial Academy in Neapolis Capitola, and wore their mage badge."

"Isabeau? I never heard of a Healer-Mage Isabeau at Neapolis Capitola. And I would know—in my days as Court Healer, I kept tabs on all the students training as healer-mages, in hopes of bringing them to court. The imperial palace had a huge infirmary, you know." Mage Armand shook his head. "But I've exiled to this damned island for nearly twenty years now, thanks to that damned Dragon and the poor princess-royal. Perhaps your mother attended the academy after my time there."

My ears pricked up at his mention of Princess-Royal Jonquil, who'd died so tragically young. This was the first time I'd heard of her connection to King Menelaus.

Before I could ask him for details, the old man raised his magnifying glass and leaned forward to peer at me. "Apprentice Jacinthe, you remind me of someone I used to know, back at court." He frowned. "Something about your eyes and the shape of your face, though your complexion and hair color are regrettably foreign." He lowered the magnifying glass. "Ah well."

"I'm told that I look like my mother, though my coloring is different," I told him. Maybe he'd known Mama, after all!

Mage Armand made an absent humming noise, and reached for a paper on the top of another stack.

He offered it to me. "Your schedule of classes, Apprentice. Gwydion, be a good lad and show her around and make sure she has everything she needs."

"Yes, Mage Armand." He turned and opened the door. "I'll take her over to the library now."

We hadn't gotten far when I rounded a corner, Gwydion at my side, and almost collided with Lady Alondra.

She reeled back, her deep blue eyes widening in sudden fear as she recognized me.

Her appearance certainly had changed since the last time I saw her. She'd drawn a pair of replacements for her missing eyebrows with thick, dark lines that weren't quite symmetrical. A wide scarf wrapped around her head concealed the hair she had lost to Boreas' fire magic.

Her brother, Lord Ilhan, stood at her shoulder, eyeing me warily. I saw him take in my new academic robes before his gaze came to rest on my silver indenture collar.

I wondered what he thought about Gwydion forcing Lady Erzabetta to transfer me from serving in the kitchens to apprenticing with Mage Armand.

He spoke first. "Well, if it isn't our new apprentice. Welcome to the infirmary, Jacinthe." His tone was friendlier than I'd feared it would be.

I nodded respectfully at him. "Thank you, Lord Ilhan."

I glanced at Alondra. Her cheeks were flushed and she was studying the flagstones with great interest.

"We were just on our way to the library," I said, wanting to ease the girl's obvious discomfort at our face-to-face meeting. "If you'll excuse us, my lord and my lady?"

"Just a moment," Ilhan said. He prodded his sister's arm. "Alondra, wasn't there something you wanted say to Apprentice Jacinthe?"

Her flush deepened. I saw her hands clutch the loose folds of her black robe.

With visible effort, she raised her scarlet face to look at me. "Apprentice Jacinthe," she said, her voice barely audible. "I wanted to apologize for my behavior a fortnight ago. Cresta and Bernardo were wrong to attack you, and I regret my part in it."

Ilhan shifted his weight and hovered protectively over his much shorter sister. He fastened me with an intense stare, as if willing me to action.

In response, Gwydion edged closer to me. I hadn't expected him to show his support so openly, but I was grateful for it.

"Apology accepted," I said quickly. "And no hard feelings, Lady Alondra."

I smiled at her, hoping to convince her I wasn't holding a grudge.

She looked away, but not before I saw the tears gathering in her eyes. I realized how difficult she must have found it to apologize to a mere commoner, and an indentured servant, to boot.

"Excuse us," Ilhan said abruptly. "It is time for Alondra make her rounds in the ward."

Alondra cast one more fearful look at me before she followed her brother down the hallway, her scarf-covered head still bowed.

When they were out of sight, I turned to Gwydion.

"Well," I said with a sigh. "I guess that's that. I wonder how I can convince her that I had nothing to do with Cresta and Bernardo's deaths."

Gwydion shrugged. "Humans believe what they want to believe. Don't trouble yourself about things you can't control."

"Easier said than done." I hoped fervently that Alondra wouldn't make more trouble for me as I tried to fit in to my new role as a student at Darkstone Academy.

Chapter 26

Jacinthe

"Surprise!"

"Happy belated birthday!"

I stopped short just inside Tama's door as a chorus of voices greeted me. I'd mentioned my birthday in passing as I moved out of the kitchen dormitory, but I hadn't expected anyone to take note.

All my friends were crowded inside his main room, grinning at me. Even Tama was smiling, and the rare sight took my breath away.

It was just after dawn. I'd awakened at my usual time, and realized I had no duties until after breakfast in the Great Hall. A breakfast *I* wouldn't have to prepare, serve, or clean up.

I'd used my free time to take a bath in the academy's communal female bathroom, which was deserted at this early hour, then I'd brewed Tama's daily jug of peony root and fennel seed tisane in the infirmary's small kitchen. With an hour still to go before breakfast, I'd walked over to the castle's gatehouse to deliver the medicine.

Behind me, Guard Machry chuckled. "I let your little kitchen friends bribe me with a custard tart or three so that your fishman could play the host."

"I knew you would come to Friend Tama's rooms this morning," Boreas added. "So, your birthday celebration is here.

Even though my quarters are larger and better-furnished." He beamed down at me, his golden eyes glowing with their usual vitality.

Tama's mouth thinned in displeasure, but he didn't respond to his friend's jibe.

Rheda held up a basket of delectable tarts and my favorite sweet buns. They were filled with a crunchy mixture of toasted poppyseeds and sugary almond paste. "Pastry Chef Kalapania and the bakery apprentices wish you well, Miss Jacinthe!"

"Well, don't just stand there gawking, Jacinthe," Gwydion said with a mischievous smile. "Come in so that we may eat some of these delicious-smelling pastries."

Elswyth and Rheda passed out pastries to all the humans, plus Gwydion, and poured fresh milk from a tall jug. They had also brought raw treats for Tama and Boreas.

The poppyseed rolls were still warm, the dough flaky and buttery.

I closed my eyes in ecstasy as I chewed and swallowed. Gwydion's musical voice wove in and out of the fabric of Boreas's deep, rumbling voice as the two of them told the story of Tama's brush with death.

Gwydion and Boreas both embarrassingly gave me more credit than I deserved.

After all, it was Gwydion's quick thinking and his ability to harness whatever strange power lay dormant inside me that had saved my merman friend.

Boreas finished the tale with a flourish. "And that's why I insisted Friend Gwydion join us here this morning!"

Gwydion beamed at him. His usual cynical, flirtatious glaze disappeared from his expression to reveal something that looked like genuine happiness.

Maybe my new Fae friend had been as lonely as Tama and Boreas had been, despite having the freedom of the castle in his role as infirmary apprentice.

"Open your presents!" Kenric urged, wiping his mouth with the back of his hand. "Toland and I have to start work soon, and I want to see what you got!"

"We brought you the flowers," Toland said, his face red. "I know it's not much—"

"They're beautiful!" I interrupted him. "And so thoughtful. I'll put them in my room and think of you and Kenric every time I see them."

Thanks to the plentiful and regular meals on board the ship and here at the castle, the gaunt hollows had vanished from the taller boy's cheeks, replaced with a healthy glow under his golden tan.

"And we can't tell you what we're going to give you until you open Prince Boreas' present," added Surniva, her hand clutching something in her apron pocket.

Happiness bubbled up from deep inside me as I looked at my gathered friends.

I remembered the despair and terror I'd felt when Baldwin dragged me inside the DBA office. I couldn't have dreamed that being sent here would change my life for the better.

Rheda snatched a package from the table and thrust it at me. "Here! Start with this one!"

It was surprisingly heavy. I carefully unwrapped the cloth and found a mortar and pestle, both carved from the island's glossy black volcanic rock. It was the same incredibly hard material used to build the castle.

On the side of the bowl, someone had carved a lifelike hyacinth flower stalk emerging from a nest of long leaves and filled the incised lines with deep blue and vivid green paint.

"It's beautiful!" I exclaimed. "But how did you get this?"

"Rheda and I borrowed against our stipend money," Elswyth said. "The castle stonemason makes these in his spare time. We asked him to decorate it with a hyacinth, so that everyone would know it belonged to you."

"That must've been expensive!" I said, alarmed. "You two ought to save your money, so that you'll have a nest egg when your indentures end."

"Oh, let the girls enjoy their generosity," Gwydion chided gently. "They still have many years ahead of them to practice joyless frugality."

At his words, I felt bad for my hasty words. I smiled apologetically at them. "Thank you so much. I'll think of you both when I use it to grind the ingredients for medicine."

Elswyth and Rheda's uncertain expressions immediately changed to smiles. "So glad you like it, Miss Jacinthe!" Rheda said.

Tama gave me two gifts. The first was a more recent edition of the herbal reference book that Lady Margitts had taken. This book had a gilt-stamped leather cover and high-quality hand-colored engravings inside.

"The younglings told me Lady Margitts stole the book I gave you," he said, when I thanked him profusely.

"That was mean of her," Rheda said. "I know how much you liked that first book."

I hugged the new volume to my chest. "And I like this one even better."

Tama rewarded me with one of his rare smiles.

His second gift was a dagger with a faceted, glittering black blade set in a walrus ivory handle, with a walrus leather sheath.

I tested the dagger's wicked-looking edge with my thumb. It parted my skin with the lightest pressure, instantly raising a line of tiny blood-beads. "Where did you get this?" I asked him, alarmed.

The castle's rules forbade weapons for everyone except the guards.

"I gave him a piece of volcanic glass, and told him that glass blades are useful for surgery," Gwydion said.

"As a warrior, I was taught how to make my own weapons. Friend Gwydion suggested I fashion you a Knife-That-Heals," Tama explained.

"Thank you," I told him, clutching the now-sheathed knife to my bodice. "It's beautiful. But I'll have to hide it until I leave this island, or the guards will confiscate it."

Tama nodded gravely. "I understand."

"Speaking of beautiful," Boreas said. "Open my present next, Friend Jacinthe!"

Winifred darted forward and thrust a large, squishy package into my arms.

I unwrapped layers of linen bath towels to reveal a turquoise velvet gown fit for a noblewoman. A small cloth bag nestled in the gown's folds held silver earrings and a pair of silver cuff bracelets, both set with a geometric inlay of turquoise, mother-of-pearl, and red carnelian.

My jaw dropped. I couldn't help stroking the velvet, softer than the softest fur.

"Does it please you, Friend Jacinthe?" Boreas asked. "The jewelry comes from my hoard."

"Prince Boreas asked us to alter the gown as our gift to you!" Sunniva exclaimed.

She withdrew her hand from her pocket and showed me a tailor's measuring tape. "He said he bought it from Princess Branwen of the Fae, because she's tall and has red hair like you do."

That statement won a sharp glance and a raised brow from Gwydion.

Tama scowled at Boreas. "You suggested *small* gifts," he told the Dragon coldly.

Boreas grinned back at him unrepentantly. "Because I wanted my present to shine, Friend Tama! This gown and my silver will make everyone acknowledge Friend Jacinthe's beauty whenever she walks through the castle."

My face grew hot. Growing up, I'd been too tall and too foreign-looking for anyone in Bernswick to call me "beautiful."

Then I realized that this grand gesture would feed a fresh wave of gossip about me. "The dress is beautiful, Boreas, and so are the earrings and bracelets. But I can't possibly wear it to my classes."

"Why not?" he demanded. His grin faded. He crossed his arms over his broad chest, and his bulging arm muscles strained the sleeves of his tight-fitting tunic.

I scrabbled for a truthful answer that wouldn't hurt his feelings.

"Because I have to wear an academic gown to lectures. Also, the practicum classes for healers are messy," I explained. "I've been warned to wear a smock to my first Introduction to Surgery class because we'll be dissecting a dead pig." I shook my head. "I don't want to ruin this beautiful dress." Then inspiration struck. "But I promise I'll wear it to the Mother of Harvests banquet."

The festival celebrated the end of summer and the autumn equinox. And for this banquet, I'd be sitting with the guests in the Great Hall, not sweating in the kitchen.

My answer seemed to please Boreas. "You will sit at my side?"

"And mine?" Tama asked. He shot Boreas a fierce look.

"Gladly," I replied. "I'll sit between you and we'll enjoy the banquet together."

That seemed to please them.

I noticed the amused smile on Gwydion's face as he watched my two friends compete for my attention. "May I also join you? I'd much prefer to feast with friends than my fellow Fae."

"Of course, Friend Gwydion," Boreas and I said at the same time. We laughed, and Tama nodded at the Fae.

My last gift came from Gwydion.

It was a locking healer's box, with compartments for pills and herbs, a velvet-lined tray to hold medical instruments, and padded dividers to hold potion bottles and ointment containers. He'd carved the lid and the sides of the box with lifelike representations of the most common medicinal herbs of the Western Isles. A pair of blooming hyacinths framed the brass lock plate on the front.

The little gathering dispersed soon after that. My apprentice friends had to return to their work, and I wanted to fortify myself with breakfast before my first lecture at Darkstone Academy.

Winifred and Sunniva quickly took my measurements, then bundled up the beautiful velvet gown so that they could work on the alterations in their spare time.

I locked the beautiful, forbidden obsidian dagger and jewelry bag inside the healer's box. Gwydion walked by my side, carrying the jug with my flowers.

We were crossing the rose garden courtyard on our way back to the infirmary building when he said, "You know they're both courting you, don't you?"

"Who's courting me?" I asked, puzzled.

"Oh, don't play the fool, Jacinthe," he said impatiently. "Boreas and Tama, of course. By accepting their gifts just now, you agreed to accept them as suitors."

"Very funny." I rolled my eyes. "Even if it weren't against the law, I can't imagine an actual prince like Boreas would be interested in wedding a lowly indentured servant."

"What about Tama?" He tilted his head.

I didn't want to talk about my feelings for Tama. Or what wearing his Kujiranokiba pendant meant beyond symbolizing his offer to protect me.

"*You* gave me a birthday gift," I pointed out, then added sarcastically, "Does that mean you're courting me, too?"

Gwydion's smirk deepened. He clapped a hand over his heart and bowed with a courtier's grace. "I would be *delighted* if my lady Jacinthe would permit me to pay my addresses as her suitor," he said, using the most formal Capitolan phrasing.

I sighed, tired of his teasing. I'd already heard some of the salacious rumors circulating about me and my friends, and the Divine Mother only knew what *else* people were saying about me. "Please don't mock me, Gwydion."

Gwydion's smile vanished. "I wasn't mocking you," he protested. "Remember, Boreas gave you jewelry. Why *else* would a Dragon part with anything from his precious hoard, if not for courtship?"

My face heated under his knowing glance. "Because he's extremely competitive? You saw how he wanted to outshine Tama and everyone else just now. 'Small gifts,'" I quoted.

"A nice explanation for everything except the most important part," Gwydion said.

His smirk returned as he waited for me to ask.

I was tired of this game. It *had* to be a game, because if Gwydion was right, I might be at risk of losing one of my friends. "All right, what's 'the most important part'?" I asked, taking the bait.

"I read their auras," Gwydion said smugly. "They are both attracted to you. Sexually," he added, in case I hadn't understood his point. Then his smile returned. "As am I. Please consider me."

He resumed walking, leaving me staring after him. My thoughts whirled like snowflakes caught in a strong wind, then melted in the heat of my sudden, fevered rush of sensual memories.

I already knew Tama had feelings for me beyond mere friendship. As I did for him. He was beautiful. I trusted him. He made me feel safe. He was the first man who'd ever kissed me, and I craved more from him.

Boreas intrigued me. His human shape was attractive. He exuded vitality and good humor. He was loyal and strong and honorable. But he'd never flirted with me—that I'd noticed—or given me any sign that he wanted to kiss me.

And then there was Gwydion. I hadn't been able to stop thinking about his wickedly skilled lips on mine, or how he'd made me burn when he caressed my breast.

Two nights ago, I'd been ready—no, *eager*—to let this Fae prince do whatever he wanted with me. Never mind that

Boreas and Tama had been asleep in the nearby beds!

My face burned with the memory of that night. I ought to be ashamed of myself. Instead, I wanted to kiss him again. And kiss Tama, too. It was confusing. How could I yearn after two different men at the same time?

Gwydion noticed I was still standing in the middle of the courtyard.

He returned to my side. "Oh, sweet Jacinthe. I see that I've upset you."

He took my arm, the burning cold of his touch numbing my skin, and gently urged me to continue walking.

"Talk to me," he urged. "I'm your friend, after all. Perhaps I can offer you some clarity with whatever dilemma you're wrestling."

Soft warmth caressed me like a summer breeze. My skin tingled gently, and suddenly, blessed calm washed over me, smoothing my inner turmoil.

I like Gwydion. And trust him, I thought fuzzily. *I should ask for his advice.*

"So, tell me, Jacinthe. What's troubling you?" His voice was low and soothing.

I blinked, trying to remember why I'd been so torn a few moments ago.

"If what you said was true, then how am I supposed to pick one of you?" I asked plaintively.

"You favor all three of us equally, then?"

I nodded. I could tell him anything, and he'd understand. He wouldn't judge. Because he understood *me*.

"Then what's the problem?"

I blinked at him and stated the obvious. "I'm human. And you three aren't. There are *laws*." I shook my head. "Besides, if I pick one of you, it'll make trouble with the other two, if you're actually serious about courting me." Sudden tears stung my eyes. "It could never work, Gwydion. Hurting you—*any* of you—would break my heart! And I'd lose you as friends!"

He squeezed my arm comfortingly. "Never mind that stupid law. I've learned how things work in this castle. A few bribes here and there, and the castle guards won't see or hear anything, as long as you're reasonably discreet."

I stared at him. "Now why didn't I think of bribery?" I asked sarcastically. "Oh, right, because I don't have any money!"

I thought of my pitifully small store of coins, all of them gifts from Tama. My apprentice stipend wouldn't arrive until the end of the month, and it was just a token sum.

Any guard in his right mind would laugh if I tried to bribe him into risking a flogging or worse for a few denarii.

"I'm rich," Gwydion said airily. "And Boreas has his hoard. Not sure about Tama, but his clothes are fine enough that he's probably got some wealth tucked away somewhere." He shifted the jug of flowers to the crook of his elbow and snapped his fingers. "There, problem solved. What else troubles you, my sweet?"

I bit my lip. And blurted, "But which one of you should I pick?"

Gwydion chuckled. "Why not pick all of us?" he asked in a light tone.

Shock arrowed through me. "*All* of you?" I asked incredulously.

Certainly, there were men in some lands who kept multiple wives or concubines. But I'd never heard of a woman doing anything like that.

"Why not? I wouldn't mind sharing you with the Wind-Walker

and the sea-brother if it meant that we could be together." Gwydion sounded so matter-of-fact. "And I suspect we could convince the two of them to join us."

"I—I don't know." Despite their friendship, neither Tama nor Boreas seemed like the type to share. In my experience, they were both proud and possessive.

And Gwydion's suggestion was, at the very least, highly scandalous. For humans, anyway.

I realized I knew nothing about how the Fae conducted their love lives. Perhaps this kind of arrangement was considered normal for them.

"Well, think on it, sweet Jacinthe. There's no hurry." His smile turned wry. "It's not as if any of us are leaving this desolate island anytime soon."

He released his hold on me. My strange feeling of serenity vanished, and all my doubts and fears returned in a rush.

I frowned at him, unsettled. "You did something to me, just now, didn't you? Some kind of spell. I felt magic."

His brows shot up. "I didn't realize you were a sensitive." Then he shrugged. "It was just a little charm to help you unburden yourself."

Betrayal felt a kick in the gut. The Fae had a reputation for all kinds of charms and glamors, but he was supposed to be my *friend*.

He began to turn away, clearly done discussing it.

But I wasn't done. Anger rose inside me, quickly replacing the hurt.

"*Gwydion*," I said through gritted teeth.

"Yes?" He gave me a look of innocent inquiry.

"Are you *really* my friend?"

I saw a flicker of alarm before his usual cynical mask reappeared. His fine, pale-green brows rose. "Of course I am, sweet Jacinthe. Why do you ask?"

"Because friends don't put spells on friends to… to force them to obey!" I looked him in the eye. An enraging thought occurred to me. "Did you put a charm on me two nights ago, in the infirmary? When you kissed me?"

"You're angry." He looked surprised and hurt. I felt an instant of regret, then realized he hadn't answered my question.

"Did. You. Put. A. Charm. On. Me?" I repeated, my throat tight with rage.

"Did you know your eyes turn gold when you're angry?" he said softly. "So fierce. So beautiful. Perhaps you are Djinn princess in disguise, after all."

I refused to be distracted. His evasions were an answer, but I needed to hear him admit what he'd done to me.

Finally, he whispered, "Yes. Just a small charm."

"Friends don't do things like that to their friends," I said. Hurt joined the mix of anger and betrayal.

"But I didn't force you to do anything you didn't want to do," Gwydion argued. "I just eased your resistance to acting on your desires."

"I can't be friends *or* lovers with someone I don't trust," I told him bluntly. And saw my words hit home, finally.

"Oh." Gwydion's usual air of confidence melted away, leaving him with an expression of uncertainty.

"I trust Tama and Boreas," I continued. "Because I know they'd never betray me. Frustrate me beyond patience, yes, but never stab me in the back. But *you*—" I pointed at him, shaking with emotion. "How can any of us trust you if you're willing to use your magic to get your way? To convince us to act when we might have restrained ourselves?"

I remembered how he'd defused Boreas and Tama's angry reactions at their first meeting, and added, "Or to restrain us when we want to act."

"I—I only wanted to help." Gwydion looked miserable now. "To make things easier for all of you by smoothing away certain obstacles in your paths."

"And thereby help yourself, too," I pointed out.

He bowed his head, and his shining, leaf-colored hair fell forward to veil his expression. "Yes. I'm sorry."

"If you're sorry, then why in the name of the Divine Mother did you do it?" I demanded.

"All my life, I've had to use my powers to protect myself. I didn't even think… but no, I—I cannot excuse my betrayal. I can only apologize." His musical voice was low and ragged now. "I'm very sorry, Jacinthe. I've behaved badly. I've been a poor friend, indeed."

"Will you promise never to do it again to any of us?" I pressed.

This time, Gwydion didn't hesitate or try to evade. "I swear on my honor never to use magic to influence your will or the will of anyone else kindly disposed towards me, without permission."

He looked up. His silver eyes were brimming with tears and filled with anguish. "I'm sorry I couldn't be a genuine friend to you. I didn't know how, because I've never had real friends before."

My anger slid away at the sight of his naked pain. Convinced that he really meant his apology and his regrets, I took a deep, cleansing breath and made a decision.

"All right, how about this? I will give you another chance to be my friend."

He stared at me, wide-eyed.

"In return, prove you're trustworthy. Don't just manipulate us—*talk* to us. Let us disagree with you. And if something comes up, and you're not sure how a true friend would act… *ask*."

He swallowed hard. And continued staring at me in disbelief.

"Do you think you can do those things?" I pressed.

To my shock and embarrassment, he sank to one knee and took my hand in his deathly cold grasp. "I swear on my name and my honor, I'll be a loyal and true friend to you and the others from this moment on."

His icy lips touched the back of my hand, leaving behind a shimmering silver imprint of his mouth. It dissolved into nothingness almost instantly, but his touch lingered.

"All right, Friend Gwydion," I said, turning my hand in his and squeezing his fingers. "Let's smooth the wax on the tablet and start fresh."

We walked the rest of the way back to the infirmary building in silence, each wrapped in our own thoughts. Unburdening myself to Gwydion made me feel both better and worse.

I wished he'd given me a choice whether to confide in him rather than compelling me to speak with him.

And now I couldn't stop thinking about his suggestions that I choose all three of my suitors. It felt like the perfect solution to my dilemma.

Too bad it was impossible.

Back in my room, I stared at the presents lying on my bed, mentally grouping them into "safe to accept" and "carry an obligation" categories.

The mortar and pestle? *Definitely safe.* I placed it on my bookshelf, next to the jug of cut flowers, which were also safe.

Gwydion's beautifully crafted medical case? I stared down at it in indecision. As a healer, I would need it.

I still wasn't entirely sure if he'd been serious about being one of my suitors.

Beware the Fae bearing gifts. I sighed and regretfully ran my fingertips over the carved hyacinths. I'd have to see whether he proved himself trustworthy in the end, or if he reverted to trying to manipulate us with magic.

I opened the box and looked at the two remaining gifts.

Tama's book and volcanic glass dagger? *Carry obligations.* But I already wore his whale tooth pendant. And even if the books and dagger were truly courtship gifts, I wanted to keep them. The idea of being courted by Tama felt good. It felt *right*.

Lastly, the small bag holding the silver earrings and bracelets.

Now that Gwydion had planted the seed in my thoughts, I realized that a beautiful dress and jewelry were the most obvious courtship gifts of all the birthday presents I'd received today.

But Boreas had never shown any signs of affection beyond normal friendship.

What if Gwydion and I are assigning too much significance to these presents? What if Boreas is simply ignorant of human courtship customs?

And I couldn't return any of the gifts, not without hurting my friends' feelings or causing a rift by declaring my preference for one over the others.

I sighed, unsure about what to do.

The breakfast bell rang, its deep tone echoing off the buildings.

I put the healer's box with the dagger and the jewelry in the bottom of the armoire, placed my new book on the shelf, and donned my academic robe.

I recalled the advice I'd given Gwydion just now. *When in doubt, ask.*

I'd talk to both Tama and Boreas when I went to the gatehouse to deliver Tama's medicine tomorrow morning.

Asking them whether they had any intentions towards me beyond friendship would be an embarrassing and deeply uncomfortable conversation. But it seemed the only way to get the clarity I needed.

Chapter 27

Jacinthe

Hungry now and looking forward to breakfast, I grabbed my new notebook and pen-case and left my room, careful to lock the door behind me.

As I exited the infirmary building, I turned left and automatically headed for the servants' hall.

Laughing, Gwydion intercepted me halfway across the paved courtyard. "This way, Apprentice Jacinthe," he said, taking my shoulders and turning me around. "You're a student now. That means you take your meals in the Great Hall."

Overcome with sudden shyness, I halted as we entered the vast, vaulted hall. Black-robed students crowded the benches at long trestle tables, and the place echoed with loud conversations and laughter.

Gwydion took my elbow and steered me to the nearest table.

"The infirmary apprentices usually sit here," he said, sliding onto a bench at the end of the table. "But Ilhan and Alondra are always late. Sometimes they don't show up for breakfast at all. They'd rather sleep than eat."

Indeed, there were four vacant place settings around a sign on a delicate metal stand that read "Infirmary."

The students seated near us gave me the once-over. Most of them immediately returned their attention to the plates of food in front of them, but a couple of them snickered and whispered to each other.

My shoulders tensed, and I hunched, trying to make myself less noticeable.

I knew I didn't really belong here among the children of the Dominion's noblest families.

In an ordinary provincial academy, I would've been among fellow commoners. But Darkstone Academy was exclusive in the sense all its students were exiles, either for political reasons or for the misuse of magic. They'd been spared for crimes where the government would've executed commoners or burned the magic out of them.

"Jacinthe." Distracted from my gloomy train of thought, I looked at Gwydion.

He lifted the bread basket and offered it to me. "Eat," he encouraged me. "And don't worry about anyone else here."

I folded back the cloth and took a freshly baked roll. It was fine white bread sprinkled with sesame seeds instead of the crusty, chewy slices of brown bread I was used to seeing in the servants' hall.

Then one of the Great Hall's serving staff plunked a plate down in front of me. A mound of scrambled eggs fought for space with plump smoked pork sausages and a ramekin of ripe cubed muskmelon.

"Melon *again?*" someone complained further down the table. "It's cherry season. Why aren't we getting fresh cherries?"

I remembered the hours I'd spent every day de-stemming, peeling, coring, pitting, and chopping bushels of melons, stone fruit, cherries, and fresh berries from the castle's orchards and gardens.

Most of the cherries and stone fruit went to the confectionary kitchen for pies, tarts, syrups, and jams, but the kitchen staff also prepared seventy-five pounds of fruit salad every morning using whatever the confectioner didn't need.

I ate my first spoonful of sweet muskmelon and sent silent thanks to my friends in the kitchens, who'd risen long before dawn to prepare this meal.

∞∞∞

My first class at the academy was Intermediate Potions, held right after breakfast.

I couldn't wait to become a proper student, but I was nervous about joining the class several weeks into the summer quarter. Over breakfast, Gwydion assured me he'd help me catch up.

It felt good to have a mentor again. Especially one so beautiful and kind.

After breakfast, we left the Great Hall. Gwydion strode off toward the infirmary building to begin his morning rounds before leaving the castle for the apothecary garden.

I paused in the main courtyard to orient myself.

All around me, black-robed students crowded the courtyard, some standing and talking in small groups, others walking with purpose.

Nervously, I smoothed the folds of my loose academic robe, worn over my usual apprentice uniform gown.

I belong here, I told myself, trying to believe it.

Then I followed the purposefully walking students to the large, two-story Academy Building between the Great Hall and the long row of storerooms against the castle's back wall.

As I rounded a corner, I could feel the other students staring at me, and whispers following in my wake. I knew what they were saying. I could hear the contempt in their voices. I was an outsider, a commoner, and I knew they didn't trust me.

I straightened my back and walked through a set of open double-doors into the lecture hall.

My heart pounded with both anticipation and trepidation as I breathed in the scents of paper, ink, and the faint aroma of herbs.

Faced with a sea of desks, I took my seat at an empty desk in the very last row, near the back of the hall. I opened my new notebook, slid a fountain pen from the pen case, and examined my surroundings.

The professor's lectern stood on a dais at the very front of the hall. Behind it stood a set of shelves, with lines of glass jars containing herbs, roots, and liquids.

An enormous square of sailcloth hung like a tapestry from the wall next to the lectern. On it, someone had painted a pair of anatomically correct human figures, one male, one female. They were depicted opened from neck to pubis bone, with their internal organs exposed and labeled.

Above me, a high vaulted stone ceiling stretched, the spaces between the stone ribbing adorned with intricate murals depicting celestial beings and allegorical scenes. Dust particles danced in the sunlight streaming through the lecture hall's narrow windows, casting golden bars of light on the stone floor.

The large hall was mostly empty when I entered. As the minutes passed and a flood of black-robed students streamed in, I began receiving startled looks as they passed me. A buzz of low-voiced comments and sharp whispers rose. The students already seated in the rows in front of me began craning their head and turning around to look at me.

I overheard snatches of conversation: "Cresta," "Bernardo,"

"consorts with the merman," "that Dragon's sweet on her," and "torn to pieces."

Any hopes I'd had of making friends with my fellow students melted away. The castle's virulent gossip had made me a monster in their eyes.

Endless minutes passed as I stared blindly down at my blank notebook. I fought the urge to get up and flee the lecture hall.

Then my stubbornness rose and pushed down the fear. I got angry.

I wasn't going to run away and discard the precious gift Gwydion had given me because of a few nasty rumors. I was a *student* now. And I planned to attend every lecture and every practicum class, no matter what my fellow students said about me.

During the past year, I'd endured much worse.

And I was determined to become a healer like Mama, even if I wasn't a mage.

Or am I?

I remembered the strange remarks Gwydion had made about my power, and wondered once again why he sensed something inside me that Mama and the Magecraft Aptitude Examiner hadn't.

A silver-haired woman wearing a lecturer's violet robes entered from a side door and took her place behind the lectern.

"Good morning, students," she said, her voice commanding attention.

Everyone in the lecture hall rose to their feet. I hastily followed them.

"Good morning, Professor Bevitrice!" a hundred voices responded in unison.

As the students all around me re-seated themselves in billows of black fabric, Professor Bevitrice said, "Today, I will discuss the various kinds of stomach ailments and demonstrate how to prepare the treatments. Take notes, because tomorrow, you will practice making these potions during your practicum session."

As she launched into her lecture, I uncapped my pen, bent my head once more, and began writing.

All around me, I heard pens scratching against paper as the professor rapidly described lists of symptoms and the recipes for the most efficacious potions to treat each kind of ailment.

Everyone was too busy taking notes now for whispers or nasty comments.

As the lecture proceeded, I realized Gwydion had been correct. Mama had taught me the principles that the professor was currently expanding on in her lecture. I found I had no trouble keeping up with the new information she presented.

Two hours flew by in the blink of an eye.

When the lecture ended and Professor Bevitrice began answering questions, I shook out my cramped fingers. I'd taken ten pages of notes. I understood now why Gwydion had given me a stack of blank notebooks and extra inkwells.

I slipped out of the lecture hall when I sensed the questions were winding down. I wanted to avoid my fellow students, at least until the worst of the rumors died away.

As I walked back to my room to drop off my notebook and exchange my academic robe for an infirmary worker's smock and cap, I realized I was humming under my breath.

Despite the whispers and stares, I'd enjoyed myself. New information buzzed around inside my head like bees gathering nectar. I felt like my mind was finally coming back to life after the many months of hard work and grinding fatigue.

I changed my clothes, washed my hands, then went to work.

The only patient in the ward today was the young man in traction with a fractured thighbone.

When I entered, carrying a basket of clean, folded bed-linens, I found Ilhan sitting at the man's side, applying ointment to a swollen, badly bruised wrist.

He motioned me over. "Ulli here is a stonemason's apprentice. He broke his leg and left wrist when he fell off a ladder."

"*I* didn't fall off the ladder," Ulli said testily. "The *ladder* fell, with me still on it."

"Either way, you're extremely lucky you didn't break your back or fracture your skull," Ilhan said forbiddingly. He turned to me and tapped the ointment pot in his towel-draped lap. "Junior Apprentice Jacinthe, we're almost out of comfrey ointment. Gwydion said you're a competent herbalist. Do you know how to make more of this?"

"Yes, Lord Ilhan," I said. It was one of the first things Mama had taught me how to make. "Using fresh or dried comfrey leaves?"

"Dried," he said. "We have both in the storeroom. Please describe the recipe and how to make the ointment."

"The recipe my mother taught me is: take one cup of dried comfrey leaves. Finely grind them in a mortar. Then put the ground leaves in a pot with one cup of olive oil, and gently heat the mixture over simmering water for several hours. When the oil is sufficiently infused, strain it, return it to the pot, and stir in a handful of grated beeswax for thickening. Stir continuously until all the wax has melted, then pour the mixture into clean ointment jars and seal the lids."

"Hm." Ilhan sounded surprised. "So, Gwydion was right about you, Apprentice. Excellent. I want you to make a fresh batch after you change and make up the beds." He pointed at a pair of beds with dented pillows and rumpled sheets.

"Yes, Lord Ilhan," I said, dipping a curtsey for good measure.

"Never mind the 'lords' and curtseys when we're working," he said. "Just call me Senior Apprentice Ilhan."

"Yes, Senior Apprentice."

The stonemason peered at me. "Hey, Apprentice, aren't you that girl who drowned Lady Cresta? I saw you trying to help that fish-man the other afternoon."

"I didn't have anything to do with her death," I protested, despite knowing it would do me no good.

Sure enough, Ulli snorted. "Yeah, of course you didn't." He winked at me. "But I tell ya, that Lady Cresta was a nasty piece o' work. I had a run-in with her myself a few months back. She wanted me to make the window in her room bigger and didn't take kindly when I pointed out that I worked for Mason Steinhardt, not *her*."

"I didn't kill anyone," I repeated. Then I turned my back on him, walked away, and began stripping the beds.

I was in the middle of remaking the first bed when a commotion broke out in the courtyard below.

I rushed to the window and saw guards running across the courtyard. It looked like they were heading towards the castle's gatehouse. I felt a burst of worry. Had someone tried to kill Tama again?

Most of the people in the castle were afraid of him, and the stories about him were stranger and more terrifying every time I heard them.

A few minutes later, a group of six castle guards barreled up the infirmary stairs and burst into the ward. They carried stretchers with three unconscious patients.

"It's the Djinn Prince Arslan, Princess Karima, and Princess Layla," Ilhan said to me as he directed the guards to lay the patients on the infirmary beds.

Arslan's face glittered with beads of sweat and his handsome features were twisted into a grimace of pain. The princesses were barely conscious and their skin had turned a sickly grayish-green hue.

"Apprentice Jacinthe, go fetch Mage Armand!" Ilhan barked. "And Gwydion, too, if you can find him. Hurry!"

I left the ward at a run and rushed downstairs.

Luckily, Mage Armand was in his office. After I told him about the Djinn, he rose painfully from behind his desk. "Apprentice Gwydion is next door, restocking the supply cabinets. Get the lad to look at the Djinn," he ordered. "Don't wait on me to start treatment. I'm an old man and slow on the stairs."

I bobbed a quick curtsey and sprinted to the workroom to fetch Gwydion.

"They've been poisoned with iron salt. It's deadly to both Djinni and Fae," he said grimly a short time later, when he had finished examining the three Djinn. "We must treat them immediately with a chelating potion."

"Poison, again? Who would dare harm imperial guests?" Ilhan sounded incredulous. "And why?"

"Those are questions for the castellan and the chatelaine," Mage Armand said as he entered the ward. "But I would dearly like to know myself."

Gwydion snorted. "We'll be waiting forever if we rely on Lord Roderigo and his sister to investigate. They don't care what happens to anyone except for themselves." He shook his head. "I'll get started on that potion. Hopefully, it's not too late to save the Djinn."

"I would like a list of everything they ate or drank in the past twenty-four hours," Mage Armand said. "That might help narrow down the source of the poison."

"I could go to the kitchens and ask for that list," I volunteered. "While I'm there, I can find out who prepared and delivered the Djinn's meals, and whether anyone noticed anything suspicious."

∞∞∞

An hour later, I left the kitchens, list in hand, and began my walk back to the infirmary.

After speaking with Chef Vollkorn and receiving a complete inventory of everything served to the three Djinn over the past two days, she'd given me permission to question the cooks and apprentices.

It now seemed likely to me that someone had poisoned the food or drink after it left the kitchens.

Jonitha and Charmaine, the two apprentices who'd delivered the food to the gatehouse, and the gatehouse guards were my chief suspects.

But as nasty and unpleasant as those two girls were, I didn't think they would've acted unless someone had either ordered them or bribed them.

The same went for the guards.

If that was true, then one of the castle's higher-ranking officials must be responsible.

My thoughts immediately turned to Lord Roderigo and Lady Erzabetta's strangely apathetic response to the previous attacks. Who were they protecting?

Ilhan had mentioned the Duke de Norhas' plot against Domina Jacinthe. Did the recent deaths and attempted murders at the castle have anything to do with a wider conspiracy?

It seemed unlikely, given how remote this island was from the major political centers of the Human Dominion, but I couldn't dismiss it completely. I'd have to ask Ilhan and Gwydion for their thoughts.

Lost in my musings, I crossed the courtyard next to the Great Hall. Too late, I noticed a group of male mage students gathered ahead of me, blocking my path to the infirmary building.

"Hey, it's that girl who killed Cresta," I heard one of them say. "The one who showed up in Potions today."

I ignored them and kept walking. I hoped they'd let me pass when I drew near.

One of them grabbed me by the arm.

"Let me go!" I demanded loudly. I looked around, but the courtyard was deserted.

"Nah, we have some questions for you, servant girl." His grip tightened on my arm. "Did Mommy and Daddy catch you giving it away to monsters? Is that why they sold you to Darkstone?" he asked, his Capitolan accented with Monteleno.

His four friends sniggered nastily.

"Better monsters than sheep," I snapped, referring to the old joke about sheep outnumbering the women of Monteleno two-to-one. "What did your mother catch *you* doing?"

The other boys laughed, and my captor's patchily bearded cheeks flushed.

I tried to pull away from him, but he held on tight and sneered down at me. "Dumuzi's Beard, you're willing to do it with those creatures, but you're too good for some honest human cock?"

"Yeah!" one of his companions said excitedly. "You up for a little action, fish-lover?"

"I can pound her just as hard as that Dragon," boasted the student holding me. "I'll even bite her, if she asks nicely."

I was terrified, but I refused to let it show on my face or in my voice. "Let me go. *Now*."

"Not until we've had some fun," said a third youth, stepping close and leering at me. His hand darted out and grabbed my chin. "Gimme a kiss, Red."

I didn't think. I just reacted. I swung my leg up and kneed him in the groin.

He folded over, groaning loudly.

One of his friends grabbed my other arm. "You little slut! I'm gonna make you pay for that!"

Chapter 28

Jacinthe

"What's going on here?" Lord Ilhan asked, his deep voice stern. "Ormond? De Montplaisir?"

All the boys froze as my fellow infirmary apprentice appeared in the building's main doorway. He wore his long white on-duty smock, his wavy golden hair confined beneath a round linen cap.

Sudden hope energized me as I continued to struggle against my captors.

"Oh, it's just you, Parrish. Just having a little fun. Care to join us?" drawled the one holding me. "This little slut is pretty feisty now, but we'll have her begging for it in no time."

"Let go of me!" I doubled my struggles. "I don't want anything to do with these crows!"

Ilhan just looked past me, his expression unreadable. *Isn't he going to help me?*

"Don't mind if I do, Ormond," he said, smiling. The expression didn't touch his cool dark blue eyes.

I gaped at him in disbelief as he strolled towards us.

My heart sank. Six against one had been bad enough. Now it was seven. For the first time, I wondered if they intended to kill me once they'd finished sporting on me.

Were they seeing revenge for Lady Cresta and Lord Bernardo's deaths?

Lady Erzabetta and Lord Roderigo wouldn't lift a manicured finger to punish them.

But I hadn't thought Ilhan my enemy. In fact, he'd seemed to accept me as his fellow apprentice.

I'd been wrong.

He thinks I'm a threat to his sister, I reminded myself.

I kicked backwards with all my strength, and my sturdy new leather shoe drove into a leg.

"Hey!" The student holding my right arm abruptly let go. Groaning loudly, he staggered back.

I whirled on the boy holding my left arm, and drove my fist into his stomach. If I could make him open his hand, I'd give him the slip and run for safety so fast a Dragon couldn't catch me.

But he had fast reflexes. He jumped back, and my punch merely brushed his robes. In the next instant, he seized my forearm, and used my momentum to spin me like a dancer. I somehow ended up with my back to him and my right arm twisted up against my spine.

It was the same hold Guard Ivar had used on me, back in Herrewick.

I raised my foot.

"Try kicking me, bitch, and I'll rip your arm out of its socket," he growled. He twisted my arm higher, straining my shoulder.

To his remaining four friends, he urged, "Get her! Grab her legs!" They surged forward.

The one I'd kneed in the groin snarled at me.

Then Ilhan, who had approached within arm's length of me,

turned and seized the arm of the student who held me.

Ilhan's powerful shoulders flexed as he twisted the captive limb. I heard popping and a sharp snap. My captor screamed and abruptly released his hold on me.

Panting, his face gone white as the infirmary linens, the injured boy staggered back, clutching his arm against his middle. "You—you— What in the name of the three cursed mountains are you *doing*, Parrish?"

"Stopping you pipsqueaks from bullying my junior apprentice." Ilhan stepped in front of me. His broad back hid them from my view.

I felt a rush of incredulous joy and relief.

"You're protecting that little monster-fucker?" one of them spat. "Do you know what her playmates *did* to Cresta and Bernardo?"

"And yet here you are, bothering her? What are you? Too stupid to live?" Ilhan pointed at the closest still-standing crow. "Piss off, all of you, and don't let me catch you bothering my apprentice again."

"No, *you* piss off, Parrish." The one in the middle looked at his friends. "What do you say, boys? Let's teach them both a lesson about messing with us!"

"Just try it," Ilhan growled. His fists clenched.

I stepped up next to him and glared at my tormentors. I wasn't going down without a fight, but it was still four against two.

"Thanks, milord," I told him. "You worried me for a moment."

"Sorry about that, Apprentice," he murmured, his eyes never leaving our opponents. "But I needed to convince them to let me get close enough to you."

I nodded.

Then Ilhan swore in Frankish as all four of the students facing us pulled daggers from beneath their robes. The blades glittered evilly in their hands.

The castle's rules didn't allow anyone except the guards to carry weapons. But I'd learned that rules meant little or nothing when it came to the crows. No one was going to hold them accountable for anything they did.

At least they weren't using magic against us.

"Friend Jacinthe!" My knees went shaky with sudden relief as I heard Boreas' familiar, booming voice. 'Who are these earthworms with their tiny little knives, and why are they troubling you?"

Out of the corner of my eye, I saw a blur of red hair and golden silk. Then my Dragon friend appeared next to me, his giant body dwarfing even Ilhan's tall, sturdy frame.

I released a shaky breath. *Saved!*

Before I could say anything, the boy with the broken arm shouted, "It's the Dragon! Run! Before he burns us alive!"

Boreas crossed his arms and grinned. "Yes, run away little earthworms, before I roast you!"

The students scattered in all directions like cockroaches facing a lit lamp. The boy whose leg I'd kicked hobbled away and vanished into a nearby building. He slammed the door behind him, and the sound echoed off the walls enclosing the courtyard.

"You have lucky timing, Friend Boreas," I told him. "Lord Ilhan was trying to help me, but when they pulled those knives…" I shook my head and shuddered.

Those crows had been bold to try assaulting me out here in the open in the middle of the afternoon. It reinforced my belief that they hadn't worried about being caught or punished by the castle authorities.

"There was no luck about it," Boreas informed me. "Friend Gwydion, Friend Tama, and I all agreed that we should keep an eye on you. I apologize for my slowness in coming to your aid."

"Nice to know you didn't need my help after all, Apprentice Jacinthe," Ilhan said, his tone heavy with sarcasm.

"But I didn't know Boreas was lurking," I pointed out. "I appreciate you coming to my rescue, milord. You didn't have to help me, but I'm glad you did."

He crossed his arms. "I'll know better next time." He still didn't sound happy.

Ilhan gave Boreas a stiff nod. "Now, if you'll excuse me, Prince Boreas, I have patients to care for. Gwydion's potion helped, but those three Djinn aren't out of the woods yet."

He strode away. I sighed. He seemed the prickly type. And definitely suspicious of me. Was he only being nice to me because he thought I posed a threat to his sister?

"Not that I don't appreciate you and Tama watching out for me," I began, turning to Boreas. "But aren't you both confined to the gatehouse?"

Boreas grinned at me. "It's become a flexible arrangement."

"Oh? And how did you manage that?"

"After Lord Shuji died, we discussed the conditions of our stay in this castle with the guards, and came to a satisfactory agreement." His grin turned smug. "We are now free to come and go from our quarters, as long as we're discreet, don't leave the castle without permission, or hurt anyone except in self-defense."

"Thank you," I said with heartfelt gratitude. I wondered what sum the guards had demanded in return for the hostages' liberty. And whether Lord Roderigo or Lady Erzabetta would care that their prisoners were freely roaming the castle.

I began walking toward the infirmary building. I wanted to go to my room before returning to the ward. I needed a few minutes to compose myself before I went to Mage Armand's office to give him Master Chef Vollkorn's list. Now that the danger had passed, my hands were shaking, and I felt weak.

While I was in my room, I was going to arm myself with Tama's contraband dagger.

It's always easier to beg forgiveness than obtain permission, Mama liked to say. If the students were carrying knives, then I needed protection, too.

Following the rules like a good girl would do me no good if I ended up cornered by bullies again. What if my protectors didn't arrive in the nick of time? Boreas had almost been too late today.

This latest incident was a harsh reminder of how vulnerable I was in this place. I'd let my guard down after becoming one of Mage Armand's apprentices and attached to the infirmary. I thought becoming a student at the academy gave me more protection than being a mere indentured kitchen apprentice.

But those students had just shown me I'd been fooling myself. I was still just an indentured commoner among three hundred young nobles. Boys like that would always see me as fair game.

From now on, I'd be looking over my shoulder at every lecture and in every class, wondering when and where I'd be attacked again.

Boreas walked into the infirmary building with me, clearly intending to escort me until I reached my destination.

As we began climbing the stairs that led to the ward and to my room, Boreas asked me, "So, what of the three Djinn? I heard someone tried to kill them."

I nodded. "I don't know much more than what Ilhan just told us," I said. "Mage Armand sent me on an errand an hour ago, and I'm just getting back now. Before I left, Gwydion was sure they'd been poisoned with iron salts. He was going to treat them with a chelating potion." I halted and turned to him. "I don't understand why Lord Roderigo and Lady Erzabetta haven't done anything! Even if they hate non-humans, they're still answerable to the dominus—or to Domina Jacinthe," I added, remembering that Ilhan had told me she was now regent.

"It's obvious to everyone at the castle that Lord Roderigo and his sister are neglecting their duties," Boreas pointed out. "And it's not just the imperial hostages they are ignoring. Before you arrived here, one of the professors was badly injured by a student's magical prank gone very wrong. Even though the student claimed it was an accident and she didn't intend to harm anyone, you would think the chatelaine would have done something to ensure it didn't happen again. Or reprimanded the student. Instead, the chatelaine did nothing except make empty statements about responsibility and greater oversight." He shook his head gravely. "That is why it was easy to convince the guards to give us more freedom. Their morale is low because they cannot trust their leaders. And it's also the reason we must protect you, Friend Jacinthe."

"I'm so lucky to have you as my friend." On impulse, I threw my arms around his neck and hugged him. Boreas stood two steps below me, so he was only a little taller than me now.

His brawny arms circled my waist, and he pulled me against his broad chest. "I will always be here for you, Friend Jacinthe, no matter what happens."

Still feeling shaky from facing down the crows, I clung to him and buried my face in his neck. His skin always radiated feverish heat, as if Dragon-fire burned inside him like a furnace, heating his skin. I let his warmth soak into me, calming me.

I don't know what came over me next. Perhaps the seed that Gwydion had planted during our strange conversation had sprouted.

Before I could think about it, I lifted my face to his. I leaned in and kissed him on the mouth, just a quick peck.

Boreas reacted as if lightning had struck him. One instant, we were both standing on the stairs. The next instant, he'd pushed me up against the cool stone wall, and his mouth was devouring mine. His kiss was deep, demanding, and burning hot.

My lips parted beneath his, and the heat from his mouth plunged through my veins like liquid fire, blossoming between my legs in a heated throb.

Before I could react, he reached down and rucked my skirts up to my waist, baring my stockings and pantaloons. His hands slid around to cup my buttocks.

He lifted me effortlessly, wrapped my legs around his hips, and settled my core firmly against the hard bulge pushing against the front of his breeches.

I squirmed against him, instinctively seeking relief from the ache of the desire he'd woken in me.

"Jacinthe," he groaned, deep and low, against my lips. His voice vibrated through my bones.

Then his mouth left mine and trailed down my neck to my collarbones in a series of burning kisses. His tongue traced the line of my silver collar while his hips moved in a steady rhythm against me, grinding his erection against my most private and aching parts. The coarse linen of my pantaloons rubbed against my folds with every movement, a maddening, unsatisfying friction.

Panting, I closed my eyes and let my head loll against the unyielding stone wall pressing into my back. I dug my fingers into his broad shoulders as raw need coiled in my belly.

"I'm not hurting you?" he murmured, briefly lifting his head to pin me with his smoldering golden gaze.

"No. Don't stop," I gasped. I loved everything about him, from his vast strength to the way he understood how much his forceful attentions aroused me.

"I don't plan on stopping." He flashed his grin at me before settling me more firmly against his groin.

Gwydion had been right. Boreas wanted more from me than friendship. With his mouth scorching me and fanning the flames of my desire, I did, too.

Then Mage Armand's creaky voice floated down the stairwell. "Apprentice Jacinthe, is that you on the stairs? We need you in the ward."

Panic poured over me like a bucket of cold water, immediately extinguishing my arousal. Sanity returned; with it came a sickening twist of fear.

What madness had taken hold of me, that I'd thought it a good idea to kiss Boreas here, in the stairwell where anyone could've caught us?

Heart pounding, my gaze flew to the top of the stairs, expecting to see either Ilhan or Mage Armand there. I could only imagine the picture I made, pressed against the stairwell wall with my skirts up around my waist, my stockinged legs wrapped around Boreas' hips.

To my relief, the landing at the top of the stairs was empty. "On my way, Mage Armand!" I called, sounding a little breathless.

Frantically, I whispered to Boreas, "Put me down!"

He scowled, but did as I asked, gently lowering me to my feet. I instantly began smoothing down my rumpled skirts.

"Jacinthe." A hot finger under my chin lifted my face to meet the Dragon's gaze. He looked uncharacteristically serious. "We have things to discuss."

I nodded, my cheeks burning. "I'll come see you tomorrow morning after I deliver Tama's medicine," I promised. "But I have to go now!"

Then I picked up my skirts and ran up the remaining stairs to the ward. When I reached the landing, I looked down and saw Boreas still standing where I'd left him.

I waved at him and stepped through the doorway, hoping that my flushed face wouldn't proclaim what I'd just been doing.

Inside the ward, I saw Mage Armand, Ilhan, and Alondra gathered around Ulli's bed.

Mage Armand waved me over. "Ah, Apprentice Jacinthe, you've returned just in time. I was just about to demonstrate how to speed the healing of broken bones with magic."

As I passed the ward's other patients, I noticed that the three Djinn hostages looked somewhat improved, especially the two women. Only Prince Arslan was awake. His gaze unblinking, he silently watched me walk by.

In his human form, Djinn was a strikingly handsome man, with dark golden skin and eyes the color of the sky at dusk. His short hair was dark, but sun-streaked with brass, copper, and gold.

I joined Mage Armand and the others and did my best to pretend interest as the old healer-mage explained what he was about to do, and how the magic worked to speed healing in bone and flesh alike.

When he'd finished his brief lecture, Mage Armand closed his eyes and summoned the familiar blue-white glow of power. I noticed he was chanting the same verses that Mama used when she performed this healing spell.

I could recite this incantation from memory—for all the good it did me, without mage powers—because I'd seen her do it a hundred times, maybe more.

Meanwhile, my thoughts zoomed madly around the inside of my head like a flock of sparrows trapped in a barn.

Gwydion was right, after all? Boreas wants me? I could still feel his hard, hungry kisses like brands on my mouth and throat.

My body sang with frustrated desire and undiluted excitement, and my blood ran hot. I couldn't believe that Armand, Ilhan, or Alondra didn't see me burning like a torch in the night.

But after a quick glance in my direction when I joined them, my two fellow apprentices both ignored me in favor of observing Mage Armand's healing ritual. Alondra even had her notebook open and was jotting notes in beautiful handwriting.

Later, I found myself alone in the workroom downstairs. As I made a batch of comfrey ointment, I found myself comparing Boreas' kisses to Tama and Gwydion's kisses.

All of them awakened intense desire in me. But how could I be attracted to three very different men with equal intensity?

Gwydion's scandalous suggestion haunted me. Even if it were possible, how would it work?

But it could never work, I reminded myself.

Here in this castle, on this isolated island, it was becoming dangerously easy to forget that harsh laws kept us apart. If things went any further between us, there would be no mercy for me… or for my three friends.

Chapter 29

Tama

For the first time in days, I had Jacinthe all to myself.

I'd waited for the time when she would visit when Boreas wasn't also present in my rooms.

The Wind-Walker and I now spent most of our days together, sharing meals, conversing, or playing cards. Though he occasionally irritated me with his loudness and his non-stop talk, Boreas was interesting and loyal. His company was a balm to the painful solitude I'd endured my first week in this place.

Jacinthe arrived at dawn, bearing her usual jug of the medicine which had worked wonders to tame the constant cramps and aches in my storm-cursed legs and feet.

For once, she came without an inquisitive guard at her heels, a sign of the newfound freedom Friend Boreas had negotiated for us.

I wondered if I could exchange another pearl or two and negotiate a visit to the cove that served as the island's harbor. I wanted to perform funeral rites for Shuji of Dolphin Clan, since he had died away from his home and his clan.

The Drylanders had buried his body on the island, far from the embrace of Mother Sea. At my request, Guard Machry had brought me Shuji's warrior pendant, a shark's tooth with wickedly sharp edges decorated with his clan signs. I planned to return it to Mother Sea in place of Shuji's flesh and bones, hoping it was enough for her to locate his soul and guide it home.

Also, I longed to swim in the sea once more. It would feel good, even with lungs and legs instead of the gills and tail I'd been born with.

But first, I had business with Jacinthe.

She seemed troubled this morning. Unlike some of the other Drylanders, she was usually as calm and watchful as one of the Sea People, only speaking when something needed to be said.

Now, as I sat, drinking my medicine, she bustled around my prison cell with nervous energy, chattering about her new classes, her work at the infirmary, and the improving condition of the three Djinn hostages.

She did not look at me directly or meet my gaze as she normally did. That troubled me.

Finally, she sank to her knees before me in a billow of fabric, and reached for my legs.

"Let's see if the swelling has gone down enough to start you on those strengthening exercises," she said, her strong fingers probing my knees.

"The pain is much reduced," I told her so that she would actually look at me.

"Oh, I'm so glad." Her hands stilled, but she still wouldn't look at me. Something was definitely wrong. "Now, about those exercises—"

I reached down and cupped her warm face between my hands, forcing her to meet my gaze. Her eyes looked more green than usual this morning against the smooth brown of her skin, and a flush tinged her cheeks.

"Jacinthe, what troubles you?"

She gazed back at me, almost fearfully. That displeased and

bewildered me. I had worked hard to gain her trust. And I had been a good friend to her. I had to discover what was going on.

Then she took a deep breath. "I had some trouble with a group of crows yesterday. But everything turned out all right. My new senior apprentice, Lord Ilhan, helped me, but there were too many of them for us to fight. And then Boreas showed up and scared them all away." Her mouth curved in a smile. "He didn't even have to use his Dragon-fire this time."

I nodded. "He guards you during the daytime hours because the Drylanders do not fear him as much as they fear me. I have been keeping watch over you overnight, staying in the shadows so no one can see me. Gwydion guards you in the Place of Healing and outside the walls when you go to harvest the plants you need for your medicines."

She nodded, then bit her deliciously plump lower lip. It momentarily distracted me with thoughts of what I planned to share with her soon.

"This is all good," I prompted her. "But why are you behaving like a seal pursued by a pod of orca, darting this way and that?"

"I—I don't know how to tell you this," she began, then stopped.

I waited, curious and also worried.

Then she blurted, "Gwydion and Boreas both kissed me."

Her flush deepened, spreading down her cheeks and down her throat. I felt the heat against my palms.

"Gwydion said he and Boreas are each courting me... and he says you are, too. Is that true? I mean, the way you kissed me... it felt like more than friendship."

I did not want to lose her. A coward's fear writhed in my guts, tearing at me with shark's teeth. Boreas and Gwydion were both my friends and honorable men. Of course they would see Jacinthe's value, as I did.

I had never courted a mate before. But I knew how the game worked. A man could not simply claim a mate. The choice lay with his intended. He had to convince, to seduce, to prove himself *worthy* of the intended's choice.

Over the past weeks, I had repeatedly warned myself against courting her because Drylanders considered a union with Sea People taboo.

But I wanted her so badly. I hadn't been able to stop thinking about her warm skin against mine, or her heated response to my kisses.

From the first, she had regarded me fearlessly and with compassion. My affection and regard for her had only grown stronger during the time we spent together on the ship. She made me feel complete in a way I'd never felt before, even at home among my people.

Now I was worried that Boreas or Gwydion would win her. Or, if Jacinthe chose me, that they would no longer wish to be my friends.

The Forest Brother had a smooth tongue. His words flowed like water to caress and persuade. It was a gift I did not possess. I spoke only when something needed to be said and stayed silent otherwise. It was the warrior's way.

The Wind-Walker was bold and confident. He knew how to choose the right gifts for courtship. He'd given Jacinthe beautiful garments and shining jewelry. What had I given her? A few coins and books and a glass knife, when I should have showered her with pearls and water-polished gems.

"Yes, I am courting you, Jacinthe," I told her. "I gave you my Kujiranokiba, after all."

But she still looked worried. "Are you angry I kissed the others?" Her gaze dropped, and she tensed beneath my hands. As if she suddenly feared me.

That I liked even less than discovering I had courtship rivals.

I'd seen how the Drylander men treated their women. But that was not the Sea People's way. I had killed the sailors who raised their hands against her.

"Why would I be angry?" I asked, bewildered. "You are a desirable woman. It is understandable that others would court you. Boreas and Gwydion are my friends. I know they are worthy suitors." I paused, trying to think of what else to say. "But I want you to choose *me* for your mate."

Her smile returned, radiant this time. Her eyes glowed with happiness at my words, assuring me she still favored me.

I decided the time for talking was over. I needed to show her how I felt in the way I knew best.

Her mouth was sweet and hot as Dragon-fire beneath mine as I drew her up. She returned my kisses with fervor and didn't object when I lifted her onto my lap. I impatiently pushed her skirts out of the way until her strong, sleek thighs straddled mine in a near-mating position.

I still wore my loose night-robe instead of the constricting Drylander clothing. As I deepened our kiss, exploring her soft, slick mouth, I felt Jacinthe push apart the halves of my robe. Her warm hands stroked my chest, inviting me to take things further.

I usually tucked away my pair of tentacles and sex in the protective genital slit at the base of my belly, where my tail was broadest. When the mage's shape-changing spell ripped my lower body asunder and reshaped it into legs, my slit remained where it was, just above the place where my legs joined my body.

I used my tentacles now to slip between Jacinthe's legs and creep beneath her undergarments while we kissed. When she didn't object, I tentatively began exploring her hot, wet sex, so different from the women of my people.

Jacinthe jerked upright and gasped against my mouth at my first gentle touch. Had I gone too far? "What's that?"

"My tentacles," I explained. "They're meant to hold a lover close in the weightless underwater world. But they have other uses, too."

"Oh?" She looked intrigued rather than repelled. "Like what?"

"Let me show you." I lightly stroked across her slick folds. She rewarded me with another gasp. "You must tell me if I do something that does not please you."

"This is strange, but I like it." Then she rocked against me with an assertiveness I liked.

I captured her mouth in another kiss as I continued to explore her, letting the hitches in her breathing and the small noises she made teach me what pleased her most.

She was deliciously responsive, especially when I scooped her breasts up out of her bodice and used my lips and tongue to tease the soft tips into hard points. Then I cupped the soft rounded weights in my hands, stroking her with my thumbs, and captured her mouth once more with mine.

I pushed the tip of one tentacle inside her opening. She squeezed it with slick heat, so tight I wondered if my sex would fit inside her.

As I slowly pushed further inside her, I used my other tentacle to stoke the small, firm bud that appeared to be her most sensitive place.

Jacinthe panted and squirmed against me in the most flattering way as I penetrated her further.

Her warm skin grew even warmer under my attentions. I swallowed each soft gasp and whimper as I devoured her mouth, mimicking the actions of my tentacle with my tongue.

"Touch me," I urged her, capturing her hands in my own and guiding them down to where my stiff sex emerged from my slit, yearning towards her wet heat.

I had never experienced sex in human form. It would be interesting, and from what I could tell, just as satisfying as what I'd known before. Maybe even more so.

Her fingers were tentative at first. But with a little guidance from me, her touch became more confident as I continued to caress her inside and out.

Each stroke of her hands sent sparks through my body, making me shudder with pleasure. She cupped and petted and teased until I was panting against her lips, barely able to keep myself from finishing before she reached her peak.

The courted must always climax first. That was the first rule of Sea-People courtship.

Moments later, she gasped my name, then moaned and writhed on my lap. Her hot, slick inner flesh pulsed and rippled around the tentacle inside her.

I vividly imagined what this moment would feel like when my sex was inside her, sheathed to the hilt in her heat and tightness. My release broke free of my control and rushed through me like a cresting storm-wave.

My hips jerked and thrust helplessly with the overwhelming torrent of pleasure as Jacinthe continued shaking in the throes of her climax, her body as warm as a Wind-Walker's now.

When the last ripples of her pleasure subsided to mere shivers, I slowly withdrew my tentacles and tucked them away safely, along with my sex.

Jacinthe pulled a handkerchief out of her pocket and cleaned her hands, sticky with my release, before running the soft cloth over my belly and around the edges of my genital slit. Then I gathered her against me.

I felt relaxed and happy. Jacinthe draped herself over me, resting her cheek against my head. Her soft breasts pressed against my throat and chin most pleasantly, and her soft, hot breath ruffled my hair.

I hoped no one would come to interrupt us. I didn't want this courtship session to end as quickly as our last one had.

"Did you enjoy my pleasuring?" I already knew the answer, but I wanted to hear her acknowledge it.

"I—I enjoyed it a bit too much, I think." She chuckled softly. "Those tentacles give the Sea People an unfair advantage over human men. I bet that's why doing what we just did is illegal."

That made me smile. "I look forward to our next courtship session." I moved my head just far enough to kiss the tip of her breast. "We could begin it now, in my bed."

She kissed my hair. "You tempt me, but I'm not ready for more right now. For one thing, a guard will be making his rounds any minute. You know we can't get caught doing this."

I looked up at her. "I would not put you in danger. I can hear when a guard or anyone else approaches. We will have sufficient warning of any interruption."

"That's a relief. But there's one other thing." She hesitated, and I saw she was uncomfortable again. "If we go any further than this in our, ah, courtship sessions, I'll need to brew some contraceptive tea and begin drinking it every morning."

"I won't dishonor you, Jacinthe, or put you in danger by giving you a child before we are formally mated. I do not know how it is for Drylander males, but I am not fertile right now, nor will I be until we seal a mating bond."

Her mouth formed an "O" of surprise. "I didn't know that."

Shyly, she added, "I'll tell Boreas and Gwydion you're courting me. And that I'm, ah, letting you."

She smiled at me, and my heart leaped with joy.

Then she added, "I don't want you to be angry at me or them." She bit her lower lip, as she did whenever she worried about something. "I hope they won't be angry, either. We're all friends right now, and I don't want to ruin things between us."

I forced myself to tell her the truth. "Jacinthe, I do not know how human courtships work, but If Boreas and Gwydion wish to court you also, it is your choice whether to permit them."

"But won't it upset you if they, um, kiss me again?" Her face had now turned deep red.

"I will not be angry." She still seemed unsure, so I clarified. "I want you to choose me as your mate. My victory will be sweeter if you test them and see that I am the best one for you."

Her apprehension disappeared, and I knew I'd said the correct thing.

She laughed. "I love your confidence, Tama. So, you're encouraging me to accept Boreas 'and Gwydion's advances to prove you're the best?"

"Yes, that is what I am saying," I replied. "Now that I know how to pleasure you, our next courtship session will be even better."

That won me another radiant smile. Her flush spread to her breasts. "I have a day off from work tomorrow, and just one practicum in the morning." Her eyes crinkled at the corners. "And my new room has a door that locks from the *inside*."

Perhaps Drylander laws forbade our courtship. But Mother Sea was telling me that Jacinthe was meant to be my mate.

Perhaps our union could help reconcile humans and Sea People after centuries of conflict.

I couldn't wait until tomorrow. I knew exactly what I wanted to do with Jacinthe once I had her alone and naked behind a locked door.

Chapter 30

Jacinthe

I left Tama's apartment feeling like I was floating a few inches off the floor. He had more than fulfilled the sensual promises of his earlier kisses. I was simultaneously wrung-out and energized by the intensity of what I'd just experienced with him.

As a healer-in-training, I had learned all about human reproductive anatomy and sex. But until now my knowledge had been purely theoretical.

And I had never imagined *tentacles.* Or all the wonderfully wicked things they could do.

A silly smile stretched my mouth as I walked toward the spiral stairway leading down to Boreas 'rooms.

I couldn't wait for Tama to visit my rooms for another "courtship session," as he called it.

As I picked up my skirts and descended the stairs, I realized how selfish I'd been just now. The vortex of sensual delight had so overwhelmed me, I hadn't even thought about Tama's pleasure until he'd asked me to touch him.

I shivered pleasantly at the memory of his cool, hard length sliding through my fisted hands, and wondered what fresh revelations lay in store for me on my day off.

But first, I'd promised Boreas that we would talk.

The prospect of facing him with my insides still warm and

jellied from Tama's extremely thorough explorations instantly sobered me.

Had Tama truly been sincere when he told me it was my choice whether to let Boreas and Gwydion court me? Especially if "courtship" meant anything like what I'd just done with Tama?

I remembered Boreas pushing me up against the stairwell wall yesterday and making his intentions known. And the way Gwydion's kisses had left me in a sensual haze.

But years of living with Baldwin left me wary. Was Tama's willingness to let me meet with his rivals secretly a loyalty test?

Baldwin had tested us all the time like that, my sisters and I. We never knew if his permission in response to a request was sincere, or a test to see whether we would do "the right thing."

Would I be betraying Tama if I took him at his word? Or, even worse, would I hurt him by not refusing the choice he'd offered me?

My palms were suddenly sweaty, even with cool morning air coming through the window-slits.

I stopped and wiped my hands on my skirts, trying to clear my head and *think*.

Was it a test or true generosity? If I guessed wrong, I might lose one or more of my dear friends.

But I *wasn't* dealing with Baldwin, I reminded myself. This was Tama. And he was the most straightforward person I'd ever met. He didn't lie, and he certainly didn't play mind games.

He had told me he was comfortable letting Gwydion and Boreas court me. I had to believe he was telling the truth.

Feeling more confident, I resumed walking.

My nerves returned as I approached Boreas' door. Tama had

been level-headed and astonishingly restrained when I told him about my other suitors.

Boreas, on the other hand, was hot-tempered and highly competitive. Was he also the jealous type? Would he explode with rage when he heard I wanted to give Gwydion and Tama a chance?

I couldn't help wondering if Boreas 'idea of courtship was anything like Tama's. And if it was…

Warmth flooded through me at the memory of Boreas kissing me yesterday. He was large, so powerful, so full of life. I remembered how effortlessly he'd picked me up and held me while he kissed me and ground himself against my core. He'd been so dominant in our encounter, and I'd enjoyed it.

I saw Guard Machry at the far end of the hall, coming towards me as he walked his rounds of the castle gatehouse. I waved at him. Uncharacteristically, he didn't wave back. I thought his face looked sweaty and ill, though it was hard to tell for certain in the corridor's dim light.

I knocked on Boreas 'door.

"Enter, Friend Jacinthe!" he called in his usual cheerful boom. "I've been waiting for you."

I took a deep breath and stepped inside, carefully closing the door behind me.

He rose from his usual spot on the window-seat and approached me with long strides. "I've thought about nothing but you since yesterday," he declared at a lower volume.

"About that," I began.

But before I could go on, Boreas swooped in and interrupted me with a passionate kiss. His arms wrapped around me, lifting me up as if I weighed nothing at all. His lips were hard and demanding, his body hot as fire against mine.

My prepared speech flew out of my head as I melted into him.

Suddenly, the door flew open and crashed against the stone wall with a resounding bang.

Caught! Sick with sudden terror, I tore myself free of Boreas' embrace just as Guard Machry burst into the apartment.

Sword drawn, he rushed towards Boreas. That was when I spotted the glowing rune on Machry's forehead, between his brows. He was wild-eyed, his complexion a strange greenish hue, like someone deathly ill.

I reacted without thinking and darted between him and Boreas, my arms outflung.

"Mach—" I began.

Before I could even speak the rest of his name, Machry thrust his sword deep into my belly. It happened so quickly I didn't have time to scream.

Disbelieving, I looked down. Dark blood soaked the front of my skirt, and I felt the sticky warmth of more blood spreading beneath my clothes and trickling down my legs.

I clutched my hands to my belly. *It doesn't hurt*, I thought in wonder.

The room spun around me, my vision blurring in and out of focus.

Behind me, Boreas screamed in fury, an inhuman sound better suited to his Dragon-shape. He lunged past me, his hands outstretched.

I felt a surge of power, like lightning, race over my skin as Boreas 'earring glowed first red, then orange, then pure, brilliant gold. My indenture collar sang a shrill note as a torrent of fire burst from his palms, enclosing Machry in a great cloak of flames.

The guard screamed. An instant later, the smell of cooking meat filled the air, and I gagged. Even worse was the sight of his body burning like a torch in the midst of the flames.

I tried to take a step forward. My legs collapsed under me and went down. I lay on my side, curled around my belly.

It still didn't hurt. But I was cold… so cold.

Then Boreas was there, kneeling beside me, his face filled with anguish. His burning lips kissed my forehead. Then he gathered me carefully in his arms and stood.

"In…firmary." It took all my strength to whisper that one word.

Then everything went away.

∞∞∞

Boreas

"Prince Boreas, why did you kill one of my guards?" Lord Roderigo demanded as he entered the infirmary ward. A larger-than-usual group of bodyguards surrounded him.

He and his men halted in the infirmary's wide center aisle, keeping a healthy distance between us.

As well he should.

I looked up from my place at Jacinthe's bedside. "Self-defense. Guard Machry burst into my room with his sword drawn." I put my hand on her shoulder. She didn't stir. "He stabbed her when she tried to intervene."

Shame flooded me as I spoke the words. I should've been the one to protect *her!* Not the other way around.

I still couldn't believe that Guard Machry nearly killed her right under my fucking nose! If I'd been in my Dragon shape, that guy wouldn't have gotten the chance to stab her.

Fucking human reflexes. I hated being this slow and puny.

I'd failed her just as badly as Lord Roderigo had.

A little over an hour had passed since I carried Jacinthe into the infirmary. Despite keeping my hand pressed over her wound, we'd left a trail of blood all the way from my room to this ward.

Luckily, Friend Gwydion was on duty, along with a human girl who wore a colorful scarf wound around her head. I recognized her as Lady Cresta and Lord Bernardo's friend, and one of the crows whose feathers I'd singed.

The girl shrieked and pointed at me when I appeared in the infirmary, Jacinthe's bleeding body in my arms.

Gwydion had immediately sent her to fetch the old healer-mage. Then my Fae friend sprang into action, examining the wound and questioning me about what had happened.

I'd freely loaned Gwydion my small store of magic when he requested my help to staunch the bleeding.

The old mage hobbled into the infirmary a few minutes later, wheezing from his climb up the stairs, and had set to work with his healing spells to close the wound.

Jacinthe hadn't stirred once, though she still breathed and her heart still beat. After he'd healed the worst of the damage, Healer-Mage Armand had laid his hand on her head and closed his eyes, frowning in concentration. Then he'd given us bad news.

"It looks like someone cursed the blade. Do you sense it, too, Apprentice Gwydion?"

Gwydion passed his hands over her, his palms skimming the air an inch or two above her still body, and swore in Fae. "Yes.

Can you dispel it, Mage Armand?"

The old healer-mage shook his head. "I don't recognize this working. I'll have to get one of my colleagues to look at it. There's an Air-Mage on the academy staff I could consult—"

"No. Don't tell anyone else about this," Gwydion ordered. He added, "*Please*. From what Boreas just told me, someone put a compulsion on the guard to make him attack."

"But that's forbidden magic!" Mage Armand croaked. "A capital crime, just like this curse!"

Gwydion nodded. "These are both mage-level spells, Mage Armand. And so were the curses laid on Lord Tama and Lord Shuji. That tells me we can't trust any of the mages here. Except for *you*, of course," he added.

"I only know about curses and compulsion spells in theory," the old man assured us. He shook his head. "They're filthy magic. Not something a healer should ever use!"

"You can't fix it?" I asked, despair flooding the fire of my anger.

"We'll dispel it, Boreas. I promise." Gwydion's tone was grim, though.

When Mage Armand departed and Friend Gwydion left for the library, I remained at Jacinthe's bedside.

Maybe guarding her now was too little, too late, but I didn't like the idea of leaving her alone and vulnerable. Especially with Alondra of Parrish working in the ward... though I hadn't seen the girl since she left to fetch Mage Armand.

Then Lord Roderigo showed up to question me.

"An unprovoked attack, you say?" he asked. "By Guard Machry, of all people?"

"Burned him alive, milord," one bodyguard muttered. "Didn't you tell us the monsters couldn't use magic?"

Frowning, the castellan surveyed my human friend lying deeply unconscious on the bed, her face bloodless beneath her smooth brown skin.

His gaze halted at the silver collar circling her throat. His mouth twisted in distaste. "Wait, isn't this the kitchen slut who's been spreading her favors around? Jacinda or Jonitha or something like that?"

"Her name is *Jacinthe*," I growled. "And don't you fucking *dare* speak of her so disrespectfully. She's a member of your aerie and under *your* protection, Castellan. You failed her!"

I sprang to my feet and pushed his bodyguards aside before they could react, sending them stumbling and falling in a clatter of armor.

Lord Roderigo's face blanched as I loomed over him. My human shape was only a fraction of my real size, but I was still larger than anyone else in this castle.

I leaned in and jabbed my finger into the castellan's chest, indenting his deep red velvet tunic as I repeated my earlier words.

"Guard Machry ambushed me in my rooms and attacked me out of the blue. Friend Jacinthe tried to stop him and almost died for it."

"Prince Boreas, please calm yourself!" Lord Roderigo exclaimed, taking a hasty step back. A false smile stretched his mouth, but his eyes remained wary. Hostile.

"I think I can guess what happened. You're a young man— young *Dragon*," he corrected himself. "It's natural that a pretty young girl's, ahem, *attentions*, turned your head."

What the fuck did courting Jacinthe have to do with anything? I glowered down at him, wondering what he was getting at.

"Given this girl's reputation, I believe Guard Machry was one of her lovers, too. I think he saw her entering your rooms, and it drove him mad with jealousy. This fit of temporary insanity drove him to take extreme action. But *you* were never the target, my lord, just an unfortunate bystander."

He gave me an oily, self-satisfied smile.

"How convenient," I snarled. "Except, how are you going to explain away all the *other* attacks against my fellow hostages? Are you going to blame Friend Jacinthe for those, as well?"

Just in time, I stopped myself from mentioning the curses and the compulsion spell.

If Lord Roderigo was the one behind these attacks, no need to inform him about what we knew.

He flinched. Then his eyes widened. "Well, she *was* working in the kitchens—" he began.

I leaned in until my face was level with his. "Not another fucking word, Castellan, if you value your life."

Lord Roderigo's eyes widened.

"I see what you're doing," I told him. "You're trying to avoid your responsibilities by blaming Friend Jacinthe. Well, that's not going to happen."

"Prince Boreas, please calm yourself and be *reasonable*," he pleaded. "This girl is nothing! She's just a servant. An *indentured* servant. And a known troublemaker. She got what was coming to her. Nothing you need concern yourself with!"

I stared at him in shock. Was Lord Roderigo really trying to blame Jacinthe for poisoning the Merfolk and the Djinn hostages?

Gwydion was right. This fucking earthworm will never take responsibility for what's been happening in his castle!

Enough talk. Jacinthe is mine. *Mine to protect.*

I growled.

Lord Roderigo's eyes narrowed. "Careful with your threats, Dragon Prince. Or it might be time for an *adjustment* to your earring."

Well, he might be a damned earthworm, but he wasn't a coward.

But I wasn't about to let him do whatever he wanted to *my* Jacinthe.

Rage flared up inside me like the flames that had consumed Guard Machry. Magic roared through me, an unstoppable force fueled by my fury. I knew what I needed to do.

Eyes wide with sudden terror, Lord Roderigo stumbled backwards as I moved. His guards, who had regrouped around us, scattered to all corners of the infirmary. Two of them even fled down the stairs.

I returned to Jacinthe's bedside and seized her limp hand in mine.

Without thinking, I chanted the Accepting Words spoken over new hatchlings to make them part of an aerie.

A small flame momentarily danced over Jacinthe's bare upper arm. When it vanished, I saw my clan's aerie mark branded into her human skin. It looked just like my mark.

"Maybe you don't give a fuck about your own aerie, Castellan," I snarled. "But Jacinthe belongs to *my* aerie now. And even if your fucking dominus doesn't give a fuck about what's been happening around here, King Menelaus and Lady Aeolia will!"

The last time a Wind-Walker aerie adopted a human had been almost a thousand years ago. Back then, the legendary King Agamemnon had abandoned his Dragon shape to wed Princess Asphodel of Espola, bringing peace between the warring kingdoms.

Lady Aeolia had always told me I acted before I thought. I hoped that my clan-mother and my king would agree to my rash revival of the almost-forgotten old custom.

Assuming they find out about it.

In my anger, I hadn't stopped to consider how I'd send them the news. The castellan and chatelaine controlled all messages leaving the island.

"Well, if claiming one of my indentured servants makes you happy, Prince Boreas, then you can have her," Lord Roderigo said, his voice shaking. He crossed his arms over his chest and attempted a sneer. "If the little slut keeps you busy enough, perhaps you'll stay out of trouble from now on."

"Get out," I growled.

Lord Roderigo bowed sarcastically. "As you wish, Prince Boreas. I wish you much joy with your new pet."

Friend Tama arrived next. "Why didn't you tell me?" he demanded. "The guard brought me the news."

"I'm sorry," I said. "I thought only of bringing Friend Jacinthe here, and then I did not want to leave her."

Tama's dark eyes swept over me, lingering on the front of my tunic and breeches, both stiff and reeking of Jacinthe's blood. "Understood."

I still held Jacinthe's hand in mine. Tama went to the other side of the bed and took her other hand. "Tell me what happened."

∞∞∞

Friend Gwydion returned from the library an hour later. Tama and I both looked up hopefully when he entered the ward.

He shook his head. Discouragement radiated from him.

But he said only, "I'll ask Mage Armand to loan me his Level Four library pass. I'll tell the librarian he sent me to do research since he's nearly blind. I'm sure there's something helpful in the restricted books." He flashed me a shadow of his former cocky smile. "There's a *reason* they're restricted, right?"

He rolled up his sleeves and went to the washstand. When he returned, a few droplets of water still gleaming on his bare wrists, he said, "I'm going to examine her now. Please step away and give us some privacy."

Reluctantly, I released Jacinthe's hand. In Gwydion's absence, her breathing and heartbeat had remained slow but steady. But the cold steadily creeping up her limbs concerned me. Even my touch hadn't been able to warm her.

Tama and I stepped away from the bed, and Gwydion drew the privacy curtains suspended from the ceiling.

I paced up and down the center aisle while I waited for Gwydion to finish. Unaccustomed anxiety roiled my soul.

Tama stood next to the doorway, arms folded and radiating his usual imperturbable calm.

But when my steps brought me close to him again, his hand shot out. He caught my elbow, halting me in my tracks.

"Stop, Boreas. This was not your fault," he said, then astonished me by pulling me into a hard embrace. "Gwydion will break Jacinthe's curse, just as he broke mine."

I embraced him in return, but couldn't stop myself from blurting, "Friend Tama, if only I'd *done* something instead of standing there, gaping like a fucking idiot when Guard Machry came at me with his sword!"

"We both thought Guard Machry trustworthy," murmured Tama, patting my back.

"I think he *was* trustworthy, poor pawn." I'd had a couple

of hours to think through the morning's unsettling events. "That's why whoever's doing this chose him and put a compulsion on him."

"Nevertheless, Friend Boreas, you are not to blame," Tama insisted.

The bed-curtains rippled, and Gwydion emerged. Without a word, he walked over and put his arms around us both.

My heart sank, and Tama and I gathered him close. We all stood there for a long moment, drawing comfort and reassurance from each other.

"I have good news and bad news," Gwydion said at last. "First, the good news. Mage Armand did a good job healing that wound. Did either of you know Jacinthe has a tattoo on her belly?"

I shook my head.

Tama said gravely, "I have not yet seen her without her clothes."

"Well, it's an odd one." Gwydion frowned. "The wound destroyed most of the design, but the bit that's left looks like a sealing sigil. My people use those to imprison destructive or evil spirits."

"What is your bad news?" Tama asked, apparently uninterested in Fae sigils.

Gwydion sighed. "She lost a lot of blood. And that curse is getting stronger by the hour. It appears to be feeding off her power."

"How much time left to break it before it's too late?" I demanded, sickened by the thought of this evil parasite drinking Jacinthe's life.

Gwydion shook his head. "I don't know. Maybe a day… maybe

less." He looked at each of us. "I'm going to get that Level Four library pass from Mage Armand now, and then I'm heading back to the library. Don't leave her alone."

"We won't," I promised. Tama nodded gravely.

Chapter 31

Gwydion

I failed. Moon and stars, I *failed*.

I spent hours in the academy's utterly inadequate library, paging through each volume in the tiny Restricted Books collection, looking for any references to curse spells.

I found nothing except repeated prohibitions against using them.

When I finally left the library, the sun had long since set. I'd missed dinner as well as lunch. My heart was heavy. Despair and hunger gnawed at my vitals.

Now, only a single option remained to save Jacinthe.

But when I returned to the infirmary ward, the mouthwatering smells of fresh bread and something savory greeted me.

I was pleasantly surprised to see Jacinthe awake at last, though terribly weak. Lord Ilhan sat at her bedside, feeding her soup.

Tama and Boreas had stationed themselves on the other side of the bed. The hope in their expressions as I entered sent a spear of guilt through my chest.

I shook my head and saw that hope dwindle and die. "Nothing. I looked through every damned book. *Twice*."

"Oh, you're back, Senior Apprentice Gwydion," Alondra exclaimed from the rear of the ward. "Have you eaten? Two girls from the kitchens came by a while ago and delivered dinner for Apprentice Jacinthe and her friends. There's plenty of food left."

"Some food would be wonderful. Thank you, Apprentice," I told her, pulling up a chair to the foot of Jacinthe's bed.

She beamed at me and vanished into the infirmary's kitchen. I heard her reciting a reheating spell. A few minutes later, she brought me a tray with a steaming bowl of vegetable soup, roast chicken, and sliced bread thickly smeared with soft cheese.

"Thank you for staying past the end of your shift," I told her. "You can go now."

There was something I needed to discuss with Boreas and Tama. And I didn't want an audience.

Alondra cast an anxious glance at Jacinthe. "You're sure there's nothing else I can do to help?"

I shook my head, surprised she cared. I'd heard she was one of the students who'd attacked Jacinthe several weeks ago.

"All right. Let me know if anything changes. Otherwise, I'll return in the morning." She left.

I looked at Ilhan. "You can go, too, if you want to, Apprentice Ilhan. I know it's been a long day for you. I'll watch over her until dawn."

Ilhan's jaw set mulishly. "I want to stay." He turned to Jacinthe. "Do you want me to stay?"

Her chapped lips moved, and the barest whisper emerged. "Yes."

Ilhan looked at me. "Mage Armand came by while you were gone. He told us to make her comfortable and remain with her until the end. So that she—she won't be alone when the time comes." He swallowed hard. "It—it won't be long now. Maybe a few more hours."

What? No!

Desperately hoping the old man was mistaken, I examined Jacinthe more closely.

To my horror, the vile yellow magic had spread in my absence. It now covered most of her body like a blanket of foul slime, oozing slowly from the freshly healed scar on her belly.

"Fuck," Boreas groaned. He glared at me from a face ravaged by grief and guilt. "Friend Gwydion, is there *anything* you can do for her? Like what you did for Friend Tama when he was cursed?" He dropped his face into his enormous hands. "I'd *die* for her, if it would only fix this."

"As would I," Tama said quietly. "I gave her my protection, but I've failed her repeatedly since arriving in this stone box."

I took a deep breath. "Apprentice Ilhan, will you leave us, please? I wish to speak to my friends in private."

Ilhan didn't look happy, but he rose, bowl in one hand. "I'll heat more soup," he muttered. "This has gone cold."

He rested his hand briefly on Jacinthe's hair. Compassion illuminated his face.

Since Jacinthe had joined the infirmary, the young Frankish nobleman and his sister had been distantly polite and openly wary around her.

What had changed in these few hours? Was it merely the knowledge that Jacinthe was dying?

When Ilhan had left the ward, I looked at my two friends. "I have one last option to try. But it's a dangerous one, with a high price, and only a tiny chance of success," I warned.

"Understood," Tama said.

"I'm willing to try anything at this point," Boreas added. "What do you have in mind?"

"When Jacinthe, Boreas, and I broke the death curse laid on Tama, I drew on Boreas and Jacinthe's power to overcome the restriction of our earrings and cleanse the magic," I began.

Hope lit Boreas 'face. "Yes, let's do that again!"

I shook my head. "It only worked last time because Jacinthe isn't restricted by an earring, and she's an extremely powerful mage, though something sealed most of her magic away. But I can't risk drawing on her power now. For all we know, it's feeding the curse infecting her. I don't want to risk giving it enough to kill her instantly."

The Wind-Walker looked crestfallen.

"But you know of another way to break the curse?" Tama's voice was calm as always, but predatory intensity radiated from his huge black eyes.

"It's an ancient Fae purification ritual," I told them. "It's only rarely used because it's dangerous. And even if it works, there's a high price to pay. Everyone who takes part in the cleansing is soul-bonded to the person being cleansed." I looked around at them. "If we survive—and that's doubtful, because the ritual requires a minimum of five mages—the ritual will bind us to Jacinthe. Permanently."

"What does 'soul-bond 'mean?" Tama asked. "How will we be bound to her?"

"I don't know," I confessed. "It could be a connection of hearts and minds, or it could turn us into her slaves. The only thing I know for sure is my Fae teachers talked about this kind of bond as one of the worst things that can happen to a person. Which is why my people only rarely perform this ritual."

Boreas didn't hesitate. "I don't care. I'm in."

"Being bonded to her would not be a price, but a blessing," Tama said.

I nodded. I felt the same way. Then I looked at Jacinthe. Her consent was the most important of all.

Little by little, I had been falling for her since the day I met her in my garden. Now, I realized I was completely and totally hers.

"I love you," I told her. "And I will do anything to save you. Please let us do this for you."

"I love and trust you, Gwydion," she whispered, and her words soothed my wounded heart like the sweetest honey-balm.

"I came to this castle thinking this would be the worst place imaginable," she continued. "But you have all made it my home. I—I love you. *All* of you. I'd be honored to be bonded to you. But I don't want you to sacrifice yourselves. Or take away your freedom."

Tears rolled over her cheeks in a steady stream, dripping onto the bedsheet pulled up over her chest.

Boreas growled and tore off the blood-stained right sleeve of his ruined shirt, revealing a small, flame-shaped brand on his impressive biceps.

Then he leaned over and tapped the matching mark on Jacinthe's upper arm. "You are now a member of my aerie. My *family*, Friend Jacinthe. A soul-bonding sounds like just another kind of aerie mark."

She inclined her head, minutely. "Do what you think is best."

Her lids drooped. And then she fell asleep.

I turned to Boreas and Tama. "We'll need to prepare a cleansing circle with salt around Jacinthe's bed. Between the three of us, we represent Fire, Water, and Wood powers. Ideally, we should also have an Earth mage and an Air mage for this ritual, but I am hoping three elements are enough to overcome the curse's strength. Once we have cast the circle, I will channel our combined power to purify the curse and cast it out of Jacinthe's body. "

They nodded.

Because I didn't think Boreas or Tama had any mage training, I added, "Once the ritual has begun, it is important that none of us break concentration or leave the circle. If any energy is lost or misdirected, then it could cause irreparable harm. I will serve as the focus, drawing and directing your powers to where they are needed most."

Another set of nods.

"Without the full contingent of five mages, this ritual could burn out our magic forever, or even kill us." I felt compelled to offer Boreas and Tama one last warning. "Especially with these restrictor earrings we're all wearing."

Suddenly, Ilhan reappeared in the infirmary. For a brief moment, the room felt charged with electricity. His dark blue eyes glowed with determination as he walked towards us with empty hands.

"Forgive me for eavesdropping," he said, sounding completely unrepentant. "But I volunteer as the fourth mage for your cleansing ritual. I have dual affinities for Earth and Wood. And unlike any of you, I'm not burdened with a restrictor earring."

We all stared at him in shock. Then I said, "Did you overhear the part where this ritual could burn out your magic or kill you? Or turn you into Jacinthe's slave?"

"Yes." He looked at me with a defiant expression. "You *need* me if you want this to work, Prince Gwydion."

"Why are you willing to risk this ritual for someone you barely know?" Boreas demanded. "We are her friends. We love her.

But who are you?"

Ilhan sighed. "I heard they found De Montplaisir's charred body in the courtyard garden today. Someone wanted it to look like Boreas and Jacinthe took revenge on him." He spread his hands. "And I might've believed it… except Jacinthe was already here in the infirmary when the murder took place. And she's in no condition to even feed herself, much less get out of bed, walk across the castle, and burn a mage-student to death with magic." He smiled grimly. "I also know for a fact that Boreas has been here at her bedside the entire time."

"Someone cooked that little earthworm?" Boreas laughed nastily. "Serves him right! But you're right. It wasn't me who did it."

Ilhan spread his hands in a conciliatory gesture. "I've been wrong about you all. Something's rotten at this academy, and I'm determined to get to the bottom of it. But first, I need to repay the debt of honor I owe Apprentice Jacinthe for falsely believing she killed Cresta and Bernardo. I feared she wanted to kill my sister next."

"A very pretty and noble speech, Apprentice Ilhan," I said. "But I remind you once more that this isn't just a regular healing spell. The price could be death, losing your powers, or being soul-bonded to her along with the three of us." I shrugged. "Or maybe you'll lose your powers *and* become her slave. I don't know."

"I heard your dire warnings the first two times, Senior Apprentice Gwydion." He smiled crookedly at me. "But I'm a healer-mage in training. I have a sacred duty to do whatever I can for a patient… especially if that patient is my junior apprentice and my responsibility."

I told myself I'd done everything I could to give him an honest warning about the risks. And I didn't *really* want to discourage him, since we badly needed his help. "If you're absolutely certain about this, then we welcome your aid, Apprentice Ilhan. We are all deeply grateful."

He nodded in acknowledgement. "Tell me what supplies you'll need for the ritual."

We moved Jacinthe's bed away from the wall while Ilhan went to the storeroom and fetched salt and herbs for the cleansing circle, as well as the other items I requested.

When we'd finished creating the circle, Ilhan and I placed the ritual focus items within it to represent the elements we would use today: a lit candle for Fire; a large spear of clear quartz crystal for Earth; a bowl of water for Water; a potted cedar tree for Wood; and a swan's wing fan for Air.

I explained the steps of the ritual, and walked my companions through the actions that each of us needed to take.

Then, we could delay no longer. It was time.

We gathered around Jacinthe's bed. Each of us took the items we would use as our focus.

I began the ritual with an invocation. Then, I drew on Ilhan, Tama, and Boreas and fed our combined powers through the swan's-wing fan I held.

At first, our earrings glowed and heated, but nothing seemed to happen.

Then, gradually, a shimmering aura gathered around the snowy feathers in my hand. Colors—scarlet, deep blue, silver, and vibrant green—flowed together until the fan blazed with opalescent light.

As the ritual dictated, I touched the fan to Jacinthe's forehead, and recited the ritual request that she accept the power we wielded as a gift.

Then I leaned down and kissed her mouth. Her lips were

alarmingly cold beneath mine.

Deep inside me, something snapped into place, like a sword fitting into a sheath.

And suddenly, Jacinthe was there, inside my mind. I knew everything about her: her shining soul, crisscrossed with deep emotional scars and her tearing grief for her lost mother; her compelling need to help others; her resolute strength and lively intelligence. And woven through all that, her powerful attraction to me, her respect for my abilities, and her deep affection for me as her friend, all tinged with wariness and the hope I could live up to my promises.

She plumbed the depths of my soul in return, and knew me for the flawed and unworthy Dark Fae I was. And yet, miraculously, she *still* loved me.

I wanted to fall to my knees and weep with joy and gratitude. I wanted to climb into the bed and make ecstatic love to her.

But first, I had to cleanse the dark magic that clung to her, sucking the life out of her like a ravenous parasite.

One by one, the others came forward, recited the same phrase, and kissed her.

As I fought to recover from the surge of emotions that had momentarily overwhelmed me, I saw each of them sway as their bonds formed.

Boreas, ever at the mercy of his emotions, dropped to his knees and wept openly. Tama's usual dourness dissolved in radiant joy. His entire being glowed with happiness and hope.

And then there was Ilhan…

My fellow apprentice's face glistened with sweat as he stared at Jacinthe. Huge, damp patches stained his tunic under his arms and over his chest. His overwhelming fear and uncertainty flowed through me, carried on the stream of his magic.

Mercifully, he kept enough control over his churning panic that he didn't bolt or cut off the flow of magic. If he had, it would have spelled disaster for this ritual.

I gave our group a few moments to regain their equilibrium while I maintained a steady flow of power and tried to project soothing and calm.

Then I raised the fan once more. I swept it over the length of Jacinthe's body, using our combined powers to sweep up the curse-magic clinging to her and collect it. My healing power of Wood split off sections of the loathsome spell and directed them to my friends and my apprentice.

Tama caught his share and drowned it in the water. The pot at his feet boiled furiously and raised a cloud of vile-smelling steam.

Boreas purified with fire magic. He forced the candle's flame to shoot upwards into a swirling vortex of blinding white-gold that surrounded and devoured his share of the curse. His wet cheeks caught the light and threw it back in a sparkling profusion..

Ilhan, his expression now serene with deep concentration, raised the spear of quartz in his hand. It captured the magic as it streamed towards him, absorbing and trapping it. As it did so, the clear stone gradually turned a sickly shade of yellowish-green.

The final portion of the curse was mine to dispose of. With a whispered word of thanks to the tree, I channeled the magic into the cedar. Its trunk swelled and its branches immediately released a cloud of fragrant perfume. Then it grew as it fed on the curse's energy, new twigs branching out and unfurling masses of tender green spikes.

I looked at Jacinthe, and saw that her body was now free of the awful coating of curse-magic.

We'd actually done it! We'd cleansed her!

Then, to my horror, more curse-magic began oozing up from the site of her stab wound, like pus from an infection.

I tried to draw more power, but we were all at our limits now.

"No!" I shouted, unwilling to accept defeat just when we thought we'd banished the curse.

Take what you need from me. Jacinthe's voice flowed through my head like a summer breeze.

"No," I said again, out loud. "Your power will only feed it."

The curse is badly weakened. It won't have time to regrow if you burn it away quickly.

Could I risk it? *Should* I?

I studied her, trying to think past my sudden weariness and my conflicted emotions.

Gwydion. I trust you, my love.

I made my decision. I closed my eyes and put my palm on the sheet covering her belly. Then I drew on her power.

Something had changed inside her. The walls enclosing her vast pool of power had mysteriously crumbled. Energy unlike anything I'd felt before surged up and flowed into me at my call.

It felt glorious as it rushed through me, caressing every cell, every nerve. I was instantly more aroused than I'd ever been in my life. Pleasure ignited and burned inside me like a Wind-Walker's fire magic.

Intoxicated with the potency and the splendor of her power, I struggled to remember what it was I needed to do.

Burn away the source of the curse. Save Jacinthe.

I took her power and fashioned a staff of light with it. Then I plunged it like a white-hot cautery iron into the heart of the putrid magic bubbling up from her belly.

Golden fire exploded like a shooting geyser, pouring over Jacinthe's body in a torrent of searing heat that left her flesh strangely untouched. In the fountain's glowing heart, I saw a dark mass shriveling into nothingness.

Then Jacinthe's back arched. She shook violently. Her mouth opened and she moaned, a low, sensual sound.

An instant later, her climax rushed through our bond, and triggered my own release. I collapsed onto my knees, gasping as overwhelming pleasure crashed through me, borne on the tide of her power.

I was dimly aware that the same thing was also happening to Ilhan, Tama, and Boreas.

The Wind-Walker was still on his feet, his arms outflung and head thrown back, his face contorted. Like me, Tama was on his knees. The sea-brother bowed forward, his long hair a dense silver curtain that concealed his face and spilled onto the floor.

Poor Ilhan was curled into a fetal position, his knees drawn up to his chest. Dimly, I worried about him. Had the young nobleman bitten off more than he could chew?

The fountain collapsed and the fire died away. I realized the curse was gone. Jacinthe's fire had completely cleansed it.

She was safe now.

I grinned and opened myself fully to the pleasure streaming through me. It felt like a victory celebration.

Ah, sweet Jacinthe, you are full of surprises.

I couldn't wait to see what happened next.

Epilogue

Jacinthe

One month later

"We finished your dress!" Sunniva announced.

She draped the shimmering expanse of turquoise velvet over my infirmary bed. It was even more beautiful than I remembered.

I stroked the soft fabric tentatively, unable to believe that the Fae princess' dress really belonged to me now.

"I hope it fits," Winifred said, bouncing a little on her feet. "Try it on!"

It was their day off from work. The two girls had arrived as I was finishing my breakfast. Now that I was finally feeling stronger, I had been thinking about going for a walk.

I desperately wanted to leave the infirmary and go back to my room. I'd only spent a couple of nights there since moving in.

I swung my legs over the edge of my bed and tried to stand. A shower of sparks blinded me, and the room felt like it was spinning slowly around me.

My two young friends rushed forward to steady me.

"Do you want to lie back down?" Winifred asked, sounding anxious.

"I've done too much of that lately," I answered. "I'll be all right in a moment." I smiled down at them. "I'm dying to wear something that isn't a white linen robe."

They laughed and set about helping me into the clean chemise and stays they'd brought with the dress.

The weeks since the purification ritual had crawled by in a strange, timeless haze. Weak and exhausted from blood loss, the rapid healing of my wound, and whatever Gwydion had done to burn away the curse, I spent most of the time sleeping.

Each time I woke, I found one or more of my friends there at my bedside, ready with food, drink, and other necessities for a bedridden patient. I did my best to stay awake and talk to them, but sleep always claimed me again after a short time.

Gwydion had warned me it would take several weeks, if not months, to recover my full strength and previous energy. No amount of mage healing or mystical fire could replace the large amount of blood I'd lost.

But I was alive and on the road to recovery. That was a miracle, and I owed it all to my friends.

Elswyth, Rheda, and my other friends from the kitchens came every day and delivered an endless supply of nourishing soups, custards, pastries, and other dishes normally reserved for the academy's mages and the castle's highest-ranking staff.

The new bonds in my head took some getting used to, though.

Even on the rare occasions when I woke and found myself physically alone in the infirmary, four distinct presences always felt like ghostly entities standing or sitting right next to me.

I quickly discovered that, except for Gwydion, I couldn't talk to them through our strange new bond. But I could feel their emotions, and that was often unsettling.

To say the least.

Gwydion, Boreas, and Tama repeatedly assured me they didn't mind our new connection. But still, it couldn't be easy for them.

The one I truly worried about was Ilhan. We hadn't known each other very well before he volunteered for the ritual. Now, we knew each other all too well.

Beneath his even-tempered, kind, and chivalrous exterior roiled a tempest of emotions—anger at being exiled for Baron and Baroness Margitts' poor judgment, frustration at the restrictions that now governed his life, and a roiling mix of protectiveness, love, worry and resentment at becoming his headstrong sister's guardian.

Ilhan of Parrish *was* strong, chivalrous and kind, but our bond revealed the startling array of doubts and insecurities racking him. His greatest fear was never measuring up to his father's stern measure. His second-greatest fear was failing to save his sister from the trouble she courted.

I badly wanted to hug him and reassure him he was already the noble, strong, and thoughtful man he yearned to be.

But he had avoided any personal contact with me so far. I saw him every day, of course, but he performed his infirmary duties with cool, professional detachment.

At first, I tried to talk to him about our strange new bond, but he put me off by telling me, "Later. When you're stronger and feeling better."

"Leave him be," Gwydion counseled me during one of my short periods of wakefulness, after I expressed my hurt and frustration at Ilhan's continual rejections. "He didn't really understand what he was agreeing to, and he was too proud to admit it, the fool!" He chuckled ruefully. "Just give him space. Let him come to you when he's ready."

It was sensible advice, even if I didn't like it. I felt guilty about binding Ilhan to me with no way to free him now.

My other regret was seeing how the pink scar from Machry's blade defaced my tattoo. It had been the last remaining keepsake from my mother. I vowed that once I was free of my indenture, and had saved some money, I would find someone to restore the design.

Sunniva and Winifred had finished lacing me into the gown, and were brushing out my hair, when Boreas strode into the infirmary. He carried a rolled-up document in one hand.

"Friend Jacinthe, it pleases me to see you out of bed and standing at last! You're feeling better?" he asked in his usual loud, cheerful voice.

He stopped and openly admired me. As always, his inner and outer emotions matched. He felt pleased and a little smug to see me wearing his gift. And he truly found me beautiful. That sent a burst of warmth through me.

Still feeling a little wobbly, I turned slowly around, so that he could admire his gift—and me—from all angles.

"Ah, I knew that dress would suit you. Wear it often!"

"We didn't even have to make a lot of alterations," Sunniva told him.

He grinned down at her, then reached into his pocket and handed each of the girls a small gold aureus, the equivalent of a month's wages for a tailor's assistant.

"Thank you, Prince Boreas!" They both darted forward and hugged him.

He put his hands on their heads. Through our bond, I felt his surprise and happiness. Tama and Gwydion had both told me that since Guard Machry's death, most of the castle's inhabitants now shunned my large friend.

Outside, the lunch bell rang.

"We should go." Winifred sounded regretful. "Do you want us to help you undress?" She shot a shy glance in the Wind-Walker's direction.

"I would appreciate that," I replied, reaching for the privacy curtain.

He sank into a visitor's chair and crossed his long legs. "Go ahead, do what you must," he said expansively. "I have something to tell you, but I'm in no hurry."

At least he isn't here with bad news, I thought as I drew the curtain. The girls quickly helped me change back into my loose patient's robe, then hung the dress and undergarments from the clothing pegs driven into the wall next to my bed.

His amusement seeped through our link, along with a tinge of his usual fierce protectiveness. Whatever he wanted to tell me, he considered it funny but also mildly alarming.

Once Winifred and Sunniva had bid me goodbye and left for the servants 'hall, and I I was comfortably settled in my bed, sitting up against a stack of pillows, Boreas handed me the document.

He sat back, grinning and waiting for my reaction.

I began reading, then stopped. "What in the world are you doing with my indenture contract?"

"Keep reading," he urged. "And then I'll tell you what happened when Lord Roderigo visited the infirmary after Guard Machry attacked you."

I reached the final page. My apprenticeship assignments were listed and countersigned below my signature and Clerk Petri's official stamp.

The first assignment was *Kitchen Apprentice, Level 1. Monthly*

Stipend: 5d. [Petri's signature and seal]

The second assignment was *Infirmary Apprentice Level 1/ Healing Arts Student Level 1 Monthly Stipend: 25d.* [Mage Armand's signature and seal]

My eyes widened. I hadn't realized my stipend had increased five-fold with my transfer to the infirmary.

Then I saw a third assignment. I read it with disbelief. *Personal servant/valet to Prince Boreas. Monthly stipend: 25d.* [Lord Roderigo de Norhas' signature and seal]

"Personal servant? What *is* this?" I demanded in outrage.

"A monthly stipend of fifty denarii and permission to court you!" Boreas laughed, his golden eyes glowing with good humor. "Don't worry, Friend Jacinthe. I don't intend to make you leave your studies and your work in this place. They will have to pay you both amounts if you remain here, but are officially in the other position as well."

I put down the contract and glared at him, failing to see the humor in this sudden and unwanted change to my contract. Not even the promise of extra money settled my unease. "You said there's a story behind this?"

He told me about his confrontation with Lord Roderigo here in the infirmary, and why I now had an aerie mark. And how the castellan explained away Machry's attack as the culmination of a sordid love triangle.

"You're telling me that Lord Roderigo *gave* me to you as your concubine?" I asked with mingled outrage and horror when he was done talking. "Because he thinks I'm a whore?" I looked back down at the contract, and felt my stomach twist.

Any sense of security I'd felt after transferring to the infirmary vanished. I hadn't known that the castellan could alter my contract without my consent.

Maybe Boreas found my reassignment as his personal servant funny. But I certainly didn't. It was only by luck that Lord Roderigo had signed me over to a trusted friend.

What if he had decided to give me to someone else as their "personal servant"?

And what if Lord Roderigo sent me to the guard barracks the next time I displeased him? I knew his men blamed me for Guard Machry's hideous death. They would not treat me gently.

I felt a rush of sick terror.

Boreas read my feelings through our bond and sobered immediately. "Ah. I was thinking only of how this official permission would make my courtship easier." He looked abashed. "I had not considered how upsetting it would be to you."

He took my hand in his heated grip, and I immediately felt better.

"I will not allow him to assign you away from me, or from this Place-That-Heals," he assured me. "The contract is yours to keep safe. If Lord Roderigo requests it from me to alter it again, I will tell him I destroyed it."

I touched my collar. "I'm an indentured servant, Boreas. Even without the contract, he can still do whatever he wants to me."

In reply, Boreas pushed up the short sleeve of my robe, baring the new mark on my upper arm. "He cannot. You are a member of my aerie now, and under my protection, as well as my clutch mother's protection. Lady Aeolia is the king's vizier, and the second-most powerful person in the kingdom. You have powerful allies now, Friend Jacinthe. Remember that."

His thumb brushed the mark, sending a pleasant shiver through me.

He was right. When I set foot on the ship a few months ago, I had been alone and friendless in the world.

But now, at my lowest and most vulnerable, I was overwhelmed by the love, care, and affection shown to me by my new friends.

By the people I love, I corrected myself. Because I did love them. *All* of them, but especially my four soul-bonded companions.

Even if Ilhan wasn't ready yet to acknowledge what we shared.

I belonged to them now, and they belonged to me. The ties of friendship and exile and strange magic had bound us all together into something strong enough to survive whatever Darkstone Island threw at us next.

∞∞∞

One week later

"Are you certain you feel well enough to resume our courtship sessions?" Tama asked as he entered my room.

I noticed he was careful to lock it behind him, and I smiled. There would be no interruptions this time.

Night had fallen, and the warm summer breeze filled my room with the scent of salt and sea. I wore my loose sleeping-robe, and nothing else.

I smiled at him and opened our bond, showing him how I felt.

My strength still hadn't returned to its previous level, but Mage Armand and Gwydion had both declared me fit enough to leave the infirmary, move back into my room, and resume my classes.

Gwydion had also proposed I enroll in mage-craft classes.

My brush with death had changed a lot of things. I now had some kind of magic, though I hadn't been able to summon it or do anything with it.

Most of all, almost dying had removed my blind obedience to unjust laws. Life was too short and too uncertain to hesitate when it came to those I loved.

Besides, the castellan already thought I was sleeping with half the castle, including Boreas and Tama. And he had literally given his stamp of approval for non-human lovers on my indenture contract.

"I love you," I told him, though he already knew that because of our bond. "You are my rock. You make me feel safe."

He inclined his head. "I am not sure what 'love' means for Drylanders, but I want you as my mate, Jacinthe. I have wanted this since we first met on the ship. You have given me a reason to endure my imprisonment far from my home and people."

I stepped into his arms. "Are you willing to share me with Gwydion and Boreas? Since they're also bonded to me."

"I am," he said gravely as his arms came around me. "While you were recovering from your wound, we met and discussed this matter. You now belong to all of us equally. It is acceptable." He hesitated. "And what of your fourth soul-bonded? Ilhan?"

I sighed. "I don't know yet. I think he needs time to accustom himself to this. We weren't enemies before this, but we weren't really friends either. I hope we can work things out. I don't want him to hate me."

Tama nodded.

I went up on tiptoes and kissed him, deep and slow. Here alone together in my room, with the door locked, I had time to enjoy the feeling of his cool lips against mine.

"I've spent the last few weeks thinking of our courtship

session," I said when the kiss finally ended.

"As have I." His large, webbed hand cupped my cheek, his claws lightly indenting my skin. "I have been remembering how you tasted and felt, Jacinthe. I want to touch you again and pleasure you. And this time, I want to mate with you."

I smiled up at him. "I like your plan."

The old Jacinthe would have been shy and worried about getting caught in a forbidden embrace with a merman. The new Jacinthe only wanted to consummate our relationship at long last. We'd both waited long enough.

Tama lifted me with ease and carried me to the bed. I felt safe and loved in his powerful arms.

He set me down gently and kissed me again, his lips tracing along my jawline and down my neck. His hands found their way under my robe, feeling the warmth of my skin. I felt a rush of heat as his cool fingers stroked my breasts, making my nipples harden.

He kissed and licked his way down my chest. I moaned softly as his tongue circled my nipples. He took one into his mouth, sucking and biting gently, while his hand played with the other. His sharp teeth scraping my sensitive tip made me gasp as a thrill raced through me.

I ran my fingers through his long, soft hair, urging him on. I wanted to feel him inside me again. And I wanted more than just his tentacle this time. I wanted all of him.

He shifted his attention lower, trailing kisses down my stomach. His lips lingered over the pink, raised line of my scar.

"I almost lost you," he whispered against my belly. "I never want to feel that fear again."

He moved lower. I parted my legs for him, welcoming him between them. He trailed kisses down the sensitive skin of my inner thighs, then his tongue explored my wet folds, tasting me deeply and hungrily. I moaned in pleasure as he licked and sucked, his talented mouth stoking the flames of my arousal.

His webbed hands clamped my hips as I tried to arch under his wicked caresses. I saw his tentacles and long, thick manhood emerge from protective slits as he became aroused.

All too soon, he moved back up my body, his mouth and fingers returning to my breasts. His tentacles slid between my legs, resuming my pleasuring. I gasped as they stroked and teased my pearl, sending jolts of pleasure racing through me, then entered me, preparing me for his mating.

He brought me right to the edge of release again and again before finally withdrawing his tentacles and replacing them with the thick, rigid shaft of his manhood. I panted as he filled my virgin passage bit by bit, stretching me around him until he'd sheathed his entire length inside me.

Tama waited until my inner walls adjusted to his invasion and the burn inside eased. Meanwhile, he continued kissing me and playing with my breasts, keeping my arousal high.

Finally, when I was squirming with renewed need, he slid partway out and began thrusting, slowly building up a steady rhythm that drove us both wild with desire.

I clung to him, my hands running over his strong back and shoulders as his tentacles continued to caress my lower body. Sparks of pleasure raced through me, each teasing flick and circling stroke intensifying the feeling of his manhood sliding in and out of me.

His pleasure raced through our bond, stoking mine higher and higher.

Tension deep inside me swelled, until I thought I'd explode with sheer need.

Then Tama's teeth closed on my breast. At the intense sensation, my release finally burst free in a wave that tore a cry of overwhelming pleasure from my throat.

At the same time, a curtain of brilliant orange-red fire surged forth, licking at Tama's pale skin, reddening and blistering it.

With blinding speed, he pushed himself away from me and leaped off the bed, leaving me bewildered and empty. Pain and shock radiated through our bond, instantly quenching my residual pleasure.

Horrified, I saw ugly, blistering burns marring the smooth skin of his chest, arms, and torso.

"What in the name of Mother Sea was *that?*" he demanded.

I looked around wildly. Who was attacking us? Was it the same sinister assassin who'd burned that student to death?

"Why did you burn me?" Tama's bewilderment flowed through our bond.

He thought *I'd* done this?

"I—I didn't—" Trembling in shock, I stared down at myself. I felt a strange mixture of awe and fear as I saw tendrils of smoke curl up from the charred remnants of my robe. Surrounded by ash, my skin remained completely untouched by the flames.

I did this? But how was it even it possible?

"Oh, Tama, I'm so sorry!"

What in the name of the Divine Mother was happening to me?

How could I suddenly possess fire magic now? Only Wind-Walkers and Djinn could wield fire magic and survive.

Was Gwydion right when he doubted I was human?

But if I'm not human, then what am I?

To be continued in A Kiss of Flame and Fury

∞∞∞

Want sneak peeks at chapters from my upcoming books in this series? Join my mailing list (https://tinyurl.com/4dcp4f95) and receive goodies like a high-res copy of the map at the front of this book, bonus scenes from the cutting room floor, and weekly sneak peeks from works in progress every time I start writing a new book!

The End

Books by Bliss Devlin

Darkstone Academy
- *A Kiss of Salt & Sea*
- *A Kiss of Flame & Fury*
- *A Kiss of Roses & Moonlight*

Beast Warriors (co-authored with Ophelia Sexton)
- *Fugitive (Beast Warriors Book 1)*
- *Hunter (Beast Warriors Book 2)*

The Children of Lilith

The Children of Lilith is an ongoing paranormal romance series, set in various periods of history from the legendary past to the present.

- *Won by the Three Satyrs* (The Children of Lilith, Book 1)
- *Taken by the Incubus* (The Children of Lilith, Book 2)
- *Saved by the Incubus* (The Children of Lilith, Book 3)
- *Claimed by the Incubus* (Book 1 & Book 2 bundle)
- *Her Roman Wolf* (The Children of Lilith Book 4)
- *Her Incubus Knight* (The Children of Lilith Book 5)
- *Her Incubus Master* (The Children of Lilith Book 6)
- *Submitting to the Incubus* (The Children of Lilith Book 7)

- *Tamed by the Incubus* (The Children of Lilith Book 8)

Made in United States
North Haven, CT
02 June 2024